I0685627

EVIL LIKE ME

STEVE BRADSHAW

EVIL LIKE ME©

No part of this publication may be reproduced in whole or in part, or
stored in a retrieval system, or transmitted in any form or by any means,
electronic, mechanical, photocopying, recording, or otherwise, without
written permission of the author, except for the inclusion of brief
quotations in a review. For information regarding permission, please write
to: steve@stevebradshawauthor.com

Copyright © 2012 Steve Bradshaw All rights reserved.

1ˢᵗ Edition 2016

FORENSIC MYSTERY/THRILLER ©

ISBN: 978-1-948059-56-5

Library of Congress Cataloging-in-Publication Data

EVIL LIKE ME/Steve Bradshaw

Printed in USA

EVIL LIKE ME© is a work of fiction.

Names, characters, businesses, organizations, places, institutions, events, and incidents either
are the product of the author's imagination or use is fictitious. Any resemblance to actual
persons, living or dead, events, or locals is entirely coincidental and fictitious

BOOKS BY STEVE BRADSHAW

The Bell Trilogy
Bluff City Butcher
The Skies Roared
Blood Lions

Evil Like Me

Serial Intent

ACKNOWLEDGMENTS

A special thanks to A.J. Scudiere for her investment of time and talent in the review of my draft manuscript. I thank Margie Colton for teaming up with me on this project—her skillful editing and thoughtful perspectives were greatly valued. I want to thank Griffyn Ink authors for their input along the way, and Eli Jackson for the special care and attention given to this publication of ELM each step of the way. Thank you Susan Reichert for your dedication to the art of prose, the honing of my writing skills, and your valued advice. And—as always—I want to thank my family for their unwavering support and understanding as I often drift away into research or disappear into my world.

"All we know is still infinitely less than all that remains unknown."
William Harvey

A story inspired by true events

In 1972 the U.S. Government began research into psychic-phenomena for potential domestic and military applications. After testing thousands of self-proclaimed psychics, few were contracted—remote viewers. Within six months the project was reclassified top secret.

In 1995 the CIA abruptly terminated the 'Stargate Project' claiming the research produced no actionable information utilized by intelligence operations. Independent reviewers disagreed. Declassified documents later released to the public were incomplete. Remote viewers vanished.

Many parapsychology experts claim the twenty-five year government research had been successful, and that a secret international effort to develop and control psychic-weapons of mass destruction was underway.

PRIMARY CHARACTERS

Baily, Cameron	Memphis Homicide Detective
Baldwin, Alfred E.	U.S. Attorney General
Cankor, T.L.	Defense Intelligence Agency
Cottam, Henry	Director Memphis PD
Jackson, Buford	Parapsychologist
Keller, Hunter	Drifter
Middleton, Elda	Landlord
Patterson, Abby	Private Investigator
Petty, Victoria	Shelby Medical Examiner
Swenson, John	Bethesda Research
Wilcox, Tony	Memphis Homicide Detective

ONE

Memphis, Tennessee

Two days after Donald Deckle died with a knife in his back and six pints of blood pooled on the floor at the Benton Bank & Trust, there were unexpected developments. Test results linking unsolved homicides in the Midsouth could be made available to Dr. Victoria Petty under certain conditions.

That day she had two suicides, two accidents, and three naturals—six required full autopsies and one an inspection. Since Deckle had died on South Main there were no other homicides in the county. The lull in activity had given her precious needed time. Completion of her transition from Dallas to Memphis meant no loose ends and no turning back. Dr. Petty now carried the full weight of the office on her shoulders—the new Chief Medical Examiner for Shelby County.

Setting ground rules for staff proved more difficult than anticipated. She would not allow the scheduling of day meetings without prior consent. Her days were dedicated to inquests starting at seven o'clock sharp and continuing unabated until completion. Her nights were for reading histology slides and assessing toxicology results, reviewing police and CSI reports, and tying it all back to the autopsy findings. An expeditious release of bodies to families was Petty's second priority, her first, determining cause and manner of death.

When her assistant poked a head in her office after hours announcing unexpected visitors from Washington DC, Petty made yet another exception.

"I'm astonished Bethesda Research sent three representatives to Memphis to hand-deliver test results," she said tongue-in-cheek pointing to the long, leather sofa across from her desk. The advanced testing she wanted was only available at Bethesda—Deckle her fourth brain tissue submission.

Her cramped, dank office was a floor plan afterthought. It sat at the east end of the basement under the two-story brick building converted to a county morgue. Squeezed between the autopsy room and walk-in refrigerator—with accommodations for twenty-five—Petty grappled with the shortcomings of her new forensic home, nothing like the pristine facilities in Dallas. Regardless of the number of light fixtures or thermostat setting, her office remained a small cold medieval dungeon minus the bats and torture apparatus.

"Welcome to Memphis," she said as they filed in. The three blue suits, narrow ties, and starched shirts sat down in unison. Each had the same lapel pin, short haircut, and wire-rimmed glasses pushed up the nose.

"To what do I owe this visit?" Petty asked. Their soft, pale faces and dainty hands were giveaways. She scrutinized the three lab rats like bodies on her autopsy table—absorbing clues to solve her next mystery. The oldest sat in the middle on the edge of the sofa with his small, round mouth poised to speak. The other two melted into the cushions with odd, catatonic stares.

Why come to see me? Is it because I'm the new ME? No. It's something about my tissue submissions? Four cases, amygdala tissue sections could be a bit unusual.

"Thank you for seeing us without a scheduled appointment, Dr. Petty." His lips barely moved until the awkward smile at the end.

"Seems impromptus are the norm around here," she replied with a hint of sarcasm as she glanced at the stack of pending cases on her desk.

Agent Brimley shuffled into the office with his nose in a file. Before speaking, he looked up and put on the brakes. Brimley flashed a surprised look at his boss, spun around, and left the room. The closing door behind him wafted in the sweet smell of human flesh and fresh blood. Petty noted two of her visitors squirmed.

"An endangered species," she said to her guests. "Mr. Brimley is one of my most valued field agents. I do not know what I would do without him."

The one seated in the middle seemed unaffected by the interruption, her words, or the smell. His eyelids flickered like a moth as his mouth transformed into a short straight line, and a tiny hole opened in the center. "I am Dr. John Swenson. This is Dr. Green and Dr. Blanchard." Both nodded with empty eyes staring at the closed door.

"And why are you here?" Petty asked.

"We are here to discuss five deaths in Shelby County."

Not my tests? "Since when did Bethesda Research take an interest in regional deaths?"

"Bethesda's primary interests will always be the provision of specialized testing services and the pooling of morbidity data. However, this meeting is different."

Petty glanced down at the three lights dancing on her phone. "One minute." She hit intercom. "Mary, take numbers. I will return calls when I can."

"Detective Wilcox called three times," squeaked from the dusty box. "He is on the line."

She saw the three visitors blink at the name. "Tell Detective Wilcox I will call him the moment I conclude my meeting. Tell him I hope to have the test results he is looking for." She hung up. "Please, continue Dr. Swenson."

"We are medical doctors and research scientists—histology and toxicology specialists by profession. Because of our credentials and government clearances, we were recruited. We are one of four teams on special assignment with the FBI."

"The FBI?"

"Yes doctor. We've been on assignment three years now. Time is running out."

"Sounds ominous. What's that got to do with me?"

"The matter of interest appears to have emerged in Shelby County. Five recent deaths. Four unsolved homicides and one ruled natural, all occurring over the last eighty-three days."

"Does this have something to do with Donald Deckle?"

"Yes. But the Thomas Derby homicide triggered our interest."

"Mr. Derby's death has been less than eighty-three days ago, Dr. Swenson."

"Mr. Derby's tissue specimens were the first received by Bethesda. It got our attention. Called for a closer look. Now our interests go back to Mr. Frank Pella."

"I remember the Pella case, one of my first during my transition to Shelby County. He is a natural death. I ruled on the case the first week in August."

"August 2 to be precise, Dr. Petty. We are quite confident

after exhumation and a closer examination you will want to change your ruling."

Petty leaned elbows on her desk. Her eyes sharpened. "Frank Pella died from congestive heart failure." She fingered a stack of files and pulled out one. They watched her flip the pages. "His cardio history confirms my findings. Mr. Pella had been diagnosed with *Graves Disease* three years ago. He has a history of rheumatoid arthritis and type-two diabetes. There was no trauma or questionable circumstances surrounding his death." She flipped pages. "No toxicology flags. This is a natural death, gentlemen. I see no reason to dig him up. Exhumations are expensive propositions, complicated, time-consuming, and disturbing to the families."

"The Pella inquest, was it an inspection or full autopsy, Dr. Petty?"

"I'm sure you know the answer, Dr. Swenson. The death certificate has been filed."

"Quite true. External inspection—collection of body fluids, routine toxicology screen, and standard chemistries. You had added a thyroid profile."

"That's more information than appears on Mr. Pella's death certificate, but yes." Petty leaned back and stared at the three. *Where is this going?*

Swenson ignored the implication. "Exophthalmos, did it trigger the thyroid profile?"

"Yes it did." Bethesda or the FBI had an interest in deaths under her purview. Petty heard the stories. The feds had ways of getting information they wanted.

"Bulging eyeballs and medical history did not raise flags," she said. "A deeper investigation was not justified or appropriate. You do know that if Mr. Pella had an attending physician his body would have never been brought here. He would have gone straight to a funeral home."

Swenson's face stayed Botox-blank. "Three years is a very long time for a man with his condition to go it alone, don't you think Dr. Petty?" Swenson buttoned his coat with his white stick fingers and buffed nails. "It's as if Mr. Pella was avoiding someone or something."

Avoiding someone or something? What a peculiar comment. She stared with growing suspicion and disguised emotion as Swenson crossed his skinny legs like a girl.

"If I didn't know better, I would think you read my case file," Petty baited. "But it has been in this stack on my desk since Mr. Pella's death."

Swenson flashed a tight smile. "Did you inspect Mr. Pella's ears?"

"Yes. Of course. A cursory look."

"Cursory as in superficial and hurried, Dr. Petty?"

"No. Cursory as in perfunctory and standard protocol, doctor —a medical history, no trauma, and an unremarkable death scene."

"Granted, but . . ."

Petty flipped pages in the master log. "The day we brought Mr. Pella in for a look, we had three homicides, three suicides, two accidental deaths, and five naturals." She closed the log with a resounding thud. "We're very busy here. The cursory inspection was beyond appropriate. What is your point, Dr. Swenson?"

"I'm sorry," he said. "I ask for informational purposes, not to challenge."

"Why the interest in Mr. Pella's ears?" Petty pushed.

"We suspect damage similar to Mr. Derby's, three more homicides, and possibly others passing through your morgue."

She leaned back and spoke with the authority of a chief medical examiner. "It is best you stop asking questions and start talking to me, Dr. Swenson. I do not have much time to give this."

"Yes. I understand, of course. This is where it gets a bit more complicated."

"You best uncomplicated it," she said rapping fingers on her knee.

"At this juncture we are authorized to speak with only you. Your staff, associates and colleagues, and local law enforcement cannot be involved until certain medical anomalies are assessed, and all affected are identified. Even then we operate in a confidential and proprietary manner."

"I am uncomfortable with your construct. I am part of a legal system. You need to do better."

"As the chief medical examiner for Shelby County, on your quest to ascertain manner and cause of death, you have the power to authorize and conduct confidential collaborations with anyone you so choose. You need not share information with anyone until you are ready. The laws governing the medical examiner medicolegal jurisprudence are quite clear on this account."

You think you can motivate me with legal recitations? "I am satisfied with my rulings, gentlemen. Your unsubstantiated claim —a natural death in my county is a homicide—is weak. My responsibility ends after my ruling unless new and relevant information emerges. At this juncture, I have none. I see no reason to reopen the Pella case."

"Rulings on five deaths under your purview are in error or held in abeyance," Swenson said with growing authority. "This is not the way to start as the chief medical examiner. There are things you do not know, Dr. Petty." His tone softened. "I'm sure you want to rectify any and all errors. It is—of course—now your duty to leave no rock unturned."

Petty straightened the stack on the edge of her desk a second time as she searched for the perfect words. "Yes, I have the authority you describe. Dr. Swenson, you have no authority here. And, you have not given me reasons to reconsider my rulings or to open confidential files with outsiders. Quite frankly, I do not respond well to federal government interventions that violate laws of a sovereign municipality. You are free to pursue in the courts the information you seek. If you are successful there, I will certainly cooperate."

Petty stood and opened her office door with cold eyes on her visitors. "I have people waiting. We're done here, unless you have my test results."

The three remained seated. "We have no intention of seeking a court order," Swenson said.

Petty opened the door wider. "And that would be your decision. Goodbye gentlemen."

"Our only chance for success is to collaborate with the presiding medical examiners and law enforcement in the locales of interest," Swenson persisted as he passed her an envelope. She held it to the light like a cheap trick and flipped it over. The wax seal looked official, an eagle atop a shield with crossed sabers. She broke it and opened the flap as she sat down. Unfolding the stiff parchment, her eyes scanned the three odd scientists—any slight move would trigger a gunfight.

"This is addressed to me," she said. "Signed by the U.S. Attorney General." She read the four short paragraphs in the silent room. "You have regained my attention."

TWO

"I started out with nothing. I still have most of it."
Michael Davis

Tony Wilcox sat alone in a smoky corner of the Lamplighter Lounge sipping a beer and lining-up four burnt fries with a butter knife—they represented the unsolved homicides in his city driving him batty. Since August 22 he got a new one every twenty days. They were stabbed in the back or strangled, and all had bizarre facial deformations he'd never seen before—like they had seen a ghost.

Wilcox had made zero progress since the night he stood over Donald Deckle on South Main. So far the new medical examiner had been zero help—still waiting on some oddball test results from D.C. that "may" tie his latest problems together. To add to the misery, at the Deckle crime scene Wilcox screwed up his debut with the new ME. She was nothing like he had expected. Petty rebuffed his every use of artistic profanity, and she was clearly unimpressed with his raw investigative style. To top things off, Dr. Victoria Petty caught Wilcox looking at her legs as they knelt over the body. All else considered, he had to admit it was a classless move. But the top Memphis homicide detective would get over it. He was too set in his ways to change anything, not even for a good looking medical examiner.

Waiting on the ME was not all he did since the Deckle homicide. His interviews with the three detectives handling the other—potentially linked—cases had not gone well. His in-your-face accusations of gross incompetence and piss poor detective work ended two meetings with middle fingers waving. The third, they had to pull Detective Cameron Baily off him.

Even the interview of the only eyewitness had gone nowhere. Although Wilcox's gut told him the guy was more than an innocent bystander, he did not have enough to hold Hunter Keller, or to even justify a tail. As Wilcox lined up the burnt fries on his crumpled napkin, he knew his clock was ticking. He had seventeen days to figure things out or he would need to add another burnt fry to his napkin.

Each time the door opened, the outside world poured into the dark smoky burger joint like a convoy of semis on high beams. From the last table, he made out the large African American standing at the door scoping out the room. When the door closed, the behemoth started toward him through the scattered tables pushing chairs out of his lane. Wilcox had made a lot of enemies over the years, but he could not make out the face of the one coming at him. He didn't want to shoot the man, but he would. With his hand on his gun he remembered the Memphis Redbirds baseball bat mounted above the jukebox. A dive over a pool table would give him enough space and time to come out swinging.

The black man stopped in the dark room a few feet away. "You're one ugly son of a bitch."

"Yeah, well my mama loves me," Wilcox said, still unable to

make out the face. His left foot pointed at the pool table. "What in the hell do you want? I'm eating my dinner."

"I want to pound your skinny, white ass between the cracks of this crap linoleum."

"Well get in line you big black—Cameron?" He pushed the hanging lamp out. The light splashed on the mystery man's face. "Detective Cameron Baily, you almost got a baseball bat upside your head."

"You and what army's gonna bring it?" Baily flopped down a stack of files on the table knocking the loose silverware onto the floor and tipping over the salt, pepper, and sugar. Tony stared at Baily as he caught his four fries in midair.

Baily pulled out a chair like a toy and sat, the swinging light over the table never got above his nose. "I started feeling sorry for you, Wilcox."

"Aren't you sweet." Tony rearranged the fries on his napkin thinking about the big man now sitting at his table. *Anybody who played right tackle for my Tigers can't be a total son of a bitch. And he's third generation cop to boot. His old man was one of the best—Kent Baily—shot in the head by a punk in Orange Mound—another drug deal gone bad. Thought it would have kept his son out of the brotherhood, but he just came in faster.*

"What're you doin' here?" Wilcox asked.

Baily pushed the stack of files to the center of the table. "I brought you a present, you mean old coot." He waved at the bar and tilted his hand to his mouth. A beer would arrive in minutes.

"You tryin' to get on my good side?" Wilcox said. "My eye's still sore."

Baily smiled. His white teeth lit the table and changed the moment. "You upset me the other day. Don't ever say I don't give a shit about catchin' bad guys. You're lucky you only got one shiner. All I saw was red."

Tony lit a cigarette. "Guess it was a little insensitive," he said under his breath.

"You pissed off half the detectives with that 'holier than thou' crap. We know you're the best at catchin' bad guys, but don't think you care more than any of us."

"You come here to tell me how to be, rookie?" Wilcox leaned back sucking his smoke.

"Nope. Guess you'll always be an asshole. Right now I'm cutting you some slack. You've been through a lot. Just remember, Alex was my friend too. We came up the ranks together. I miss the hell out of him—a damn good man. But there's nothin' we can do about it now. Sometimes the bad guys win. They got my dad and they got Alex. It can't stop us. It must make us stronger."

Wilcox looked over his tilted bottle a hundred miles away. The memory of the day he found his rookie partner tortured and dead was still raw. It could still be his end game.

Baily grabbed a file off the top of the stack. "You want to finish eating your sick lookin' burger and those four grungy fries you're playin' with, or you wanna get somethin' done? I brought the case files of the unsolved homicides that could tie to your Mr. Deckle."

Wilcox mentally returned and focused on the stack. He took a slow drag. "Guess you've looked inside those files since you think they're connected. The boys have been less than cooperative with details," Wilcox muttered.

"'Cause you've been a pain in the ass tryin' to get your way, the hell with everyone else. It's a new day, Detective Wilcox. You actually have to be nice to people you work with." Baily opened the first dog-eared file and knocked over a beer. Wilcox caught it like the fries and didn't spill a drop. Baily's beer arrived. They sat and drank and stared at each other—thinking.

"August 22. Thomas Derby, a thirty-seven-year-old white

male," Baily scanned. "Found hangin' out the window, fourteenth floor of the Sterick Building."

"Damn abandoned building for decades. Tell me why this is not a suicide?"

"The autopsy. Petty said Mr. Derby had to be dead before he got strung up." Baily looked up from the file. "Guess he couldn't hang himself dead, and I'm no doctor." He grabbed his longneck and stuck it in his smile. Wilcox frowned rubbing his unshaven jaw.

Smart ass. "Then how'd the ME say he died?" Wilcox asked.

"Strangled. One hand. A crushing grip. Petty said it shattered the thyroid cartilage and fractured cervical vertebrae—neck spine bones. She made these notes in red ink—three of the seven cervical vertebrae were snapped clean in two. Strangulation pressure had to be great. Trauma to the thyroid cartilage and trachea—the front part of the neck—is always expected in strangulations, but the damage to Derby's spine was excessive."

"Can that damage happen other ways like running into something, or the body dropping some distance and stopping with the rope around the neck? Seems to me body weight directed to the noose could do serious damage."

"Petty says no. There's telltale tissue damage fitting both fracture sites, one large hand wrapped around the guy's neck—a fat thumb over the thyroid cartilage and four fingers clampin' down on the back of the neck. Dr. Petty says the finger indentations almost left prints."

Wilcox downed his beer and waved two fingers. "Someone went to great lengths to make it look like a suicide. Takes effort and strength to hang a dead guy out a window."

"Yeah, and Mr. Derby looked strange according to these notes—eyes popping out his head like fried eggs sunny side up, and a snow white face. But all you guys look like that to me." He chuckled into his longneck again.

"Funny—racist. We can't all be melanin gifted. What else you got?"

Baily leaned into the file flipping pages with big fingers. "Don't see anythin' major in detective notes. Wait. Somethin' about a weird smile. Derby's mouth was wide open, corners pulled back to his ears. He swallowed his tongue, too. Petty's notes are full of medical terms. I think 'contorted anterior facials' means face was screwed up."

"We need more on the Sterick building and what Derby was doing there? What did he do for a living? Who wanted him dead? Did anyone report the guy missing? I want to know who saw Derby hanging outside the fourteenth floor window. Really! When's the last time you even looked at that eyesore of a building? It's damn invisible downtown."

"You're the old fart with the history of the city. I'm the rookie. Look. I got a suggestion, somethin' I've been readin' about—the art of closing in on linked killings."

"You read?" Wilcox scoffed.

"Keep that up and I'll pound you again. It says it's best to start with overviews of cold cases, don't get hung up in details early. Take these three cases and Deckle for example, what ties them together that's simple? After we get the big picture, we can dive deeper and see if it holds together or falls apart. This technique is supposed to speed up the process. Gets us lookin' at the relevant stuff first. We don't get lost in the minutia."

Wilcox pushed his cigarette into his burger bun. *The 'graduated assessment process' is how it's done. Glad to see someone's writing this stuff down.* "Go ahead, Baily."

"Okay. We got William Hudson next, another white guy but older than Derby, forty-five. He's an accountant in private practice. Petty puts time of death early morning September 11."

"A decomp. Died twenty days after Derby," Wilcox said.

"Right. But Mr. Hudson wasn't strangled. He got a knife in

the back."

"Like Deckle."

"Correct. They found Mr. Hudson in an office building, White Station Tower. Unlike the Sterick Building, this place is open for business," Baily said.

"Except the tenth floor where the body was found," Wilcox added.

"They closed the floor for remodeling scheduled to start year end. Had controlled access—locked doors in stairwells, elevator programmed to skip it. You needed a key to get on the floor, one only security had."

"That's bullshit. Anyone can get a key, especially bad people," Wilcox said. "It's like damn guns. Never understood the logic of the idiots wanting to take guns from the innocent people."

"Yeah, for another day. Good news is the elevator is monitored 24/7. The last stop on the tenth floor was seven days prior to Hudson's time of death—September 4. The building manager and a couple of architects found the body on the seventeenth, a bad smell complaint."

"What about surveillance, they gotta have cameras."

"They do," Baily said. "But the cameras on ten were turned off when they closed the floor back in July."

"What about stairwells, elevators, and lobbies on all the other floors? Hudson had to get to ten somehow. He didn't just materialize. If we haven't done it yet, we need to look at video from the fourth to the seventeenth. Hudson's gotta be there, and maybe our killer.

"What we have on the knife wound?" Wilcox asked.

Baily kept a nose in the file dragging a finger. "Tell me if this line's out of the Deckle M.E. report. Knife entered posterior thoracic region, deep penetration between T4-T5. Lacerated aortic artery, exsanguination—fatal blood loss."

Exactly like Deckle. "The poor bastard bled to death in minutes," Wilcox said under his breath. They both stared at their beers as they relived the heinous act. Wilcox lit another smoke. "What else?"

Baily blinked his way back to the table and flipped the page. "Same as Derby, the white face and bulging eyes and weird smile, lips pulled back to the ears. Swallowed his tongue. It's like something scared the hell out of 'em."

"What else you got?"

"Petty says he was dead a week before he was found."

"Any signs of a struggle?" Wilcox asked.

"No."

"You got Pemberton's file?"

"Yes. Mark Pemberton, another white guy, age forty-six," Baily said as the waitress walked up behind. "Yes, I want another beer."

"I'll take another long neck," Wilcox said as she took the remains of his burger and cleared the bottle collection. "Leave my burnt fries alone, please ma'am."

Baily's nose dipped back into the open file. "I can tell you a lot about this one. He's mine. I found him in a dumpster behind the Peabody Hotel October 1. You were out of town chasing your favorite serial killer."

Wilcox rolled his eyes. "Don't remind me."

"Mr. Pemberton got killed twenty days after Mr. Hudson. Strangled identical to Mr. Derby. The ME said damage to the neck was a forensic match. Hudson and Derby are connected."

"Slow down, Baily. Who found Pemberton?"

Two wet longnecks hit the table. "Hotel employee taking out the trash. Saw a leg hanging out the top of the dumpster. Mr. Pemberton had to be tossed up there."

"And how did you reach that conclusion?"

"The guy that found him had wheeled out his first pile of

garbage bags. Tossed the bags seven feet up into the jumbo dumpster. He saw nothing. He returns with a second pile of bags five minutes later and sees Pemberton's leg. It had to happen in the five-minute window. Pemberton was on top of the first pile of garbage bags the guy tossed."

"We got pictures?"

"Somewhere in here." Baily dug through the file. "Mr. Pemberton's a big guy, two hundred and thirty pounds. I looked for a ladder or somethin' in the alley to stand on. I found nothing."

"Or he came from high above, Baily."

"Damn! The roof."

"Is the parking garage next to that dumpster?"

"Yes sir. I missed it," Baily sighed.

"Derby, Hudson, Pemberton, and Deckle: four unsolved homicides twenty days apart, two identical strangulations, two identical knifings, four weird faces, all around the same age. Derby's the only one repositioned to look like a suicide," Wilcox said.

"Maybe the killer stopped trying to hide his work after Derby?"

If that's true, there could be kills before Derby. "We need to take a closer look at all deaths in the city twenty day increments prior to the Derby death. I mean all homicides, suicides, accidental, and naturals. We need to look for more connections."

"You think we got a serial killer?" Baily asked.

"I don't know. It's too soon to go there," Wilcox said. "Could be organized crime taking out the trash, or just coincidental. We need something more definitive to connect the cases."

"Your Mr. Deckle's the only one with an eyewitness," Baily said as he opened the file.

"Right. Hunter Keller, a strange little guy. Works in a used book store across from the bank—Rare Books," Wilcox said lighting another cigarette. "Says he saw someone go in the bank. Claims he tried to warn Deckle—called him on his cell. Couldn't get him to answer, so he called 911. The ME said Deckle was dead before the call to 911. I have Deckle's cell. Keller never called him."

"Sounds a little screwy, but it would not be the first time an eyewitness couldn't remember. What else did Keller tell you?"

"He described an old model sedan that crawled by the bank with its lights off. Claims it parked in the alley. He said he was closing the book store when it caught his attention. He gave me a 'comic book' description of a guy leaving the car and entering the bank—a large, dark man floating over the ground wearing a long, black coat, the collar up, and a wide brimmed hat with a round top."

"Sounds like the 'Darkman', an old sci-fi movie."

Wilcox put down his longneck and flipped his Zippo lighter between his fingers "I talked to Deckle's wife that night."

"You went to see her?"

"Nope. Talked to her on Deckle's cell phone. She called right before I crossed Main to talk to Mr. Keller. She knew something had happened. A Memphis cop answered the phone and passed it to me."

"You told her on the phone her husband was killed?"

Wilcox lit another smoke. "Had no choice. But that's not what I'm trying to tell you, Baily. His wife was on the cell phone with her husband the same time when Keller claims he called Deckle. The two were talking when the car parked in the alley. That old sedan belongs to Deckle."

"Strange, but I don't think Keller did this."

"Is it your gut or brain talking?" Wilcox shot back

"My brain says any one of the four dead guys could crush that little guy like a bug."

"I don't know. I interviewed him all night. He's more than an eyewitness. He's hiding something."

Baily pulled out a small notepad. "I saw that comment in the Deckle file, so I did some checking on Keller." He flipped a few pages and squinted at his bullet points. "Abandoned at birth. Bounced around foster homes until adopted by Arnold and Alma Keller. Grew up in Oklahoma on a farm south of Stringtown."

"Abandoned at birth?" Wilcox rubbed the stubble on his chin watching the door.

"Keller was found in the snow around midnight in December. Don't have a year. He was found stuffed in a cardboard box left at a train stop in Stringtown. Hadn't been a train go through that town for decades. It was abandoned even back then."

"Surprised he didn't freeze to death."

"Some lady found him. She was walking her dog."

"Walkin' a dog at midnight in a snowstorm? What're the chances?" Wilcox scoffed.

"Hospital report said he was wrapped in a bloody blanket with his umbilical cord still attached. They estimated he was less than an hour old when they got him. Said he almost died 'cause the drop in body temp. His name came from the blanket—a Hunter blanket.

"The guy's described as a quiet bookworm type," Baily said. "I think he came into our world because he saw somethin' outside his window at closing time. Maybe he screwed up some of the details, but there's a chance he did see Deckle's killer."

"I couldn't confirm a thing he said."

"Maybe he was smoking pot or somethin'." Baily held his notepad up to the hanging lamp. "Here's something I forgot. His adoptive parents died five years ago."

"No shit, Baily!" Wilcox slammed his longneck to the table. "What in the hell's the matter with you? Don't you think you should have led with that little piece of information?"

"It seems way more important now, after talkin' about the four cases."

"Shut up, Baily. How did they die?"

"Oh God. Double homicide."

Wilcox's cigarette hung on his lip. "I'm going to shoot you in the face. Someone needs to take your kind of stupid off the streets."

"Look. I'm sorry. I didn't think."

"Just tell me how the adoptive parents were killed."

"Get your gun out," Baily mumbled as he stared at the page. "The father was stabbed in the back, and the mother was . . ."

"Strangled!" Wilcox sucked a half-inch off his cigarette with his eyes burning a hole through Baily. "Do you read? Did you read before coming here to interrupt my dinner?"

"I scanned it. I was runnin' around pullin' it together. Everybody was givin' me shit."

Wilcox took a deep breath. His opinion of youth had once again been substantiated. They don't have a clue. "What else do you have?"

He pulled a page from Deckle's file. "This is a copy of the email I got before coming here. I stuck it in your file and did not look at it." Baily read to himself. His eyes moved from the page to the Wilcox.

Wilcox grabbed the paper. "Says the investigating officer is a Deputy Carl Bennet—first on the scene. He found Arnold Keller on the front porch, a bowie knife in the center of his back. Bennet went in the farmhouse. It was a shambles—drawers pulled out and upside down on the floor, bookshelves emptied, torn cushions off sofas and torn mattresses off beds. Bennet found Alma Keller in a bedroom." Wilcox squinted. "Coroner ruled death by affixation, strangulation."

"You think Keller killed his parents?" Baily asked.

Wilcox kept reading. "Says Keller was in Maryland at the

time. Atoka County Sheriff kept the case open three years. They think the double homicide was likely a home invasion gone bad. No suspects. Cold case."

"And what do you think?" Baily asked.

"It's not a home invasion. You don't tear into cushions and mattresses when you're robbing someone. They were looking for something. Alma and Albert Keller were executed." Wilcox leaned over the table. "You got any other bombshells to share, Detective Baily?"

"Keller's a genius."

"Really. Now there's another useless piece of information."

"There's a notation in the Stringtown police report. Hunter Keller took an IQ test his senior year in high school. His IQ was listed as unmeasurable. It made the Stringtown newspaper. He got a ribbon at the county fair."

"You think it might be a little bit odd that our squirrely eyewitness is a genius working in a secondhand bookstore, and his parents were killed like our four homicides?" Wilcox punched speed dial—the ME office. "Maybe Petty's got something. She sent brain tissue to D.C. on all four victims. Said she saw something peculiar. I have no clue what that means."

Baily read from the file. "'Multiple lesions found on a normal amygdala of a healthy male are linear in nature.'"

The phone rang. "Stop reading and start pulling this shit together," Wilcox barked.

Baily deserved it. Under Wilcox's stare, he gathered the loose papers and stuck them in the Deckle file. A file on the bottom of the stack slid off the table and exploded on the floor, and paper and photos skidded across the grimy cracked linoleum.

Wilcox waited for someone to answer the phone as he glanced down at a photograph centered in the only light. "Baily, what's that?" Wilcox picked it up and held it to the lamp.

"Crime scene pics from the four homicides." He kept

scooping papers and pictures. "It's okay. They're labeled on back so I won't get them mixed up." Baily stuffed the last fistful into the file and joined Wilcox. Both stared at the one picture. "That one is from the Hudson crime scene. People just standin' outside the White Station Tower watchin' the medical examiner's people remove the body. Always draws a crowd."

"Look closer, Baily. What do you see?" Wilcox asked.

Baily squinted. "I see a bunch of white people drinking and rubbernecking. They're holdin' their bottles smilin' and havin' a good ole' time."

"You're a racist, Baily."

He laughed at the crusty homicide detective who saw racism in everything.

"This is not a black/white thing, Detective Wilcox. It just so happens in this picture you got a bunch of white people standing around without a care in the world. They're oblivious to the fact that some poor bastard got killed. They're not thinking about the hell the guy went through, or the mama who's gonna have her heart broken. Your right. All I see is a bunch of cold white people enjoying their special evening entertainment."

"Okay, now set aside your judgments. Take a close look at each face in this picture. Do your damn job, Detective Baily. Tell me what you see."

Baily grabbed the picture like a kid forced to take his medicine. Wilcox gave up on the ME office and pocketed his cell. Petty was still in her meeting and now no one was answering the phones at the county morgue.

"Holy shit!" Baily sat down dazed. He swallowed hard with his eyes fused onto the photograph.

"Now tell me what you see, Detective Baily."

"In the crowd, on the back row, I see Hunter Keller."

THREE

"Is this other stack of pictures from the Derby case?" Wilcox asked. Baily kept staring at the picture in his hand.

"Snap out of it, son. Are these pictures from the Derby case, a simple yes or no?"

Baily nodded. "I can't believe I missed this. You're right, I am racist."

"Stop pouting and look at the Pemberton photos." Wilcox fanned through his stack like he was hunting for the aces in the deck.

"I'll be a son of a bitch. Keller's standing outside the Sterick Building. He's at the bus stop across the street." *What in the hell are you doing at my crime scenes?*

Baily's head hung over his handful of photographs. "He's here, too."

Wilcox punched MPD on his cell. "Jennifer, I need to send a car to Hunter Keller's place. Address's on file. Eyewitness to Deckle homicide. I want the man watched until I get there. Under no circumstance let him leave. If he comes out of his apartment, pick him up for questioning. I don't have enough to hold him, but I got to talk to the guy."

Baily slouched back in his chair.

"Snap out of it," Wilcox barked.

"I'm useless." Baily pined as he dropped his head. Wilcox smiled at the broad shoulders and bald patch shining under the hanging lamp. "I can't believe I'm a racist," Baily muttered.

"Hell, Baily. You know black people aren't racist."

"Stop. I'm serious." He stuffed pictures into the file and sat up straight in his chair.

"Look, if it helps any I'm racist too. We're all racist, judgmental pricks to some degree."

"What you just said makes no sense," Baily said.

"It's human nature to think you're better than everyone else. We think we got all the answers. We are the smartest and fairest person on the planet. Truth is that none of us have all the answers. We're all trying to figure out life. We have our fears, skeletons in our closets, and crosses to bear. And to make it worse, we're all at a different place in our life." Wilcox rubbed his face like he just rolled out of bed. "I can be an asshole at times, but I mean well. I try not to be judgmental. I don't care anything about color or race or gender or anything. I care about right and wrong. I care about stopping bad people from hurting good people—simple as that."

"That's different. Everyone knows you're an asshole."

"Shut up, Baily. I'm giving you some fatherly advice."

"I'm just sayin' you're not racist. Some people are racist, but I never thought I was one of them."

"You met Elliott Sumner. He's the guy who opened my eyes. You know why he's the most successful forensic investigator out there?"

"Easy. Everyone knows the guy's a genius with a photographic memory."

"Nope. You're wrong. He'll tell you. It's because he knows how to focus. The man's got self-discipline. He told me anyone can do what he does. He simply eliminates mental clutter, all the meaningless bullshit. He's a master at it. Sumner said human emotions and opinions are major detractors from finding truth where facts exist. People are so busy with the bullshit that they lose the ability to recognize reality. When you lose touch with reality, you're totally lost in a complex world. Then it only gets worse."

"Guess that makes sense," Baily said.

"Good talk. I gotta go."

"Wait," Baily said. "We need to work these four cases together."

"Don't even go there."

"Why not? It makes perfect sense."

"No, it makes imperfect sense. It is a bad idea. I work alone. You would slow me down. I will work the Deckle case and you will work the Hudson case. When and if they connect, that's when we get back together. Right now we got nothing but pictures of a nut in a crowd and some scary-looking, white, dead people."

"These cases are connected and you know it. I'll do whatever you tell me. I'll play second fiddle. You're the boss."

Wilcox sucked his cigarette reaching for his keys and eyeing Baily. *I do need someone to go to Stringtown to do some digging. I'm not looking forward to that drive. If Keller's a serial killer, I'm gonna have a chase on my hands. Gonna need help building the case.*

Alex flashed in his mind. The raw pain washed over him taking his breath. "No Baily. I work alone." Wilcox saw Alex hanging in the Memphis public library naked, tortured to death. They used Alex to get to him. *I can't be the reason someone else dies—never again.*

Wilcox dropped a twenty on the table. "I'm picking up Keller for questioning. You can sit in on the interview. That's it, Baily."

"I don't think so."

"Suit yourself."

Baily got up and blocked Wilcox's only path out of Lamplighters. Baily was a head taller and hundred pounds heavier. "These cases are connected. If Keller's the monster we think he is, there will be more killings. You can't let your feelings get in the way of the right decision."

"Move out of my way or I will shoot you, Baily."

"Not working together puts innocent lives at risk, Detective Wilcox."

"Move now," he demanded with his hand on Baily's rock hard chest.

"Give it a week. If Keller's not the one, I disappear and you go back to being an asshole."

"This is the last time I'm gonna politely ask you to move your fat ass out of my way." He pushed, but Baily didn't budge.

The rookie detective, rooted to the floor like a giant oak, said, "A smart man once told me good detectives put aside emotions and opinions. They focus on reality where facts live. They are not distracted by personal shit." Baily leaned into Wilcox's face. "This is the right thing to do. Give it a week. You're in charge of everything. Let's find out if we got a serial killer."

Wilcox stared. *The son of a bitch has a point. I gotta vet Keller before he has a chance to kill again. Nothing else should matter. Keller's now the prime suspect. Hell, he's the only suspect.* Wilcox picked up the empty longneck like a club. *I can't lose another partner. But I can't let a serial killer get away.*

"We work one week," Wilcox said. "It's enough time to vet Keller."

"Agreed." Baily relaxed his muscles—no longneck upside the

head. He brushed off Wilcox's lapel. "French fry salt on your blazer, sir."

Wilcox slapped his hand away. "No touching. And you say nothing about this arrangement to Cottam. I don't need him thinking I'm taking on a partner, because I'm not."

"Yes sir." Baily turned and gathered up the files. "The director will think you're being a team player. It will keep him confused for a week."

"You're already pissing me off."

"Don't worry; I'll make sure you continue to look like a pain in the ass, sir."

Wilcox rolled his eyes and focused. "You go to Stringtown tonight. I want to know everything about Keller's parents and the day they were killed. You better be able to answer every goddamn question I have when you get back. I want to know Keller's whereabouts on the day they died. That means you check it out and get a hundred percent confirmation."

"I will handle it," Baily said.

"Find Atoka County Sheriff Bennet. Tell him we got homicides in Memphis that may be a possible connection to the Keller family killings. You say nothing about Hunter Keller. You let him bring up the guy and just listen."

"I gotta get a look at those police files," Baily said.

"Bennet should open them to you if you do your job right. He'll think we can help him solve his cold cases, probably the only homicides in his county for a hundred years."

"I'll go to the Keller farm myself, poke around some."

Wilcox did not let on he was pleased Baily thought of it himself. "After you get backstory, spend a day at the farm, alone. Take time to look at things from multiple vantage points. Reconstruct the crime scene. Talk to neighbors, teachers, shopkeepers, and people around town. Stringtown is a small place. Everyone knows everyone."

"I'll find someone who knows Hunter Keller's life story, learn more about his abandonment. It could be an important part of the puzzle—who found him and what they were doing out at midnight in a snowstorm."

"Find out if they were close to the Kellers. What was the connection? Trouble is they might not be alive today."

"It is going back thirty-five years," Baily said.

"If Hunter Keller is a serial killer, his making started back then."

"Most people will be dead or old as hell," Baily said. "I may get my hands on some physical evidence from the Keller family homicides."

"Probably tucked away in a dusty evidence room. They should have the knife. If we're lucky we may be able to get DNA. And their clothing, the killer, or killers, had to be all over them. Back then they weren't thinking DNA."

"Should I ask for copies of the autopsy reports for Dr. Petty to look at?"

"Hell yes," Wilcox said. "She can tell us if there are forensic connections. We got matching 'unidentified' DNA off our four victims. If it matches with the Kellers, we got something important."

"How do I take this trip? Director Cottam will ask questions."

"You say you got a family matter. Stay away from the details. Fill out the paperwork. Cottam doesn't see that stuff. If he notices you're gone, I'll tell him I took on the Hudson case to help." Wilcox looked down at the photo of Keller standing outside White Station Tower. He grabbed it. "I'm holdin' onto this one."

They walked out the backdoor of the Lamplighter. Their two-hour talk felt like ten minutes. Bumper to bumper cars had filled the small parking lot squeezed between three two-story brick buildings. When Wilcox lit his cigarette, an engine started a half block down the side road. They watched the old sedan roll past their parking lot. The car lights were off.

"What in the hell was that about?" Baily asked. He pulled out his gun and ran to the road. Wilcox didn't move except to puff on his cigarette and smile.

Baily returned with his gun dangling at his side. "You gonna shoot a car?" Wilcox chided.

"Yeah, if it shot at me first."

"You young cops are all alike," Wilcox sighed.

"But did you see that? It was an old model sedan like the one Hunter Keller had described. And what the hell, no lights all the way down the road. Normal people don't drive like that. Very strange."

"The clock is ticking, Baily. A storm is rolling across Arkansas. We have no time for lame distractions. It has been three days since Deckle died. If the twenty-day rule holds, we got two weeks and three days to solve this thing before someone else dies."

"I understand," Baily said as he holstered his gun.

"Go to Stringtown tonight. I've got a date with Hunter Keller —if he's still in town." *And I need my PI to check out some people like no one else can.*

"Someone was out here waiting for you," Baily said. "Your picture was on the front page of *The Memphis Tribune* today— the Donald Deckle homicide you said you would solve. Maybe someone doesn't want you to. Maybe that someone was parked out here waiting for you to come out alone."

"If any of that's true, they'll be back. Enough talking. I want you to focus, Baily. Go to Stringtown."

FOUR

Dr. Petty stared at the threaded parchment graced with a gold flaked government seal. The four paragraphs were ominous and vague on purpose. *If this is big enough to get the attention of a U.S. Attorney General,* she thought, *what kind of hell has found its way to Memphis?*

The old refrigerator motor, perched on dusty grease laden springs, wobbled in the crawl space behind her office wall. It struggled to keep twelve bodies cold in the next room. The rumbling shook her diplomas and framed certificates and the picture of a younger Petty with her eye in a microscope—a departing gift from her staff at the Institute of Forensic Science. They did not want her to leave Dallas. Now, she was a million miles away from those memories. Dr. Petty was more than ready to take the chair of chief medical examiner.

After scrutinizing the letter, she again studied her three visitors from Bethesda, this time with even more discerning eyes. Drawing upon her eidetic skills, she revisited each spoken word and subtle clue since they had taken a seat on her sofa. Petty would miss nothing going forward. She was very good at solving puzzles. Now, the forensic sleuth would find the guarded portal into their secret world.

Dr. Swenson's rigid posture relaxed when he removed the small leather notebook from his coat. With the smile of a child, he cradled it on his lap like a kitten. The sealed letter from the attorney general seemed to empower the odd, little man. Petty observed the subtle facial transition as he moved to the next level of revelations. Assessing Dr. Swenson's authenticity was as important to her as the information he would deliver for the federal government.

"The five in Shelby County died at the hands of a 'real monster'," he said.

"A 'real monster'? I've not heard those two words used together professionally."

His catatonic gaze found her. "I've chosen the words carefully. This is not my first time to have this discussion. I assure you my intent is accuracy." He looked at the ceiling, took a deep breath, and found Petty's challenging eyes.

"'Real' means it is true, not merely ostensible, nominal, or apparent. It exists or occurs as fact. It is actual rather than imaginary or fictitious. 'Monster' is any animal or human grotesquely deviating from normal shape, behavior, or character. It is a person who excites horror by cruelty and wickedness."

Petty showed nothing. The motor in the wall stopped churning on the word "wickedness". Only the laminar airflow blowers in the autopsy room broke the morbid silence of the dead county morgue. She watched Swenson swallow and his eyes dart to the closed door.

He's afraid of this "real monster", she thought. *He thinks it is out there following him. All three of are nervous, pensive, and absorbed. What is this thing they fear?*

Swenson's eyes jumped back to Petty. "The Shelby County victims died like all the others."

"How many others?" she asked.

"Thirty-eight and counting."

"Including my five?"

"Yes," Swenson shot back.

"And what is the *cause of death*, doctor?"

"'Lethal telepathic manipulation of the amygdala'. As you've already experienced, your four unsolved homicides with amygdala lesions were staged as either stabbing or strangulation homicides. And, I will add here, some were hidden in the natural death category like Mr. Pella."

"You can't be serious," Petty pushed at the open letter on her desk like it was a failing term paper. "Are you telling me the U.S. Attorney General is hunting someone with some science-fictional murder weapon?"

"Yes. And it's not just the Attorney General, Dr. Petty. This has the attention of certain members of Congress, the CIA, and the White House."

"This sounds absurd," Petty scoffed.

Swenson held up a hand, more to gather his thoughts than to stop her rant. "The person we hunt operates outside known sensory channels, Dr. Petty. This monster kills without physical contact. We classify this 'new' manner of death as 'remote homicide'."

"Dr. Swenson. A telepathic induced brain lesion is an enormous reach." Straightening the already neat stack of files on her desk, Petty processed the obscure concept attempting to manage her tendency to dismiss new concepts—a known weakness following her through life. "You'll excuse me if I have a problem with your theory."

Dr. Swenson paused to allow her to search her medical databank. Immediate denial was not a surprise—he saw it every time. Each ME brought into the program handled the information the same way. First they completely rejected the possibility. Then their curiosity took over. Grasping the concept would always be difficult for the scientifically advanced. It broke every rule in their book.

"Spontaneous tissue alterations caused by external forces other than electrical, chemical, and physical are theoretical at best. Telekinetic manipulation of tissue is unproven fantasy. Scientific evidence does not support the existence of such a bizarre paranormal phenomenon," Petty orated as if correcting a medical student in front of the entire class.

Swenson sprinkled more on her fire of doubt. "There is a clairvoyant component."

Dr. Green spoke for the first time. "With advanced extrasensory skill sets, our psychic killer obtains current and future information, including the location of the next victim."

"When the time is right, we will provide proof," Swenson said.

Petty tapped her ink blotter with a painted nail. "This is not going well for you, doctor. Two of my unsolved homicides died from strangulation, and two died from exsanguination following massive, aortic lacerations. All four are traumatic deaths due to observable, physical attacks. And Mr. Pella is a natural death. Nothing you've said to me changes those realities. You have made unsubstantiated, grandiose, laughable claims, and I still have nothing on my amygdala lesions, the tissue samples I sent to Bethesda in good faith."

"I believe we need more . . ."

Petty cut him off. "Rather than results, I get this malarkey."

Swenson smiled pushing his wire frames tighter to his face waiting for Petty to stop talking. "The amygdala is a fascinating structure with enormous responsibilities."

"I learned that my second year in medical school—processing memory, decision-making, emotion, and behavior to name a few. We are all doctors here. We are well versed in the anatomy and function of the human body. That's not the point."

Swenson pushed forward. "I'm sure you're aware of the universally accepted fact the amygdala modulates aggression, fear, and anxiety. Can we agree on this simple point?"

"Of course. The function and role of the amygdala is not in question."

"You are a forensic pathologist, Dr. Petty. You need physical evidence." Dr. Blanchard opened a small briefcase and passed a file to Swenson. He removed a report and passed it to Petty. "These are the MRI's of four of the five Shelby County cases. You are familiar with the lesions on each victim's amygdala. Note they are identical in location, frequency, and dimension."

Petty studied the report scrutinizing the MRI frame by frame. Each was labeled: patient name, processing date, identification markers, and various government seals of authentication. She passed the report back to Swenson. "This only confirms my findings, the reason I sent the tissue to Bethesda for additional assessment. I was expecting more from you."

"When we exhume Franklyn Pella, you will see the same lesions, Dr. Petty."

"The presence of acute lesions has been established in four cases. How they got there is my focus. Without any proof, you claim a 'clairvoyant monster' willed them there. Medical examiners do not do well with outlandish theories and unfounded speculation."

"Medical examiners deal in facts," Swenson said. "Yes. Bethesda confirms your findings, Dr. Petty. Is that enough? Are you now able to do your job?" This time he could see the hesitation in her eyes. "Would you agree the replication of brain lesions is peculiar? Replication four or five or thirty-eight times would be more than peculiar, I would think. Would it be bizarre?

EVIL LIKE ME   35

Would it be strange? Or would it be impossible? I suppose it could not be impossible because we can both agree it exists at least four times."

He passed Petty documents. "The toxicology screens are negative, Dr. Petty. The histology does not support electrical, chemical, or physical intervention. There is no evidence of searing, hemolysis, or disease—past or present. The lesions are spontaneous, acute—not chronic in origin. The lesions are targeted and encapsulated at the cellular level. There is no associated trauma. Electron microscopy shows the brain tissue disruptions come from within."

Blanchard left the sofa and leaned over her desk with a photograph of the EM imagery. After she studied it, he passed a photograph of her four unsolved homicides. "Bulging eyes, ashen complexions, and contorted facials—those horrible grins—are symptomatic of the spontaneous, amygdala lesions."

Petty's eyes moved from the photographs to Dr. Blanchard. He backed away and straightened his stance. "You've not observed the paralysis, the back arching to the snapping point and joints locked," he said.

"The victims of this kind of psychic-attack experience a level of terror so intense their autonomic nervous system takes over," Swenson said under his breath. "Life support systems shut down. In the end, the heart simply stops." He blinked back into the moment. "Do you recall the death of Oklahoma Senator Willingham some time ago?"

"I recall news reports—cardiac arrest, senate floor."

"A story for public consumption. Actually, Senator Willingham died in the basement of the U.S. Capital building. It was the first time we witnessed death by remote manipulation of the amygdala. I'm sorry. The term's still new. I meant to say *lethal telepathic manipulation*."

"I'm listening," Petty said.

"It happened in the heart of our nation's capital. I'm sure you can appreciate the potential implications. We had to view it as a possible attack on our government. Was Willingham's death a test? What were we dealing with: a killer virus, a poison, or a game-changer? Who is the next target? Could it be the president?

"This new and bizarre national security risk engaged all government investigative bodies. The senator's corpse was studied. We ran every test known, and some not known. The top forensic minds in the country processed the death scene and conducted the autopsy. Someone attacked Senator Wilber Willingham, Dr. Petty. Unlike your homicides, he died from amygdala lesions alone."

"The senator's autopsy and related files will be downloaded to your computer," Blanchard said holding his cell phone.

Swenson's confirmatory nod pulled Petty back. "You'll see some proprietary testing methods revealing the cellular aberrations unique to the senator and others. After you review this material, I'm confident many of your questions will be answered."

"The files should be on your computer now," Blanchard said.

Petty jiggled her mouse. Her screen came alive, but it was not her regular desktop. She saw the gold seal on the letterhead centered in a sea of blue. Below were two words—Rejdak Project.

"What is the Rejdak Project?" Petty asked.

"This is Dr. Green's area," Swenson said nodding to the silent one on the sofa.

He had the voice of an old woman with bronchitis—weak and raspy. "Zdenek Rejdak is an Eastern Bloc parapsychologist most noted for his work, 1950s through the 1970s. He led the way on psychotronic research, the study of the ability to sense places and events from great distances. It is remote viewing."

"I've read about 'mind control' and 'remote viewing'," Petty said. "The research is lean at best. It generates more questions than answers."

"Are you familiar with the term 'psychic-weaponry'?" Swenson asked.

"No, but I think I can grasp the concept."

"Psychic-weaponry has received serious attention from the world's top governments. At this juncture I'm not at liberty to discuss the extent of U.S. involvement. However, I can tell you we are involved and significant military applications do exist."

"Did one of your lab rats escape, doctor?"

Swenson blinked as if a book slammed on a table behind him. "The level of psychic manipulation we are seeing is beyond our laboratory experience."

"The so-called threat is new. Is it home grown or imported?" she asked.

"New. We think home grown. Based on the ramping kill rate, we project a catastrophic future. If left unabated, lethal telepathic manipulation, or LTM, of the amygdala could be a top five cause of death in our country."

"If your psychic-monster increases targets or the skill set spreads," Petty scoffed.

"I suggest you begin to consider adjusting your flippant view of a delicate matter you do not understand," Swenson scolded. "This is not the government's problem alone."

"Our only chance of stopping this is to expand knowledge it exists," Dr. Green said.

"You want me to believe psychic-weapons suddenly exist," Petty said rolling her eyes.

"What you believe changes nothing. They do exist. Entities developing them threaten our nation. If they use them to attack us, they will likely be successful. The advance will alter the balance of power in the world and change the course of history."

"LTM is the ultimate weapon of mass destruction,"

Blanchard said. "When future wars are fought with it, there is no battlefield. The enemy population dies where they stand in their homeland."

"Efficient geopolitical and socioeconomic genocide," Dr. Green said.

"And our government is the one who needs to control LTM," Petty said with disdain.

Dr. Swenson stared without emotion. "Can you think of another place safer?"

"I'm sorry you view me uncooperative, doctors. My life is about operating with empirical information. Everything I do is based on known science and verifiable observations. I do not do anything based on wild theory and pure logic. You've only begun to share information." Petty picked up the letter and waved it at them. "I suppose working with the 'feet on the ground' is the best way for the federal government to get ahead of this. Tell me the other cities involved?"

"Henryetta, New York City, St. Louis, Washington D.C., and Boston."

"Our work is top secret. The public cannot know. If knowledge of this *dire situation* got out, it would have an increased negative impact our projected morbidity calculus. We would need to factor in collateral deaths due to mass hysteria and alerting our nemesis."

"When can I talk to the other medical examiners?"

"Only after we validate the Memphis cases."

"And if they're not linked?" Petty asked.

"We won't bother you anymore," Dr. Swenson said as he got to his feet.

The old motor in the wall jumped back. The frames and bookshelves rattled. Petty watched Dr. Swenson tuck his leather notebook in his coat breast pocket. Dr. Green closed his briefcase and stood at the sofa like a boy waiting for a school bus. Dr.

Blanchard hung over Petty's computer screen tapping the keyboard with spread-handed flurries.

She turned in time to watch a horizontal bar fill and close. "I can access data?" she asked.

"You are cleared for phase one," Blanchard said.

"SgME6 is your unique, proprietary access code," Swenson said.

A simple code I'm sure, she thought.

"Thank you for your time, Dr. Petty." He paused and smiled. "And yes, it is a simple code for sure." Swenson winked and the three filed out of her office.

The motor in the wall stopped. The fume hood fans in the autopsy room stopped. The lights flickered and a light popped out. Victoria Petty was not alone with her thoughts.

FIVE

"If you're going through hell, keep going."
Winston Churchill

He let me live . . .

Billy Dodson pushed back in his seat toweling off and releasing the airbrakes. He started crunching the gears. The semi crawled onto the empty highway with two objectives, build speed and get distance. Every three seconds Dodson shifted and the tractor trailer lunged forward for a short-lived whining climb and the swallowing of another thirty yards. When he got the nerve, he looked in the side mirrors. The man in the hoodie was gone.

Dodson held onto the wheel with a shaking hand and lit a cigarette dangling from his taut lips. Then he pressed every button on his dusty console opening every window and vent for precious air. He even turned on the small cab fan and aimed it at his face.

As he gained distance from his imminent threat, the sixty-mile-an-hour whirlwind cooled his wet head, soaked shirt, and burning skin. Dodson's ears popped and heart slowed—at last.

Sound exploded back into his world like he broke the water's surface after a deep dive. With five miles of black asphalt behind him, he could breathe normally again.

In the middle of the flat, dead cotton fields of northeast Arkansas, the forty-ton tractor trailer lumbered along I-55, and Dodson kept looking in his long rectangular side mirrors. When he pitched his second butt out the window and saw the exploding ashes, he started to worry again.

What if he climbed on the back? I'll call police. They'll find me. I won't stop until I see them on my tail. Dodson checked his mirrors again—still nothing. *But he could be on top of the trailer or behind my cab waiting for an opportunity.* Dodson hit the door locks and raised the windows.

He fished for his cell phone swerving the rig. *I'm not calling some Podunk police department in east Arkansas. All I need is a Barney Fife type to get me killed.* He regained control and swallowed hard. *The weirdo said he was out of Memphis. Maybe the cops are looking for em. If they're not, they should be. The guy's dangerous.* Dodson called the MPD.

"Memphis police, how may I direct your call?" The voice was female and strong. It helped his nerves.

"I was almost killed," Dodson said.

"Identify yourself."

"I'm Billy Dodson. I drive a truck—Louisiana Missouri Express." He slapped his face and blinked sweat from his eyes.

"Mr. Dodson, are you in danger now?"

"I don't know. He got out my truck. I'm driving away. He could be on the back. I just don't know for sure."

"Keep driving. Don't stop. Lock your doors. Did this person threaten you?"

"Yes. Well, I don't know. It felt like he did. I think he's a serial killer. He said he's responsible for a lot of people—dead. I'm still not sure why I'm alive. He said I was going to die tonight. I thought he was gonna take me with him."

"Where are you now, Mr. Dodson?"

"Interstate-55 north of Blytheville. I picked him up outside Memphis. He was walking on the side of the highway. I shouldn't have, but it was raining hard. He looked harmless. I just wanted to help."

"I'm transferring you to homicide, Detective Wilcox. Please hold."

"Wilcox here, who's this?"

"I'm Billy Dodson. Driving a truck on I-55 a few miles north of Blytheville."

"Why're you callin' Memphis PD?"

"I picked up a man. He said he killed people. He said he had problems with police in Memphis. I thought you guys would be looking for him. Country cops will get me killed. I think the guy's on my truck, behind the cab or on top of my trailer. He got out. I pulled away. He was gone too fast. Then I started thinking."

"I'm coming your way. Slow your truck to fifty. Whatever you do, do not stop. Are your doors locked and windows up?"

"Hell yes. I was thinking he'd try to climb in my cab."

"Give me your license, Dodson."

"BD48817, Louisiana."

"Did the man identify himself?"

"Said he was Hunter Keller."

Son of a bitch! But why use your name, Keller? "What else did he say?"

"Said he is responsible for a lot of dead people."

"Were those his exact words," Wilcox asked, turning onto I-55 with grill lights flashing.

"He said he couldn't stop it. Said he let them all die."

"I'm on my way, keep driving. Don't exit. Needle on fifty. Tell me more about Keller."

"He's a skinny man, six-feet. Had on a black hoodie and backpack."

"What made you think he was gonna hurt you, Dodson?"

"The way he acted, all quiet and mysterious, hardly talking, keeping his face covered. He tells me about all these people dead because of him. When he said I was going to die, I knew I was next on his list."

"But he didn't kill you when he could. You say he got out of the truck."

"He told me to stop. I thought he would do it to me then. He slid out. Said thanks and closed the door. I pulled away as fast as I could. I was thinking I just might live to tell this one."

"Go back to the people you said he killed. Try to remember his exact words. It's important Dodson," Wilcox pushed.

"He said when he shows up people die. He said he could not help himself, I mean 'stop it'. He told me he takes full responsibility."

"I'm twenty minutes out. I want you to stay on I-55. Do not slow down. If he's on your truck, we don't want him jumping off and getting away."

Wilcox traveled at ninety in the left lane. He put his cell on speaker and set it on the seat. He grabbed his radio mic. "Where did Hunter Keller get out, Mr. Dodson?"

"A mile south of the Hayti exit. Nothin' there but dead cotton fields."

"Hold on. I need to talk to my people on the radio."

He held the mic close so Dodson couldn't hear. "Get me Miss Prior, this is Wilcox."

"Sally Prior. Go ahead detective."

"Get a hold of the Hayti PD and Pemiscot Sheriff's Office. Tell them there's a semi traveling north on I-55, Louisiana plate BD48817. Tell them we have a possible serial killer on the truck driven by a Billy Dodson. Hold on.

"Mr. Dodson, did Hunter Keller say where he was going? And give me his exact words."

Dodson swallowed hard. "Said he had to be in Sikeston tonight."

"Miss Prior. Get Sikeston PD on the lookout for a skinny, white male, six-feet-plus wearing a black hoodie with a backpack. Name is Hunter Keller. He could be walking on the side of the road, Hayti exit off Interstate-55." *If he's not on the damn truck.*

"Mr. Dodson, local police will pull alongside. I'm still a ways out. The Hayti PD will make contact with you very soon."

"I don't know if I can do this."

"They know what's going on. They will inspect your truck in motion and guide you to a controlled stop. If Hunter Keller's on your truck, they'll get him."

"I can't," Dodson said.

"You can do this. You must do this. They will be there soon. The HPD is blocking the highway as we speak. You will be alone on open road with police cars surrounding your truck."

"I'm scared. I really don't think I can do this."

"Tell me more about your time with Mr. Keller." *Stop thinking and keep talking buddy.*

Dodson checked his mirrors and hit his door locks every few seconds. "Keller was quiet a long time. Just sat there looking straight ahead, his hood covering his face. I thought he was tired or the unsociable type. After Blytheville he started talking. Pulled off his hood and leaned back in the seat with his eyes closed. He rambled like he was in a trance or something."

"In a trance?" *What the hell does that mean?*

"Yeah. He said he was drawn to death. Then he said I was gonna die tonight. Told me to exit the highway. I refused. Then he got quiet. Said it wouldn't matter for me anyway."

Wilcox flew down the highway through the dead cotton fields in northeast Arkansas. He saw the roadblock ahead when his radio crackled alive. "Memphis PD, this is HPD in pursuit of Dodson truck on I-55, over."

"Memphis PD, Wilcox here, go ahead HPD, over."

"We're about a mile out from the Dodson truck. No visual at this time. Will initiate CB radio contact and take it from here, over."

"Roger that, HPD. Over and out."

"Mr. Dodson, I'm hanging up now. HPD is close. They will get you on your CB."

"Got them now." The cell phone went dead.

On the inside shoulder Wilcox passed a mile of sitting traffic. Then HPD squad cars opened a path and waved him through. Wilcox's flashing blue streak of cold metal exploded through the roadblock leaving a cloud of dust and burnt rubber. He would not let Keller escape again.

Why tell a random truck driver he's gonna die tonight? Wilcox wondered as he eased back onto the asphalt and checked his watch. It had been almost fifteen minutes since he first spoke to the trucker. *Keller tells him to exit the highway. Dodson refuses. Then Keller has him stop the truck so he can get out. If Keller was gonna kill Dodson, he'd kill him then? Makes no sense he'd climb onto a moving truck.*

The needle touched a hundred as Wilcox shot down the empty highway. His radio and cell were silent. The world flew by in a night blur for another eight minutes. Then, an orange glow filled the horizon straight ahead. Wilcox hit his brakes and skidded out of control. His cruiser spun down the hot asphalt. His smoking tires spit gravel as he fought to keep her on the road. When the car finally stopped and the smoke settled, he could see out his side window. The burning cloud climbed into the night less than a mile ahead.

SIX

"Evil enters like a needle and spreads like an oak tree."
Proverb

After the three from Bethesda left the medical examiner's office, Petty sat alone with her newest mystery. Staring at the letter addressed to her and signed by the attorney general, she studied the four paragraphs—each word seared into her brain. But memorizing a hundred words was not her goal. Her photographic memory had it the first pass. Petty was launching her process, the beginning of an investigation. At the moment, the letter had become the most important piece to her new puzzle.

It was the only thing credible—her visitors and their bizarre claims were in question. Up until Swenson placed the envelope in her hand, Petty searched for a polite way to conclude the bizarre meeting. Now she was scrutinizing an official document. Were there any conflicting statements, errors, or hidden meanings? The letter she held could be the start of the most hideous hunt of her forensic career, or it could be an absolute hoax.

She removed tweezers from her lab coat, inserted the letter into a paper evidence bag, and attached a label. She wrote: Proprietary—Dr. V. Petty prints and DNA isolated top left & bottom right corners of document. *I should find Dr. Swenson and Attorney General Baldwin on this.* She pulled out her cell and scrolled contacts stopping on Richard B. Tanner, M.D., PhD, Vanderbilt Medical School, and Department of Genetic Research.

"Hello Victoria," Tanner said. "I must have dozed off."

"Richard. I'm sorry to call at this hour."

"Nonsense, I was looking in a microscope as usual. It's been a while. How are you doing?"

"I'm good. Thank you for asking. I'm now a Tennessee resident."

"Memphis. I read about your appointment, chief medical examiner. Nashville is happy to get back our M.E on loan to your fair city. Terrible about Dr. Henderson Bates. We heard all the gory details over here in the music city."

"Dr. Bates is recovering. He's offered his support once he gets back on his feet."

"Congratulations to you. I'm confident Memphis will reap great benefits. Your exceptional forensic skills and intuitive investigative spirit are major assets."

"Thank you Richard. I'm calling on a confidential matter. I need a favor."

"Interesting. Please go on."

"I have a letter from the U.S. Attorney General. He seeks my personal assistance on a secret government matter. Without some objective confirmation, the value and content of this letter is in question. I need a closer look, a forensic look."

"I think I understand."

"The people who delivered this letter must be vetted. I can do some myself. One handled the letter. The attorney general should have handled the letter too. It has his signature. I'm looking at it now. It's been preserved in a sterile evidence bag."

"You want me to check it for DNA. If found, you want me to confirm the identity of the one bearing gifts—confirm it was indeed handled by Alfred E. Baldwin?"

"I don't know if a known sample of Mr. Baldwin's DNA is available to compare. If it is possible to check, I would be grateful. Confirmation of participants in an unfolding mystery would help. You know I would not ask if it was not important."

"Victoria, please, of course I can help you. And yes, I have ways of obtaining DNA samples from all prospects. I suppose I've gotten pretty good at trash-diving. Well, I guess I can't take all the credit. My younger generation associates deserve the accolades. They've made me a believer. We all live in our garbage," he chuckled.

"I'll arrange for a courier to deliver the letter overnight," Petty said.

"I know the identity of the U.S. Attorney General. Give me the name of the person who handed you the letter. I can get my people on it immediately."

"I suppose both are in the DC area. Dr. John Swenson is who passed me the envelope. He's an employee of the Bethesda Research Center. I know nothing about him."

"Name is all I need, Victoria."

"I think it best I not go into details with you. The less you know, probably the better."

"I understand fully. A little excitement in my life is a good thing. I'm growing weary harvesting cultures and looking into electron microscopes for fractured strands of DNA. Sometimes it's good for us researchers to get out of the lab and into the real world."

"Thank you Richard. Please be careful. I'll tell you more when I can."

"Will keep an eye open for your overnighter."

Before sliding it into the larger envelope, she took another look at the opening paragraph. She would expect it from the top legal authority in the U.S. Government—vague, full of emotive words and flowery phrases, and applauding the courageous spirit of Americans. The dark second paragraph described the unknown danger born in our country—words like 'untethered', 'hideous', and 'evil' sprinkled with care. The third paragraph, dedicated to Dr. Petty, celebrated her forensic accomplishments and new role as the chief M.E. in Memphis. The last paragraph got most of her time. The attorney general did not request her assistance, he directed her to serve her country without question or pause. He demanded confidentiality. He instructed her to accommodate all of Dr. Swenson's requests in great haste.

The knock on the door went almost unnoticed. The courier stepped inside, stood in the shadows with his clipboard and cleared his throat. Petty returned from her world and handed him the envelope and signed. It was done. The currier left. She made her first move. If Dr. Petty was monitored, she needed to know. If not monitored, information from Tanner would set her course.

She left the county morgue alone after ten. Rain moved through leaving the ground wet and air thick. Her walk from the empty loading dock to her car required carful navigation. Countless water-filled potholes waited to sprain an ankle—something she did not need now. Under the dismal glow of the lone flood at the far end of the secured lot, Petty walked the gauntlet.

Every night for the last three months she began her journey to her car feeling caged. She questioned the need for a ten-foot, chain-linked fence with coiled bobbed wire. It seemed to be there more for protection from danger than to maintain a secured environment. But on this night Petty was uncomfortable. She sensed a new danger—possibly her Bethesda visitors making her overthink everything. She walked in cold silence and felt the hair on her neck stand on end. *What was it?* Petty slowed when she smelled the salty perspiration. She froze.

The man in the long coat and flat-brimmed hat stepped from the brick wall feet away. He stayed in the darkest shadow.

"Who are you and what are you doing on private property?" Petty asked, with as much authority as she could muster.

"Who I am will mean nothing to you, Dr. Petty." The words dripped from his lips as he seemed to get bigger and she smaller. Her fingers searched deep in her purse for her gun. *My lockbox at the Peabody, I took it out last night. I was going to a range this weekend. I'm alone in a new city.* Her finger touched her keys. *I'll press the car alarm.*

"Don't touch your car alarm, doctor." He stepped closer, like a hungry wolf. His coat opened. He hovered. His acrid odor mixed with hot foul breath. "If you cooperate, you may survive this encounter."

How did you know I was thinking car alarm? "What do you want?"

"I ask questions one at a time. If you lie to me, I will kill you here and now."

Her stomach knotted. She backed away. Petty had no defense, and no escape options.

"Why is Dr. Swenson here?"

I can answer that one. "He believes a serial killer is in Memphis."

"Is he asking for details on Pella, Derby, Hudson, Pemberton, and Deckle?"

How do you know those names? "Ah . . . Yes."

"Did Alfred Baldwin send Swenson, or did Dr. Swenson come on his own?"

"Sent by Baldwin. Tell me. Why are you here?"

"Where is Hunter Keller, Dr. Petty?"

The eyewitness on Main, the Deckle case . . .? "I don't know Hunter Keller."

The intimidating silhouette straightened, now looming more than a foot above her. His hot breath now shot into the nightglow. "These people are bad. They are not who they claim to be. They want Hunter Keller for their own, twisted purposes. If you help them, more people die."

"Tell me who you are. What is your interest in Dr. Swenson and Hunter Keller?"

On her last word headlight beams shot into the mist and a car pulled up to the gate. Petty turned when it clanked alive and started to open. The beams reached across the wet pavement and found her car. *Thank God, my field agent.* Emboldened, she turned back to confront her threat. He was gone.

SEVEN

"There is nothing that man fears more than the touch of the unknown."
Elias Canetti

Like a broken freezer in a butcher shop, meat hung on the front of the truck and flies gathered.

Wilcox could do nothing. He pulled up to the inferno, the firemen standing back. In the middle of nowhere, even they had their limits. The 1,500-gallon tanker sat almost empty and the fire raged on.

When he saw the blaze on the horizon, he knew something went terribly wrong. Wilcox parked behind the fire truck and walked the length of the hose to the firefighters and the underside of the blazing tractor trailer. They warned him the contents could blow—it kept them all at bay, rescue attempts were never an option. They could only wait for the fire to burn itself out as they kept a hose on the explosive payload.

The morning sun broke before the fire was a smoldering pile of twisted metal. It sprawled across two lanes. Endless lines of traffic crawled access roads on both sides of the highway. Some stopped to load an unexpected surprise—the police allowed it.

"I've never seen anything like this," said Officer Edelman—Hayti police.

For the first time Wilcox did not want a cigarette. He stared at the grill of the overturned semi. It was the only place not burned beyond recognition.

"Tell me again how this happened," Wilcox said.

Edelman stared at the grill. "I had Dodson in sight. We were on the flattest span of highway around here. I'm talkin' to him on the CB. He knew what to do. About a half mile ahead I saw his rig move to the center of the two lanes as instructed. He had left room for me to pass and two squad cars to get on each side and one behind. But, we never got the chance. Never got close enough."

"Did he say okay to everything?" Wilcox asked.

Edelman blinked away from the singed meat hanging on the grill. "Yes sir. He was talking to me, and pretty much settling down, okay with everything. I watched his taillights. Like I said, maybe a half mile ahead. We were closing in on him at a good clip.

"Then the CB went dead. We saw the explosion. A bright orange-yellow flare shot straight up and out. Lit up the place like a morning sun. We slowed down and watched three more explosions. Had the HFD on the way from the start, but it didn't matter."

"Did Dodson say anything before the explosions?"

"Yes. He asked God to forgive him for something. I couldn't make out what."

"And what about all these animals?"

"Never seen anything like it before, and I've lived here all my life."

"Don't leave anything out. It could be important."

"Okay. It must have been some kind of migration. I've heard about it in places like Alaska but never around here. Dang whitetail deer moving from the cotton fields to the river. Maybe something to do with food source or fear. They got plenty of water in the woods 'round here. Doesn't make sense, detective." Edelman scratched his head and hung a hand on his holstered gun.

"So, a bunch of deer decide to cross the highway in the middle of the night." Wilcox squinted at the rising sun. "Am I hearing it right?"

"Yes sir. We almost hit some, too. If we weren't slowing down for the explosions, we'd run into them too. There were hundreds of whitetails crossing the highway—unbelievable. Mr. Dodson ran into the center of a moving herd. After things settled down some, I saw dead and dying deer all over the road on my way to the burning truck. We had to take it slow to dodge a bunch more of them standing in the highway."

"I don't know if you can answer this, but did they act funny, look spooked?"

"Nope. Looked like they were where they needed to be. Our presence didn't bother them. They didn't pay attention to us, just the truck. Maybe the fire, I guess."

Wilcox watched people stop on the shoulders of the access road to drag a carcass to the bed of their truck or strap it on their hoods. "You don't have a problem with people taking road kill?"

Edelman smiled. "You're not a hunter are you, Detective Wilcox?"

"Only people."

"We hate to see fresh venison go to waste around here."

"That's just sick," Wilcox muttered.

"If people don't drag them off, the city will have a heck of a job cleaning this place up. They'd just toss good meat into Beatty's land fill to rot."

"You sure this never happened before?"

"This is a freak of nature," Edelman said. "The big ones hung around the burning truck a while, like they were waiting for something to happen. After a while they left together. Very strange thing if you ask me. I know it doesn't make any sense, but it was kinda like they were making sure Mr. Dodson didn't get out of that truck alive."

"You're right, that makes no sense. *Unless there's more going on here than any of us know,* Wilcox thought as he stepped closer to the smoldering grill.

The county coroner walked up holding a handkerchief to his nose stepping over the carnage. "This is just lovely," he said.

"Morning Jake," Edelman chirped.

"Your people gonna snag me one of those bucks?" he asked.

"Can do." He pointed to Wilcox. "Jake Mandel, county coroner, Memphis Homicide Detective Tony Wilcox." Wilcox didn't look up. He stared at the steaming metal, his mind on the unexplainable. He had to get inside the cab for a look, but the heat was still too intense.

"Memphis? You're a long way from home," Mandel said. "What's your interest in this accident, or are you just passing through?"

Wilcox didn't acknowledge Mandel's presence.

Edelman answered the question. "We think Mr. Dodson, the truck driver, picked up a hitchhiker. A person of interest linked to homicides in Memphis."

"My understanding there's only one 'crispy critter' in the cab," Mandel joked.

"We think there's one person. We won't know until the metal cools down enough to get in there. Detective Wilcox is here because the man they're lookin' for—the hitchhiker—could be in the cab with the truck driver."

"I see." Mandel stepped between Wilcox and the smoking truck. "I thought you might be here to tell us how the big city does things."

Wilcox lifted his cold eyes. "Put your dick back in your pants and do your job."

Mandel smiled. "Guess the city boys are touchy," he chided.

Like a cobra strike, Wilcox grabbed Mandel's shirt, pulled him in. "I'm in a bad mood. I'll show you how I do things if you keep this shit up." Edelman avoided the confrontation heading to the side of the cab where a fireman leaned a ladder. Wilcox released Mendel and followed.

He expected a shattered windshield and Dodson burned beyond recognition. He saw a 500-pound buck poking through a dead man's abdomen. Wilcox closed his eyes to get a grip.

Reconstruction of events told the story. Dodson had cut the wheel sharp to avoid the herd. His semi flipped onto its side and skidded down I-55 rupturing a gas tank. Sparks ignited the spray and the flames heated up the illegal load of butane canisters. They blew and the legal load of mattresses and bedding fed the fire. Dodson's covert money-maker did not kill him, but it did eliminate any chance at survival. The buck's head buried in Dodson's abdomen killed him instantly.

There were no signs of Keller. Wilcox dropped from the ladder to the smoking tarmac to head to his car. Mandel watched from a crowd with his mouth closed. The local insurance salesman elected county coroner learned an important lesson at his first death scene—don't get in the way of the professionals. Wilcox's hunt for another sick bastard left no room for amateurs. Mandel was fortunate the top homicide detective in the Midsouth had released only a sliver of the rage boiling inside.

Wilcox returned to his car without a word. Everyone left him alone. He had seen enough. With the circus winding down, he needed time to think. Looking through his bug splattered windshield, his empty stomach growled. If he had eaten, he could puke and feel better. Instead, he lit another cigarette and watched them slide Dodson's charred remains into a crash bag. They left the stag's head fused to man's gut. They cut off 450-pounds at the neck. Mandel grew a brain. He signed the papers authorizing transport to the Shelby County Medical Examiner's Office.

As they shot the last animals kicking and they dragged them away, Wilcox watched the tow truck roll up to the smoldering pile of twisted steel. It was time to connect the dots. He hit speed dial, a number normally reserved for personal occasions. Although Abby Patterson could be described as a crazy blond, she was the top private investigator south of the Mason-Dixon.

"Hey, baby doll."

"Hey, Tee. I was just thinking about you. How's the homicide business, baby?"

He watched them sling the body bag onto the ambulance. "Picking up."

"You don't sound like your normal negative self. This must be a business call."

"I love your investigative mind, darlin', and perfect body."

"I know you do. You know both so well. When're you coming to see me?"

"Depends on you. I'm up to my ass in cadavers."

"Here it comes, unbillable hours." *You never talk to me about business. This must be bad.*

Abby Patterson ran one of the most successful private investigation firms in the country. As a rule, Wilcox never mixed with PI's. Most were law enforcement wannabes with small brains unwilling to take on real risk. In Patterson's case, Wilcox made an exception. Her professional prowess caught his interest.

However, the knockout blonde with the attitude caught him first.

She could keep up with his shot glass, liked marathon sex, and told a story better than a man. Early in their relationship Wilcox realized Abby was one of those natural born sleuths. The modern day Sherlock Holmes on heels pulled down six figures working with top law firms in the southeast. Busting cheaters and tracking down anyone or anything hiding from the truth, she played the ditzy blond with the skill of a Broadway Diva.

"Cadavers!" Patterson kicked off her heels and lit a cigarette. "I'm on surveillance, sitting in another rental car in another gated community waiting on another loser."

"It is how you roll."

"Right. When you gonna take me out of this hell hole, Tee? A sandy beach somewhere, emerald waves breaking and a harvest moon. I see us sipping Pina Coladas and rolling around under puffy comforters."

"Sounds good to me. How about when I'm a millionaire. Hey what are you doing later?"

"I need to blend at a semi-formal brunch later, dear. A networking event."

"The event's where *he's* going to meet his mistress?"

"Nope. She's going to meet her boy toy."

"Keep forgetting it takes two," Wilcox said.

"Seems like I've been following a lot of cheating women lately. Tis a brave new world."

"I miss you girl. Bet you look great."

"Get to Atlanta and I'll let you undress me."

Tony cracked a window and flicked his cigarette. "Don't get me all worked up, Patterson. I have half a mind to head east, but I'm chasing a bad guy at the moment."

"Enough fun, talk to me. Where are you and what's this call really about?"

"Where I am is irrelevant. What is relevant, I have four unsolved homicides."

"*Four!* A record for you."

"They may be connected. Still waiting on forensics. My new ME—Petty—is sending brain tissue to DC for some kind of advanced testing."

"So why call me, outside of wanting to arrange a night of bliss."

"I need the Patterson probe, someone with more than a half-brain to do some old fashion detective work. I need to find out how these guys are connected. So far I got nothing."

"Your people can run names as easy as me," Abby said.

"True, but the likely linkage is not obvious. And it may not be too recent. Could go way back like a multigenerational thing."

"What got you there?" she asked as her subject got in a car four houses down. "Tee, I need to roll, but I can listen." Abby zipped her windbreaker and pulled on her baseball cap.

Hypnotized by the fireman hosing the highway, Wilcox snapped back when a whitetail jumped his hood. "Shit!" Then he saw a dozen more standing at the edge of the cotton field. *Seems like you guys lost your incentive and direction,* he thought. Only their heads followed the tow truck as it pulled the twisted steel away. Then they backed into the field.

"What just happened, Tee?"

"Not sure." He blinked and refocused. "Okay . . . My homicides. I have four. One killed at his place of business, a 'one-man show' savings and loan downtown, South Main. Stabbed in the back. Forensics says the killer walked him across the room with the knife in his back."

"And how do you know that?" Patterson asked.

"The ME said no knife toggle. Did not see tissue tears above or below the knife at the entry point. If the victim crossed the room alone with the knife in his back, there'd be torn tissue.

Someone had to be holding the knife steady . . . applying pressure."

"Sounds like voodoo magic to me."

"The important thing is the victim—Donald Deckle— dropped face down in front of a picture hanging on his savings and loan wall."

"Okay, and that's important because why?"

"I found a fresh fingerprint on the dusty glass. I think my killer pointed at a guy in the group picture. It was the 1968 Memphis State Tigers football team on bleachers."

"A piece to your puzzle. Your hunches often turn out to be correct, Wilcox."

"I want to give you names of my homicides without a lot of explanation. Don't want to mess with your instincts. Need you to sniff around the Patterson way."

"So far I have Donald Deckle stabbed in the back."

"Two stabbed. Two strangled. ME says the forensics are clear —stabbings with identical entry points and aortic severing. And strangulations with the identical damage to the spine, the cervical vertebrae."

"Then you could have up to two killers, Wilcox."

"It's a possibility, but I'm still thinking one. What has me scratching my head is that all four had eyes bulging out their sockets like a couple of fried eggs sunny side up—never seen that one before."

"Gawd! Are you serious? That is just hideous."

"Yeah. And all four faces were snow white and deformed. Creepy smiles. The lips were stretched back to the ears. No signs it was forced by someone or something."

"Sounds like they saw a ghost," Abby teased.

"They had lesions. Same part of the brain—amygdala. Until Deckle, never knew we had an amygdala."

"I've never heard of that. Were they hit on the head?"

"No external head trauma. ME said it's new for her too. Not in the books."

"I've got enough to get started. Give me the names."

"Thomas Bender Derby, William Trenton Hudson, Mark Tyler Pemberton, and you have Donald Francis Deckle. When I get back to Memphis, I'll send you DOBs, socials, and DMVs."

"Those squirrelly middle names will help. I'll let you know. I gotta go darlin'."

Wilcox smiled as he drove his cruiser across the grassy median and climbed onto the southbound access road. "I'm off to Sikeston on a long shot. Be careful. Not sure where all this is going yet."

He threw his cell on the seat squinting in the morning sun. His smile faded when the pickup passed. The pile of deer carcasses sprayed blood across his windshield.

That's just wonderful . . .

EIGHT

"Insanity is often the logic of an accurate mind overtasked."
Oliver Wendell Holmes

Stringtown, Oklahoma

"If you want to stay alive, you better talk to me, Bone Jackson," he called into the wilderness.

Cameron Baily got off his four-wheeler all-terrain rental and stuck his helmet on the handlebars like he knew what he was doing. He spit and looked around the miserable, rocky scrub of southeast Oklahoma with disdain. The city boy did not enjoy the teeth-rattling, ten-mile ride into the hinterlands. The washed-out road along the endless barbed wire fence drove him nuts. He knew he had to at least try to find Bone Jackson.

The battered teal camper was covered in bird droppings,

broken sticks, and wet leaves. It squatted in dead grass under a fat tree on the edge of more tangled woods. Baily surveyed the immediate area wondering if anyone could possibly live in the God forsaken dumpster on wheels. Next to it was an abused 1982 Ford pickup with rusted fenders and bald tires. Under the weight of corroded junk heaped in the bed, it sunk into the mud up to the hubcaps. Then he found the prize, the backend of a mud-caked Sportsman XP 1000 four-wheeler.

A drop from the fat cloud that followed him hit his nose when the grizzly-bear shaped man squeezed out of the camper. Baily reached for his gun instinctively as the man's boots hit the ground and the crappy camper lifted eight inches. Under rage-filled eyes, a scraggly beard scraped the basketball belly. Sleeves got pushed above elbows in stride, as the man grabbed a metal pipe from the back of the Ford and approached in a straight line.

"Are you threatening me black man?" barked the behemoth with the swirling metal pipe.

Baily leveled his gun. All he saw was another white bigot coming after him.

I don't know who the hell you are, but I can shoot . . . you backwoods, racist redneck. I can scratch that lifelong itch right now once and for all. I'm not standin' in the streets of Memphis under a damn microscope. I gotta be fifty miles in the middle of nowhere.

That's it—I'm gonna shoot this KKK-lovin' redneck. I'm gonna get my justice. Baily pulled back the hammer and aimed at the head of the charging white rage with the pipe. Baily yelled, "You stop right there!" *Please keep coming.* But the approaching angry eyes dipped more and the pipe went even higher.

Are you thinkin' you can take a bullet you dumb hillbilly? You must be dying to put that pipe upside my black head. Baily instinctively pulled his badge and waved it. "I'm a Memphis cop looking for Bone Jackson." *One more step and I shoot. I scratch my damn itch once and for all. Come on. One more step you mother . . .*

The man stopped in his tracks and lowered his pipe. "A Memphis police officer? But you threatened me."

"I did not threaten you," Baily said with his gun on his target.

"You used extremely threatening words and tone."

"I said Jackson was in danger and best talk to me."

"No you didn't. Your words were more like—if I want to stay alive, I best talk to you." The man stroked his beard flat and tossed the pipe in the back of the truck. "Sorry about this. I've had a few negative experiences in these woods. Some people think remote areas offer opportunity to misbehave."

Still rattled Baily huffed, "You came out that camper mad as hell. And I've been bouncing my brains all over Oklahoma for the last three hours. Been on that pitiful dirt trail way too long." He holstered his gun. "Guess I'm not thinking polite." He extended his hand. "I'm Cameron Baily. Yes, with the Memphis police."

"I saw your badge. I am Buford Jackson."

"Buford?" *I don't know a Buford. That name did not come up in my talks in Stringtown.* "You know where I can find a Bone Jackson? Maybe cousin or something?"

"You're looking at him. Bone's my nickname."

"Really. That's a strange nickname, if you don't mind me sayin'."

"I know. I found a Sasquatch femur when I was a kid. I've been called 'Bone' ever since. Nobody ever let me forget I found that bone." He turned back to the mobile home. "Are you permitted an alcoholic beverage, Officer Baily?"

"I guess I'm off the clock."

Bone grabbed a wet bag of beers from the camper and led Baily to a cluster of bushes in front of an enormous boulder. He pushed through, Baily followed. They climbed a steep trail emerging atop the giant rock. There was a weathered picnic table sitting in its center.

"What the hell," Baily mumbled. "A picnic table in middle of nowhere. Hell of a view."

"Took me a month to get it up here. Highest point for miles. I spend hours sitting here looking for Bigfoot. One day he is going to cross that field over there. He's going to enter the woods over there. It's an ideal route into dense terrain, ample food and water. I am sitting in the perfect location. When I'm not here, I have a camera hooked up to a laser beam, motion detection."

"I don't know 'bout that Bigfoot stuff," Baily said as he studied the dirt road he came in on. "I can see way the hell up there—one side of the crappy road and barbed wire fence it's flat fields, the other side is thick woods. Guess the change means somethin' in the scheme of things, in Sasquatch's world," he chuckled. "But it is kinda peaceful up here. Do you leave those binocs out all the time?"

"Yes. They are waterproof. On a clear night, I can see a couple miles with them. Sometimes I sleep up here." Bone watched Baily scan the horizon with the binocs. It was time to find out what was going on. "So, what brings the Memphis police to Oklahoma looking for me?"

"I'm a homicide detective. I'm working a case that we believe is connected to the Keller family homicides—now five years ago in Stringtown."

"I remember," Bone said under his breath. "It was the worst day in Atoka County history. They never found who was responsible."

"I spent a few days in Stringtown talking to people. You're right. Nobody knows much about what happened or who did it, not even the Atoka County Sheriff's Office."

"Do you think I know something?" Bone asked.

"I think there's a possibility you do know something. I am

here because your name keeps coming up, Bone. You are one of Hunter Keller's few friends in the world, maybe his best friend."

"I am his friend, but Hunter's always been a loner. We grew up together. Would go fishing and look for Bigfoot. We always enjoyed the outdoors. I don't see him much anymore."

"What happened? And why're you out here alone?"

"Things happen. After high school I went to Norman—Oklahoma University. He went to Tahlequah—Northeastern. Now I teach at Oklahoma State. After the parents were killed, we lost track of each other. Hunter took it hard."

"I was told you were the only one he trusts."

"Well, I don't know about that. He has other friends—Hennings, Dacus, and Tinderson. The five of us ran around together growing up. I guess I lost touch with them, too. People do grow up. We're in different orbits now."

"I'm sorry to tell you, all three are dead." Baily watched for Bone's reaction. Would he show surprise, fear, sadness, curiosity, or would he show nothing?

Bone set down his beer and looked up the empty dirt road. "They are dead?" he said under his breath as he pinched the bridge of his nose.

You're upset but don't appear to be surprised, Baily thought. *Were their deaths an expected outcome? If they were, Wilcox was right to get me to Stringtown. But maybe there's something much bigger going on here than either of us imagined. Maybe our four connected homicides just became seven.*

"People in Stringtown don't know about these deaths," Baily said. "I got the names from my interviews. Then I had them checked out by my people in Memphis."

"How did they die? Were they all together?"

"Hennings committed suicide in Chicago a year ago, a gun in the mouth. Dacus died in a car accident 300 miles away, St. Louis, around the same time. Dacus ran his car off a bridge into the Mississippi River—no witnesses. They found him dead in his car on a sandbar about three miles downriver." Baily noticed Bone's fingers trembling.

"I don't know what to say. What about Tinderson? What happened to him?"

"Last month they pulled him out of White Rock Lake in Dallas. The police report said it was a boating accident. I found that odd because Tinderson didn't own a boat. The DPD found his body floating by the dam. Tinderson was chewed up by a boat propeller."

Bone picked up his beer in his shaking hand and stared at the empty road.

"I think someone killed all of them, Bone."

"But you said one was a suicide, one an accident, and one still an open case. You also said the deaths were in three different locations at three different times."

"That's right, but I think their deaths were staged," Baily said.

"Why would someone kill them?" Bone barked. Then he turned back to Baily. "Do you think I did this? Is that what this is all about, why you're here? You think I killed my best friends!"

"Everyone close to Hunter Keller is dead except you. Keller's parents and friends are gone. You're still kicking, Bone Jackson. I think that is an issue."

"I did not kill anybody, Detective Baily."

"Well then, if that is the case, you are next on someone's kill list. I tend to think that is the case. I don't believe you killed your friends. I believe you're on a kill list . . . and I believe you know why."

Bone crushed his beer can. "And I think you're over thinking, detective. If anybody's trying to kill me—which I doubt—they would have one hell of a time trying to find me out here. Trust me; I can take care of myself."

"I found you," Baily shot back. "I think your luck's running out, Bone. I ran into the guy who sold you that crappy camper. He works at the only damn gas station in Stringtown. He gave me three places to look—this was number one. He said you hunt Bigfoot every fall semester break. The guy even gave me a map and highlighted the route to your camper in the woods."

"Jacob Smyth did all that?"

"Yes he did. And he will do it for other people claiming to be your buddies wanting to join in on another Bigfoot expedition. Best you start talking, Bone. They're coming for you next. You don't have long to live. These people are determined to eliminate you boys, and I think you know why."

"I don't know why they would want to kill us," Bone declared.

Baily turned to the weed-covered, rock-strewn, deep-rutted, dirt road that connected to the interstate fifty miles out. Sitting on the boulder at the edge of a hundred-thousand acres of tangled scrub and woodlands unfit for a wild goat, he knew it was the perfect place for a murder.

"I suggest you stop stonewalling and start talking."

With beer suds on his beard, Bone said, "I don't like the idea of being hunted."

"Like you do to Bigfoot? What goes around comes around."

Bone stroked the weather-worn table like a cherished pet. "This is the one thing I got left. My parent's house burned to the ground. Lost them and everything else but this."

"House fire. What happened?"

"I don't know. I never found out how the fire actually started. It happened the year the Keller's were murdered, a month later. I was a little suspicious, but I didn't quite know what to do about it."

"We don't have a lot of time. I don't need the epic version of things. I've got questions. Your answers will decide if you're going to spend some time in a Memphis jail, or if I'm gonna help you stay alive."

"I need to talk to somebody. Go ahead. Let's do this."

"What do you know about the Stargate Project?"

Bone flinched at the topic. "You're going there?"

"I know you're heavy into parapsychology stuff—the paranormal and psychic phenomena. You know all about telepathy, precognition, clairvoyance, psychokinesis, near-death experience, apparitions, and reincarnation just to name a few."

"True. But I'm not interested in apparitions and reincarnation," Bone muttered. "Those areas are even a stretch for the open minded."

"Your three dead friends and Hunter Keller were into paranormal stuff too."

"We were attracted to 'fringe science' all our lives. Is that a problem, detective?"

Baily ignored the shot. "You believe in cryptids, too. And you're a devout Bigfooter."

"You act like there's something wrong with us. Cryptozoology is the study of animals and plants not yet known. Most discoveries are eventually accepted by the scientific community. We consider ourselves explorers."

"Yes but you teach cognitive psychology." He unfolded a tattered paper and read. "Cog psych is the scientific study of mental function—learning, memory, perception, reasoning, conceptual development, and decision making." He looked up. "Did I get most of them?"

"Close enough," Bone muttered. "Is there a question in there somewhere?"

"You gotta be smart to teach cognitive psychology at a major university."

"You think?"

"You're not the dumb redneck you try to project with your beard and attire, Dr. Jackson."

"Is there something wrong with my appearance?"

"You're not hunting Bigfoot. I think you're a PhD hiding in the woods. Tell me, doctor. Do you believe the human brain is capable of things science cannot explain?"

"I think so."

"No. You know so," Baily said. "Stop the bullshit. We don't have the time."

"Okay. I know so," Bone said.

"A lot of people in Stringtown talked to me about the Stargate Project when I asked them about Hunter Keller. I had to wonder why. First, why do so many people in a small town in southeast Oklahoma have an interest in a top secret government program? And second, how does it relate to Hunter Keller?"

"The U.S. Government does a lot of speculative research with our tax dollars, Detective Baily. In the early '70s they recruited psychics to study the paranormal. They put ads in the newspapers looking for these people. We had a few psychics in Stringtown. They applied. As you can imagine, there's not a lot to talk about in a small town. It was an event to have some people participate."

"So this is how you want to play it?"

"What do you mean?"

"I mean . . . you are a PhD in psychology teaching at a major university. I mean . . . you need a damn good reason to dabble in the loony world of parapsychology."

"Dabbling in the 'loony' does not put my reputation in jeopardy, detective."

"But none of this is 'loony' for you, Dr. Jackson. Your best friend's psychic abilities were driving him insane. You had to get involved to help him. Isn't that true?"

"You are reaching, detective."

"You're trying to help him. But now he is out of control. He is unfixable. Now he is some kind of monster. Hunter Keller is killing people and you know it!"

"Oliver Wendell Holmes once said insanity is the logic of an accurate mind overtasked. You are reaching."

"I'll make this easy for you, Dr. Jackson." Baily leaned over the table. "You did your thesis on the Stargate Project because it was connected to Stringtown, Hunter Keller, your dead friends, and my four unsolved homicides in Memphis. I guess you can live with all that. But now it has to do with you living or dying. As far as I'm concerned, you have chosen death. I've decided to leave you here to die. We will stop Hunter Keller without you."

Bone jumped to his feet. Baily was ready for Bone to start talking. But instead, Bone stood there staring at the west horizon. He whispered, "We gotta go."

Baily turned in time to see the headlights bounce across the creek on the rutted dirt road.

NINE

"Man is manacled only by himself; thought and action are the jailers of fate."
James Allen

Memphis, Tennessee

I f Ben had looked at the overdressed man taking a walk in the middle of the night, maybe he would not have gotten a knife in his back.

The Super 8 on West Illinois was the most inconspicuous choice. A few hundred yards from the Mississippi River the weathered hotel in ill repair blended with the abandoned buildings, scraggly trees, and barren grounds. The location, and less scrutinizing clientele, made it the perfect place for Swenson and associates. They could come and go as they pleased, and they could monitor tails. The Dr. Petty visit was unsanctioned.

Ben Nutley checked-in the three but paid little attention. His primary interest was under the counter, the warm bucket of chicken and a cold beer. The sooner he got rid of the three suits paying in cash the better.

The retired Memphis school system janitor took a night manager position for supplemental income—Ben's Social Security would never be enough. Last spring his wife had been diagnosed as morbidly obese. She tipped the scales at 512 pounds. She lived in bed 24/7 for several years. Unless something drastic changed, Ben would feed and clean her until the day she died in their doublewide down by the river.

At three in the morning Dr. Green asked for the best way to walk to the river. Ben still did not look at the man. With his nose in a newspaper, he pointed. "You go out the front doors, go left across the parking lot and across the field. Head to the trees. River's on the other side."

Ben did not see Dr. Green's $2,000 three-piece Zegna suit, or the starched cotton shirt with diamond studded French cuffs, or the $1,200 Louis Vuitton alligator wingtips. Even if Ben had studied the doctor from Bethesda, he would not know he was looking at a four-figure outfit. Ben was too busy living his miserable life to think it odd a man would walk to the Mississippi River at three o'clock in the morning.

The three had gotten separate rooms on separate floors. The plan was to meet for breakfast each morning. Only then would they review the prior day's findings, discuss strategy, and plan the current day's agenda. At the end of each day they would leave the Shelby County morgue together and in complete silence—the bugs. At the hotel they would go to their rooms. Nothing could be said there until breakfast.

On the third day in Memphis, Dr. Green deviated from the

agreed routine. He left his room at three in the morning for a meeting he would not share with his associates. Green failed to plan ahead. He did not pack casual clothes, and his scrubs were left in his locker at the morgue. Regardless, he would not risk drawing attention wearing them in a cheap hotel in the wee hours.

When the night manager kept his nose in the paper, Green could only smile inside. He would not be remembered. Heading out the glass doors he found a new worry, soiling his expensive suit.

Dr. Green sailed across the crumbling driveway and empty parking lot as instructed. Light from the half-moon and continuous sweeps of headlights turning onto the Arkansas-Memphis Bridge helped him avoid mud puddles and debris in the poorly cut field. As he approached the west edge, he saw the lights on the Hernando de Soto Bridge a mile to the north. He could hear the river sliding by a hundred-yards away. Green entered the stand of trees and found the fattest one with the darkest shadow. There he waited like an unfortunate fox stranded in an unfamiliar neighborhood surrounded. When he felt comfortable, he would make his phone call.

He hit speed dial and waited, his eyes darting from one shadow to another.

The phone crackled. "Do they know where he is?"

Green shivered in the breeze that swept up the bank and lifted his hair. Was it the cold or nerves? Did he feel a presence? Was it nothing?

"No," Green whispered. "They have no idea who they are dealing with."

"Where is he?" The voice demanded.

"Memphis Detective Wilcox tracked him to Sikeston. He hitched a ride with a trucker. We know he got out at the Hayti exit. About thirty minutes later the trucker, dead. Killed in a freak accident."

"He had a reason for being there—always does. What do we know about this dead trucker?"

"Name's Billy Dodson," Green said. "He's got a record in Louisiana. He's a serial child molester, although he's never been prosecuted."

"Parents protecting their kids, not going to trial."

"Dodson's been charged a dozen times over the last five or so years. Always walked."

"That history's not admissible, legal loopholes. Appears our Mr. Keller wanted to have a little chat with this child molester."

"Dodson will never talk to us. He ran into a herd of deer crossing the highway. It was reported as an 'unexplainable migration'. Dodson's truck flipped onto its side, slid down the road, caught fire, and blew up. The police report, we obtained surreptitiously, said he was hauling illegal combustibles."

"Keller knew it was going to happen."

Green took a deep breath. Another gust lifted his hair and rattled leaves. He scanned the field between him and the hotel. It appeared to be empty.

"Did Dr. Petty mention her 'parking lot' visitor?"

"No. Who visited Petty?"

"It's not important now."

A twig snapped. This time it was not the wind or the river. Green leaned out and surveyed the small stand of trees. He whispered into his phone. "Dr. Petty's on board. She's cooperating, but cautious. She is gathering her own information."

"That's to be expected. It's manageable. What about Blanchard? You know he cannot leave Memphis."

"The timing's not right. They exhumed Pella today. Body didn't arrive at the morgue until late. I need Blanchard for the inspection. Trust me. He won't be a problem in twenty-four hours. What about Swenson?"

Another twig snapped. Closer.

"What are you doing out here, Dr. Green?" The words floated on the river breeze cutting through the cluster of trees. Green spun around and recognized the silhouette. Stumbling backwards he left the woods. Green dropped his cell phone. He didn't stop. He just ran without looking back. He could only pray he would not fall—that would be his end.

Tripping over the crumbling asphalt, he crossed the empty lot and went for the darkest shadows by the hotel. Green was no athlete. He awkwardly skirted the brick wall dodging the shrubs until he reached the back of the building. He hid behind a dumpster and stared at the only light—it flickered above the only door on an empty loading dock.

I will wait here until daylight and a crowd. Moving now would be suicide, he thought. *How did they know?*

He had crouched in the shadows for an hour, when the backdoor whined opened. Green tried not to move, but the temptation was too great. Maybe he had waited long enough. Or was the quiet and rank smell too much? Were the unknowns lurking in the dark more than Green could bear? He was no secret agent. Green rationalized that staying too long would expose him more.

I will be safer in the company of another. I don't care if it's just one, he rationalized. *They wouldn't do anything in front of an innocent bystander.*

Ben Nutley held the door with his foot as he flung the fat plastic bag into the top of the giant dumpster onto the garbage heap. Before the bag hit the pile, Green had bolted up the steps with arms waving. "Excuse me, sir. I'm afraid I got turned around."

Like he was watching an alien step from a flying saucer,

Nutley stood half in and out at the metal door staring at the man in the suit waving his hands.

"Excuse me, sir. You do recall I asked for directions to the river earlier. I wanted to take a short walk. Get some fresh air. Maybe see the river at night. Somehow along the way I got lost. Here I am. I would like to enter the building, please sir."

Ben Nutley stood in silence. Green leaned closer. Nutley's eyes widened as if he was ready to respond. Then Nutley's eyes rolled into his forehead. The man swayed inches and dropped forward like a dead tree. Green had stepped aside in time to avoid Nutley making contact. He watched Nutley's face slam into the concrete and blood fill the back of his shirt. When Green turned back to darkness of the opened door, the knife sunk into his belly.

"It's you," Green gasped.

With a firm upward thrust, the blade moved up Green's abdomen to his chest slicing open his sternum and severing his aortic artery. Green's last words were lost in the splash of his steaming blood onto the dock. It poured from his gut over his Louis Vuitton alligator wingtips, and he dropped.

The metal door closed. The river rats squeaked.

TEN

"The world is a contradiction, the universe a paradox."
Kedar Joshi

Southeast, Oklahoma

"You think he wants to kill me?" Bone asked.

"I don't know. Are you expecting anybody?" Baily watched the headlights climb out of the creek onto the road.

The two slid down the trail behind the boulder. "Expecting nobody," jostled out of Bone as he bounced off the last rock and planted his feet like an experienced hiker.

"We've got a twenty-minute head start. You better know how to lose them."

They rounded the corner. Bone reached in the camper and grabbed a backpack and rifle. "Start yours and keep up." He stuck his rifle in a holder and pinched his pack on the rack. Bone cranked his four-wheeler several times before it grumbled alive. He hopped on and the Sportsman XP 1000 shot around the back of the camper. Baily did all he could to keep up.

The fat, bushy man snaked down the bunny trails crushing shrubs and leveling saplings knowing the way. Minutes later they broke onto a pasture. Baily looked. Bone disappeared. *Well this is just great,* Baily mused. *Hell, I'd lose me too, if I were him.*

Seconds later Baily's four-wheeler dropped down a steep slope into an unseen eroded creek bed. He immediately saw Bone's tail lights bouncing ahead. They moved down the creek bed like the lead wave of a sloshing flood lapping up the walls at turns, avoiding boulders, and sliding under fallen trees and nests of debris. For the next thirty minutes they navigated the ravine of countless forks—most of which led to dead ends. Bone knew the way through nature's intricate maze. Their hunters could fail in navigation, but their skills were unknown. Baily and Jackson had to assume the worse.

At the end of the creek bed was a small canyon. Bone stopped at the edge and offed his motor. Baily killed his. They sat in the dark silence except for the cooling engines popping.

"Can they get here another way?" Baily asked.

Bone stretched his legs. "I've been all over this part of Oklahoma. There's no other way from the camper on wheels that I know about. This place has too many cliffs and the woods are too dense. The trail we took is too tight for a horse in many places. A mountain goat would have a tough time out here. And if they try to do it on foot, we're a good ten miles ahead."

Baily rechecked his gun. "We best keep moving, Bone. These people seem highly motivated to find you. We need to get where we can talk and breathe. Then I gotta get you out of Oklahoma so you don't join your buddies."

"That's it?"

"And I gotta return this rental."

Bone passed a beer from his backpack. "You need to hydrate, Detective Baily. And you can forget about returning that rental. We'll just leave it on the side of a road when you're done with it. The thing's got stickers all over it. People do it all the time, abandon them. Nobody's going to steal a crumby rental four-wheeler. It will get back to the rental place before you get to Memphis."

"I can't just leave it on the side of the road. I'm a law enforcement officer." They looked at each other and broke out laughing until Bone slid off his seat and spilled his beer.

An hour passed. "I'm glad I didn't have to beat the 'city' out of you with my pipe."

"Don't worry. I would have shot the 'country' out of you first." Baily holstered his gun and looked over the canyon. "I need to know about Stargate and the connection to Stringtown. I saw that name on documents I found at the Keller farm. I did some diggin' in the attic." Baily downed his beer and passed the empty to Bone. "You don't have much time to get help, Bone."

"You're making me nervous," Bone said as he slid his rifle back into the side mount. "We need to get to Marston's. We will be safe there. Trust me. We can talk then."

Baily nodded as they cranked the four-wheelers. They crawled from the creek bed onto the rim of the canyon twelve miles east of the camper.

"We got to get to Hochatown State Park," Bone yelled over his shoulder. "Marston's cabin's on Mountain Fork River. It's a hard place to find even if you've been there. I fished with Marston a year ago, a college acquaintance. Marston uses the cabin in the spring. The place is empty the rest of the time. It's perfect."

* * *

Aimed for a quick departure, they put the four-wheelers under enough evergreen branches to blend with the terrane. If they had to leave, the best route was a winding trail to the river. It also went to the main road if need be.

The log cabin was under the towering pines next to the Mountain Fork River. Baily jimmied a window. Inside, Bone poked around for a lantern. When he found the matches he bumped into Baily. "We don't light a lantern. We do not want to draw attention. It's best we sit in the dark like a raccoon."

"Like a raccoon? Why would a city boy say a raccoon? I'd expect a city boy to say a sewer rat. I'll bet you haven't ever seen a raccoon and you have seen hundreds of those big rats."

Baily shook his head opening the window another inch and peering out. "I'm just sayin' we need to become a part of our surroundings. I don't see any activity out there."

"There are two ways out of this cabin if we need to depart," Bone said. "We go out the window we came in or out the front door." He pulled beef jerky from his backpack and passed one Baily. "We need protein."

"You're a regular dietician. First we need to hydrate and now we need our protein. You wouldn't have any mustard in that backpack of yours, would ya? I need mustard with my jerky."

Bone passed a mustard packet. "Help yourself. I rarely use it myself. I keep a little of everything in this backpack." He poked around inside his bag. "I've got mayonnaise, ketchup, relish, hot sauce, and just about every other condiment that exists in packet-form that you can get between here and Stringtown."

They sat on the floor of the musty cabin eating their beef jerky and hydrating. An hour later the woods were still quiet. Moonlight fell in the window and through the burlap curtain on the cabin door. Baily's cell phone had no bars and his battery was at thirty percent.

"You said some things back there," Bone mumbled.

"Springtown's got somethin' going on, Bone. The people are starting to talk about it. They are one big family, if you ask me. It'll all get out sooner or later."

"Everybody knows Uncle Joe's a pervert and Aunt Martha had the mailman's baby."

"It didn't take me any time to get the details on the Keller homicides, and that's after five years of silence. People are uneasy. Like you said, it was one of the worst things to ever happen in Stringtown."

"Worst thing to ever happen in Atoka County," Bone said under his breath.

"They wanted to talk about Hunter Keller," Baily baited. "They told me what kind of guy he is, how he spent his time, and who he ran around with. They said you guys were always together. Said you were not typical kids growin' up. Said you were always mysterious and secretive. Then one day you all left town."

"It's called having a life," Bone barked.

"Yeah, but none of you guys ever came back." Baily looked out the window. "Stringtown doesn't know three of you guys are dead, Bone. You know what really got my attention after all the interviews and reading my notes and case files?"

"I'm sure you're going to tell me."

"People die around Hunter Keller," Baily said. Bone stared at his shoes. "So you're a PhD, Psychology," Baily mumbled after giving Bone a few minutes to think about his friend at the center of the storm. Bone had to know why.

"Yes I am," Bone said still staring at his shoes.

"And you're heavy into parapsychology, like we already talked about some."

"No. I'm not heavy into anything."

"Can you at least admit your interest in the paranormal is because of Keller?"

"You keep trying to weave that web, Detective Baily. What makes you think that?"

"Psychology PhD types don't buy into fringe science. You scientist-types work with facts. Your training teaches you to reject wild concepts. I read about parapsychology. It's a pseudoscience. You know 'pseudo' means false, Dr. Jackson. There's only one obvious reason why you would invest such a big part of your life into the study of psychic phenomena."

"You must be a brilliant detective," Bone scoffed.

Baily sat on the dust laden floor next to Bone. "You don't have any more time to hope things work out. People are dropping dead all around you, Bone. Someone's coming for you right now. I can't protect you if you don't help me understand what we're up against."

Bone rubbed his head and took a deep breath. "You're right. I can't do this anymore. This whole thing has gotten out of control. I honestly don't know how much it will help, but I will tell you everything I know. Let's start by you asking what's most important to you."

"Is Hunter Keller a serial killer?" Baily asked.

"No. I do not think he is capable of hurting anyone."

"Then why is he at my homicides? Why's he running? And, why're you helping him?"

"It's not how it appears. For you to understand, I need to go to the beginning."

"Best be brief," Baily warned. "They're coming."

"In the early '70s our government learned the Russians were spending millions of rubbles a year on psychotronic research, a term coined by a parapsychologist, Zdenek Rejdak, the Eastern Bloc. It's about mind control and remote viewing and other psychic abilities."

"Tell me about this remote viewing?"

"Remote viewing—or RV—is sensual perception at great distances through other than known senses."

"Like mind reading?" Baily asked.

"Similar, but more. Someone in Dallas, for example, is able to obtain specific and detailed information on an object, person, or event in Tel Aviv as if they were in Tel Aviv observing it directly. Some RVs can do this in the past, present, and future state. These few RVs have extremely advanced precognitive skills."

"Do you really believe this stuff is real?" Baily asked.

"I know it is real. So do most governments in the world. Remote viewing is the ultimate intelligence gathering tool, and more. Remote viewing has been a top secret program with our government for the last forty years, detective."

"I'm not a scientist. This sounds like a magic act. However, I did find some files stored deep in the Keller's attic. I saw newspaper articles dated back to the '70s about people in the Scanate Project found a secret Soviet military base and an R&D facility."

"In the beginning, it was public. The few RVs contracted by the government found Russian subs in the ocean with pinpoint accuracy. Soon the program went underground. The government said they shut it down."

"Sorry, but this all sounds like fantasyland," Baily scoffed.

"I don't have time to convince or educate you, detective. If you want to get anywhere, you best accept it so you can start dealing with the bigger picture."

"And what might that be?"

"If enemies of the United States develop an RV program first, they can access everything and shut us down. They can sit in top secret meetings at the Pentagon—psychically speaking. They can even sit in the Oval Office with the president, and we wouldn't know they were there. Imagine our enemies having total access to our national secrets, plans, and strategies. Imagine them countering us at every turn. You best understand and accept that psychotronics is a world-changing weapon system with an unlimited reach."

"I understand what you are saying. I struggle with the possibility."

"The world as we know it will change, detective."

"How does it tie to Hunter Keller?" Baily asked.

"Let's go back to the Defense Intelligence Agency, the DIA. They launched research into all forms of psychic phenomena in search of potential military and domestic applications. They recruited self-proclaimed psychics nationwide. Over time the fakes were harvested. The testing was rigid."

"This psychic recruiting, was it a public or secret process?"

"In the beginning it was promoted. The U.S. Government ran ads in every newspaper around the country. They tested all military and government personnel. After elimination of the frauds, or weak psychics, they had a small elite force. They did not call them psychics or clairvoyants. They named them 'remote viewer' to give their program scientific credibility."

They must have found something, Baily thought. *Maybe this is for real.*

"Identities of their elite force were aggressively protected. Their capabilities were no longer discussed publically. The program moved from Menlo Park—the Stanford Research Institute—to Fort Meade. There the CIA, DIA, and military took their turns sniffing around. The RV program had numerous names over the ensuing twenty-five years—Scanate, Gondola Wish, Grill Flame, Inscom Lane, Sun Streak, and . . ."

"The Stargate Project."

"Right. In 1995 the CIA terminated Stargate and declassified."

"So it did not work?"

Bone chuckled. "Come on, detective. You're smarter than that."

"I'm not into government decision process, Bone."

"Let me help you with this one. You don't interview the country looking for psychics, test them, narrow it down to a few, immediately take the program underground and spend millions of dollars over twenty-five long years only to suddenly discover it does not work!"

"I get that."

"The U.S. Government then dumped a mountain of incomplete, complicated, and useless documents on the public claiming it did not work. But people like me read everything. We saw the gaping holes, the heavy redactions, the hiding of tests and results. People like me knew they had something that they did not want to share with the rest of the world."

"So, they took it deeper," Bone said as he got up and went to the door. He peered out the edge of the burlap curtain and studied the shadows in the moonlit woods.

"To add to the covertness of it all, the government's contracted remote viewers vanished in 1995. In that same year things changed at Fort Meade. The once active military base became the new home for the most secretive agencies in the federal government—NSA, DIA, and DOD combat support. These government entities live outside the mainstream. They do not report to Congress or the people. They are unaccountable. They are connected to the White House."

"Again, how does this relate to Hunter Keller and Stringtown?"

"Hunter is the Keller's biological son. Alma and Arnold Keller were the most powerful RVs in the government's psychic-weaponry program. The two ran away from Fort Meade one night. They settled in Stringtown in 1978. Or, I should say they hid in Stringtown in 1978."

"My information says he was adopted by the Kellers."

"This gets complicated. Alma hid her pregnancy. She secretly gave birth to Hunter in a car one night in December. They had made arrangements for their baby to be found. He would be a nameless, abandoned child. A few years later Alma and Arnold Keller adopted him."

"Why go to all that trouble?" Baily said as he dropped the curtain.

"The Kellers knew their child would be different. He was the genetic product of two powerful psychics. They had to protect him from the government and the world."

Bone returned to the floor next to bone. "So, Hunter Keller is important or he's dangerous. Which one is it?"

Bone looked at the ceiling as if he could see into space. "Hunter used to get headaches, bad headaches, paralyzing headaches. One day they just stopped. Hunter then started to talk about things before they happened. I thought he was crazy and lucky. Didn't take any of it seriously. But he knew scores of baseball games before they were played. And he knew the next day's headline—verbatim. For a while I thought it was a trick. Then I knew different."

"What convinced you?" Baily asked.

"It was the week before Christmas. He told me my father's truck would be in a terrible accident. He didn't want my father in the truck that day. Then he demanded I at least make my father wear his seatbelt—something my father never did."

"Was he in the accident?"

Baily's head dropped under the load of the memory. "Yes. The next day. He would not wear the seatbelt. I begged him." Bone shook his head. "Broke his back on Main Street, downtown Stringtown. Paralyzed. My father died a month later."

"I'm sorry," Baily said as the fog of confusion lifted some.

Bone rubbed his face like a man rolling out of bed, but this was to fight back the tears. "I knew right then Hunter was gifted. Right then I decided to help him live his gifts. Hunter saw everything—past, present, and future. He needed to be able to turn it off. The information flow was too much to cope with. It would drive him crazy. I had to help him. Nobody else would."

"That 'reality' leaves all this open to question," Baily said. "Maybe Keller is crazy. Maybe you can't help the man. Maybe he's responsible for all these dead people. The facts are the facts, Bone. He's at each death. It's hard to explain away."

"You're a savvy homicide detective. I'm a savvy PhD in Psychology. I investigate things, too. I have my process like you have your process. I've observed Hunter Keller for twenty-three years as a friend and as a professional. I've tested him on many occasions over the last decade."

"And your point . . . ?"

"His psychic abilities are off the charts. It cannot be explained. It is a first. His precognitive skills are a hundred percent accurate. He sees the future with the same detail you can see me sitting on this floor in front of you right now. He is a paradox."

"What in the hell does that mean?" Baily asked.

"Hunter's abilities seem absurd and false, but they are rational and true."

"You know he could be dangerous, Bone. There's a very good chance he's gone well beyond you now."

"He told me some time ago that all the government contracted RVs were going to die. He said their direct descendants were going to die, too." Bone sank. "When he told me the close friends of RVs were at risk, it never hit me that he was also talking about us."

Baily leaned closer. "But you honestly do not know if Hunter Keller was telling you then that he was going to make it happen. You assumed it was someone else."

"I do not believe he is a monster. It never crossed my mind because Hunter would never do that."

Baily jumped to his feet and went to the front door waving his hand for quiet. He slid the burlap curtain to the side and put his eye to the dark edge of the window pane.

"You hear something?" Bond asked.

"Get your rifle ready. We've got company . . ."

ELEVEN

"The devil doesn't know how to sing, only how to howl."
Francis Thompson

Memphis, Tennessee

B en Nutley became a human doorstop. The other corpse in the Zegna suit and muddy alligator shoes was slumped over Nutley's head.

"This changes my vow of secrecy," Petty said staring at the fresh kills pulling on gloves.

Wilcox stepped over the bodies and reached in the back pocket of the expensive suit. "You know these people?"

Petty knelt over Green as Wilcox rifled through the alligator wallet. "I know one."

A dozen squad cars, two ambulances, and a fire truck

surrounded the Super 8 on West Illinois. The two dead were found by Memphis Waste Management on their 5:30 a.m. pickup. The bodies were on the dock by the dumpster. There was no effort to hide the carnage. Like a fat line of red army ants marching, the blood streamed twenty-feet down the steps and across the driveway to the drain.

Petty pronounced both dead at 6:02 a.m. and estimated TOD at 3:40 a.m. She and Wilcox standing on the stained cement stage backed away so Brimley could take pictures. A covey of Memphis police waited next to the dumpster for instructions.

She pointed to the suit. "Dr. Jacob Green."

Tony pulled the ID from the wallet. "And we have a winner —Jacob Green, MD. Did you kill this man, Dr. Petty?"

"Yes. And my plan is to take you out next." She rolled her eyes and flipped her long, blond hair over her shoulder. Brimley lowered the camera as she returned to the bodies. "Mr. Brimley, you can move Green off the other body now. I'd like some shots of the knife wound."

Wilcox hovered.

"This is an aggressive cut," she said. "Green's abdominal entry wound is followed by an abrupt upward movement bisecting sternum cartilage and clipping the aorta. Our killer is strong and efficient. I need to check, but I've seen this technique before."

"And how do you know Dr. Green?" Wilcox asked, knowing the answer.

"He's from Bethesda Research, one of three doctors in town. I met them three days ago. They've been coming to the morgue every day since."

"Bethesda Research? You've had my test results three days and did not tell me?" Wilcox fumed as Petty avoided eye contact.

"I wouldn't say that. No. Not really." She checked for

defensive wounds and spoke into her recorder. "No bruising, cuts, or lacerations to the hands or forearms. No signs of a struggle."

"So you do not have my test results, is that what you are saying?"

"Deceased number one—Dr. Green—was surprised or he knew his killer. That would make him an unsuspecting victim." She turned off the recorder. "I don't have test results to share, Wilcox."

"You say Green is one of three? I need names, now."

"Dr. Swenson and Dr. Blanchard," Petty said. "Although this hotel is not the place I would have expected them to stay, it is highly possible the other two are here. They traveled together."

Wilcox turned to the police. "Find me Sergeant Tucker. We need to locate Dr. Green's associates. Petty thinks they're at this hotel. Look for Dr. Swenson and Dr. Blanchard. Move with extreme caution, gentlemen."

He swung back to Petty. "If no test results, what the hell are they doing in Memphis?"

"They have an interest in our unsolved homicides."

"Oh really."

"They also have questions about a natural death I handled when I first got here."

"And you didn't feel it important enough to share with me because why?"

"Their presence was proprietary. They believe the Memphis cases could be part of a national killing spree."

Wilcox popped on gloves. "Get lost Brimley. I'll help her hold shit." Petty nodded her approval and Brimley disappeared into the hotel.

"What the do you think you're doing?" Wilcox seethed. "I don't know how they do things in Dallas, but the medical examiner and homicide work together in Memphis. I could run your pretty, little ass in for willful obstruction and tampering in four active homicide investigations. M.E. or not, you could find yourself in jail for this shit."

With bloody gloves and a smile she said, "Are you trying to impress me?" She leaned back into Green's gut wound with a penlight. "You're not going to do anything about this. May I call you Anthony, or do you prefer Tony?"

"You call me Detective Wilcox, goddamn it."

"I've heard you called Tee. I like Tony. I think I'll call you Tony."

"Stop Petty," he huffed.

She looked up, inches from his face. "Memphis is a part of some kind of national crisis—allegedly. Until Dr. Green, Dr. Blanchard, and Dr. Swenson completed their cursory review, I was bound to secrecy. It was a national security matter. I'm sorry if you do not understand that."

"Who the hell binds a county medical examiner to secrecy?"

"The United States Attorney General."

"The U.S. Attorney General is sticking his fat nose into my cases without my involvement or approval? I don't think so, Petty."

"Your cases?" she sighed. "You're not the least impressed are you?"

"I know the damn law, Petty. I know my powers, and they are many. I do not trust the government or any federal agency sneaking around my world. I own homicides in Memphis, Tennessee. On my watch, they're my business unless the President of the United States gets nailed here. Even then, after screwing up the Kennedy assassination, we got laws to keep the feds out of our hair. The fuckers are incompetent and up to their asses in hidden agendas."

"I lost count of the bad words, Tony. It is very distracting and unprofessional." She looked into Green's mouth. "But, I agree with most everything said. I suggest you start trusting me."

Wilcox rocked back on his heels. He never won a verbal exchange that he knew about. Brimley poked his head out the door more to rescue Petty than to offer assistance.

"What the hell does your leprechaun want?" Wilcox barked.

Brimley smiled at his new boss. "Do you need me, for anything?"

"No. But I am done with Dr. Green. I need to examine the next body."

"Benjamin Nutley, the night manager," Wilcox said.

"I've seen more knives in backs in the last three months than five years in Dallas."

"We like knives here," Wilcox grumbled.

Petty smiled but didn't look up. She let him stew.

"Nutley was leaning out the door when he got stuck in the back," Wilcox said as he scanned the dock chewing on the Bethesda revelations and frustration with his new ME.

It was the second crime scene together. Petty had to find out for herself—was Wilcox as good as his reputation. So far the double homicide held few if any clues.

"What do you think happened here?" she asked as she busied herself over the body.

He took his time lighting a cigarette. "Green's clandestine phone conversation was interrupted. Nutley was in the wrong place at the wrong time."

"Clandestine phone conversation . . . really?" Petty scoffed.

"Yeah, really. Probably in a cluster of trees by the river," Wilcox said pocketing his lighter.

"How did you reach your conclusions?"

"Simple logic, Petty." He blew smoke at the dumpster looking toward the Mississippi.

"Humor me."

"Oh. You want information from me, like we're a team?" He turned his back. "Here's a crumb. I bet your Dr. Green's room is bugged."

"Seriously! Bugged? And his body's a long way from trees and Mississippi River. You're reaching, Tony." She lifted Nutley's shirt and leaned into his bloody wound with her light.

"Why leave the comfort of your room in the middle of the night? If it were me, I would only leave to meet or talk to someone on the phone. His room was not secure. He couldn't talk on the phone there. Green left the hotel for the woods to not be seen on his cell. I'd choose trees on the other side of the empty parking lot. Not too far. There's enough moonlight to cross the field without stepping on a damn snake or in a mud puddle with my damn expensive shoes. Nobody can see or hear me in those trees."

"Are you serious with this elaborate theory?"

"Green has river mud on his shoes." Wilcox pulled a leaf from Green's pant cuff. "I think you will find this to be river birch. They are by the river, not the hotel."

"And how'd he get on the loading dock?"

"Something went awry in the trees by the river. Green bumped into his killer, dropped his phone and ran like hell."

"You know all this from looking at Dr. Green lying on the loading dock?"

"I've done this a few times. I'm not new like you."

"Come on detective, you have no idea if Dr. Green was talking on his phone, or he was running from the river chased by his killer. You're rambling. You're trying to impress me."

"People like Green always have their phone on them. His is missing."

"People like Green? You don't know anything about Dr. Green."

"He's wearing a $4,000.00 outfit. He's got styled hair, a

manicure, and probably a pedicure. His teeth are capped. He plucks his eyebrows, nose, and ears. People like Green never misplace or forget their keys, wallets, or phones. Something bad would have to happen for him to leave his phone behind."

"You said he was running for his life, how do you know? Maybe he couldn't sleep and went for a walk. Maybe he was not running from anything."

"Listen and learn, Petty. Green's polished and buffed shoes are scuffed on the toes from the ragged asphalt parking lot he tripped across—the guy's no athlete. His white, starched shirt is untucked on both sides but not front and back. His arms were pumping like hell. And it was a short run, no sweat. We're gonna find his shoe impressions in the field, long strides, and a bee line to the hotel. The orange peel stuck on his heel came from behind the dumpster."

"What's he doing at the back of the hotel, Sherlock?"

"Sherlock—cute. Easy. He ran along the side of the hotel so he could hide from the guy he knew would kill him."

"Why go to the back of the hotel? Why not go in the front door and back to your room to call the police."

"No police, Petty. Dr. Green's entangled in something clandestine. He knows his killer. He thinks there are more bad guys waiting for him in the lobby or his room. No. It would be best for him to disappear for a while."

"If any of this is true, you're more amazing than your reputation and bloated ego."

"I don't carry around a crystal ball, and I'm no psychic. I have hunches. My hunch is Green chose the shadows of the building, thick shrubs, and a dark hiding place behind the dumpster so he could wait things out. He had every intention of staying in his hiding place all night. If I was hunted, I'd wait for daylight and a crowd."

"But, something changed his mind."

"Right. Mr. Nutley opened the back door. Green saw an opportunity and took it."

"I think that scenario is too risky," Petty said.

"Green is a city boy sitting in the dark behind a dumpster scared shitless. He got sick of breathing garbage, swatting mosquitos, and scaring off rats. Nutley was Green's gift from heaven. He opened the back door to toss a bag of trash. Nutley was enough of a crowd for Green to escape his little slice of hell."

Petty dropped her gloves on the bloody back. "Mr. Nutley was an unsuspecting victim."

"Mr. Nutley got it in the back and fell past Green."

"Then Green saw his killer," Petty surmised.

"And he had no time to react. Green gets filleted and bleeds all over his expensive threads."

Sergeant Tucker poked his head out the back door. "Excuse me Detective Wilcox. We have a development. We found Dr. Blanchard."

"Oh good. I need to talk with him," Petty said.

Wilcox shook his head. "I'm afraid that's not going to be possible. Go ahead Tucker."

"He's dead, Dr. Petty. We found him in room 301." He turned back to Wilcox. "One of the magnetic cards was still in the door. We're waiting for CSI. Appears the doctor was sleeping when he was attacked. Stabbed through the blanket, sheet, and pajamas. He didn't move."

"What about Swenson?" Wilcox asked.

"The doctor checked out last night at seven o'clock."

Petty held up her hand. "Wait. They were scheduled to be at the morgue two more days. The Pella exhumation and autopsy is what they've been waiting for."

"Where's Pella's body now?" Wilcox asked.

"The morgue. He was exhumed yesterday afternoon. Delivered last evening."

"Maybe Swenson got a private look at the body. Maybe he already has all the information he needs."

The morning sun pushed the river mist off the field, but not from the stand of trees west of the Super 8. Wilcox and Tucker followed Green's tracks along the side of the hotel and into the field. In the shadows of the cluster of trees Dr. Swenson backed away from the bobbing heads coming his way. He moved through the river birch like a cat and slid down the bank onto the weed infested cobblestone road. Swenson's small motorboat was waiting at the water's edge.

Unlike Dr. Green, he had packed a change of clothes. Swenson was organized to a fault. Before Wilcox and Tucker reached the trees, he was afloat wearing an old fishing hat and weather-worn, Tigers windbreaker. He pushed the throttle and watched the east bank slide by as the bobbing heads stopped on the edge of the bluff. The fishing poles propped at the stern bent with the waves of the majestic river—a nice added touch.

When Wilcox and Tucker disappeared back into the stand of river birch trees, Swenson tossed Dr. Green's cell phone into the swirling currents under the Harahan Bridge.

TWELVE

"Never open the door to a lesser evil, for others invariably slink in after it."
Baltasar Gracian

Henryetta, Oklahoma

"I'm here for Hunter Keller."

Elda Middleton yanked the tattered belt of her terrycloth robe looking through the old screen at the imposing silhouette. He wore a long, black coat and flat-brimmed hat. A late model, dark sedan sat in the shadows under her oak tree, and someone was up against the trunk out of the scattered patches of moonlight. Her eyes shot to the trampled garden and followed the dirt tracks up her front steps to the muddy boots on her porch. Her eyes narrowed even more in the dark.

He leaned in like a crow landing on a post. A sliver of moonlight traced his edgy face and found a thin smile. *"Can you hear me?"* he boomed at the old lady.

Elda looked dead—like she climbed out of a casket instead of a bed. Her sparse, white hair laid flat on the side that left her pillow. Sagging skin, etched lines, blotches, and moles had taken over long ago, but like a dormant rose in a winter snow there was still a hint of lingering beauty and tenderness.

"I hear ya," Elda carped. "It's three in the mornin'. Who are ya and what're ya doin' knockin' on my door at this hour?"

She flipped the switch. The porch light stayed out. She toggled it. Still nothing. *Was workin' this evenin',* she thought as she checked the latch with a casual finger and caught the man's darting eye in the band of moonlight. A child could pull the latch-screw from the doorstop. Elda checked more out of habit than purpose, but that changed when the man straightened.

"Sorry about the hour, ma'am," he said. "I'm Major T.L. Cankor with DIA." He looked up the empty road like he expected someone, and turned back to the old lady with more purpose in his voice. "I'm here on a matter of upmost importance." When he looked the other way, Elda saw the forced smile was now a flat line.

"What's a DIA?" she asked, even though she knew the answer.

"Defense Intelligence Agency—U.S. Government." They stared in the dark.

"Government? All I know is you're standin' on my porch in the middle of the night with muddy boots makin' a big mess for me, mister." *I knew you people would come . . .*

Major Cankor looked at his boots and cleared his throat. "Hunter Keller, we know he's here. He's staying at your boarding house. I need to see him, now."

"Who said the man's stayin' here?"

"We don't have time. Failure to cooperate has consequences."
He reached for the door."

Her eyes followed the gnarled fingers on the muscular hand.
"You got some piece of paper says ya can come in my house?"
Now I remember you—been forty years.

He pulled back, looked over his shoulder, and nodded to the
man by the tree. This time his coat fell open blocking Elda's view
—but it didn't matter, she knew.

Major Cankor leaned his nose to the screen. His anger leaked
out his exploding whisper, "I don't *need* a piece of paper."

"Why ya lookin' for this man ya call Keller?"

"It's classified," he snapped, spittle stopping at the screen.

"Seems it would be somethin' important for me to know if ya
want inside my house."

Cankor had expeditious ways to get what he wanted, but
there were benefits to be had from a smooth extraction on Dewar
Avenue. Managing the news events was preferable.

"Mr. Keller is a homeland security risk, a danger to the
public. If he is innocent, he will be back in two days. This is only
an investigation."

"Doesn't feel like one to me. Feels like you're pretty darn
certain this man's guilty of somethin' ya won't talk about."

"Elda Middleton," he bellowed. "It is my responsibility to
locate and transport Mr. Keller to a government facility for
questioning. If you interfere with this process, you are viewed as
an accomplice, a new person of interest aiding and abetting an
enemy of the state."

She tightened her belt as her thinning, white eyebrows
dipped in the shadows of her entry. "Enemy of the state, ya say?
How'd ya know my name, Mr. Cankor?"

"Your mailbox," he shot back without thinking.

Elda didn't hesitate for a reason. "Never said I had this Keller
feller in my house. Still don't know how ya can just come here at

three in the mornin' and get me out of my bed with nothin' but demands."

"This man is dangerous. He's killed and is on the run. You, your tenants, and your neighbors could get hurt. Hunter Keller is a sick, deranged man. He appears to be normal, but he has severe mental problems. I have seen what he can do. I have seen his victims. You must cooperate. It is for your own good. Allow me to secure the area and neutralize the threat before it's too late."

"Shoot, that doesn't scare me, Mr. Cankor. I'm an old lady. I lived in Henryetta eighty-four years. This house, fifty. Lots of people stay here. They come and go. I mind my own business. I never had one problem with my tenants."

Cankor contained his wrath. "He is a psychopath! He is a serial killer! You have no idea what this man's capable of doing. My presence on your porch is enough to set him off. Hunter Keller could be moving into position to hurt you and many others right now."

"It doesn't make sense, my government chasin' serial killers. That's what police do, or FBI. Never heard about DIA lookin' for serial killers . . .

"You and the man by my tree need to leave. Go get papers to let you come in my house in the morning. Judge Hughes is up the road a mile. Knock on his door in the middle of the night and see what he's got to say about all this psycho stuff. Good night Mr. Government man."

She reached back for the heavy wood door with the deadbolts, the one she seldom closed in the summertime. Elda liked the breeze from the garden snaking through the house—the trampled garden next to the mailbox with no name. When Elda widowed, she painted over the name and left the numbers. Ruby Tantabaum—her best friend—said it was the safe thing to do. But Elda Middleton had other reasons she hid her name, reasons only she and Ruby knew.

Cankor straightened his hat and sucked in the night air as Elda reached back for the door. He glared through the screen he could rip to shreds with a single swipe. But Cankor saw movement in the dark recesses of the entry by the stairs behind the old lady. When the door muffled closed, his thin smile returned.

* * *

Ruby Tantabaum could not sleep. Halfway into her mystery novel she heard Beatrice creak down the back stairs.

"You see Elda's got company?" Bea said, as she eased into Ruby's light, flashed a smile, and scurried to the window blinds.

Ruby squinted at her watch. "It's awful late for company. What makes you think Elda's got any? Probably just a tenant getting in—most are young, still running 'round at all hours."

"Never saw that old sedan before. Wasn't there when I walked Pepper." She pressed her nose to the glass. "I don't think it belongs to anyone stayin' with her."

Old sedan doesn't mean a thing, Ruby mused as she closed her book. "You're just snooping around sister. You're making stuff up in your head. Shouldn't be spying on Elda and her tenants in the first place."

"I saw someone under the oak tree by the car," Bea said. "Looked like he was hiding."

"Bunch a shadows movin' in the moonlight," Ruby sighed.

"And I saw a big man standing on Elda's front porch. He had on one of those long coats like those scary people in the movies." Bea leaned to see around the azalea bush covering half the window. "I couldn't see his head from upstairs. I think he was wearin' a hat. Don't see people wearing hats much anymore, not unless they're sneaking around if ya know what I mean." She moved to a lower slat and lifted. "I don't see either now. And the car's still there, Ruby."

"Then they're inside the house with Elda." Ruby slid into her slippers and got up.

"Wonder who they are?" She dropped the slat and spun around. "Elda didn't say anything about expectin' late visitors. I spoke with her when I was walkin' Pepper."

"Guess I'll never hear the end of this. Let's go out on the porch where we can see better."

At the crape myrtle hanging over the railing they peeked through the gaps in the foliage. "Whoever they are, they parked away from the sidewalk. Looks like they got under the oak tree to avoid the moonlight," Bea said.

Ruby lifted a limb. "Moonlight stops at both bumpers. And someone walked straight through Elda's garden."

"Bet she's havin' a hissy-fit. She loves her garden."

"I guess it is late for visitors," Ruby muttered.

"Maybe they're delivering some bad news. Maybe someone died in Elda's family."

"Elda doesn't have family, sister. Everyone's dead but her. What other kind of news could someone be delivering to an old lady in the middle of the night?"

"I don't know the answer to that."

Ruby got out her cell and scrolled contacts as Bea moved branches. "You got Oglebee's phone number?"

"Didn't bring my phone. Why you calling the sheriff?"

"Like you said, we've never seen that old sedan around here, and we don't know who'd be coming in the middle of the night. If something bad happened, there would be a Henryetta police car parked out front, sister."

"You're right, Ruby. Call the sheriff. No. Call 911. No. Wait. Call Elda first. People are gonna think we're a couple of meddling old ladies." Bea bent down. "I just saw a shadow move in an upstairs window."

The cell phone lit the side of Ruby's face. "Elda's not answering. If she's up, she would pick up, always does. Something's wrong, sister."

"Turn it off. The light, it's all over your face, Ruby. They're gonna see you."

A dark figure moved from second floor window. "Oh dear," Bea whispered. "I think someone just caught us snoopin' honey. You better call 911 right now."

THIRTEEN

"Suspicion is a heavy armor and with its weight it impedes more than it protects."
Robert Burns

Broken Bow Lake, Oklahoma

T wo hours and twenty minutes from Henryetta the knob on the cabin door rattled. Baily raised his Smith & Wesson head high. Bone rested his Browning 30-06 rifle on his knee and took it off safety.

They ran all night. The beer and beef jerky were gone and Baily's brain hurt. Bone's Stargate story and bizarre linkage to homicides in Memphis bordered on insane. Now someone rattled the knob to their cabin in the middle of nowhere. Baily lived on the razor's edge since Stringtown and the revelations in Arnold and Alma Keller's attic. Each minute there were more questions and fewer answers. Now, people were going to die.

They both stopped breathing when the door whined open. Only Baily's thumb moved. He pulled back the hammer on his 38 releasing the metallic click into the cold, dark cabin.

The door stopped moving. Nobody blinked.

The childlike whisper entered the room, "Please don't shoot me."

Confused but cautious, Baily barked, "Then don't move. Identify yourself."

Bone wiped sweat from his eye and kept the silhouette in the doorway on top of his bead. He would not go down like his friends.

"I am Hunter Keller."

More confused and unsure, Baily ordered, "Say more," as he glanced over at Bone's shadow and shoulder shrug. Both guns stayed on the target.

"What do you want me to say?" The door opened wider. The moonlight surrounded him. The tall, skinny figure wearing a hoodie came into the room. He stopped. His hands hung at his side. Unsure, Bone focused ready to shoot, his nerves frazzled. It could be a trick. He knew Hunter had to be more than a hundred miles away.

"I grew up in Stringtown. You are Cameron Baily, a Memphis homicide detective sent here by Detective Tony Wilcox. You're investigating me. Bone Jackson's my friend. He's over there with a rifle aimed at me—the safety's off, but he forgot to cock it. Bone won't shoot me. And you won't shoot me, Mr. Baily." He closed the door and turned the deadbolt. "We don't have time for this. They're coming. They want me. And they want both of you dead."

Bone set down his rifle and struggled off the floor. Baily watched him cross the room like a water buffalo. He wrapped his sweaty arms around the skinny man. "What're you doin' here, Hunter? I thought you were hiding somewhere in Henryetta."

Baily kept his gun on both. Maybe Keller's wrong. Maybe Baily would shoot the guy before he did something bad. From his vantage point the skinny guy is still the prime suspect in the multiple homicides back in Memphis.

"Slow down," Baily said. "Bone, back away. Do exactly as I say. Back away now and go back to the damn window. Pick up your gun. Cock the damn thing and put your eyes out that damn window. This is not over. This could be a trap. We don't know anything right now."

Bone backed away from Keller and went to the window. "It is Hunter. He is not an imposter." He looked out the window. "And nothing's moving out there."

Baily ignored Bone. "Sit on the floor, mister. The middle of the room. What I know about you makes me very nervous. You think you know what I'm gonna do. Hell, that's impossible because I don't even know what I'm gonna do. I promise you, if you freak me out I will shoot you and ask questions later."

"They killed Brad," Bone said with his nose pressed to a window pane. "They killed Jeff and Jeremy, too. They're all dead, Hunter."

Baily watched Keller sit on the floor with his head down. His long, scrawny body folded like a dead spider. *How can this anemic wimp kill four big guys,* Baily wondered? "Stop talking, Bone. Focus on the woods. There are people out there trying to get in here."

Bone ignored Baily. "Is *he* out there, Hunter? Is *he* coming tonight?"

"Who the hell is *he?*" Baily asked as he opened the burlap curtain on the front door and his gun clicked on a glass window pane.

Keller said, "He had to leave. He won't be back. He won't risk it."

"Both of you stop talkin' until I figure things out," Baily ordered. "Who won't risk what?"

"I don't like hearing that, Hunter. He's determined," Bone said.

"All right goddamn it. That's enough." Baily barked.

Keller whispered, "He won't risk me, Detective Baily."

Trying to make sense of it all, Baily turned and stared at Keller. "I have no idea what any of that means. No offense, but my little sister could whip your ass."

Baily could not see Keller's smile under his hoodie. "Did you tell him about me, Bone?"

"Told him about Stargate, your parents, and some of your abilities."

"What abilities do people fear, Mr. Keller?"

"It's complicated."

"Simplify. The more I know the better it is for you."

"He is a bad man. I can get inside his head. He does not like it. He must always be in control. The only way he can keep me from getting inside him is to maintain distance."

"Mental telepathy? Okay. So how far away does this guy need to be?"

"A minimum of fifty miles," Keller said.

"Then why are we hiding?"

"Because his people are coming. I am here."

"Why does he want you, Keller?" Baily asked.

"I am an obstacle. People around me are disposable inconveniences."

Baily shook his head and went back under the burlap to scan the woods. "This is way above my pay grade. Makes absolutely no sense." He pulled back out. "Just tell me; did you kill Thomas Derby, Mr. Keller? Did you kill William Hudson, Mark

Pemberton, and Donald Deckle? And before you think about lying, we have you at each crime scene."

"I am responsible for their deaths."

"That's what I thought. You're going to get the chair in Tennessee," Baily said.

"Wait a minute." Bone left the window and stood in front of Keller like a father. "This is what gets you in trouble. Think about your words, not your feelings. You feel responsible for these deaths because you see the future. You did not prevent the deaths. We've talked about this. It does not make you responsible, Hunter. You did not kill these people."

"Is that true, Mr. Keller?" Baily asked. "You did not kill them?"

"I knew they were going to die." Keller's head dropped. "I did not stop it."

Baily lowered his gun. "Detective Wilcox told me what happened on highway 55 a few days ago, the trucker that drove into a herd of deer and was killed."

"What's that got to do with anything?" Bone asked.

Baily stayed on Keller. "You were in that truck, weren't you? You got out right before the accident, didn't you? Tony Wilcox talked to the trucker before he died. He told Wilcox you got out of the truck. He knew your name. That trucker told Wilcox you told him he was gonna die that very night. I guess you didn't help him either, did you Mr. Keller?"

"Is all that true, Hunter," Bone asked. "Did you tell the man he was going to die?"

"Yes, to both questions."

Bone returned to the window shaking his head. "You didn't help the poor guy. You knew about the deer. Why didn't you say something? Why did you just get out?"

"I tried to warn him. He would not listen. He was not going to change."

"Not going to change what?" Baily asked.

"You saw something you're not talking about," Bone said. "You located this trucker for a reason, didn't you? After you talked to him you made a decision."

Keller got to his feet and walked over to Bone standing at the window. "We must talk about this later. Now, you must shoot the man kneeling by the tree thirty yards out. He is sliding onto his gun a night vision scope. If you do not act now, you will be killed, Bone."

With his head under the burlap curtain at the front door, Baily listened to the bizarre instructions given to Bone. *Are you kidding me? What in the hell is Keller trying to do?*

"Detective Baily," Keller yelled. "You're in a gun sight. Do not question me. You have two seconds. Lean back now!"

Confused, Baily backed away inches and the glass shattered lifting the curtain. A bullet ricocheted off the stone fireplace across the room. Immediately Bone's Browning exploded. Burnt gunpowder filled the room and a cracking echo rolled down the river valley.

"I think I got him," Bone muttered.

"You did," Keller said. "Detective, your shooter is running. He believes he hit you. They will be back for me, and to finish Bone. We all need to leave now."

"Wait!" Baily peered out the edge of the splintered wood through the shattered glass in time to see a dark figure scramble over the wooded hill and out of sight.

"We must leave now to have any chance," Keller said.

"There may be more out there. We could run right into them," Baily said.

"We are alone for a short time. We must go now."

Baily joined them at the window. "Go where?"

"Broken Bow Lake. There's a boat by the dam. We go south

on Mountain Fork River. We have a narrow window—less than an hour—before many more get here."

"Not a good idea," Bone said. "The river, we'll be exposed. We'll be sitting ducks."

"When they find we are gone they will first check the roads, then the lake, and then the river. It is the only way now."

The moon slid behind a bank of clouds as they left the cabin. The darker woods and craggy hills made their trek slow. When they pushed through the last line of foliage and saw the dam, most of their hour was gone.

Exactly as Keller described, they found the boat by the dam. The nose was grounded under a pile of debris. Bone pulled it out like a bear going after a honey pot. "Not bad. And there's a trolling motor on this bad boy," he said.

"You use logic to do this stuff, Keller," Baily said under his breath. "This is common sense, a fishin' boat on a river by a damn dam. I'll bet there are ten or more around here. And this big dam, it was on the poster at the cabin, the one I saw you studying."

Keller watched Bone clean debris from inside the boat.

"What? No comments?" Baily chided, when Bone slid the boat into the water.

Keller turned to Baily. "It's not important you believe. We need to go."

"I told you he sees things, detective. There is much you do not understand. I suggest we leave it at that."

But Baily pushed. "Keller, did you see this boat sitting by the dam under branches?"

"No. I saw us getting in a boat here, by this dam."

"Are you telling me logic is not a big part of what you do?"

"I do not know the answer to your question."

"He took us in a straight line from the cabin to this boat," Bone bellowed. "You see any other boats around here? No. And this boat was hidden. Did you see it before Hunter pointed at the pile of debris and after I started digging? No you did not, sir."

Bone fiddled with the motor as they bobbed in the boat at the edge of river. Then the current grabbed their bow and pulled them downstream. "We need to get control soon."

"It is the battery cable," Keller said. "It is disconnected."

"What battery cable?" Baily barked.

"It is under your seat," Keller replied.

Baily found the two cables and pushed them together. "See. Nothing." Then the small motor hummed.

Bone worked the tiller hugging the east bank, dodging low hanging tree limbs, and watching for moving shadows. The clouds opened and the half-moon transformed the river to white glass.

"The events at the cabin, and finding this boat, demonstrate some of Hunter's gifts, detective," Bone said under his breath as he surveyed their surroundings.

"Some are assets. Others are liabilities," Keller sighed.

Could you be for real? Baily wondered as he eyed the banks with gun in hand. He had enough trouble dealing with reality—the world had always been a complicated place for him. Now, he was being hunted by unknown people for unclear reasons and the person at four of his homicides now sat across from him in a stolen boat.

Keller answered Baily's unspoken question. "For a long time I did not understand what I was seeing in my head. I believed they were dreams. But there were too many. I could not turn them off, and I started to see them come true—the good and the bad. I did not control them."

Bone checked the safety for a third time and looked down the river. "I started working with Hunter ten years ago," he said. "We didn't make real progress until I got smarter."

"Got your PhD?" Baily said.

"Yes. It gave me the tools for a deep dive into the world of parapsychology, a far less understood world, and one on the fringe of reality as we know it. We eventually learned how to turn things down and then on and off. It was important because the flow from the past, present, and future was crippling him."

"Danger is near," Keller said. *And you two will not escape.* "I wish I could be of more help, but there are no more options."

Baily scanned the woods. "I don't see anything."

"They have night vision," Keller said.

Ahead the river narrowed to fifty-feet. Both shorelines were lined with trees, overhanging branches touched the water creating leafy caves they could navigate. Staying in the shadows and dodging debris on the edge of the main current provided the most cover.

"We're moving at about five knots," Bone whispered. "How far do we need to go?"

Keller ignored Bone's question and ordered Baily to call Wilcox on his cell. "Do it now. Tell him we are on Mountain Fork River seven miles north of Eagletown, Arkansas."

Baily pulled out his phone. "I haven't had reception since Bone's camper. What makes you think anything has changed? Son of a bitch, I've got bars."

"Call now," Keller demanded. *I'm sorry Bone. It is too late for you and the detective.*

The half-moon draped over the water as their black mass with three bumps floated in and out of hanging shadows. The occasional wind gusts whistled through the trees and the branches lifted and settled on the water like giant breathing animals. Then the swirling leaves started to rain down on the water. The river got silent. Only the hum of the boat motor mingled with the empty night sounds.

"Where the hell are you Baily?" Wilcox yelled. *"You're phone's been out of service since five yesterday, goddamn it!"*

"I'm still in Oklahoma. Calm down. I have Hunter Keller."

"Keller's in Oklahoma? Tell me you have him tied up like a Christmas turkey, Baily." Wilcox slid out of bed, grabbed his cigarettes and lighter, and went out onto the balcony in his underwear. "I think he could be more dangerous than we thought."

Baily saw movement in the woods. "Hold on a minute."

"Hold on for what?" Wilcox said.

Baily leaned into Keller. "Tell me why people around you are dying?"

Keller's eyes stayed on the west bank as he spoke. "The elimination of remote viewers and their descendants," he said.

"But why?"

"To control psychic-weaponry." Keller held up one finger as he stared into the woods. "We are not alone anymore. Tell Detective Wilcox our location now!"

"Keller wants me to tell you we are on the Mountain Fork River in east Oklahoma."

"Does he have a gun on you?" Wilcox asked. "Just cough, if yes."

The phone crackled. "We are on the river south of Broken Bow Lake, seven miles north of Eagletown. It doesn't look good. Keller is . . ."

The first bullet exploded through Baily's head. He slumped over and dropped the phone to the floor of the boat. The next two missed Keller. The third hit Bone in the chest. He fell back onto the tiller. The boat cut sharp into the east bank. A spray of bullets riddled the boat as it disappeared in the overhanging foliage and clouds covered the moon. Everything went black.

"*Baily! Baily!*" Wilcox yelled into his dead phone. The last thing he heard was Keller's name and gunshots.

Wilcox looked at the worthless piece of technology in his hand and threw it into the bedroom. After kicking the iron chair across the balcony, he glared at the Mississippi River as if he could see all the way to Oklahoma. He flicked his cigarette into the sky as his rage swallowed him whole. The growling monster inside wanted out of its cage. It was the same monster that stirred the day Wilcox found his partner hanging in the Memphis Public Library.

I'm gonna find you Keller . . .

Henryetta Daily Herald

Serving Okmulgee County Since 1924

October 27, 2014

Five Found Dead on Dewar Avenue

Henryetta PD was called to 2175 Dewar Avenue around 11:00 a.m. and found three people dead. Shortly after answering the call they made another gruesome discovery at the neighboring residence (2165 Dewar) where two more were found dead taking the total count to five. HPD launched a house-to-house search for more possible victims and witnesses to the bizarre deaths. The medical examiner places time of death between 3:00 and 4:00 a.m. October 27.

Elda Middleton was found dead in her living room. Middleton, a longtime resident of Henryetta, is the owner of the boarding house at 2175 Dewar. Two of three known tenants were found dead in their rooms; names are being withheld until notification of next-of-kin. A third tenant, Hunter Keller, from Stringtown, Oklahoma, was not at the Dewar address. Sources close to the investigation say it appears Keller checked out. There were no personal effects found at the crime scene. At this time, he is a person of interest. Anyone knowing of Hunter Keller's whereabouts is asked to contact HPD. Police warn the public not to approach the man. He may be armed and dangerous.

Ruby Tantabaum, owner of the neighboring residence at 2165 Dewar address, and her sister Beatrice, were found dead on their front porch. The two were sitting in chairs. More details about cause of death are not available at this time. The Tantabaum family is known in Henryetta, kin to early settlers on Creek Nation land leading to the founding of the city in the early 1900s.

Police are not commenting on the Dewar deaths at this time. Bodies have been taken to the Okmulgee County morgue for autopsy. The medical examiner, Dr. Benjamin Proust, was contacted. "We have begun our process, our look into cause and manner of death of these five people," Proust said. "We are treating these as homicides and will carefully assess all physical evidence and provide more definitive information to the HPD and sheriff's office in the days ahead."

County Sheriff T.E. Oglebee said, "We are very disturbed over this terrible tragedy. Elda, Ruby, and Beatrice were friends of mine. Their deaths, and Elda's tenants, and the timing and proximity are upsetting. Although we will wait for Dr. Proust's findings, the HPD and county sheriff's office will treat this heinous crime as a mass murder of the worst kind to ever occur in our community. We are aggressively moving forward with our investigation. Trust me when I say we will find those responsible."

Unnamed sources report the five dead had necks broken. The bodies were positioned after death. Home invasion is unlikely, but has not been ruled out. Anyone with information is requested to immediately contact the Henryetta Police Department at 918-HPD-HELP.

FOURTEEN

"A half-truth is a whole lie."
Proverb

Memphis, Tennessee

The naked bodies of Dr. Green, Dr. Blanchard, and Benjamin Nutley laid supine on gurneys in the walk-in refrigerator at the Shelby County morgue. The bloody Y-shaped incisions and sunken chests confirmed the autopsies had been completed—all organs removed, examined, and sections sent to the histology lab. The remaining viscera were returned to the empty thoracic cavities of the deceased to be buried or burned along with the surgically ravaged corpses.

The three were not going anywhere soon. The city transported Nutley's morbidly obese spouse to The MED. She fell into a catatonic state when she learned her husband would never come home again. The bodies of the two Bethesda doctors would be held by the county until true identities were known—records of Green and Blanchard at Bethesda Research and with the U.S. Government did not exist. Records for the missing Dr. Swenson did, but required clearance from the highest level in the DOJ—the U.S. Attorney General.

Classified information that had been promised to Dr. Petty had never arrived. Prior to Swenson's disappearance she bought into the slow grinding wheels of the unwieldy federal government. But even the few electronic files transferred the night they had met had been blocked.

Each morning the Bethesda-three came to the morgue to examine the bodies of the four unsolved homicides. Each day they waited for the legal clearances to authorize exhumation of Pella. Dr. Swenson reassured Dr. Petty the government delays were just a part of the complex vetting process. Now, after the Super 8 kills and Swenson's odd disappearance, Petty questioned the government's true role in the Stargate Project, and she questioned their culpability in the bizarre deaths in Memphis.

When her phone rang, she opened her eyes lost in the dark, cold room in the basement of the county morgue. It had been another exhausting day as the new chief medical examiner. And it was another night on the old leather sofa in her cold office.

"Dr. Petty?" She recognized the voice immediately.

"Dr. Tanner. Hello." She tried to climb out of her stupor by turning on a light.

"Sorry for the late hour, but I thought you would want this information right away."

"My letter? It's about the DNA?"

"Yes."

She swung her legs over the side and found herself in the mirror across the room. She pushed at her hair without thinking. "Please go on."

"We can confirm the letter was handled by the U.S. Attorney

General. We secured his genetic material and got a perfect match. I must say I am proud of our team. They witnessed Mr. Baldwin discarding a Starbuck's vanilla latte. We retrieved the cup in the DOJ cafeteria, a place he rarely frequents. I suppose we were in the proverbial right place and time."

"I recognize the risk of obtaining the DNA of a sitting attorney general. This will remain confidential. I needed to confirm the letter was from Alfred Baldwin."

Petty jumped when the refrigerator motor banged on and her pictures began to shake. But now the familiar hum and vibrations oddly relaxed her. The sounds had become part of her new home. Like a familiar creak in the floor or squeaky ceiling fan, the old motor in the wall would be missed if it were ever replaced. Alone at night with dead bodies should not bother educated medical professionals—especially a forensic pathologist. Although Petty knew ghosts and goblins were fantasy, it was that sliver of the unknown that would keep her forever vigilant.

Petty could hear Tanner rustle through papers on the other end of the phone. "You gave me the name Dr. John Swenson," he said. "One of the three doctors from Bethesda, I believe. He was the one you said handed you the envelope."

"Correct," Petty said now eager to find out more about the missing doctor.

"Was he wearing gloves, Victoria? Did he handle the envelope in a peculiar way, by the edges maybe?" Tanner shuffled more papers.

"No gloves. He presented the envelope to me holding it in both hands—fingers beneath and thumbs on top. I thought it a bit dramatic at the time."

"I see. That is odd. We 'did not' recover Dr. Swenson's DNA on the envelope."

"I assume an insufficient transfer of biologic material—skin cells, perspiration."

"Today we have advanced nano-technology. It requires infinitesimal DNA transfer. May I confirm this? Are you certain the envelope was sealed when he passed it to you?"

"Yes. I would assume a private document from a high ranking government official would be signed and sealed by the author."

"We found your DNA and Mr. Baldwin's DNA on the envelope and on the letter. We found Dr. Swenson's DNA on the letter, but not on the envelope, Victoria."

"I can assume Dr. Swenson prepared or proofed the letter for the attorney general. That seems plausible."

"We found DNA from a fourth person on the letter."

"A fourth person handled the letter?"

"Yes. We ran it through the national data base."

Petty got to her feet and walked to the mirror as more papers rustled on the other end of the phone. Staring at herself she tried to separate her lack of self-confidence from the growing fears. "Did you find a match?"

"Yes we did. However, based on what you shared with me, it makes no sense. The letter from the attorney general was also handled by Dr. Benjamin Proust. He is the medical examiner for Okmulgee County, Oklahoma."

* * *

The McCurtain Democrat

October 28, 2014

Two Dead, One to Regional Med Center

Broken Bow, Oklahoma – Police were called to investigate a possible shooting on Mountain Fork River south of Broken Bow Lake Dam. Early this morning officers found a gunshot victim by a cabin north of Beavers Bend State Park. Three miles south, on the river, a boat was found with two gunshot victims. One was dead at the scene. The second was taken by Life Flight helicopter to the Regional Trauma Center in Memphis, Tennessee.

BBPD was contacted by Memphis Police on a possible shooting involving one of their homicide detectives investigating a case tied to unsolved deaths in Memphis and Oklahoma. "I can't remember the last time we had a homicide in McCurtain County," said BBPD Chief Darryl Strider. "However, we are capable of handling all police matters in our area. I have been in communication with the Director of the Memphis PD. He has assured me that they would work hand in hand as together we solve this heinous crime."

Campers in the area reported shots were fired around 4:00 a.m. this morning in the Beavers Bend area. Around 4:45 a.m. another flurry of shots echoed throughout the Mountain Fork River valley. Some said it sounded like the Fourth of July.

Names of the dead and injured are being withheld until notification of next of kin. The shootings on the Mountain Fork River are under investigation. Anyone with information is asked to contact the BBPD.

FIFTEEN

"True genius resides in the capacity for evaluation of uncertain,
hazardous, and conflicting information."
Winston Churchill

Memphis, Tennessee

The Regional Medical Center is always busy. Wilcox met
the Life Flight helicopter from Broken Bow when it
touched down. All he could do was watch the team whisk the
gurney into the trauma center—a cluster of surgical greens and
white coats holding IV bags and pushing a pile of bloody sheets
across the tarmac.

He smoked a half pack outside the ER exit—Baily hung by a
thread. Even if he survived, they said he may never know. The
bullet had entered above his eye and exited the top of his head.

The good news—not a hollow point. If it had been, Cam Baily would have lost the back of his head and died on Mountain Fork River. The fact he was still alive had everyone scratching their heads.

"Why was Detective Baily in Broken Bow?" Director Cottam asked Wilcox.

He took a drag and stepped out his cigarette in no hurry to answer Cottam's question. Wilcox respected the new director, but he didn't like explaining himself to anyone. The question reeked of second guessing.

"Answer my question please sir," Cottam ordered.

"I sent him." He stared back with angry eyes.

Cottam had been reluctant to put Wilcox back in the field so soon after losing his partner, and on the heels of the bloodbath in Dyersburg—five dead and Wilcox the only one there to explain. Even though the five dead ones were international wanted killers holding empty guns, Cottam knew Wilcox had help. But like the disciplined POW, Wilcox stayed with the minimum. His story, although weak in many places, held up. Cottam believed Wilcox got a lead, but he did not believe Wilcox just found the dead guys at the abandon farmhouse. He could not explain his head wound or the all the knife wounds on five dead men.

"Relax detective. How does Broken Bow connect with the unsolved homicides?"

The doors opened and two paramedics left the ER. Wilcox waited for them to pass. "I'm working the Deckle case. Baily had the Derby case. We compared notes and discovered my eyewitness was standing in the crowd at Derby's crime scene. After a little digging we found him at the other two."

"Who is he?"

"Hunter Keller."

"Why go to Oklahoma?"

"Keller's from Stringtown. His parents were killed in 2009. They died like our four."

"So Baily went on his own time to do some sniffing around?" Cottam asked.

"Yes."

"What do you think he ran into out there?" Cottam took the pack of cigarettes and lighter from Wilcox's trembling hand. Wilcox hated authority figures, his fist tightened behind his back. Cottam shook the pack and gave him another. He lit it. Wilcox relaxed.

"Did Baily confirm Hunter Keller is our man?"

"I can't answer that question. *Keller shot Baily, and I don't need you getting in my way. There's no place this skinny psychic can hide. I will find him . . .*

Cottam stood tall studying Wilcox. The slender, black man had paid his dues. He survived the streets of Memphis as a beat cop for twenty-five years. The only reason he came inside was because the city mayor begged him after Director Collin Wade took a bullet that left him a paraplegic. Cottam did it more for Wade than the mayor.

"What do we know about the shooting and dead man in the boat?" I understand you were on the phone with Detective Baily when he got shot."

Wilcox wrestled with a dozen loose ends he would not share with the director. From experience, he knew too much information shared too early screwed up things. The brass always thought they knew best. They always knew the least.

"I talked to Strider, Broken Bow Chief of Police. He identified the dead guy in the boat as Buford Jackson, a PhD in psychology, nickname Bone. What's his connection?"

"Childhood friend of Keller. Baily got names of four. Now they're all dead. The other three died in the last six months, all suspicious circumstances."

"You think Hunter Keller is killing these people?"

"Don't know. It is possible he's erasing his history for some reason, or something bigger is going on. First thing, I need forensics on Bone Jackson and Detective Baily. I want the ballistics. Keller was in the boat. I need to know if he shot Baily and Jackson. I need to know soon."

"They found another body at a cabin up the river," Cottam said.

"I know. The guy was naked. No ID. I'm sure he's related."

"I'll make some calls," Cottam said. "You and Dr. Petty need to go to Broken Bow for the autopsy and crime scene. McCurtain County has a coroner, not a forensic pathologist. I'll synchronize with Strider. I'll make sure they don't mess with the bodies."

Cottam had information he knew Wilcox did not. How Wilcox reacted would decide if he was pulled off the case. "Strider shared information they're keeping under their hat," he said. Wilcox looked up for the first time. "Strider said the boat was Swiss cheese. Your theory that Keller is the shooter would be wrong. It appears the three were running. Looks like all were targeted. Give yourself some room on this, detective."

"Interesting information, but it doesn't change much for me right now. I don't know anything about those bullet holes. They could be real. They could be old. And they could be staged. I need a closer look. Keller's a smart guy. Jackson took one in the chest and Baily took one in the head. I find it odd and suspicious that Keller was the only one to get away."

Cottam smiled, more like a father than the director of the Memphis police department. "Looks to me like this Keller fellow is the reason they were hunted."

"I don't know about that," Wilcox muttered as he flicked his cigarette over a shrub.

"It's possible Hunter Keller was captured, the other two left for dead. All I'm saying is to keep an open mind, detective. Don't make this personal."

Cottam put his hand on Tony's shoulder. "I am very close to pulling you off the case. If I sense you are losing control, you are done. Do you understand me, detective?"

Wilcox got the message. And it mattered because he knew Cottam was right. It was personal. Ever since he heard Keller's name and the shot in the phone, he wanted to kill the man in the hoodie.

"Yes, sir. This is not personal."

"Your visit to Broken Bow will give us more answers. God knows we need them." Cottam backed off the sidewalk and punched numbers on his cell. Wilcox lit his last cigarette and watched another ambulance pull up and another crowd of paramedics push another bloody gurney through the glass doors.

"Can you leave in an hour? Dr. Petty's good to go. Chief Strider's on board. The MPD chopper will take you to Broken Bow, ETA sundown."

"I keep a toothbrush and extra pair of underwear in my glove," Wilcox said.

The glass doors opened and a white coat walked up with a scowl. "I'm Dr. Mathews. You must be Detective Wilcox and Director Cottam." They swallowed hard and both nodded. Was there a chance? Can there be one miracle?

"I've never seen an injury this bad," the doctor said.

Wilcox shook his head denying the information he most feared. Fire filled his eyes as his shoulders cramped and fists tightened. *I will find you, Keller.*

Dr. Mathew's continued. "An injury this bad that one would survive."

"Survive?" Wilcox asked. "Are you saying Baily can survive a bullet to his head?"

"Yes. Mr. Baily is going to survive, but."

"Here we go. I get it. 'But' he will never know what the hell's goin' on," Wilcox scoffed.

"Not a true statement. There's no reason why Mr. Baily cannot recover fully. There are numerous cases when damage to the frontal lobe is overcome. His wound is significant but isolated. I expect functions controlled in that area will relocate to other parts of the brain. This is not an unusual experience."

"This is better news than expected," Cottam said.

"Can I talk to him?" Wilcox asked.

"Not for a while. He's in a drug-induced coma until brain swelling goes down and vitals stabilize. In about a week we might be able to bring him out of that coma. It can take another week or so before Mr. Baily can speak."

"You are sure he will recover?" Wilcox asked.

"Yes."

"Will he lose anything?" Cottam asked.

"He will experience loss of memory. Some loss will be temporary and some permanent. His muscle coordination will be impaired for weeks or months. His speech could come back right away, or he could struggle. We'll know more after we wake him up."

As Dr. Mathews departed Cottam patted Wilcox's shoulder. "We got some good news for a change. Now, get to your chopper and find out who did this. We'll take good care of Baily."

SIXTEEN

"In hell, the Devil is God."
Kedar Joshi

W ho would agree to meet a killer in a cemetery at
midnight?

The streetlights on South Lamar were sparse, and most were
dysfunctional. Roger Tinley sat at a table in the backroom of an
abandoned gas station where the only light for blocks hung at the
end of a grimy, dust covered cord inches above his head.

He lived in the boarded-up structure behind the six-foot
chain-linked fence. One cold February night after a heavy snow
he found a loose board. When he climbed inside and discovered
MLG&W had failed to disconnect the service, he thought he had
died and gone to heaven. The one night of refuge from the
elements turned into a nine-month abode—his longest yet.

"It comes from the Latin word 'occultus'. It means
clandestine, a hidden secret, knowledge of something

unmeasurable." Roger pushed back from the table and scratched the side of his belly. He had a rash from sleeping on the floor. The cold cement by the small heater had sucked up decades of gas spills and oil. The cardboard used for bedding made for a bad barrier.

Hayes coughed up something and spit in the cup he always kept handy. After a few more hacks he focused on Tinley's words. "I don't believe in the occult stuff."

"There's been widespread belief in ghosts throughout history. You need to catch up."

"I may be a bum now, but I do have some education. Those misty, airy things floating around make no damn sense to me—deceased souls stuck down here and all. It's crazy if you ask me."

"We've known each other a while now. I told you I see things I can't explain. Just because you don't, doesn't make it's a bunch of hooey." Roger pulled a beer from a crumpled bag and popped it open. "You want one?"

"Nope. Had enough." William Hayes—a tall, stringy man in an orange jumpsuit—managed to keep most of his wiry hair in his knit cap an inch above his tiny, black eyes and bushy brows. The one-time respected college professor had his breakdown fourteen years ago. He checked out. Now the streets of Memphis were home and Tinsley his only connection to the real world, the one he feared beyond words.

"You don't need to meet with the man you told me about. I don't like him. He sounds evil."

Tinsley smiled and looked up at the rusted metal girders covered in cobwebs. "I think he's a demon, too. But I'm tired of running." *This place isn't even fit for insects,* He thought. *I haven't even seen a lousy rodent around here.*

"He can't find you. The call was to a phone booth on Perkins a couple miles from here."

"He knew my location, William. He can find me."

"He saw you sitting on the curb there one day, got the number, and called."

"I don't think so. He's like I used to be. He can find me."

"We are bums. Nobody cares about us. No offense, but you're not important to anybody." Hayes wobbled to his feet and ambled past his bed of folded cardboard. He got to a corner, unzipped, and peed.

Tinsley took a gulp of beer and looked back at the matted webs thinking about his life and the turns it took. "I never should have answered the newspaper ad in Phoenix. I'll never forget April 23, 1973, the day my life changed forever."

Hayes returned to the table and stood with his mouth open and zipper down. His perpetual look of confusion hid his substantial intellect. "What'd the government call you guys?"

"We were psychics. They gave us the name 'remote viewer'. They wanted to give it more credibility to justify the research project and to get funding."

"That's right. You were a bunch of clairvoyants, mind readers. What could you do?"

"I could see things without being there. Some of us could see the future. Not me. I signed up because I had some psychic abilities—not many. I thought I could do somethin' positive with it. The government paid well and took good care of us for a while."

"I still don't get why that program went south."

"All governments are sneaky, William. They do a lot of things and don't tell anybody. I don't know why they got to lie to people all the time. They contracted with a bunch of us and started testing. Never told us a thing—zero feedback. They bounced us around too. We were the property of the DIA, the military, and the CIA at different times. I never understood why they moved us around."

"How do you know they kept things from you?"

"Are you kidding? We're psychics. We knew what they were doing and their plans. A bunch of us didn't like it and got the hell out of there."

"What didn't you like about it beside secrets and no feedback?"

"We were used, like other covert weapon systems. They took better care of their U-2s and SR-71 aircraft. They never treated us like people with lives."

"So remote viewing worked?"

"Most of the time," Roger said as he looked at the broken professor sitting across from him. He answered the questions because it felt good to talk about the things bouncing around his head for the last thirty-five years.

"We were tested all the time."

"What kind of testing?"

Roger leaned back in his chair and traveled back decades. "They asked me things like what's in a box. Then they'd ask where they hid the box. I always got it right. Then they would put people in rooms and ask more questions."

"They wanted you to name the people in the room?" William asked.

"Yes, and sometimes we didn't know the people. They asked us to describe how they were dressed and what they were talking about. Later they had us locate people in various cities and do it all over again." Roger blinked back into the room. "Sometimes I wondered if they wanted to be able to find people to hurt them."

Hayes ignored the comment. "Were you any good?"

"I'm pretty sure I nailed it most of the time. I don't know for sure because we didn't get feedback. They said feedback interfered with our psychic skills. It affected judgment and therefore interfered with our psychic sensitivity."

"Made you second-guess yourselves?"

"They treated us more like lab rats than people. Hundreds of

self-proclaimed psychics from all over the country applied in the
'70s. Only twenty-three got contracts."

"I don't think you're a hunted man, Roger. You haven't done
anything to anybody. And you've been out of the program a long
time—you said 1984."

"It wasn't like quitting a job. I had to run away—escape. I left
in the middle of the night like the others. I know they've been
looking for me ever since. They look at us like we're a secret
weapon available to the enemy. Every bone in my body told me
to disappear."

Tinsley chugged the rest of his beer and pulled the string on
the dangling lightbulb. The two sat in the weak glow of the
portable heater. "I know who's huntin' me," he mumbled. "I'm
just not sure why. My psychic abilities are not what they used
to be."

"Maybe you can't read it because it's just your imagination.
You're paranoid like me."

"No it's real. Some of the remote viewers I knew are dead
now. I did some research."

"People die all the time, Roger."

"I knew cities where they lived. I went to the library and
looked up obituaries. Found seven. They all died violent deaths,
William. No witnesses."

"Like how?"

"Two drowned in the Mississippi River. Nobody knows how
they got there. Three others committed suicide—I knew them,
William. They were normal people with good families."

"We talk about killing ourselves all the time. Suicide's more
prevalent than people think."

"Two died recently with their families, single car accidents,
no witnesses. I thought it odd there were no investigations. Both
cars burned to cinders."

"That's terrible, but bad things do happen. Seven out of twenty-three over thirty-five years is not that strange."

"How often do cars explode, William? How many times have you seen a car engulfed in flames? Families do not run off quiet roads after Saturday movie matinees. And seven is all I could find. I know others have disappeared. I think someone's killing remote viewers."

In the soft glow William Hayes stared at the wall and watched his demons dance. The chat conjured up some of his most paralyzing memories. If he did not regain control soon, he would wake up in a week in a fetal position in a hospital bed.

"Let's leave Memphis tonight. We can catch a boxcar to New Orleans."

"I'm tired of running. I'm tired of living in dumpy places eating tuna fish and drinking warm beer. I need to go meet this guy and find out what it's all about. He wants to discuss the Stargate Project. He said he'd pay me a thousand dollars for my time. I'm going."

"Okay. You go and talk and get some money. Then let's get out of Memphis. I'm going with you tonight. Two is better than one. I'll take my tire iron."

Roger smiled. He could not talk William out of going. Roger knew more about this night than he would share. He knew it was time.

This is how it ends for both of us, William. It just is . . .

Elmwood Cemetery was a mile from the abandoned gas station. They left at nine o'clock with more than enough time to walk to the west side of the historic property and make a midnight meeting. Roger had a way onto the grounds after hours—a hole in the fence on Neptune by Provine Avenue. He often slept at the old cemetery on warm summer nights. The manicured grass on the grave sites felt like an expensive, sponge mattress, and the place was quiet and safe after dark. The only visitors in a cemetery at night are the ghost hunters. When they came, Roger had his fun.

The small stone house on the southwest corner of the grounds was surrounded by tall oak trees. Roger was standing in the shadows twenty minutes before Cankor was scheduled to arrive.

Cankor said he was retired military and claimed to be an original government remote viewer. He told Roger he had lost confidence in the program years ago. Now he was connecting with other RVs to share information. It seems most RVs were in hiding. Cankor also claimed the meeting in the cemetery at midnight was for their privacy.

Kneeling next to a large tombstone a hundred feet away, William and his tire iron waited in another shadow. He did not have psychic skills, and could not feel any presence. Unfortunately William did not see the man in the flat-brimmed hat standing behind him like another gothic stone monument. Roger felt a presence but did not hear his friend's neck snap like a small twig.

"I did not expect you to come tonight, Mr. Tinsley." The words seeped from the inky shadows and hung in the air around the stone house.

William searched for the source of the words. "Is that you, Mr. Cankor?" On his last word his heart seemed to crawl into his throat and beat. He gagged. *Are you doing this to me? We don't need to . . .*

"Your skills are weak, Mr. Tinsley. I'm disappointed in you. The alcohol and your lack of discipline have taken their toll. You should have been more careful with your gifts."

"How do you know the condition of my gift?" He spun around searching for Major Cankor.

"You ask what you should already know. Regardless of your below average state, you pose a risk. I'm certain you have known for a long time that this day would come."

"No! Please let me live," he begged. He turned to the line of headstones where William Hayes was waiting with his tire iron.

Cankor cackled. "Your friend is dead. Surely you at least know that."

There was nothing left to do but run. Roger backed away from the voice drifting from the wavering shadows of the cemetery. He ran from Cankor and the stark images of his impending death.

Cankor walked. Tinsley stopped among the tombstones lost in another night breeze. Dead leaves lifted off the thin layer of snow. Before they settled, Roger was holding his aching head and gasping for air. His eyes had begun to swell and his face twisted and mouth stretched. His teeth bled as the unbearable terror grew inside him.

It only took a couple minutes. Roger Tinsley's heart stopped and he joined his friend on the frozen turf of the Elmwood Cemetery.

Cankor brushed ice crystals from his sleeves and adjusted his hat. *Who would agree to meet with me in a cemetery at midnight . . .?*

SEVENTEEN

"What happens to the hole when the cheese is gone?"
Bertolt Brecht

"We got off to a bad start," Petty yelled over the pounding chopper blades as they crossed the Mississippi River on a straight line to Broken Bow. "We can't do our jobs without trust and communication. When I was in Dallas I . . ."

"Maybe you need to go back to Dallas," Wilcox said and turned to his small window.

"I can't believe you would say such a thing," she huffed. "You're mad because I didn't tell you about the Bethesda Research people." Petty turned her back. "I did not keep information from you. I was directed by a sitting U.S. Attorney General to maintain confidentiality. It was a matter of national security."

"You think you're better than me," he said. "That's what this is all about. You're a big, important doctor from Texas working with a big U.S. Attorney General, and I'm some stupid, backwater cop who cusses, and smokes, and drinks scotch, and has nothing to give but trouble." He jerked his head back to his window.

Petty grabbed his arm. Wilcox flinched. He wasn't expecting such a painful grip or the nails clamping into his bicep like a jaw trap.

"You do have a filthy mouth. And you do smoke cigarettes. And everybody knows you're a scotch man." She loosened her grip. "I personally prefer Chardonnay." She squeezed again. He tried not to wince. "But this goes back to the Deckle case, the first time we met. I caught you looking at my legs. You got embarrassed and still haven't gotten over it."

"Are you kidding me?" They sat in silence pressed against their windows for an hour long thirty seconds.

"*I personally prefer Chardonnay,*" Tony mimicked. "I could puke! It's so hoity-toity to say that. And for the record, I was not looking at your legs. I was thinking and looking in the direction of your legs."

"You were looking at my legs," Petty muttered.

"This is all about you screwing up with your Bethesda boys. The big, smart medical examiner, new to Memphis, screwed up big time in her first ninety days—*boom!*"

Wilcox waited for a response. "If you touched base with me, I could have told you they were fakes ten seconds after I met them. But I never got the opportunity to meet the clowns, did I doctor? The highbrow, forensic genius on heels did not feel like telling Detective Magoo a thing."

"That's not true," she whispered as she stayed at her window watching treetops whisk by.

"You may be medical smart, but you got zero street smarts. You did not live amidst the scumbags and sneaky, conniving, wheeling and dealing freaks. It's why the smart forensic docs team-up with the scurrilous homicide dicks. Shit happens in this dark damn world, Petty. It comes in all flavors. It has always been about the good guys against the bad guys."

"You looked at my legs when I climbed into the helicopter," she said.

Wilcox spun around. "What is it with your legs? Granted they are pretty good, but I was strapped in the damn chopper in a shoulder harness. You were late—as usual. My head can barely move four inches left or right. You climbed up here and put yourself in my face."

"Oh, I got in your face. What a contumelious explanation," she scolded.

"Contum—what? There you go again with the big sophisticated words. Why not just say I'm insulting or got a dirty mind? I'm not near as stupid as I look, Petty. And another thing, if you don't want men looking at your great legs, you need to wear pantsuits." Wilcox turned back to his window snickering, and heard Petty doing the same.

The small speaker crackled alive. They turned. Their eyes met for the first time. They stared and listened.

"This is the pilot. Welcome aboard Dr. Petty and Detective Wilcox. We are cleared for a direct flightpath to Broken Bow, ETA 1800 hours. We've got clear skies and zero turbulence. We'll try to stay above the trees and keep things interesting. Sit back and enjoy. It's our privilege to transport you. If you need anything, press the yellow button on this speaker—over and out."

"I despise pantsuits," Petty said.

"Me too." They laughed.

Petty opened her purse and pulled out a small bottle of scotch and waved it at Wilcox. "If you stole that from Delta I will need to arrest you."

"Actually, I collected them on my trips between Dallas and

Memphis the last few months after I heard you were a scotch man." She passed one to him and pulled out a small Chardonnay.

Wilcox eyed her Chardonnay. "Now that's just ridiculous."

"The world's a big place," she said. They unscrewed their caps and clicked bottles.

"How many of these did you bring?" he asked.

Petty rolled her eyes. "We have some work when we land. I was hoping we could talk this through, have a drink, and start over."

"If you stop with the big words, I'll try not to look at your legs." He downed his bottle.

Her smile faded as she changed gears. "I've got information you need to know."

Wilcox swallowed. "You got my attention."

She passed the letter. "This is a copy of the attorney general's letter to me. I sent the original and envelope to a friend at Vanderbilt Medical School. Dr. Richard Tanner is the head of the advanced genetic research program. I asked him to check it for DNA. I wanted to know who handled the sealed letter. I wanted to confirm it was from Alfred E. Baldwin—the acting attorney general—and I wanted to confirm the identity of Dr. John Swenson, the Bethesda team leader who has disappeared."

Wilcox nodded as he read the letter and Petty sipped her Chardonnay. When he finished, he passed it back and asked, "What did you find out?"

"Alfred Baldwin's DNA on the letter and the envelope has been confirmed."

"You do know the bad guys expect forensic pathologists to look for DNA."

Petty nodded. "Dr. Swenson handed me the letter."

"You got his DNA, too?" Wilcox asked.

"No. Swenson's DNA was not on the envelope, only the letter in the sealed envelope."

"Okay. Swenson was with Baldwin when it got signed. Not a big deal."

"I agree. However, what is peculiar is the letter was handled by a third person."

"And the plot thickens. Got another scotch in there?"

"The third person's DNA belongs to Dr. Benjamin Proust."

Wilcox leaned back forgetting his scotch. That name's familiar."

"He's the medical examiner—Okmulgee County, Oklahoma."

"Yes. I remember. The name came up during the Deckle investigation."

Petty grabbed his arm and squeezed. "Tell me what you know."

"Damn." He pulled back. "Please loosen your grip and remove your nails from my skin. Do you work out?" He gently pried her hand from his arm like he was opening a bear trap.

"I'm sorry—a reaction. And yes, I do work out. Now, talk to me Detective Wilcox."

"Here's what we know. The dead man in the bank on Main Street is not Donald Deckle. Oh. I'm sorry. Did I forget to tell you?"

"And I'm sure you had good reason, detective," she shot back. "And you know this how?"

"I never bought the 'wife act' on the phone. We talked on my way to my eyewitness—Keller. She was faking emotions. Women do it all the time. I can always tell."

"There's so much wrong with that, but I just don't have the energy. Get to the part he's not Donald Deckle. Who is he and what does it all mean."

"For someone claiming to have talked her husband all the way from home to him parking his car downtown, she just didn't breakdown enough when she got the news of his death."

"Very perceptive," Petty said under her breath and exasperated at his chauvinism.

"She did not fit. I put her in the category—intending to mislead."

"So you have categories for people?"

Wilcox ignored the dig. "She had an agenda. There were multiple possibilities. Maybe she didn't love the guy and could care less he was dead. Or maybe she had the poor bastard killed. Or maybe she was an imposter involved in some bank scheme and my corpse was someone else entirely."

"You got all that from a minute phone conversation?"

"Yes. I don't trust easy. You remember the photograph on the wall—the Memphis Tiger football team?"

"Of course I do. You pointed it out to me. There was a smudge on the glass over a face. I remember you thought it could have something to do with the case."

"Well, I found a guy who had played on the '68 team. He was the captain. He knew everyone in that picture—had the same one on his desk. We talked. Turns out the man under the smudge is Bradley Johnson, a booster."

"I'm sure this is an interesting football story, but . . ."

"Bradley Johnson died in a car wreck this year, a one-car accident without witnesses. The car was found burning in a field."

"It happens."

"Not really. Few burn in a field after a fender bender."

"And this matters why?" Petty asked.

"Bradley Johnson's son Randle Johnson was not in the car that day. Randle Johnson was the dead man in the Benton Bank & Trust on South Main."

"Why would anybody . . . ?"

"Did I tell you Bradley Johnson and most of his family died in Okmulgee County? The ME who worked the case was Dr.

Proust. I say 'worked the case', but there was no investigation. There was only a routine accident report."

"What are you saying?"

"I had a friend do some digging. Bradley Johnson was not your typical guy. He took part in a secret government program back in the '70s. It had several names. Most know it as the Stargate Project."

Petty wanted to see if Wilcox's had connected Stargate to the Attorney General and the Bethesda boys. "And why is that significant?"

"Oh, I don't know," Wilcox muttered. "Imagine the United States Government spending our tax dollars on paranormal bullshit for twenty-five years."

"Imagine that," Petty said passing a scotch. *Should I tell him what I know now, or wait?*

"Do you know why Cam Baily was in Oklahoma?" Wilcox asked.

"To look for your eyewitness—Hunter Keller."

"Right. He lived in Stringtown, Oklahoma. Do you know Keller's parents are dead?"

Petty lowered her little bottle. "I did not know that. How is that relevant?"

"Five years ago Arnold Keller was stabbed in the back on the front porch of their farmhouse and Alma was strangled in a bedroom. I think we will find the forensics tie back to our four unsolved homicides."

Petty sat up straight. "You think Hunter Keller killed his parents and our four?"

"Baily and I talked the day before he was shot. He gave me a brief update. He went to the Keller's farm to look around. I gotta give the boy credit. He poked around the place for a day determined to find something important to the case. He was following his instincts. Things stunk."

"He was alone?"

"Yes. We didn't need to waste time looking at nothing with the locals. Baily climbed up into the attic and found a box of papers tucked deep in the back, a place people did not look. Inside the dusty old box Baily found a government contract. Turns out Alma and Arnold Keller were part of the same government program as Bradley Johnson. They joined in 1972."

Petty downed her Chardonnay. As the Arkansas treetops slid beneath the chopper, she processed the chilling connections and realized she needed Wilcox as much as he needed her.

"What really got me scratching my head was that Dr. Proust came all the way down from Henryetta to Stringtown to do Alma and Arnold Keller's autopsies. I find that very odd."

"Okay," Petty said. "You've made a point. There is more going on here than any one person can pull together alone."

"Full disclosure," Wilcox said. "I have not been completely forthcoming either. I knew about your Bethesda-boys the day they showed up at your door."

"What're you talking about?" She asked.

"I had a car watching the morgue 24/7."

"You spied on me?"

"Yes I did. You were new, dragging your feet, not talking to me. Very suspicious."

"I didn't have anything to give you, or I would have."

"Not true. The Bethesda pricks, you had their information. I knew they were not legit day one. Bethesda would never send three to Memphis. They wouldn't even send one, the tightwads."

Petty opened another Chardonnay and passed Wilcox a scotch. "I guess I should have found a way. You're right. I am new and don't know you. Maybe I could have benefitted from your Memphis experience." She checked her watch. "We have a half-hour before we get to Broken Bow. We best make good use of this time."

"Randle Johnson is the owner of Benton Bank and Trust on South Main."

"Why the Donald Deckle masquerade? It was only a matter of time before we would have uncovered the true identity," Petty said.

"Maybe the killer needed twenty-four hours. Or, maybe the killer was hanging around South Main for some other reason. Deckle's in this somehow. I found him in the national registry. There were prints and DNA, but pictures and personal data have been erased."

"Who can do that?" Petty asked.

"I don't know, maybe a sitting U.S. Attorney General." Wilcox downed his scotch and eyed the sunset through the bottom of the empty bottle.

Dr. Petty pulled out the last one from her purse. "I'm sure you've developed a tolerance." She slapped it in his hand. "This is it."

He cracked the seal. "Tell me more about the Bethesda boys."

"I don't know much. According to my Vanderbilt connection Dr. Green and Dr. Blanchard do not exist, and Dr. Swenson is known but his files are sealed."

"We know Green and Blanchard were executed at the Super 8. Were you at a turning point? Was there anything different the day they got stuck?"

"Bethesda had an interest in the five Memphis cases, the four homicides with amygdala lesions and one natural death—Frank Pella. As you know, we exhumed the body the day Blanchard and Green were killed."

"And Pella was delivered to the morgue that evening?"

"Yes. He was lying in my refrigerator."

"Dr. Swenson could have visited Pella and obtained what he was looking for?"

"Yes. He could have."

The speaker between the seats crackled alive. "We are approaching Broken Bow. Touch down, five minutes. Chief Daryl Strider will meet you."

The sun was now down. They stared out the small window at the lights dotting the horizon—the town of Broken Bow. "What's going on, Tony?" Petty asked.

He finished the last of his scotch. "Something very big, Dr. Petty."

Flying over Arkansas, Petty got a good look at the real Tony Wilcox. He used distance, dry wit, and a gruff persona to hide his sharp mind and sensitive side. The man she got to know today was at the top as a Memphis homicide detective for a reason. She needed to stay close.

"You can call me Victoria."

Wilcox stared at the sparkling lights. "We have seven more bodies."

"The Randle Johnson family, the Kellers, and two dead a Broken Bow," Petty whispered.

"We need to get our eyes on the two at Broken Bow and their boat."

"Why the boat?" Petty asked.

"We have two common denominators. We need to narrow it down to one."

"The Stargate Project is one," Petty said. She crossed her legs and left her hem above her knee. Wilcox smiled. Their lips were inches apart. "What's number two?" She asked.

They lingered. "Hunter Keller," Tony said.

The Memphis Tribune
Groundskeeper Finds Bodies at Elmwood
October 29, 2014

. . .

Memphis, Tennessee: At 5:30 a.m. a groundskeeper at Elmwood Cemetery found a dead body on one of the graves. Memphis police were called. Soon after their arrival a second body was found. Police believe the deaths are connected and may be a robbery and beating of the homeless.

The dead are white males in their seventies, identities unknown. "We are dealing with two homicides," said MPD Detective Steven Marcus. "I cannot discuss details of an active investigation. The medical examiner is out of town but will return tomorrow and we will learn more."

The groundskeeper that found the first body said, "I was not startled when I saw the man. It happens around here. I thought he was sleeping. He was lying on his back. When I got closer, I saw his eyes were open real wide and he was smiling. It was kinda scary. Then I saw he was not moving. He was dead. I called the police and got out of there fast."

Elmwood Cemetery was established in 1852. Today the 80-acre grounds are on the historic National Registry and the final resting place for 75,000 inhabitants. Anyone with information on the Elmwood deaths is asked to contact the Memphis police department at 901-MPD-HELP.

EIGHTEEN

"Death is the cure for all diseases."
Thomas Browne

It was the perfect place to kill again, without those messy details—witnesses.

Built in 1928, the Queen of Memphis was the pride of the Midsouth skyline. Now, the Sterick Building was not even an eyesore. The twenty-nine story, gothic edifice on the corner of Third and Madison was invisible to Memphians. Dying from within, the renovation nightmare abounded with acres of poisonous asbestos, structural impossibilities, and miles of legal entanglements. The only future for the forgotten landmark was suicide by implosion.

Even though they knew he was coming, Hunter Keller would wait for his time to be right. He slow walked the streets of Memphis watching (and feeling) his surroundings like no other could. On his last pass down Madison Avenue he stepped into the alley, stood in shadows, and confirmed he was alone. He backed along the dark, brick wall of the Sterick Building to the last dumpster in the line of three.

Keller always did his homework. From the top of the dumpster he could reach the second floor window and loose board. Braving the putrid stench rising from the battered metal box used by neighbors, he climbed the paint-chipped wall and shimmied into the decrepit building through broken glass, matted webs, and a disgusting trail of rat droppings. Gagging on the stale mold and ancient dust he found the north stairwell in his dream. There would be metal doors on each level. All would be closed and locked except the nineteenth floor, that door would be off its hinges resting against the wall.

He climbed the muculent stairwell skirting gaping holes and cement clumps on crumbling risers. Each step could be his last, sending him plummeting to his death. Keller clung to the plaster walls and tested his footing, and he climbed undeterred in the hollow silence.

Maybe this time can be different.

Touching the metal numbers on the doors, he made his way from the stairwell down the dark hall—first 1962, and then 1958, and then 1954. When he reached 1900, he pushed the double doors into the cavernous room. Somehow city lights found their way up to the shattered windows of the nineteenth floor and painted the walls with a pale fog. Keller took in the torn carpets, and piles of debris, and crumbling walls of the desolate room. Like the aftermath of a massive earthquake, shattered memories strewn about melted in a dying world above the city.

From the soft grays and sharp black edges Keller watched clouds slide over the moon and the room dim. He didn't need to see. He felt another's presence.

"You're early." The words were sharp. They cut through the room like a sabre.

"So are you," Keller replied with his eyes on a moving shadow.

"No games this time. Join me at the table by the windows."

He saw a silhouette. "It is not you."

"You can't stop, can you?" The hideous cackle snaked through the debris.

Keller stayed down. *You're blocking. It does not matter.* Keller had to learn to trust his instincts even though he did not understand them.

"You killed each one of them, Hunter Keller. You are responsible. Don't you think enough have died? You killed your parents. You killed your friends. Now you threaten to kill perfect strangers with your gift."

And imperfect ones still live, Keller seethed.

"I feel the negativity. I feel the loathing, disgust, and anger. But it is okay. I understand you better than you understand yourself. I always have. As I promised you, I have delivered Donald Deckle. He stands at the table by the windows. Do you want to kill him too?"

"Donald Deckle is dead. He died on Main Street. I was there. I saw you."

"Are you certain it was me, Hunter? Are you certain it was Donald Deckle?"

"You left before the police came. They told me Donald Deckle was dead. I saw them remove his body."

"Someone died. Are you sure you did not kill him? Are you sure you control your gift?"

"I'm here. I'm alive," Deckle yelled. "He's telling the truth. I am Donald Deckle. We met at the bookstore—remember?"

Keller leaned out from the pile of debris. He recognized the voice.

"We spoke. I gave you my business card," Deckle said. "We exchanged numbers."

Keller got to his feet and scanned the room. "Show yourself, Major Cankor."

"I am right here with Mr. Deckle." The large, dark figure broke from the shadows and walked up behind Deckle.

"Who died at the bank, Mr. Cankor?"

"You know the answer to your own question. Use your gift, Mr. Keller."

He knew the answer before Cankor stopped talking. *You found Randle Johnson, the son of another remote viewer.* Keller's eyes narrowed. *It's too late for Deckle. He made a deal for his life. Cankor won't let him be.* Keller slid his hands in his pockets and backed away.

"Don't do it, Mr. Keller," Cankor ordered. He towered over Deckle. "I'm the only one who can help you. The killing can stop."

"I had no choice," Deckle said. "I am a direct descendent. I have some gifts. I can't run forever. Randle Johnson was my only way to live."

The clouds opened and the moonlight fell across Cankor's flat face. "Our deal was I let Deckle live and you come with me. I am your only way out of the carnage."

"You killed the Johnson family." Keller said as he took another step back and glanced at the opened doors he had passed through moments before."

"No. You killed the Johnson family." Cankor's sick smile grew. "You killed Randle on Main Street. None of it had to happen. You could have come to me in Stringtown five years ago. You lost your parents that day. Now you've lost your friends. And you could have come to me in Henryetta, but you did not. Middleton and Tantabaum would be alive today if you had— alive and living their decrepit lives," he spewed.

"Everyone died on Dewar," Keller sighed.

"Their blood's on your hands. Come with me. All this can stop. I'm the only one who understands you."

He felt for his gun, the 357 magnum he took from Broken Bow. *Baily was hit, and then Bone. The boat turned into the bank under the trees. I had seconds—I took it and ran. I knew what I had to do.*

"Why's your head at Broken Bow?" Cankor said. "Focus on me."

The bullets were hitting everywhere. I heard you. I agreed to meet you in the Sterick building. Keller wrapped his fingers around the gun in his pocket blocking Cankor.

"You're the worst kind of serial killer," Cankor scoffed. "Donald Deckle is nothing. He can leave here alive if we leave together."

"Why were you at Elmwood Cemetery?" Keller asked.

"You found a way through my block. I am impressed. Try harder. Find the answer to your question."

"You killed two," Keller said.

"Very good. Try harder," Cankor pushed.

"You killed Roger Tinsley and his friend."

"Tinsley is a remote viewer. His friend is nothing but an inconvenience." Cankor smiled. "And, you won't shoot me with that gun your holding in your pocket."

Deckle gasped and fell forward onto the table, his arms outstretched. Keller watched Cankor remove his bloody left hand from the knife. "You are responsible for another death."

Throbbing blue lights climbed the Sterick from the streets nineteen floors below.

"They are coming," Cankor said. "They are on every floor. This building is surrounded, and you will not escape unless you come with me now."

Keller pulled the gun as Major Cankor backed into the shadows. He fired six times and dropped it like a hot iron burning in his hand. More lights bounced in the hallway as Keller rounded the table and leaned over Deckle.

"I'm sorry. He made me do it. He made me hurt Randle," Deckle whispered. White light broke into the room, and a single beam found Keller's face above the dying man.

"Don't move. I will shoot you, Hunter Keller," Wilcox boomed.

NINETEEN

"Destiny has two ways of crushing us—by refusing wishes and fulfilling them."
Henri Frederic Amiel

Lights bounced through the double doors and moved around the room. Keller fell backwards into the shadows and pushed through a hole in the wall. Wilcox ran to the man draped over the table. "He's still alive! Get paramedics up here now!" Wilcox found the hole and dove through rolling to his feet. "Hunter Keller—Stop," he yelled into the dark room. Shots were fired.

Minutes later he slid out the boarded window onto the dumpster. Guns rose. "Put those down, goddamn it." The four officers backed away as Wilcox dropped onto the crumbling alley cement. Squad cars in a line hugged the building, and dozens more lined both sides of Madison and Third. Blue lights flashed around the city block as streams of police flowed in the unboarded doors of the Sterick.

"Anybody come out this window?" Wilcox asked as his eyes darted from shadow to shadow.

"No. But we just got into position, detective."

"Great way to secure a perimeter," he muttered as he stomped up the alley. He knew it would have been a miracle to seal an entire city block in seven minutes, but it did not make him feel any better.

Wilcox got to Madison and another herd of cops in combat gear. "You men see a skinny guy in a hoodie run out this alley?" As heads turned to the detective, a late model sedan exploded through hedges a block away. They watched it fishtail eastbound.

"Let's go, go, go! Don't let that bastard get away!"

Running to his cruiser, Wilcox watched the old sedan clip parked cars and squeal into the center lane. He holstered his gun and patted for his keys as squad cars around him came alive. Flashing lights and screaming sirens hopped curbs and skirted pedestrians and traffic caught in the chaos.

"Where are my damn keys?" Wilcox got to his car and went through each pocket watching the chase and piling possessions on the hood. *Did I lose 'em in the Sterick?*

His keys were gone. The parade left him behind. Kicking tires and pounding the hood of his silent cruiser, Wilcox watched the armada roll down Madison Avenue and disappear over the crest. *A dozen cop cars should be enough,* he fumed. *It's an old car. It can't go that fast.*

After ten minutes and no word, he went back inside the Sterick and retraced his steps from the second floor window to the nineteenth floor crime scene. The potential routes were many. Escaping the entourage of cops and dogs and moving lights would have been easy even for the mentally challenged.

"Anybody call the ME?" His flashlight found the dead man's

face. "Hello Mr. Deckle. Why am I not surprised?" Then his beam found Brimley in the shadows holding the stainless steel suitcase—Petty's medical photographer.

"I see the vultures are circling," Wilcox poked. "Hello, Sir Brimley."

"Yes. Hello, Detective Wilcox," he replied in his thick English brogue. "Dr. Petty is out of town."

"Right," he said moving his light from Deckle's wet head to the bloody knife in his back.

"After returning from Broken Bow, Dr. Petty handled all pending cases prior to departure."

"*She said the Elmwood homicides were connected to all this.* "Good to hear it, Brimley." *Washington D.C.—what's that girl thinkin'? Meet with the Attorney General without a damn appointment—fat chance of that happening. And if she does get to the over-stuffed liberal prick, he's not about to tell her the truth.*"

"Okay Brimley, you're in charge. The dead guy is Donald Deckle. Don't ask. Just take all your pictures and transport. You better take him face down. Petty's gonna want that knife left there."

I caught you red-handed this time—Keller. I saw you holding the knife in Deckle's back. I'll bet the knife's in the same exact position as the others. This removes doubt. But I still have some loose ends, like the bullet riddled boat in Broken Bow. Still, the physical evidence points to you. As always, things eventually come together.

Wilcox walked to the window and looked at the street nineteen floors below. *But who's helping you? Who's driving that sedan? Or, is it you?*

Twenty minutes passed before the news reached him—the old sedan got away. Brimley had removed Deckle's body. Now the real Deckle was tucked in bed—face down in the county morgue.

Two hours later the MPD had abandoned the building search and resealed the Sterick. Police melted back into the city and Wilcox sat in his car waiting for new keys.

"Are you kidding me?" He fumed. Wilcox's knee touched something under the steering column. His keys hung from the ignition.

Shit! You get the call from Keller. He says he's ready to turn himself in. He says he's on the nineteenth floor. I get here. Slide to a stop in the alley. Jump out. I was first on the scene. I heard the sirens as I'm scrambling to get to the nineteenth floor . . .

Wait a damn minute. I didn't turn off the car. I left it running. That's what screwed me up. Someone turned off my damn car. They left my keys in the damn ignition.

"It's me. Cancel the backup keys. Don't ask."

Wilcox threw his cell phone on the seat and stared at the dark and empty alley. He turned the key. The car came alive. The familiar rumbling of his engine would be the last thing he remembered.

TWENTY

"Nothing happens by itself."
Ben Stein

The sounds fit his dream perfectly. With his bazooka, he moved through the electronic maze shooting everything that moved, avoiding traps, and racking up points. The flashing lights and pings and buzzes and bleeps marked his progress. But the musty smell of the bar was missing. And the smoke was not burning his eyes. And his mouth felt like he sucked a tube of toothpaste and drank a gallon of mouthwash. But Wilcox never entered battle lying down.

When he opened his eyes, tape snapped off his lids. He saw the blur of movement in a sea of white. He blinked and focused and knew he was not in his favorite bar playing his favorite video game. Wilcox felt the straps holding him down. He was in a hospital bed surrounded by monitors. Why was he tied to the bed? Why was he in intensive care at The Med?

"Welcome back, detective." The tall, black man stood at the end of the bed. Wearing a blue uniform with starched creases and shiny gold bars and stars and a badge, Director Cottam smiled at his now struggling soldier. His men and women were his family. Tony Wilcox was returning from another street war—alive. "You've been out a while, Detective Wilcox."

"What's going on?" He tugged at his restraints and tried to reach the tubes in his body.

Cottam stood at the end of the bed with the confidence of a five-star general on the front lines of a war they would win. With his arms folded and legs spread, he advised his injured man. "I wouldn't do that if I were you. Should you pull out a tube, you will set off an alarm. They will come in here and tie you down even more. They will stick the tube right back in you."

Wilcox's eyes darted around the room, and then back to Cottam. "What happened? Why am I here?"

"You don't remember?" Cottam asked.

"No. I don't know. Have I been shot?" Wilcox asked.

"No. You have not been shot."

Wilcox didn't believe Cottam. He had to raise his sheets to search for himself, but he couldn't move his arms or legs.

"You're not telling me." He threw his head left and right. "I feel like shit. Tell me everything. Don't hold shit back. You know me."

Cottam held up his hand. Wilcox closed his mouth and sunk back into his pillow. "Let's try to relax or they will ask me to leave." He reached back and swung the door closed. "You're at The Med, private room in ICU. It is for precautionary purposes. We can watch you better here while the doctors run their tests."

"So you can watch me better and what tests?" Wilcox pushed.

"They don't know much about your medical condition. Tests are necessary."

"What happened to me?"

"Your cruiser was on fire in a field off West Person Avenue down by the river."

"I was in a wreck? I don't remember."

"Your car was not damaged. It was on fire," Cottam said.

"That makes no sense. I'm not burned, am I?"

"No. We found you lying in the field unconscious. The fire trucks almost ran over you getting to your car. You were very lucky, Detective Wilcox."

Cottam untied a hand. "Don't do anything that gets me in trouble." He poured a cup of ice water and passed it to Wilcox. "They said you needed liquids."

Wilcox eyed the flashing monitors. "Thanks for checking on me. But I still don't know what to think about all this. I don't remember a damn thing."

The door opened. A white coat entered with two nurses. "Good. You're awake. I am Dr. Whiteside. I've been taking care of you." He studied the bank of monitors.

Wilcox did not like doctors. He never had a good experience. Their God-complex often got in the way of his God-complex and investigations. White coats blocked him questioning injured and dying scumbags. But Wilcox did like nurses.

"Do you remember anything about last night, Mr. Wilcox?" the doctor asked.

"I remember chasing a serial killer in the Sterick Building. He stabbed a man in the back and dove through a wall. How's that doc?"

Wilcox could see the nurses were impressed—some women are drawn to the thrill of danger and his Dirty Harry persona. At six four with sandy brown hair, a chiseled jaw and badge, he attracted a lot of women. It was his intense demeanor and shallow view of the opposite sex that drove them off.

"Can you put a timeline to events, Mr. Wilcox?"

"We got done at the Sterick around three in the morning. I was the last to leave."

"What else?"

"I remember sitting in my car. Had a headache. Was tired and frustrated. It's possible I dozed off in the ally. I wanted to watch the building for a while. Been a long day and a monster got away." He pinched the bridge of his nose as the doctor wrote in his chart. "I remember starting the car. Then I'm blank." The nurses stared at Wilcox with glassy eyes.

"What's going on?" Wilcox huffed. "What's wrong? When can I get out of here? I've lost a lot of time. I've got a serial killer to catch."

"Detective!" Cottam stopped him. "Please continue, Dr. Whiteside."

"Your memory of lost hours could come back or not. We just don't know. The brain is a complex organ, not fully understood."

"Damn wonderful to hear that, doc. Let's call it a day. I'll just leave now since nobody knows what in the hell is going on with me."

"You came to me unconscious, Mr. Wilcox. I was told your police car was burning in a field. You were found a distance away. There were no witnesses to the event."

"Tell me something new."

"We do not know if you were thrown from the vehicle or got out on your own. I doubt you were thrown. There are no signs of external trauma. When you arrived here, we thought you had suffered an acute cardiac arrest or cerebral vascular episode, had a stroke."

"I'm too young for either."

"Age is only one factor. Genetics is another. Lifestyle is another. Your physical condition can be greatly affected by non-physical factors like stress. Regardless, our tests eliminated the possibility of a cardiac or vascular incident. While restoring fluids we've been running many tests. Are you familiar with MRI, Mr. Wilcox?"

"You're checking to see if I got hit on the noggin."

"Actually I am looking for internal trauma. We also checked for drugs. Your preliminary toxicology is negative and chemistries normal."

"My only drugs are scotch and Marlboro."

"You should stop both," Whiteside scolded. "I was looking for a sedative. A knockout drug. I found nothing. However, your MRI did show something else."

"What's an MRI again?" Wilcox's interest perked with the doctor's negative comment. He would pay closer attention now.

"Magnetic Resonance Imaging utilizes magnetic fields and radio waves to examine organs and other structures inside the body. In your case, we found something peculiar, lesions—internal wounds—isolate to one part of your brain."

"Are you saying I have brain damage?"

"Technically yes, but no observed consequences as of yet. The lesions—injuries—could be serious. Modern medicine has limited experience in the area."

"Then they could be nothing. My head feels fine now. No headaches."

"I suppose your statement is true to an extent," Whiteside said. "But I doubt it."

"And what is your specialty, doc?" Wilcox jeered.

"Neurosurgery."

Shit. "Can I drop dead all of a sudden?" Wilcox asked. Cottam stared at the floor.

"Yes. But there is a caveat," Whiteside said.

"A proviso?" Wilcox said. Cottam's wet eyes returned to his detective.

"I've not seen this type of brain injury before. Yours is

isolated to one area with no related external trauma. It appears to be a targeted, internally perpetuated injury."

Wilcox knew the answer before he asked. "What part of my brain has these lesions?"

"Your amygdala."

TWENTY-ONE

"The only difference between me and a madman is I am not mad."
Salvador Dali

Washington DC

"Mr. Baldwin will be with you shortly, Dr. Petty." The attractive, leggy administrator worked at being cordial—it did not come naturally. She wore sling back high heels, a black pencil skirt, and puffy white blouse. Like crossed sabers on a royal coat of arms, pearl-handled spears stabbed her precision woven, flaxen bun.

"Would you like coffee, tea, or water while you wait?" Her robotic smile widened in curious increments beneath eyes unable to hide the monotony of her life.

"Nothing. Thank you." Petty accepted the polite nod and watched the aging beauty turn and her smile die in the mirror across the small reception room. The quiet felt tedious immediately.

It took two hours to travel the last hundred yards. Inside the DOJ countless checkpoints, frisks, accusatory inspections, and repeat questions were more intimidating than necessary. Petty would not succumb. She lacked the reverence for the absurd security process and the awe for the liberal politician she hoped to meet, the U.S. Attorney General. He was a big piece in her puzzle.

Her calls were dropped or bounced around for days. Not until she said the *two words* did the wheels in the U.S. Department of Justice turn in a favorable direction. After Broken Bow and the Elmwood autopsies, Dr. Petty synchronized with Tony Wilcox. The "two words" he gave her in the helicopter would shoot through the halls of 950 Pennsylvania Avenue like a sizzling rocket on the Fourth of July. In the beginning Hunter Keller meant eyewitness. At the DOJ, Hunter Keller meant the epicenter of a gathering storm.

Asleep on her office sofa with a case file in hand, the phone rang and papers rained down. The Associate Attorney General—third in line—returned her calls to the U.S. Attorney General. He made an awkward attempt at an exploratory interview, but Petty made it clear she would be doing all the *asking*, or troubling information connected to the U.S. Department of Justice would go public.

The phone call ended when she advised the AAG he meet with his boss's boss if he wanted to know the contents of the sealed letter from the AG to the Shelby County Medical Examiner—the one delivered by Dr. John Swenson. To further expedite the process, Petty said she would only discuss Hunter Keller with Alfred Baldwin.

She had almost nodded off a second time when the next call

came. This time the Deputy Attorney General—second in line—opened with an apology. Although a more sophisticated approach, the DAG soon revealed his lack of knowledge and agreed to try to set up a meeting with Baldwin at DOJ headquarters in D.C. She decided to go without an invitation. Time was of the essence.

After six o'clock the administrator led Petty into a wood-paneled conference room with bars on the windows. When the door closed, Petty explored the view of the courtyard three floors down. She then sat down at the cherry conference table and took in the eleven foot, sculpted ceiling and walls of bookcases packed with thousands of legal books. She could smell the ink on the million pages mixed with the dust of the gothic structure built in 1935. Running her hand over the smooth cherry table her thoughts went to Franklin D. Roosevelt who probably met with his Attorney General—Homer Cummings—in the same room. It was a better time then, one of great men with great character and vision. *What ever happened to the world?*

Alfred Baldwin swooped into the room like a politician at a county fair. "Welcome to Washington D.C.," he bubbled.

In seconds she assessed the expensive three-piece suit, protruding belly, and dead toupee atop the salt-and-pepper curls flipping over his rodent ears. His bright red cheeks and petechia revealed high blood pressure and poor diet. The sparse but wild mustache under his bulbous nose revealed a self-perpetuated worldly flare.

They sat. His smile melted into an anxious grin. "We are familiar with your work in Dallas—the Institute of Forensic Science—and appointment to Shelby County's Chief Medical Examiner, all tremendous accomplishments in the face of numerous obstacles: the tragic loss of your parents, raising your siblings, and working your way through medical school. You are another great American story, Dr. Petty."

Her customary greeting smile stayed on her face as she buried her ire. *How dare you invest time and resources looking into the private life of any American? You're trying to intimidate me with your reach? You think I'm shallow?*

"I am pleased to be in Memphis," she said. *You far left despots always claim to carry the flag of freedom, to be the champions of human rights, but whenever you get the privilege to serve you abuse the power, trample the constitution, break laws, and create a mess for others to fix. Regardless, I must wade through and get some answers. I know you are in the middle of this.*

He didn't waste time. "Do you know the whereabouts of Hunter Keller?"

She didn't either. "Maybe." She would leave that door ajar. Baldwin just confirmed the importance, as Wilcox hypothesized.

"Why is Mr. Keller important to the Department of Justice?" *This will be interesting.*

Baldwin brushed off the non-existent lint from his coat sleeves. With a neck stretch, he pinched the knot on his fake tie and kept control of the meeting. "Why did you come here?"

Oh really! This is how you want to play the game? I don't think so.

"This might go better if you were mindful of my expertise." She smiled and leaned back. "I trained my whole life. I'm very good at solving puzzles with little or no help—your research should have told you that." Her smile melted. "You have a choice, Mr. Baldwin. Tell me nothing, I leave you with a failing effort. Talk to me, maybe new doors open."

He slid his hand down his tie and fidgeted with the tip. "You are direct, Dr. Petty."

"We both know two of the three doctors sent to Memphis are dead. Dr. Swenson, the leader of your envoy, has disappeared. He gave me 'the story' and passed your letter."

"I am aware that Dr. Green and Dr. Blanchard are dead, Dr. Petty."

Interesting you did not say "we" are aware. How narrow is this covert operation? And you did not confirm Dr. Swenson's disappearance. Maybe you've not misplaced him?

A door opened and a silver tray entered—coffee service. Baldwin waited on the intrusive delivery in silence until the door closed behind the flaxen bun.

"I'm sorry for the interruption."

"Your letter spoke of a national crisis. You sought my support, but offered little explanation. You leaned on my patriotism. In the beginning, I cooperated even though Dr. Swenson prohibited the involvement of local law enforcement—which I found very peculiar. He asked I personally collaborate with the DOJ on a regional matter of national security interest. At the time there were five dead Memphians of interest to you people. I will never forget Dr. Swenson's words—*they died at the hand of a real monster.*"

Baldwin poured a cup. "I'm aware of the words he used." He held up the pot. "They have been carefully chosen and approved by me."

She declined with a wave. "There are eleven deaths linked so far. I returned from Broken Bow, Oklahoma where I conducted an autopsy on a man named Bone Jackson. He was with Hunter Keller when he was shot, a 30-06 round to the chest. One of our homicide detectives lays in ICU now. He took a bullet to the head while attempting to bring in Hunter Keller. We found an unidentified body holding a rifle in the woods by a cabin. I have two more dead at Elmwood Cemetery in Memphis—I believe they are connected. Your people have lost control, Mr. Baldwin. Or maybe you never had control."

"I'm sorry to hear this, Dr. Petty." He sipped. She watched

his eyelid twitch and face turn purple. "This discussion's not moving in a good direction."

"Dr. Swenson said the cause of death was the telepathic manipulation of the amygdala."

Baldwin looked into his coffee cup. "Yes. A terrible new way to die, I'm afraid. One with enormous national security implications."

"What does that mean?" she asked. "How is Hunter Keller involved? Is he your monster?"

They sat in a confusing silence. Petty watched Baldwin stare into his cup. The Attorney General seemed unable or unwilling to share information. Petty concluded he knew nothing or he knew everything. She would return to Memphis and untangle the mystery her way.

"Well then." She got to her feet. "I am sorry I took the time to come here. I see this is a matter you believe the government can and should handle alone. As an American citizen, and one who understands the methods and madness of serial killers, I can only wish you luck. You will need it. I will return home and do what I do."

"No. Wait." He swallowed hard and pushed his cup away. "My silence is not what you think. I am thinking. I am consumed by an unfathomable national crisis. I allowed this meeting because I intend to tell you more. You are right. We must employ experienced professionals."

"You may have those intentions, but I still see it is not something you want to do."

"Too many have been killed. Many more are going to die, Dr. Petty. There is a very dangerous man out there. This demon has managed to evade the unlimited resources of the most powerful government on earth." His hands trembled. Petty sat. "I want to tell you more, but you must understand this office has limits—

national defense responsibilities. Everything I do is governed by strict policy and procedure, and the President of the United States."

"I understand limits, but if you want help you must share information."

"I am going to tell you things known only to a few. The stakes are high."

"I'm not the enemy. Anything you say will be used to bring this nightmare to a close."

Baldwin flashed a nervous smile. He locked both doors and stood looking out the window. "Senator Willingham was the first. The senator from Oklahoma was my personal friend."

"He died five years ago. I recall reading about it in the *Washington Post*."

Baldwin nodded. "What you read is not what happened. Wilber dropped dead in the basement of the U.S. Capital Building. We thought a heart attack. They rushed him to George Washington University Hospital, lights and sirens. He left dead. They thought he had a massive stroke. He had all the signs."

"Cerebral vascular accident," Petty said.

"We were told an artery in his brain ruptured. He hemorrhaged."

"And what did the autopsy reveal?"

Baldwin wiped his eyes with a crumpled napkin. "We flew in our pathologist to do the autopsy. We've used him in the past. Do you know Dr. Leonard Dryden?"

"Of course. He is a respected forensic pathologist, second only to Dr. Elliott Sumner."

"Dr. Sumner was our first choice. At the time he was hunting an international serial killer. I believe Europe and South America. He recommended Dr. Dryden, who subsequently has been working with us on a flurry of fallen CIA operatives.

Dryden is a specialist, well versed in the exotic weaponry used against our people by the most clandestine forces in the world.

"Dryden found no evidence of a stroke. Willingham's cause of death was unknown."

"Imaginations went wild—our nation's security breached," Petty surmised.

"Precisely our concern. Did we have a killer on Capitol Hill? Is it organized? Are others in danger? We spared no expense finding out how Senator Willingham died. We could not show our concern. Only the highest level of the government knew our true fears."

"Did you find the cause of death?" Petty asked.

Still staring out the window, Baldwin spoke in a trance. "The bulging eyes and contorted facial muscles and snow white complexion, we kept it away from the media." He turned to Petty. "We found lesions on the amygdala. Dr. Dryden concluded they were induced at a cellular level. Trauma to the amygdala explained all the exhibited external anomalies."

"What killed him?"

"Senator Willingham was scared to death," Baldwin sighed.

"Lesions to the amygdala can create an overwhelming sense of terror," she confirmed.

"The frightening experience—although self-manufactured—threw Willingham into shock. The realization shut down his heart."

Petty went through her diagnostic models searching for a feasible cause, but continued to hit a wall. There was no precedence. "Did Dr. Dryden explore the etiology of these lesions?"

"Yes. Extensive study. He concluded the lesions had to be telepathically produced."

"I find that hard to believe," Petty said shaking her head. "Do you realize how significant that would be—mental manipulation of biology outside a host?"

"Following the senator's death, Dr. Dryden's hypothesis was confirmed. We know a lethal telepathic weapon exists. We also know that if a United States Senator can be targeted and terminated in the heart of our nation's capital, we are an exposed nation."

"May I meet with Dr. Dryden to learn more about his findings and confirmations?"

"No. Dr. Dryden is dead."

Petty leaned back in her chair shocked. "I did not see anything about his death. I would have known."

Baldwin continued to stare out the window. "It was handled as a natural death. Kept low key. There was a quiet family funeral."

"But I never . . ."

"He was killed while reporting his findings. I was there, Dr. Petty. It was horrible. Dr. Dryden collapsed in front of the elite committee. We watched the grotesque deformations, the convulsions, and the terror the poor man experienced. We saw him die and could do nothing."

"Oh God." Petty froze. *Could this all be true?*

In a distant daze, Baldwin whispered at the glass window pane. "Leonard described everything as it happened. His face changed first. His eyes bulged with the terror. He talked as long as he could. Then the cramping. His arms locked. Legs. His back arched. He flopped on the floor like a marlin pulled from the ocean. We couldn't get near him. We could not save him"

"I'm sorry," Petty sighed with glassy eyes.

"The autopsy revealed the most extensive lesions we've ever seen. His heart exploded."

Petty could do nothing but stare at the table as Baldwin returned to his chair. "Someone attacked that man with malice,

Dr. Petty. They wanted to send a clear message to the United States Government."

"Your letter authorized my access to the Rejdak Project."

"And you are unable to enter," Baldwin confirmed.

"I've done my own research. You could have come up with a less transparent name for your secret program. I know all about Mr. Rejdak's work in the eastern bloc—psychotronic research."

"There's a lot of information out there on the topic, but it is incomplete and speculative. It lacks the research necessary to establish an acceptable validation model—no double blind randomized studies the scientific community would expect."

"Psychic-weaponry is a hot topic in paranormal circles. Like most fringe science, the scientific community is the last to get on board."

"That is true."

"Seems to me discrediting 'breakthrough science' for national defense purposes would be risky, Mr. Baldwin."

"Maybe, but we're quite good at it, Dr. Petty. We do not like to share breakthroughs with the world, especially those with potential military applications."

"I must admit I cannot believe you would admit the obvious to me," Petty said.

"You are an educated woman. You know most communications in the world are propaganda with intended outcomes. Manipulation of the masses is the mantra of the global news media. Information is selected, packaged, and presented based on objectives of world powers."

"I would not lose too much sleep over it, Mr. Baldwin. The masses are not that easily fooled. On the contrary, we now search for truth in many more places. The established news media will evolve and one day serve the people again. Power is like a summer storm. It is fleeting. Truth finds a way. I know it's hard to imagine, but one day you'll not be in this office."

"Our actions will be part of the historical record," Baldwin said.

"You decide if you are forever honored, or forever despised," Petty said.

Baldwin smiled. "The Rejdak Project is a good example. The best way to keep a secret is to put it out there. We leak information to unreliable sources. Do it all the time. The topic is discredited and not taken seriously by the main stream. Promoters are viewed as crackpots."

"I'm sure you're very proud of that. Have you ever considered the honesty route?"

"All governments have secrets, Dr. Petty. It is impossible to keep them when so many people are involved. Well managed leaks put things into the black hole of crazy speculation."

"Like UFOs, Bigfoot, time travel, and antigravity?"

"No comment on fringe science and cryptozoology. I can tell you this, levitation is our newest leak. Take that for what it's worth."

You were dying to tell me something, to show off. But why levitation? Does it have some relevance here? How would the revelation further his veiled agenda? Petty pondered.

"Psychic-weaponry research was not a secret in the '70s. However, it did go underground fast. The CIA declassified it in '95. I'm afraid many people are not buying the current charade. Remote viewing and telekinesis are not going away soon, Mr. Baldwin."

"You think the search for this truth can outlast the determination of a government?"

"I'd like to believe truth prevails and time is but one variable."

"The concept of remote viewing resides in the diatribe of the parapsychology cults. There it will die under the weight of the skeptics and scientific community."

"If amygdala lesions are telepathically induced, it will get out there one day."

"You think so?" Baldwin sighed.

"Medical examiners around the country will not sit on it," Petty said. It was time to throw a curve ball. "Tell me why were Green and Blanchard killed, and where is Dr. Swenson?"

"Dr. Swenson is in a safe place. Dr. Green and Dr. Blanchard were Russian spies. We've been following them for years. They obtained sensitive information."

"Were they terminated by our government?"

"No comment."

"Do the Russians possess psychic-weaponry?" She asked. "Are we playing catch up?"

"Again, I have no comment," Baldwin said without hesitation as he brushed his sleeve.

"Do you know a man by the name of Randle Johnson?" Petty asked.

After a few seconds of thought he said, "I know Bradley Johnson. I assume Randle would be a son."

"We found Bradley's son with a knife in his back on Main Street in Memphis. He had amygdala lesions. Someone wanted us to think he was Donald Deckle. I just did an autopsy on Roger Tinsley. He too had massive, amygdala lesions."

Baldwin winced. "Tinsley is dead?"

"He's there with William Hayes. They were found dead together. Amygdala lesions."

"I don't know Hayes. We have been looking for Tinsley for years."

"Who are these people, and why are they being killed?"

"I cannot answer those questions," Baldwin said looking down at his hands.

"Do you believe Hunter Keller is the one doing all this?" Petty asked.

"I will tell you this. Hunter Keller is extremely dangerous. He is a person of interest to the United States Government. If you know of his whereabouts, I urge you to tell me."

"And if you're wrong about Hunter Keller?" she pushed.

"I'm not wrong about this man. If you're not careful, Dr. Petty, an encounter with Hunter Keller could very well be the last thing you do in this world."

TWENTY-TWO

"A hero is a man who is afraid to run away."
Proverb

Memphis, Tennessee

The nails started at his neck and moved down his spine digging into his skin. His face was pressed into his pillow—he was having the perfect dream. They spread at his waist and slid under his boxers. He opened his eyes, the perfume familiar. And he knew when the cutting tips would turn into soft, exploring fingers. "I died and am in Abby heaven," he said.

"You're sweet, Tee." She kissed the back of his neck and reached deeper into his boxers. He slid his hand up her thigh. He felt her smile move to his ear. A rush of air escaped her soft lips. "You must be drunk."

Tony rolled over and pulled her close. They kissed hard. "I was sleeping." They kissed again. "I've missed you. Take off your clothes and get in here with me."

"I would, but I see an empty scotch bottle. You're impotent, love. Are you medicated?"

Abby reached over and turned on the lamp. She examined him. "I don't see bruises or cuts or bandages. Wait a damn minute." She got to his arms. "I see you've been taking drugs or had an IV. Talk to me, Tee."

"It can wait. The important thing is I'm not taking drugs." He laughed until she held his head and leaned into his face. He looked back and fell in love again with her big eyes, soft smile and inquisitive stare. He loved the way she looked when she was thinking.

"You've had a head injury, damn it." Abby was the only person on the planet who cussed more than Wilcox—one of her most endearing qualities. "But no bumps or scrapes. I got it; you passed out and they don't know why. I'm right. It would explain the hospital and IV. You're on something, honey. Talk to me. What happened?"

"You're the best PI in the world. Look, I'm not sick. None of it is as important as you being here right now. I swear that I will tell you everything—later. First, take care of your patient."

He watched her long legs slip out of her dress and kick off her panties. She fell out of her bra and sent it spinning to the top of the lamp. She slid under the sheets. Their legs tangled, locked, and bodies melded, tongues touched as they pulled closer, hands moved everywhere with a familiar, tender rage. Then Abby stopped. She rolled Tony onto his back and straddled him, her firm thighs outside his, her breasts resting on his chest, and her lips inches away.

"I have things to tell you that cannot wait. Things so important I drove my pretty little ass all the way from Kentucky to Memphis." She fluttered her eyelashes and pecked the tip of his nose. "I mean it, Tee."

He knew the look, but tried to keep it light. "Wait a minute. You mean to tell me Abby Patterson left a case to bring me information? I like you, but who are you and what have you done with the hot blond private investigator extraordinaire?"

She squeezed his cheeks and kissed his puckered lips. "I just put another cheatin' wife on hold. She'll be there when I get back. I already got her and the boyfriend on HD. My client can wait another day."

Wilcox sat up. "Seriously, it's not you." He opened the drawer and passed a pint of scotch and searched for his Marlboros. "You got some bad information or you wouldn't be here."

She broke the seal, took a shot and passed it back. "Some very bad shit, Tee. I'm worried for you. I know you're good, baby, but this could get out of control fast." He passed her a lit cigarette. "I thought you were in over your head with the last serial killer, but this is convoluted, creepy bad, government stuff."

Damn it, he fumed. *I knew those Bethesda boys were up to their eyeballs getting people killed. They were gutted for a reason.* He smiled at Abby. "Shine your light."

"I need my laptop." She pulled it from her purse. "You gave me names of four dead guys. I did not expect to go far, but I ran into some odd shit and got blocked. You know how I hate people messing with me."

"Those bastards," Tony joked. He looked around for his watch. "What time is it?"

"A little after midnight," she said as she swiped her finger sliding screens and pounded PI access codes. "You also know I hate cyber-dicks. They try to spoil my investigative process by throwing up walls. It just motivates me more."

"I know darling."

"I decided to take a deep dive for you. I got interested. Wanted to find out what was really going on with these dead guys you were *so damn sure* were linked. You're lucky it was a challenge."

"Thank you, baby." They kissed and she returned to her computer.

"It took a while. And I used some of my government sources —they owed me." She swiped a few more screens dragging her finger and clicking her nail with each command. "Thomas Derby, William Hudson, Mark Pemberton, and Donald Deckle had parents who worked for the federal government in the '70s. It is the only thing connecting them. Paths did not cross in the usual ways: schools, sports, military, jobs, residences, or friends."

"Parents of my homicides worked for the government?" *Could they all be connected to the Stargate Project?* He thought.

"I knew I was onto something because they tried to bury the info. I found a backdoor. There's always a way in if your smart and patient. It's significant the four killed are connected to something forty years ago."

Wilcox lit his cigarette. "What about the government connection?"

"I got really pissed. I was doing my basic search, going in protected files where I always checkout my clients and subjects. When I entered Deckle's name on a government site, someone started watchin' me—cyber peek-a-boo. But I've got a program filter. It tells me when that shit's happening."

"So they let you look but wanted to know who you were and what you were looking at?"

"A bit more complicated, but close enough. I let them shadow me for a while. In minutes there was a car parked outside my condo; two sitting inside, lights out, smoke drifting from the tailpipe. The least they could have done is turn off the car—damn rookies."

"Your computer search got you a visit—from who?"

She nodded. "I went out there. Good guys. I knew one. He's not a very good PI—a retired cop." Tony pushed her. "Not like you, Tee. We talked a while. I told them I was working on long shots, some cheaters. I said my search kept taking me to government lah-lah land, so I aborted. I played the dumb blonde. You guys eat it up every time."

"They left."

"Probably reported back—the dumb blonde got lost. I've been solo ever since. Never revisited the sites on my computer. Moved my searches to internet cafés. I got a new gadget—it scrambles my presence on websites. I can live on a website looking like cyber noise."

Wilcox got out of bed and went to the window. "You sure you weren't followed here?" He checked his gun and turned off the lamp. "I don't like surprises."

"You kidding me. Nobody follows me without me knowing it."

"Okay *Cat Woman*. Tell me what you found. I hate pregame."

"The parents of your four dead guys were part of a government research program funded by the CIA called Scanate, an acronym for scan by coordinate. Later it was called Stargate."

"A psychic intelligence gathering program?"

"You have some info on this, too?"

"Some, but keep going. We can compare notes later."

"In the '70s the feds got involved in psychotronic research—Stanford Research Institute, Menlo Park shit. A lot of money was spent. The program went underground."

"And what did they do in this secret program?" Wilcox asked with some knowledge but wanted to hear it from Patterson. She was the one source he believed without reservation.

"They were called remote viewers. It was all about

developing psychic-weapons. They were working with people with psychic skills. Their goal was to mentally infiltrate enemy meetings from great distances. Remember, it was the '70s, the height of the Cold War. Everyone was paranoid. They built bomb shelters for God's sake."

"I remember the stories. People were scared of Russian nukes."

"All governments were exploring the feasibility of psychic-weapons," Abby said. "CIA killed the program in '95. It was declassified."

"Parents of my homicides in a program forty years ago are dead. What am I missing?"

"Shut up and listen." Abby took Tony's cigarette. "There were hundreds of *so-called psychics* responding to the government ads. Five years later there were only twenty-three remote viewers under contract. When it was shut down in '95, remote viewers vanished."

"Did you get names?" Wilcox asked.

"I have nineteen."

"I love you, Patterson."

"I know you do." They downed a shot and kissed.

"Something knocked me off my high heels, Tee."

"You cross-checked the names with the national data bases," he said.

"I connected the dots," she said. "There's a definite cover up. Their files are gone. The remote viewers I know about are dead."

"That can't be a surprise. They'd be in their eighties today," Wilcox said.

"It was the way they died, Tee. And their direct descendants are dead too. All the deaths are traumatic and unwitnessed. In some cases, the bodies have never been found. Look here." She turned the screen. "Thomas Derby's father was a remote viewer in 1975. He died in 2010 in Boston, an unsolved homicide, stabbed in the back like two of your cases."

"How do you know?"

"Don't ask." She pointed. "William Hudson's mother was a remote viewer. She signed up in 1977 and died 2010 in New York City. She was an unwitnessed suicide with no history of depression and no note.

"Mark Pemberton's father was a remote viewer. He signed up in 1974 and died 2011 in a single car accident in the country. His car was a cinder in a field. They found him inside . . .

"And Donald Deckle's mother was a remote viewer. They say she committed suicide in 2012, but no one saw her jump off the Brooklyn Bridge."

Wilcox touched the screen and leaned in and read, "Bradley Johnson, his wife and daughter, died in a one car accident followed by a fire."

"Why'd you pick out Bradley Johnson?" Abby asked.

"I know the Johnson family's story. What I know ties in with everything you're telling me now," Wilcox said.

"Tee, all these people are remote viewers or direct descendants. They are listed as accidents, suicides, homicides, or missing."

"Did you find autopsy records?" Wilcox asked.

"I found a few. I thought it odd because they each commented on the eyes—they were bulging out of the sockets. The faces were grossly disfigured. I saw Wilber Willingham's name on the list. That man was a U.S. Senator. He died in the basement of the Capital Building. He was one of the remote viewers. They said he had a heart attack. I don't believe it."

"You're good Patterson. Are Alma and Arnold Keller on your list?" Wilcox asked expecting an affirmative answer.

"Yes." She scrolled her notes—double homicide. They were

killed in Stringtown, Oklahoma in 2009. This says they adopted Hunter."

"What if he was not adopted? What if Hunter Keller was their biological son?"

"You mean maybe the Kellers knew one day someone would kill their child? Maybe they staged the adoption so he would be left alone."

"Or maybe they are protecting a psychic-monster from the world," Wilcox muttered. "I think Hunter Keller could be the serial killer I'm hunting. Maybe he is killing remote viewers and their families for some twisted reasons."

"That would be a possibility," Abby said.

"I remember the other night," Wilcox said under his breath. "My car was burning."

"What are you talking about?"

"I remember the Sterick Building. I found Deckle. He was dying with a knife in his back. I saw Hunter Keller, Abby. He was there, leaning over Deckle when I came in the room. I caught him in the act."

"Are you positive he killed Deckle?"

"I didn't see him put in the knife. He ran. I went after him. It was dark. The skinny guy got through holes in the walls faster than a jackrabbit. He got away."

Abby rubbed his arm to bring him back. "Running says something, I guess."

"It was the second time I saw him. The first was at the bank on South Main. He was my eyewitness. Then I found him in pictures at all four homicides, just standing in the crowd."

"Now that is very weird," Abby said.

"But after the incident at the Sterick building . . ."

"What happened, Tony?"

"I remember my car on fire. I was blacking out." Wilcox

pushed his fingers into his temples. "I was pulled out of my car and dragged across a field. Cottam said my car exploded."

Headlights washed across the bedroom ceiling and down the wall. Abby slid her laptop onto the nightstand and wrapped her arms around Wilcox.

"Hunter Keller was there, Abby. He was in the field." Tony reached for his gun. His unlit cigarette hung from his lips as he looked at the window and the lights outside.

"He tried to kill you, Tee?" Abby asked.

"No. Hunter Keller pulled me out. He saved my life."

TWENTY-THREE

"Fate is not an eagle, it creeps like a rat."
Elizabeth Bowen

Washington DC

I*t is time to do something about Dr. Petty and that Memphis homicide detective . . .*

The rain pounded Pennsylvania Avenue on a Friday night. Baldwin left the DOJ building through a back service entrance. Normally he was escorted from the building by secret service and driven to his condo in Alexandria. This night was different. The Attorney General could not to be disturbed. He would be working late—he sent his staff home. Baldwin would spend the night in the private quarters adjacent to his office. The rooms were converted into an efficiency apartment for just such occasions. But this night Alfred Baldwin had no intention of using the private quarters.

He considered "stealth" one of his strengths. When he wanted to leave the DOJ building unseen, he used a certain stairwell at a certain time. He descended three flights, crossed an empty hallway, and departed through a certain service entrance into the garage. Only two pillars left enough room to squeeze his pudgy body through behind a line of hedges. On the other side an alley connected to a bustling sidewalk. A collar up, hat on, and one step into the crowd, he disappeared. Baldwin's stealth route took shape after weeks of study years earlier. As the sitting attorney general, nobody questioned his odd request for total access to all DOJ surveillance cameras. If asked, he would cite personal security reasons—he never left anything to chance.

No one looks for a U.S. Attorney General walking down Pennsylvania Avenue alone at night. He looked like anyone else in D.C. attempting to avoid the rain and eager to reach his destination. He pulled his black fedora down tight, almost touching his eyebrows, and he made sure his raised coat collar covered his large ears. The black umbrella completed his disguise. Even if someone got a glimpse of the AG, Baldwin still had no worries. All his life he had a most forgettable face.

With a growing smile, he trudged forward in the undulating herd feeling a new freedom. He received the final paperwork—it was now official. Evelyn was no longer his lawfully wedded wife. Although the documents arrived at his desk late, the news recharged his batteries—another loose end tied into a tidy knot. After five years of bliss, fifteen of hell, and two of estrangement, the marriage ended with her last act of benevolence—attending the ceremony, his appointment to the post of attorney general. At the time few knew there would be a formal announcement. The president, in so many words, suggested a delay would be in their best interest politically.

Evelyn complied—she did not want to jeopardize the generous flow of alimony payments.

In the pouring rain he walked four long blocks in the huddled masses surrounded by smoking traffic and steaming headlights. Alfred E. Baldwin, the seventh in line to the presidency, turned onto a familiar side street and this time down an unfamiliar alley —a necessary route modification due to past transgressions. His destination lay two blocks ahead, and the alleys provided additional cover, and danger. Holding his Jennings J-22 to his chest, he walked alone in the pounding rain and obscure shadows. If anyone interfered, he would shoot to kill and move on just like he did the week before. Nothing could compromise the mission, not even a two-bit punk looking for an old man's wallet.

The Washington Post had a small article on page fourteen— man found dead in alley off Pennsylvania Avenue, single shot in eye, twenty-two caliber, and no witnesses. Baldwin smiled and turned the page. He was all about practical justice.

Benny Birnbaum was a rotund bald Jew with coke bottle glasses and a genius IQ. He owned the brownstone on paper only. The butterfly collector and Chicago University CPA had worked for Alfred Baldwin since his Harvard Law School days. Benny held the titles to a lot of Baldwin's real estate and investments for tax purposes. He moved millions to the Caymans each year—government service had been a goldmine. Evelyn's high priced attorneys would never find most of Baldwin's assets. Few attorneys would question the ethics or practices of the chief law enforcement officer of the land—his greatest cover. And no one knew Baldwin maintained the brownstone six blocks from the DOJ complex for nefarious reasons.

"Good evening, Dr. Swenson," Baldwin said as he closed the door and hung his dripping hat and coat. Brushing sleeves and retucking his shirt, he found the leather chair by the popping fire in the room with soft light. Benny had already poured his glass of

Celani Cabernet Sauvignon Ardore 2011—it would be at room temperature.

Dr. Swenson sat on the arm of the dark leather sofa staring like a monkey on an organ grinder waiting to perform for a peanut. His small head and pencil body in Pee-wee Herman attire was misleading. Swenson possessed rare psychic skills and was a cold-blooded killer.

"Bad weather, Alfred?" Swenson said sipping his steaming tea with a finger up.

"The others will be here soon," Benny said from across the room.

"Did we confirm Tanner and Proust?" Baldwin asked.

"Yes. And Benny said the police were here. More questions about the man you shot."

Baldwin smelled his Celani. "They're simply canvassing the neighborhood. I'm sure they don't suspect anyone here," he said.

"Still, it does add a wrinkle. We don't need attention." Swenson crossed his legs like a woman. "I suggest you try to refrain from shooting pedestrians for a while."

"We have more important matters. The Memphis initiative is getting dicey." Baldwin waved to Benny passing through to the kitchen. "I worry about the proliferation of targets."

"We confirmed. The Memphis dead are all direct descendants. The genetics check out."

"Tell me more," Baldwin said into his wine glass with eyes on the fire already knowing everything Swenson could share. It was how he shared that interested Baldwin most. Would Swenson manipulate the facts to serve some ulterior purpose? Would he leave things out to protect his position?

"Donald Deckle was not in the first group. The kill on Main was Randle Johnson. Deckle was held captive and terminated in the abandoned Sterick building in downtown Memphis. Keller was seen by Detective Wilcox."

"And what do you know about Mr. Keller's whereabouts?" Baldwin asked.

"We know he was hiding in Memphis at a used bookstore, Rare Books. It was across the street from the Benton Bank & Trust. They knew Keller was on South Main, but not exactly where. They used Deckle as bait."

"They got closer this time. Keller's cloaking skills are superior to anything we've seen."

"He'll make a mistake. We'll get him in Memphis," Swenson muttered.

The door opened and a tall man entered in the mist. Benny helped him out of his coat.

"Good evening, gentlemen." The dark figure broke from the shadows into the fire glow. "It is a miserable night out there. I've never liked the storms on the east coast—drenching."

"Hello Benjamin." Baldwin watched Dr. Proust take a seat next to Swenson. "I assume your jaunt to the brownstone was uneventful."

"Don't worry Alfred. I was not followed, my friend."

His Choctaw heritage lived in his flat cheeks, strong jaw, and chiseled nose. Proust, seventy, was still the rugged western man with dark, leathery skin, thick, white eyebrows and long, white hair. The Okmulgee County Medical Examiner looked more like a retired professional athlete than a forensic pathologist.

Proust had handled the Henryetta homicides on Dewar and the Keller deaths in Stringtown. Only three in the government ever knew about his secret assignment in Oklahoma—to monitor Elda Middleton, Ruby Tantabaum, and the Keller family.

"Where's Richard?" Proust asked as he lit a small cigar and lifted a glass of vodka from Benny's silver tray.

"In route," Swenson said. "Plane's on time. He's caught in traffic from Dulles."

"It's been a while," Baldwin said. "We haven't talked about it much. You had Major Cankor and Hunter Keller in your zone, Benjamin. Another lost opportunity."

Proust blew a cloud into the conversation. "The Major knew I was out of the state. I assure you it was the only reason he made a move. Somehow he found Keller at Middleton's place. We had no idea—the kid can block like no other." He said under his breath, "I still don't know how Cankor found him."

Baldwin stared at the fire. "It is very disturbing about Middleton and Tantabaum."

"We lost Alma and Arnold Keller on your watch too," Swenson attacked. "Seems a lot bad happens in your state."

Proust aimed his sneer at the skinny suit next to him. "I'm not responsible for the Kellers. If you recall, it started then. And I don't like your accusatory tone, doctor."

"This kind of talk's not helpful," Baldwin said. "Benjamin's right, we were ill prepared when the Kellers were eliminated." The front door opened. "Richard. You made it."

He joined the three by the fire and waved-off Benny's tray of alcoholic beverages. "We have problems gentlemen." He chose the only open chair. It was next to Alfred. "The Memphis medical examiner—Dr. Victoria Petty—is making enormous progress. I've tried to contain her, but she and a homicide detective, Tony Wilcox, are getting close. They've met Hunter Keller, and I believe Major Cankor has visited Dr. Petty at the Shelby County morgue."

Swenson straightened his posture on the arm of the sofa. "I did not like her. I felt from the start she allowed us in her morgue to watch more than to cooperate with the government. She dragged-out the Pella exhumation to have more time to study us. I should have dug him up myself and got what we needed."

"I agree with Dr. Swenson. We should have handled Memphis differently," Tanner said.

"You can't crack open a skull and dissect a brain in a cemetery," Proust rebuked.

"You can get a head and drop it in a backpack. I could remove the amygdala in my hotel room and put it in the mail that night," Swenson crowed. "It would be in D.C. and verified before Elmwood Cemetery found the hole."

"I agree. There was a better way," Tanner said. "We revealed too much in the Memphis operation. And we gave Green and Blanchard too much time to transfer information."

Baldwin held up his hand. "Both of you stop, please. Second-guessing operations is not helpful. Dr. Green and Dr. Blanchard are no longer a problem. We go forward from here."

"Well, Dr. Swenson left a mess in Memphis," Tanner said. "We are exposed."

"Richard B. Tanner, the great Vanderbilt geneticist," Swenson sneered, "If you had refrained from telling Petty about the DNA—or lack thereof—on Alfred's letter, we would not be under a microscope. You destroyed our plan when you casted doubt over the Bethesda team. Your hipshot took away our opportunity to personally validate Randle Johnson, Donald Deckle, and Roger Tinsley. Sometimes I believe you are working for the other side."

"Gentlemen please," Baldwin bellowed. "Let us agree Memphis is a pressure cooker, the center of the storm currently. We knew this day was coming."

"Escalation of exterminations on the horrific road to world domination," Proust orated.

"I thought we had a plan. I thought this could be controlled," Tanner said.

"The enemy is very much alive, and very much underground like us. If they take control of psychic-weaponry the global balance of power will shift. The world as we know it will change."

"What about Hunter Keller?" Proust asked.

"Nobody can touch him," Swenson said.

"He's learning his capabilities," Baldwin muttered. "We must find him soon. There's little time."

"He's too dangerous," Tanner fumed. "As I have always said, Keller must be destroyed."

"Too important to destroy. He must be controlled," Baldwin said.

Tanner held his cold hands at the fire. "He's a killing machine. He'll never be controlled. We learn from him and then eliminate him. That is the best plan."

"Major Cankor is getting close now," Baldwin whispered over his glass. "Top secret senate sub-committee meetings are infiltrated by RVs. They don't know it is happening. I do."

"We should have dealt with Cankor a long time ago," Proust said. "I knew the day I met the man he would be a problem. He has always been strange, a loner with mental problems."

"I didn't trust Cankor either," Baldwin said. "But we were young and inexperienced at the time. We didn't understand the magnitude of the threat."

"I may not be a remote viewer like you three," Tanner said. "But I'm smart enough to see a future where these dangerous psychic powers are genetically reproduced and perpetuated."

"The creation of an army of lethal psychics is going to happen. We know it must be controlled," Proust said. "War will be different. Civilizations will drop where they stand."

"Tell us something new, Tanner," Swenson scoffed.

"Memphis is in our way," Tanner said. "I continue to recommend the immediate elimination of all uncontrolled variables."

"Be more specific," Baldwin said setting down his glass.

"It is time to do something about Dr. Petty and the Memphis homicide detective."

"Do what?" Baldwin asked already knowing the answer.

"We terminate Dr. Petty and Detective Wilcox immediately," Tanner said.

"Preposterous," Proust said. "You can't justify the termination of a medical examiner and homicide detective. That action does not reduce variables, it creates more."

"If we don't do as I say, we are all exposed. This mission fails. Our country is at great risk. We cannot lose any more time. We must find and stop Hunter Keller."

"On the contrary," Swenson said. "If we do as you propose; we are assured of losing Hunter Keller. Major Cankor has the advantage here. Terminating the collaterals only attracts attention and ties us up more."

Baldwin downed his last inch of wine. "I met with Dr. Petty yesterday."

"This is the first time I'm hearing about this," Tanner said with poorly managed irritation.

"She came to D.C. to talk to me about the Stargate Project, the Bethesda visitors, recent deaths, and Hunter Keller. I agree with Dr. Tanner on one account, they are making progress."

"Did you tell her anything?" Swenson asked.

"I felt compelled to give her some information. I told her about Willingham and Dryden."

"Are you out of your mind," Tanner grumbled.

"I wanted to gain her trust, Richard. She can help, if we bring her closer."

"As planned, on my first visit I told Dr. Petty about death by telepathic manipulation of the amygdala." Swenson said. "She did not buy it. The concept was a stretch in spite of histology."

"The psychic-weaponry we are dealing with is too bizarre for anyone to accept," Baldwin said. "That fact alone buys us time. The medical examiners we've engaged are all alike. They hear us but are looking for practical explanations. They are pragmatic."

"We need the help of more medical examiners," Proust said.

"That has always been a terrible idea," Tanner seethed. "We need the opposite. We must eliminate Dr. Petty and Detective Wilcox before they get too close."

"We need help finding Hunter Keller before Major Cankor. I've prepared her for a demon," Swenson argued. "They are our boots on the ground chasing a hideous serial killer."

"We all agreed that approach had merit," Proust said.

Tanner's brows dipped. "It's always been a bad idea, now more than ever. Alfred, I think you've lost your grasp of the total situation facing us."

Baldwin waved at Benny with an empty glass. "Gentlemen, we are not terminating Dr. Petty or Detective Wilcox. Enough talk on the matter."

Tanner sat up and took a deep breath. "Does she know about the Rejdak Project?"

"Yes. But she cannot access proprietary files," Swenson said.

Baldwin set down his empty glass. "Don't worry Richard. She can't see your genetic research. She will never know your involvement."

"Still, the declassified Stargate Project files give way too much information. Dr. Petty can access a lot on line. She is very bright and capable of sifting through the data to figure this out. When she does, we are all exposed. We are all ruined. This program fails."

"The information you are worried about has been out there for more than a decade," Swenson said.

"The world knows the government contracted clairvoyants in the '70s," Proust said.

"Petty and Wilcox have put it together. They know remote viewers and descendants are being systematically terminated," Tanner argued. "It's a matter of time."

"And they believe the federal government shares their concern," Proust said.

Swenson shook his head. "Dr. Tanner, I'm beginning to question your true interests in this matter." Baldwin looked into the fire and Proust dropped his head. The three knew what was going to happen next.

"This is why we have soldiers and generals," Baldwin said. "I'm the general. You're a soldier, Dr. Tanner. I have decided it is time we enlist the aid of others to find Keller and Cankor. Our mission is impossible for rational minds to comprehend. That is our veil. If Cankor and his minions find Keller first, we lose."

"This is an unacceptable direction," Tanner said. "I am no soldier. I am an officer in this battle who needs to be heard. I do not request, I insist on the termination of Dr. Petty and Detective Wilcox, and Detective Baily. If this is not our course, I must exit this mission."

Swenson and Proust turned from the fire and looked into Baldwin's empty eyes. The three knew all of Tanner's secrets. He should have been smarter.

"Well then, gentlemen," Proust said. "It appears you two need some private time. And it is a perfect opportunity for me to pay a visit to the restroom." He stood nudging Swenson off the arm of the leather sofa.

"Yes. Privacy. And I will refresh my tepid tea." Swenson slid the rest of the way off the arm and went into the kitchen. Benny closed the French doors behind.

Tanner leaned close and whispered. "I cannot live with your decision, Alfred. Mine is the right action. The terminations will give us the precious time needed. Our exposure by outsiders can only lead to failure."

"Or more boots on the ground can lead to success, Richard. Can't you see that?"

"I'm no psychic, Alfred. I do not see the future."

"But I think you see 'a' future." Baldwin slid his hand in his coat as if to retrieve a release form or checkbook. "But it's not a shared future, Richard."

"I just want out, Alfred."

"И вы должны получить выход, г-н Председатель," Baldwin whispered.

Tanner's eyes widened as he translated the Russian words —*and you should get out, sir.*

The muffled pop stayed in the room by the fire. Like a single firecracker going off in a small box, Alfred Baldwin derived yet another benefit from his Jennings J-22. Benny would clean up the mess as always.

TWENTY-FOUR

"Everyone has his day and some days last longer than others."
Churchill

Memphis, Tennessee

Wilcox joined Petty in the hallway. "What are you doing here?"

"I just landed. I had a message from Detective Baily." Petty adjusted her arm strap and pulled her leather satchel close.

"I got the call too. Baily was brought out of his coma last night. He can talk. He wants to talk."

"I met with Alfred Baldwin yesterday," Petty said without slowing her pace to ICU.

Wilcox chuckled. "So, you actually got to spend some time with that liberal prick." They rounded the corner to the bank of elevators and a small crowd. They stood quietly. Nothing was safe anymore.

The doors closed. "I didn't know you were a staunch conservative," Petty said from the side of her mouth with a half-smile." The doors opened. People scattered.

"I'm not staunch anything. I'm pissed-off at all of 'em. None do what the people send 'em there to do. The whole damn system's broke." They rounded the corner to a nurse behind the glass at the ICU gateway. She ignored Wilcox's taps. She shuffled papers with her head down. He rapped harder.

The glass window slid open. "Visiting hours are over."

"MPD. We're here to see Cameron Baily. Room number please?" he asked scrolling text messages and ignoring the sizzling eyes and pursed lips in scrubs.

"I said visiting hours are over. You can come back tomorrow morning at nine." She began to close the window. Wilcox stopped her progress with his shoulder now leaning into her space and his eyes on her nametag.

"Miss Greedy. We're not visitors. I'm a homicide detective and this is the ME. I will appreciate Baily's room number and the glass door open, please ma'am."

"I don't care who you are. You're not getting into my ICU tonight."

Wilcox turned to Petty—smiled—and turned back to Greedy with burning eyes. "Here's how this is going to go. You will give me a room number and open the glass door to ICU in five seconds. If you fail to do this, Greedy, I will break down the glass doors and arrest you for interfering with an active homicide investigation. You will be charged as an accomplice in any and all homicides that occur due to your behavior—willing obstruction of justice. I will cuff and drag you out of here to my car. You will spend the night in jail with tonight's crop of prostitutes. I will make sure it takes 24 hours to fix this small misunderstanding. Clock starts now."

The door swished open. "Room 302."

"You're such a bully," Petty muttered.

"Right. And Greedy's a bundle of joy."

The hall was empty, the smell aseptic. When they reached 302 they saw Detective Baily lying in a hospital bed surrounded by monitors. His head was bandaged covering one eye. His jaw was swollen and bruised, and his arms were tied to the sidebars.

"They like to tie people up in this place," Wilcox said as they entered and he closed the door behind them.

Baily's one eye popped open. He looked at Wilcox, and then found Dr. Petty's blond hair and red lipstick smile. "It's about time they sent a pretty lady," he said. Petty winked.

"Hey. What about me?" Wilcox teased, as he perused Baily's puffy face and bruises.

"You're ugly," Baily said as Wilcox gripped his tied hand.

"I assume you know you are flirting with our new medical examiner."

"Nice to meet you Detective Baily," Petty said. "I wish it was under less traumatic circumstances." Baily nodded. He had something on his mind.

"Thought we lost you," Wilcox said looking at the monitors.

"The docs say I'm gonna be fine." He cleared his throat. "I've been layin' here goin' over stuff. We don't have a lot of time. You guys need to pull up chairs. I gotta tell you."

"You sure about this?" Wilcox asked. "You look like shit."

Petty pushed Wilcox. Baily chuckled. "It's okay. I'm used to this insensitive old coot. Anyway, my mama always said I only used ten percent of my brain. I figure now I got eighty percent I won't be using. I'll bet Dr. Petty can keep an eye on all these monitors."

"I can," she said as she scanned them. "Your heart rate and blood pressure are good."

"Nobody's talking to me. Did Bone Jackson make it off that river?" Baily asked.

"No," Wilcox said. "Bullet in the chest—heart shot."

"And Keller?"

"Keller got away, Baily." *I'll let you choose the time to tell me he shot you.*

Baily closed his eye. "I met with the Atoka County Sheriff, Carl Bennet."

"Bennet worked the Keller family homicides in Stringtown, 2009," Wilcox told Petty.

Baily's eye popped open and locked on Wilcox. "Like you said, when he heard we had unsolved homicides in Memphis that might be connected, he showed me everything."

"We already know Dr. Benjamin Proust, the Okmulgee County Medical Examiner, did the Keller family autopsies," Wilcox told Baily.

"Did you think it was unusual the Atoka County ME. let that happen?

"Sometimes we invite other medical examiners in on cases if they have more expertise in certain areas," Petty said. "Small towns do not see many multiple homicides."

"Yeah, well Dr. Landry didn't invite Proust. And Landry didn't participate in the autopsies. I thought that was strange."

"He must have been out of town or otherwise involved," Dr. Petty said.

"That was my first thought, too. Sheriff Bennet told me Proust called him twenty minutes after he found the bodies. Proust was on vacation down the road. He offered to help. Bennet was staring at the worst kills of his entire career. He said he thought Dr. Proust was a gift from heaven."

"There you have it," Wilcox sighed. "Let's move on. We're wasting time."

Baily smiled. The puffy, bruised side of his face didn't move. "Just slow down old man and listen. Proust told Bennet the only way he'd help was if he worked the cases alone. He didn't have time for collaborations or news media. He also recommended Stringtown cremate the bodies to stop the circus that surrounds these kinds of messes."

"Those are strange demands," Petty mumbled.

"Where's this going Baily," Wilcox pushed.

"I looked at the autopsy paperwork. I didn't see anything about bulging eyes, screwed-up faces, or lesions."

"So, there you have it. They're not connected to Memphis," Wilcox said. "That's what we needed to know."

Petty held up a hand to stop the bull in the china shop. "Did you get a look at Dr. Proust's 'external inspection' narrative? Except for the lesions, the information on the eyes and facials would have been reported there."

"I read the narrative. It was not there."

"Let's move on," Wilcox pushed. "We have a lot to talk about and little time. I want to know what you learned about Hunter Keller. And what were you doing at Broken Bow Lake with a guy named Bone Jackson."

Baily ignored Wilcox. "Somethin's not right about the way these homicides got handled by some guy callin' that fast, with demands, and outside his jurisdiction. Proust had no business bein' there. How did he know twenty minutes after Bennet saw the Kellers? And who takes a damn vacation in east Oklahoma?

"I asked Sheriff Bennet what he saw when he looked at those bodies five years ago. Well, turns out he kept his notes. He read it to me verbatim. Both Alma and Arnold Keller's eyes were bulging out their sockets like fried eggs sunny side up. Both had twisted-up faces and their lips pulled back to their ears and faces white as snow. Bennet said he wet his pants." Baily chuckled. "He said that's when his phone rang. It was like he had a camera on him or something. Proust was a gift from heaven. Bennet agreed to everything on the spot."

"Didn't Bennet see all that missing from Proust's autopsy report?" Wilcox scoffed.

"He sure did. Bennet said he read the report and asked Proust about it missing. Proust told him it was not unusual when someone's strangled or stabbed in the back. Bennet bought it."

"Tony, this information is disturbing," Petty said.

"That's not all," Baily said. "Before they cremated Alma and Arnold Keller, Proust took the brains. Said he had to run more tests in Henryetta. Later told Bennet everything was negative and he destroyed the brains."

Petty's brow dipped. "We need to know more about Dr. Benjamin Proust."

Wilcox nodded. "Five people were killed in Henryetta the night you were shot, Baily."

"Five?" Baily sighed. "What's the connection?"

"Henryetta's in Okmulgee County, Proust's jurisdiction. I think I need to go up there and meet this guy. I need to take a closer look at Dewar Avenue. The newspaper reported Hunter Keller had been staying there, a tenant where three of the five died. The Henryetta police are looking for Hunter Keller, too."

"I should go with you," Petty said. "I know how to vet Dr. Proust. I'm sure he can lose you in the medical jargon. We need to know how he fits in all this."

Wilcox didn't respond. A road trip with Petty was a bad idea on many levels. First, she would slow him down because he breaks the rules and she is a rule person. Second, he did not want to spend two days with her nagging at him about his smoking and cussing and drinking. And third, there was a physical attraction that could get out of control.

"I poked around Stringtown like you told me," Baily said. "Learned Hunter Keller had four close friends. I ran checks on 'em. I think I told you all four died traumatic deaths over the last six months—one suicide, one accident, and one under undetermined still under investigation."

"And Jackson, a homicide. Did you leave Stringtown with Bone Jackson?" Wilcox asked.

"No. I found him in the woods fifty miles east of Stringtown. He was hunting Bigfoot. I think him being in the woods was the only thing keeping him alive."

"Then someone found you two. You went to Broken Bow," Wilcox said.

"Bone Jackson knew a place to hide, a cabin on Broken Bow. Less than an hour after getting to that cabin, there was a knock at the door. It was Hunter Keller."

"Did he shoot you in the boat?" Wilcox asked straight out.

"Did Keller shoot me? *Hell no*! Is that what you think?"

"Ballistics were inconclusive. I've been waiting to hear from you."

Half of Baily's face smiled. "I guess I can see how you got there. Keller's the guy in the pictures at all our homicides. No, Keller did not shoot me. He came to Broken Bow to help Bone Jackson and me. He wanted to save us."

"Save you from what?" Wilcox pushed.

"From the people hunting us all damn night. I don't know who they were, but I do know they were hell-bent on killing Bone and me and taking Keller."

"How do you know that for sure?" Wilcox asked. "Maybe Keller was playing you. Think about your training. If there were a bunch of people hunting a couple guys, why didn't they storm the cabin? They could have overpowered you easily."

"I think they would have, but Hunter Keller got there first. They fear that guy."

"What are they afraid of," Wilcox asked.

"He is a powerful psychic," Petty said under her breath.

"I have trouble believing that kind of stuff," Wilcox said. "I know about the government research and people dying with lesions, but that program was shut down decades ago."

Baily rubbed his good eye waiting for Wilcox to stop talking. "You're way off base, boss. Keller is different. He has powers. I saw him in action. And Bone Jackson is not your typical friend. The guy's a PhD in psychology and recognized expert in the field of parapsychology. He dedicated his life to helping his friend understand and control his psychic abilities."

Wilcox pushed fingers through his hair and fell back in his chair as Petty rounded Baily's bed. "What powers does he have," she asked. "Tell me some of what you witnessed?"

"We're in the cabin. He tells Bone to shoot a guy thirty-five yards out. He says the guys at one o'clock. It is pitch black."

"Are you serious," Wilcox chided.

"Keller tells Bone the guy's sliding a night vision scope onto his rifle. Keller says if you do not shoot now, the guy will kill him. Bone blindly aims his rifle. Keller lifts the barrel and moves it with his finger. Then Keller tells me to move my head away from the front door window or in two seconds get shot in the head. Shit, I backed away in one second. A damn bullet exploded through the glass inches from my nose. Then Bone pulls his trigger.

"Keller says we gotta go. We climb out the window. Thirty yards out we step over a dead guy with a rifle in one hand and night vision scope in the other. Bone nailed him between the eyes."

"I don't know about any of that," Wilcox muttered. *Is it possible?*

"That government research you mentioned, Bone told me the CIA didn't end it. He said they just took it deeper underground.

Bone has proof. He said a lot of governments are working on psychic-weapons. He said it is the next weapon of mass destruction."

"I met with the Attorney General," Petty said to Baily. "He did admit the government had an interest in psychic-weaponry, but he did confirm the existence of remote viewers. He was unwilling to go deeper. He claimed there were national security matters in play."

"Although psychic-weaponry is likely fiction, I do have a private investigator sending me the names of the government contracted remote viewers from the '70s and early '80s. Granted, most are dead or missing today. For some reason they are targets and Hunter Keller is involved."

"You gotta ask why else would an attorney general be involved." Baily said. "This is a much bigger deal than we have considered. We all need to open minds."

"These RV people are being killed. I suspect one of their lab rats got loose," Wilcox said. "Maybe that lab rat is Hunter Keller. There are logical answers to all of this."

"Maybe government people are the ones who need to be put back in a cage," Petty said. "Maybe Hunter Keller is the one trying to stop them."

"Why are you pro Hunter Keller?" Wilcox asked. "The evidence doesn't support it."

"I met with Baldwin and the Bethesda three. They want us to believe Hunter Keller is a real monster. So far they've lied about everything. I think they have an agenda, Tony. Tell me why Keller called 911. Why help? Tell me why he came to the aide of Bone Jackson and Detective Baily? The evidence against him is not that compelling. You are suspicious of him because you don't understand him. You cannot get your 'detective head' around psychic-weaponry."

"I agree with Dr. Petty," Baily said. "Keller's not a killing machine. I spent time with him. I know people. Keller's a sickly person with incredible abilities. He wants to be left alone. He avoids conflict, but they keep coming for him. The government wants to control him."

Wilcox always looked for facts, but also trusted his gut. In the past neither let him down. The addition of psychic-weapons and a clandestine government operation threw him off his game, and he knew it. But Wilcox also knew he had to find his own way.

"Although the evidence is confusing, we can't dismiss certain facts," Wilcox said. "Keller's at every death scene—the four Memphis homicides, the I-55 truck driver, the Sterick Building where Deckle got a knife in the back, the Henryetta homicides, and now Broken Bow. And we don't know 'for sure' about his whereabouts when his parents were killed in Stringtown. In every case Hunter Keller walked away."

"He does have a point," Baily muttered. "The guy is at all the death scenes. Somehow he did get off that river and we got shot."

"Those facts exist," Petty said. "But you cannot dismiss all the other facts just because we do not understand them. We can't dismiss Keller's psychic abilities, the Stargate Project, the targeting and killing of remote viewers, the veiled government interests, and most importantly, the brain lesions. When we understand these, we will solve this mystery."

Wilcox returned from the window—Petty got it right. Until she listed them, he did not realize how much he had on the back burner because he couldn't explain them.

"Time for full disclosure," Wilcox said. Heads turned. "I guess I'm gonna confuse things even more, now. I need to tell you something." He swallowed hard. "A few days ago I got pulled out of a burning car."

"My God," Petty gasped. "Why would you keep that information to yourself, Tony?"

Baily sat up in bed. "I knew it. Someone is definitely after us. We are getting close."

"I didn't say anything because you've been out of town and Baily's been out cold. We just now got together, and what Baily had to say was more important."

"To use one of your favorite words—bullshit," Petty scolded.

Wilcox rubbed his face searching for the words to explain what he did not understand. "I'm not sure what happened that night."

"Just start talking," Petty said. "Together we will figure it out."

He nodded. "I was unconscious in the hospital a while. When I woke up, they said they found me lying at the edge of a field by the Mississippi River. My car was on fire in the middle of the field. They said my car exploded. I guess I could have been killed that night."

Baily untied his hand and pulled off his head bandage. "This is not making a lot of sense to me. How'd you get out of your car and not know?"

"Seven hours were plucked out of my head. Pieces are coming back. There are two things I want to tell you. First, I remember getting pulled out of the car."

"That's not so hard," Baily teased.

"I was pulled out by Hunter Keller," Wilcox said.

"Holy shit!" Baily threw his bandage against the wall. "Keller saved your damn life just like he saved mine. Kinda screws up your 'guilty as shit' theory, boss man."

Petty touched his shoulder. Wilcox was trembling. "I saw him that night. I'm sure of it. I don't remember much before or after."

"It'll come back," Baily said. He saw a look on Wilcox's face for the first time—fear.

"Amnesia is complicated," Petty said. "After our debate on

guilt and innocence, I hate to say this. There is a chance you are filling memory gaps with imagination. It is possible Hunter Keller was not there, Tony. He has been on your mind. You need time to remember."

"No. I know for a fact he was there," Wilcox barked. "That skinny guy had one hell of a time dragging me across that field. It took him a while. I remember him tugging and grunting all the way. I remember him sweating. I remember the desperation in his eyes. It happened."

"Okay, it happened. We can talk about the 'why' later. What is the second thing you wanted to tell us?" Petty asked.

Wilcox returned to the window and lifted a slat. "Before I tell you the second thing, we need to agree to change the way we do things going forward. I am a primary target, not you. I will be more unpredictable."

"We're all primary targets, Tony. And, you have always been unpredictable."

"Not this kind of unpredictable. You don't understand. While I was in the hospital, they ran tests, lots of tests."

"Of course they did. You were unconscious, a head injury." Then it hit her. "They did an MRI, didn't they?" Petty whispered.

Wilcox dropped the slat and turned to them. "I have lesions on my amygdala."

TWENTY-FIVE

"Believe nothing and be on your guard against everything."
Proverb

"You remember the car in your driveway the other night?" Abby asked as she retrieved her latte concoction at the Starbuck's window, her phone in a dash mount on speaker.

Wilcox merged onto I-40. "Are you talkin' about the lights? People get lost on Mud Island all the time. Every condo looks alike. Why?" He glanced over at Petty busy texting. He kept it cryptic and pushed his cell tight to his ear. She did not need to know about his intimate relationship with a private investigator.

"You went to the bathroom," Abby said. "I looked out the window. I saw a Yukon SUV. It was silver. I watched it pull away. It had a decal—a Russian flag—on the back window."

"You could see that?"

"It's what I do, Wilcox—observe. That Yukon's been

following me ever since Memphis. It's parked here at Starbuck's now."

He changed hands. "Patterson, you need to be careful. We're on someone's list. I wish I could tell you more, but it's complicated and time is important now. Trust me when I say these people are dangerous. We are getting close, because we are being hunted now."

Petty looked up. "What's going on?"

He held the phone to his chest. "Remember the PI I mentioned? She's being followed." He got back on the phone. "Where are you now? I'll send our people."

"Relax Tee. I'm not in Memphis. I'm in Knoxville. Had to get back to my cheatin' spouse."

"Listen to me, in your world people cheat. In my world people die. You can't fool around with this stuff, Abby. There's a good chance the people following you know you've been digging around secret government research."

"Then they know I know about dead remote viewers," Abby said.

"And that could make you a problem."

"I think the people following me are Russian. You don't see a Russian flag every day."

"Drive to the nearest police station. Tell the cops they're harassing you. Then go to a beach for a while. I mean it, Abby."

"You're more nervous than usual, Tee. You must have more bad information?" She pulled out of the parking lot. The Yukon slid into traffic three cars back.

"Dr. Petty met with the Attorney General."

"U.S. Attorney General Baldwin?" Abby asked.

"Yes. They are in the middle of all this. Although we have differing opinions on the matter, I think we can all agree the Stargate Project has its roots in Russia. It makes sense they would be involved in some way."

"Sounds like this is not a job for a Memphis homicide detective. Maybe you need to back off. Maybe you need to take your own advice—pass the ball to the FBI or CIA."

"I hear you. But I'm gonna keep this ball a little while longer," Wilcox said.

"Why?"

"Petty doesn't have a good feeling about Baldwin. His hands are all over this stealth death match taking place in several cities. Bodies are dropping on my front steps. I don't like it."

"And if it happens in Memphis, it's your business?" Abby poked. "Did you ever consider the possibility Baldwin is a good guy chasing the bad guys like you?"

"I smell a rat. This wouldn't be the first time people in high places had their own agenda. A lot of narcissistic bastards hold top positions in government. Baldwin is on my list until I know different."

"Did you get the names I texted you?"

"Got it, but have not had a chance to look at it yet."

"You need to—nineteen remote viewers. I believe there were twenty-three contracted by the government. Can't find the missing four names."

"Is Blanchard, Green, or Swenson on the list?"

"I gotta go, Tee. Changing cars. Have one stashed in a parking garage."

"Be careful, Abby. Lose them or get to a police station."

"I'll text my new *throw-away* number. Where you and Petty headed?"

"Henryetta, Oklahoma. Meeting with the medical examiner that did the Keller autopsies."

"The Henryetta M.E. has Stringtown? They cover a lot of geography in Oklahoma."

"Actually, Stringtown is not in Proust's jurisdiction. He was visiting the area when the Kellers were killed. We think the story is thin. We're going to Henryetta to vet him and to check out a recent multiple homicide case—five killed on Dewar Avenue."

"Are you talking about Benjamin Proust?" Abby asked.

"Yes, Benjamin Proust," Wilcox said looking at Petty.

Patterson pulled into the parking garage. As she climbed levels she saw the silver Yukon pull to the side of the road. "Hold on, Tee." She parked by her stash-car on the third level, slid into the dark sedan, and pulled on a brown wig tucking her blonde hair. She fished for her baseball cap and slipped on her windbreaker.

"Okay, I'm driving out a brunette," she said.

"How do you know Benjamin Proust?" Wilcox asked again. Petty stared.

"He's on the list, Tee. Benjamin Proust is a remote viewer."

TWENTY-SIX

"It is better to meet danger than to wait for it."
Charles Caleb Colton

W ELCOME TO OKMULGEE COUNTY. The lightning
flashed at the perfect moment, or Wilcox would have
missed the ten-foot letters painted on the side of the old barn.

They flew down I-40 with the wipers slapping the pounding
rain. "Henryetta's five miles. We need to find a place to stay the
night."

After talking to Cam Baily at Baptist Hospital, Dr.
Benjamin Proust became a person of interest—what was he
doing in Stringtown five years ago, and why did he falsify
documents? After PI Patterson revealed the man was a
government remote viewer, Proust became an even more
important piece to the puzzle. But the trip to Henryetta
would not be all about Benjamin Proust. Further research
into the multiple homicides on Dewar Avenue revealed

Hunter Keller was at the house on Dewar. Wilcox was determined to find out if Keller left before or after the massacre.

Wilcox's reluctance to bring Petty to Henryetta had been neutralized. Director Cottam left strict orders Wilcox was off the case recuperating at home until he had a formal medical release on his desk. Driving to Oklahoma with a head injury would get Wilcox suspended. Driving under the care of a physician (albeit a forensic pathologist) would be arguable. Wilcox would tolerate Petty because she could confuse Cottam with the medical mumbo-jumbo, and she wanted to go to Henryetta as bad as Wilcox.

The impromptu road trip turned into a traveler's nightmare, Oktoberfest in Henryetta never crossed their minds. After an hour looking, the Relax Inn on East Trudgeon was the fourth hotel and last room available for fifty miles according to the plump, Choctaw Indian with the toothy smile. Rather than risk losing the whole night looking, Petty insisted they share the room. She would take the bed and he the sofa. The only good news was the pounding rain slowed to a miserable drizzle and they were a mile from Dewar.

"We won't be here long," Petty said as she set her overnight bag on the bed and plugged in her laptop. "You need to hear this, parts of the *Henryetta Daily Herald* archives."

Wilcox cracked the door, lit a cigarette, and pulled a silver flask from his coat. He took a sip and offered Petty a glass. He gave her an inch of scotch as she scrolled. Because commenting on his drinking and smoking would be useless, Petty didn't go there except for the irritated look.

"Headline on August 17," she said. "*Five found dead on Dewar Avenue. The Henryetta PD was called to 2175 Dewar Avenue around 11:00 AM. They found three people dead. Shortly after answering the call they made another gruesome discovery—*

the neighboring residence at 2165 Dewar—where two more were found dead taking the total count to five."

"I know. The neighbors, too," Wilcox said blowing smoke out the door. He let her read.

"The medical examiner places time of death between 3:00 to 4:00 AM." Petty looked up. "You have the list of remote viewers from Patterson, a text message attachment?"

Wilcox pulled his phone with smoke crawling up his face. "Got it right here."

Petty read on. *"Elda Middleton was found dead in the living room. Middleton, a longtime resident of Henryetta, is the owner of the boarding house. Two of the three tenants were found dead in their rooms—names withheld. The third tenant, Hunter Keller—"* Petty paused. "He was there."

Wilcox swallowed another shot of scotch. He would let Petty catch up. Telling her he read all the articles on the Dewar homicides wouldn't bring her up to speed.

"Hunter Keller from Stringtown, Oklahoma was not at the Dewar residence at the time of the killings. Sources close to the investigation say Keller checked out earlier in the day. Personal effects were not found at the crime scene. Keller is a person of interest. Anyone knowing of his whereabouts . . ." She sipped her scotch and scrolled. *"Ruby Tantabaum, owner of the neighboring residence . . ."*

"Wait." Wilcox opened the attachment on his cell and scrolled. "We found more. Ruby Tantabaum and Elda Middleton are on this list. They are remote viewers. Counting Keller and Proust, we have four of the twenty-three RVs in a town with a population of 5,000."

Petty continued reading, *"Ruby and Beatrice Tantabaum were found dead on their front porch, details on cause not available. The bodies were taken to the Okmulgee County morgue for autopsy. The medical examiner, Dr. Benjamin Proust, was contacted. County Sheriff T.E. Oglebee said deaths, timing, and proximity are disturbing.*"

"Keller's my prime suspect," Wilcox muttered as he flicked his butt into the mist.

Petty looked in the mirror above the laptop and pulled lipstick from her purse. "He's not the monster you think, Tony. Dr. Proust was at the Henryetta and Stringtown homicides. We know he's a remote viewer, and he hid information—why? 'Prime suspect' means nothing now."

"Proust was not at the Memphis homicides. Keller was at all of them. That matters."

"You can't explain your burning car," Petty said. "You can't explain Hunter Keller saving your life. You can't explain Russians tailing Patterson. And you can't explain Alfred Baldwin's involvement or the special interests of the federal government."

She puckered her lips in the mirror and put on lipstick. "This time your gut is wrong." She ran a fingertip over her bottom lip. "Are we going out or staying in tonight?"

Was Petty suggesting a romantic interlude, or was Wilcox's rogue imagination off base again. "I'm gonna visit Dewar Avenue before anyone knows I'm in Henryetta. You stay here."

"So Dr. Proust and Sheriff Oglebee are not expecting us until tomorrow?"

"Afternoon," Wilcox said. "We'll show up in the morning, unannounced. They won't be ready. They'll expect us late, the long drive from Memphis. I want a look at all the files, not just the ones they pick."

"And I would like to get a look at physical evidence and autopsies." Petty closed her laptop and stood up. "I'm going to Dewar with you."

Wilcox rolled his eyes. He did not want to explain all the things he was going to do at Dewar. "That's not a good idea."

"Why not?" she huffed.

"It's dangerous."

Petty lifted her skirt revealing her shapely legs, garter holster, and nine-millimeter Glock. "I'm protected."

Wilcox stared. She had a way of punching his buttons. He was a simple man attracted to the trifecta—beauty, intelligence, and attitude. He was repelled by the lack of any one. Petty had them all. He pocketed his flask and swung open the door. "Tonight's police business. You're a ride-along. Do everything I say. Question nothing I do."

"Or what, Detective Wilcox?" She dropped her hem. "You going to shoot me?"

"Not that drastic. I'll just lock you in the car until I'm done."

What a dinosaur, she mused as she went through the door burning a hole between Wilcox's eyes. But she was not as exasperated as she played it. She saw more of him than he wanted to show. She analyzed everything in life, including Wilcox. Among other things, she knew he was alone in the world by choice. Somewhere along the way he convinced himself the best way to stop evil was to live in the darkest parts of the world with it. Attachments only weakened him, something she was beginning to understand.

TWENTY-SEVEN

"Truth fears nothing but concealment."
Proverb

Henryetta, Oklahoma

L ike a couple rolling to a quiet spot on Lovers Lane, Wilcox turned off the car in the darkest shadow under the only tree in front of Elda Middleton's house on Dewar Avenue. The car windows were down. The smell of burnt leaves and cut grass laced the damp night air and stirred childhood memories—a time when life was less complicated and the world a safer place.

The wet stone houses loomed in gray skies like tombstones of giants. The stark structures lined side by side held the secrets of five horrific deaths and the real monster. But would this quiet night on Dewar provide more pieces to the impossible puzzle, or would Wilcox and Petty fall deeper into the rabbit hole?

The investigation process began when Wilcox turned onto Dewar. He pulled the key from the ignition and they sat in silence. Forcing twisted thoughts, they studied the moonlit landscape and empty houses where people died.

In the beginning the investigative mind is open to all possibilities. If not, the logic of the crime scene telling its story is lost. There is only one chance for the first impression, and it is often the best way into the nightmare. Windows of thought begin to close as information pours in and unanswered questions mount —it numbs the sharpest of minds. The battle between mind and gut begins. The "humanity march" to justice seeks the most direct route. It is always impulsive, hard to stop, and often wrong.

Errors allow monsters to get away.

Did you park here, under this tree, Wilcox thought. *Did you watch and wait for the perfect moment, or were you already inside with the trust of your victims? If it is you (Hunter Keller), why kill five? What horror in your world justified that carnage? If you are a psychic killer, you could use your skills from a distance without risk or compromise. Why come here—it makes no sense? Did you kill these remote viewers? Were the others just in the way? Is this revenge or is Dewar telling me it is something else?*

Why save my life? He let the thought in. *But how can you be a victim in all this?*

The half-moon washed over the manicured lawns and climbed the wet stone. Fifty years ago the Middletons and Tantabaums were two of the three structures northeast of town—the First Pentecostal Church was the third. Now the gothic houses were crowded by Highway 62 and a dozen more stone mansions. Dewar Avenue kept its country charm. The small pocket of affluence was the only neighborhood in Henryetta with houses on five acre lots.

Ruby and Elda knew they were different in the first grade—they were inseparable. Later they built houses next to each other. Unlike the others they built at their property edge so they were a whisper away. Ruby and Elda always knew when the other had something on their mind.

"Perfect place for a mass murder," Wilcox said leaning over the steering wheel.

"Location is not a factor. Someone came here for a reason," Petty challenged.

Trimmed lawns stopped at the Middleton and Tantabaum property lines. The extended vacancy was obvious—gardens overtaken by weeds, shrubs with shooters, and grass flopped over curbs and onto sidewalks. The stone mansions with dark windows had dark porches lined with dead potted plants.

"If Keller was a boarder for several weeks, I would be less suspicious," Wilcox said. "We need to check on that tomorrow." He felt for his gun and opened the car door.

Petty jumped out and got ahead of him with a flashlight. "Nice garden around this mailbox, once. Notice the tree is the only one by the road for five houses both ways. If someone wanted to be inconspicuous, they'd park where you did." She looked past the houses. "And we need to check the alley."

Wilcox knelt by the garden. "If you parked under the tree and went to Middleton's front porch, you wouldn't take the sidewalk. You'd take a shortcut through this garden. Knocks off forty feet."

"What's your point?" Petty asked.

Wilcox lifted leaves of towering weeds and shined his penlight. "I've got one boot print, thanks to this big-ass weed. Damn plant looks carnivorous."

"Are you serious? You're really interested in a boot print now?"

Wilcox studied the impression. "The toe's pointing to the porch on a direct line from the tree. I'm thinkin' a size fourteen."

"Tony! Time, weather, animals, police, paramedics, neighbors walking dogs—"

"You're like a damn fish out of water without a body to poke at. I'm not hanging everything on a damn boot print. I'm tucking it away. It could belong to the killer, and that's good news for your skinny buddy in the hoodie."

The porch was dark. Wilcox stood at the screen door and looked around. "From here I can see both ends of Dewar and nobody can see me, not even the Tantabaums, unless they're on their front porch. And where did they find the Tantabaums, doctor?"

"There's a porch light, genius. There goes that theory," Petty scoffed.

"Well, what do we have here? No lightbulb, Dr. Petty."

"You are strange. Do you always talk your way through crime scenes?"

"Yes I do, but mostly to myself." He opened the screen door and felt wood molding. "I never know what's going to trigger things. Like this hole in the wood. Appears the screen door latch pulled out the eye. Could be something."

"Miss Middleton and Miss Tantabaum were remote viewers," Petty said as Wilcox inspected the door jam. "They could have been the targets."

"I know you don't have this skill set, but my gut tells me Middleton was the target. The Tantabaum sisters were collateral damage." Wilcox tore off the crime tape and tried the knob. "Place is locked up. This is gonna take a minute."

"You reached that conclusion from a boot print, the view from the porch, a missing bulb, and a broken screen door latch?"

"Pretty much." Wilcox stuck a paperclip in the lock and

wiggled it. "Crime scenes are my corpses, Victoria. Do I question you when you lift an eyelid or look in an ear?"

"Good parallel, I guess." *He called me Victoria . . .*

"Most killers take care of the big things. It's the little things that get them caught."

"Tell me you're not picking that lock."

Wilcox smiled. "I'm inspecting the keyhole with a paperclip." The knob popped and door opened an inch.

"Breaking and entering is illegal, Tony. This is a controlled crime scene and private property. Are you seriously going inside?"

"I've been warned, Officer Petty. I agree. Both of us should not risk felony charges for the unlawful entry of a residence. My defense is that the door was open. I'm good with that. I suggest you head back and sit in the car. Call me if someone comes. I'm going inside."

"That still makes me an accessory. I'd be just as guilty."

Headlights turned onto Dewar. Wilcox wrapped an arm around Petty's waist, lifted her off the ground, and swung her into the foyer as he closed the door behind. "Don't breathe." Lights accelerated down Dewar and disappeared. Petty held onto his neck, their lips inches apart and bodies fused. He lowered her. She clung. They waited in silence for several minutes.

He reached for his gun and he whispered; "Now we are not alone."

TWENTY-EIGHT

"What is worse than evil? The inability to hear it."
C.J. Weber

"What're yawl doin' here?" The crusty words echoed through the cold house. Wilcox nudged Petty outside the line of fire and raised his gun looking for the shadow that went with the question. Petty hiked her dress and reached for her Glock.

"Put your gun away, Detective Wilcox. You're the one trespassing, not me."

"Yeah?" He cocked it sending the metallic click into the mix. "If you know my name, you also know I'll shoot first and ask questions later. You got one chance to identify yourself."

Petty took her Glock off safety. Two guns are always better than one.

The table lamp popped on and lit the face of the man on the Okmulgee County Medical Examiner's website—but the haggard, bowlegged body with it was a surprise. Dr. Benjamin Proust looked more like a retired rodeo cowboy than a forensic pathologist. He raised his hands as a jester of good faith. "You don't need to shoot me, not now anyway."

Wilcox kept his gun up. "What're you doin' here, Proust?"

"Something told me you and Dr. Petty might come to Dewar tonight. Didn't make sense to drive all the way from Memphis in the morning and sit in a room with me and the sheriff looking at paper. Sheriff said nothing about you two wanting to visit the crime scene. That was odd."

"So you thought you'd wait for us in the dark?" Wilcox pushed.

"You got here before me," Proust said. "Those were my lights out front. Saw your car. Tennessee government plates were a give-away. I scooted up the alley and got here in under a minute. Came through the kitchen—no tape or locks." He smiled and looked away. "Guess you two got a little sidetracked in the foyer." He smiled.

"Wasn't anything happening in the foyer, Proust." *Bet you're not gonna tell me your timing is because you're a psychic. You kept that secret for a lifetime.* Wilcox's eyes darted around the room. "Elda got any security cameras?"

"Nope. Elda didn't believe in technology. She thought the government watched her through the TV." He pointed at the camera in the ceiling corner, the one Wilcox saw. "FBI put that one up there after the killings. You can shoot me if you want. I'm tired and going to sit down, now."

Petty pushed by Wilcox. "I'm Victoria Petty." Proust's eyes perused her like a doting father. He held her small hand as they sat next to each other on Elda' living room sofa.

Wilcox eased into the room like a cat looking for a dog. "Is that camera working?"

"Don't know." He turned to Petty. "I read about your work in

Dallas and recent Memphis appointment. You're an accomplished medical examiner, young lady." He caught Wilcox opening the curtain with a finger. "We don't get many visitors out this way. Henryetta's not the most exciting place to be."

"I don't know about that. I would enjoy a peaceful rural setting like this one day," Petty said.

"It has benefits." He cupped his vein riddle hands on his boney lap. His website bio said he just turned seventy. He looked eighty. His dark skin had a yellow tinge only a doctor would notice—kidney failure. The facial emaciation revealed more than the aging process. By the end of the conversation, Petty would know his medical condition.

"We get a couple homicides a year here, mostly family disputes. Farm accidents keep me busy. And we get our fair share of suicides, of course. People struggling to make ends meet give up from time to time." He looked at the ceiling and a hundred miles away. "They lose the will to live." He snapped out of it and said, "Strokes and heart attacks are the number one killer."

"I suppose the Dewar homicides were a shock to the community," Petty said.

Proust eyed Wilcox's back. "Devastating," he said as he rubbed his legs like he wanted to get off the school bus. "You two can walk around if you like. I'll turn on what lights there are."

Wilcox stayed at the window as he spoke. "Give us an overview on these homicides."

"Not much to add to the police reports online. No secrets here. This case was big news, caught the attention of the national media for a while."

"And it was covered one time in the Henryetta newspaper," Wilcox said. "Don't you think that's a little odd?"

"The *Daily Herald* covered it one time? I didn't know that. I don't' read a newspaper anymore. I get my news online now, when I have the time."

"What happened here, Dr. Proust?" Petty asked.

He closed his eyes and reflected. "It was terrible. Elda Middleton was my friend." He spoke as if baring witness before his God. "The Tantabaum sisters were my friends, too. I found Elda in this room. She was sitting in the chair over there."

Proust stared at the empty chair like she was still there. "Elda wore a teal nightgown, pink robe, and pink slippers. She'd been dead seven hours. If I didn't know better, I'd think she just nodded off in her chair. But she was strangled unmercifully."

"Strangled how?" Wilcox asked.

"A hand."

"One hand?"

"Yes. Her killer was left handed, too. The thumb crushed her thyroid cartilage. Four fingers embedded in the back of her neck and crushed vertebrae. I got DNA, but no matches."

"What other trauma did you observe?" Petty asked.

"Bruising. Inferior aspect of ribcage," he said as if he was dictating in his autopsy room. "Intense abdominal pressure. I believe Elda was picked up from behind and carried into the living room. The pressure was enough to cause her to black out. Then she was strangled. I pray she was not awake for that terrible experience."

"Was her body moved?" Petty asked.

"No. She was strangled in that chair."

"What about the college kids?" Wilcox asked.

"Same, but strangled in their beds. Both were strangled, but by different people."

"There were two?" Wilcox turned in surprise.

"Yes. The other was right-handed, a much smaller grip. He sat on the two college students and strangled them with two hands, not one."

"You get defensive wounds, any DNA?" Wilcox asked. "College boys would fight."

"There were defensive wounds. The right-handed killer took the fingers of his victims," Proust said. "Wire cutters. Guess he knew enough forensics."

Wilcox turned back to the curtain and opened it an inch. Dewar felt emptier than when they arrived. The sky was spitting and Proust left Wilcox with more questions. Dr. Petty could be watching a sad movie, or be elbow deep in a thoracic cavity eating a ham sandwich. Her face stayed the same, serene and confident. Wilcox had to admire her professionalism. Even her choice of wording was always precise and targeted. He knew she was working up to the Keller autopsies.

"Tell us about the Tantabaum sisters, Dr. Proust. What did the forensics tell you?"

"They were killed by the lefty. Both necks crushed by one large hand. He left their fingers. The Tantabaum sisters were in their late seventies, Elda eighty-two. None of these ladies presented a challenge. They died quietly and quickly."

"What's the motive here, Proust?" Wilcox asked. "Why were all these people killed?" The answer would shape the next series of questions. Did he know? If he did, would he tell the truth or dance? Either way, Wilcox would tighten the screws. Proust was not leaving Dewar Avenue without telling him something useful.

"I really do not know. I'm sure the sheriff can give you more tomorrow. I can tell you it was not a home invasion or burglary. Nothing was taken from either property. There were no family fortunes to leave behind, and no descendants to leave anything to. Both properties were willed to the county—charity. There were no pending lawsuits, conflicts, or squabbles."

"Okay. Great. Thanks for the report," Wilcox scoffed. "It's time to cut the bullshit, Proust."

His tired eyes found Petty's. He was an old man with no more fight. In a way Petty felt sorry for the doctor she had just met—if he had been bad, she knew there was a time when he had been good. Petty also knew his medical problem—her diagnostic skills were impeccable. Proust had no more reason to lie, but Wilcox would not see. If anything, Proust would tell them everything so he could die with a modicum of honor.

"Detective Wilcox, please stop." Petty had the tone Wilcox would test one time.

"We don't have time to foxtrot to the answers," he seethed. "We need answers."

Proust's eyes stayed on Petty's. He bit his lower lip and swallowed hard. "I'm dying."

"I know. Pancreatic cancer," she whispered.

"Very good, doctor." Proust smiled like the senior physician praising the student. "I've known a while. Like my patients, I too have been in denial for a while. That's over now. I have maybe a month."

"I'm sorry," Petty said.

"I can't do this anymore," he said.

A flash of lightning outed the lamp. Wilcox turned and saw the tiny, red dot blink. The ceiling device was connected. They were being monitored. The lamp flickered back on.

"We really don't have a lot of time. What can't you do anymore?" Wilcox pressed.

"It wasn't supposed to be like this." His hands trembled. "I don't know what is right anymore. I don't know who to trust. I don't know what is going to happen next."

"Killing remote viewers, is that what's out of control?" Wilcox asked. Proust sunk into the sofa like he finished running his last marathon. Petty leaned in and felt his pulse. His heart rate was increasing.

"We cannot help if you don't talk to us," Petty said. "It is easy. You can trust us. We only want the killing to stop." Wilcox watched from the curtains.

"They asked me to go to Stringtown in 2009," Proust said.

"They told me it was damage control." He rested his hand on his heart. "It was Alma and Arnold Keller." Tears rolled down his cheeks. "Someone killed them. It was awful. It was wrong. They were my friends, too."

"Who sent you to Stringtown?" Wilcox asked.

"Alfred Baldwin. He wasn't the Attorney General in 2009. He was the DIA. His people located the Kellers five years after they left the program—Gondola Wish. Alma and Arnold wanted out. They wanted their life back. Elda Middleton was their friend. She insisted they leave at night. Elda instructed them to find a small town. They may get away. Alfred did not want to lose any of the assets."

"Why did Baldwin call you in on the Stringtown homicides? Why didn't the Atoka County Coroner handle them?" Petty asked.

"Because I am one of them—I am a remote viewer. I joined Gondola Wish, a precursor to the Stargate Project."

"Why are remote viewers being terminated? And why are you still alive?" Wilcox dug.

"I left the program in 1985. I signed non-disclosure agreements and contracted with the government for off-site continuance. They paid for my medical school."

"They paid your medical school," Wilcox scoffed. "Why?"

"They wanted me to stay involved. They sent me money every month. All I they asked is I watch Elda and Ruby, and be available for an occasional assignment."

"Did you watch Alma and Arnold Keller, too?" Petty asked.

"No. I never went to Stringtown. I don't know who had them."

"How does a Henryetta Medical Examiner work Stringtown homicides?"

"Alfred called me in 2009. He asked me to go to Atoka County, outside Stringtown, the second week of October. They had a hotel room for me. I checked in and watched TV a couple days thinking it was another waste of time. Then I got the call. Alfred said there's a crime scene they wanted me work for the federal government, but low key."

"Did you tell them Atoka County had their own medical examiner?"

"Of course. I told Alfred it was outside my legal jurisdiction —I had to be invited by the Atoka County M.E. Alfred said he was out of town. The investigation was mine, and the FBI would keep a very low profile. Alfred said Alma and Arnold Keller were killed. He said it was a horrific crime we needed to get to the bottom of it—someone was hunting remote viewers. Alfred said it had to stay in the family, so I went."

"Didn't you find any of it suspicious, Proust?" Wilcox asked, scratching his head.

"Yes. Scheduled into a hotel in advance, sitting and waiting, and then there's a double homicide with chilling overtones. I guess I still believed in my government. I thought the Kellers were in danger and we were unable to protect them."

"Why would Alma and Arnold be in danger?" Petty asked.

"Psychic-weaponry has the attention of governments around the world. Whoever harnesses it will be a powerful force. People with true psychic gifts are rare. Alma and Arnold Keller were the most gifted psychics I've ever known and observed. I was certain one day their powers would put them in danger. Others would want to control."

"What did Baldwin want you to do in Stringtown?"

"He wanted the details of their deaths kept quiet. I was told to call the Atoka County Sheriff and offer my services. I was to say I was nearby. Since the Atoka County ME was unavailable, Sheriff Bennet jumped at the chance for help."

"Do you know who killed Alma and Arnold Keller?" Wilcox asked.

Proust glared at the detective. "No. I do not know."

"Is Alfred Baldwin your primary contact for the terminated Stargate project?"

"He's the only contact. I was with him in D.C. two nights ago. It is why I'm here talking to you tonight, that and my cancer. Suddenly things make more sense to me."

"Explain that comment," Wilcox said.

Proust dropped his head. "I knew Alfred was going to do it. I'm a remote viewer. I know things before they happen. I did nothing to stop it."

"What are you talking about?" Wilcox asked.

"At his brownstone in D.C., he shot a man by the fireplace. Shot him in the head."

"My God, you saw the U.S. Attorney General kill someone?" Petty gasped.

"Yes. A Russian spy. He infiltrated Stargate in 1993. Our government knew from the start. They used him to mislead the Russians on the progress of our psychic-weaponry program."

"So it was time to eliminate a mole," Wilcox muttered. "Happens all the time."

"Dr. Richard Tanner had become an unacceptable risk. He is responsible for many deaths. Now, most of the remote viewers are dead. Tanner's termination order came from the top."

"My God! I've known Richard Tanner since medical school. He's an accomplished geneticist with a prestigious practice at Vanderbilt."

"He was a home grown Russian spy, a serious danger to our country," Proust said. "He may have been involved in the termination of the Kellers and others in the Memphis area."

"We have nineteen names. We know there are twenty-three remote viewers. Can you give us the four missing names," Wilcox asked.

"Me, Mr. Baldwin, Dr. Swenson, and . . ."

Wilcox threw up his hand. "Quiet. Someone's here." A motor grumbled outside. He opened the curtain a sliver. The late model sedan from the Sterick sat out front, the lights off. The moon was white on the wet roof, the steaming hood, and the flat brimmed hat. The man in the long coat stood at the passenger door watching the house.

Petty saw Wilcox reach for his gun. "Who is number four?" she asked Proust. He blinked and loosened his tie. Something was wrong. He froze.

"You expecting someone?" Wilcox asked leaning an eye to the crack in the curtain.

"He's here," squeaked out Proust's tight lips. "Number four —" Proust gagged. His eyes widened, and blood left his head.

"Who's here?" Wilcox asked as he whirled around. "And who is number four? Petty, can you do something." But Proust was catatonic. His pale face began to deform, melt like wax. The hideous smile they saw so many times before was growing on Proust's face. It was pure terror.

"What's happening to him?" Wilcox gasped. Petty could not help the man dying in front of her. Then the trembling stopped. The raspy breathing stopped. The bulging eyes and twisting facial muscles froze. Proust fell back into the sofa with his arms and legs locked and back arched beyond normal limits. Petty grabbed the man's wrist. No pulse. Wilcox returned to the curtain. He already knew what Petty was going to say.

"He is dead, Tony."

On her last word the lamp flickered and went out. Wilcox opened the curtain and saw the old sedan parked in front of Elda's stone house. It sat empty in the middle of the road. The man in the flat-brimmed hat was gone.

TWENTY-NINE

"Courage is a peculiar kind of fear."
Charles Kennedy

"He's dead. What just happened?" Wilcox asked as he scanned the front yard and Dewar Avenue. Except for him holding a gun, Petty did not know the danger outside.

"This is how they die, Tony."

"The brain lesions."

"I won't know for sure until autopsy, but yes. Why the gun?" she asked.

"We've got company."

Petty joined him at the window and leaned an eye to the sliver in the curtain.

"He showed up when Proust started shaking."

"There's more going on here than I'm ready to accept medically," Petty muttered.

Wilcox grabbed her arm and walked her to dark stairs in the

entry. "Do me a favor. Do not ask questions. Do exactly what I say. If the guy out there did this to Proust, he knows we're in here. There's a good chance he wants to get rid of Proust and eliminate witnesses."

Wilcox aimed Petty up the tight staircase. They eased down the dark hall to the last bedroom. Inside, soft moonlight came in the only window. He pulled her close in a dark corner and held his gun on the doorway. When a damp gust lifted the curtains, he realized the window was open and their visitor could be in the house.

"Did you recognize our visitor?" she whispered.

He nodded and touched his lips. *He fits the description Keller gave me at the bank,* Wilcox thought. *A big man in a long coat and flat-brimmed hat. Nobody wears hats like that. And it's the car I saw at the Sterick building.*

"Best you return to Memphis." The raspy voice sent a hot, stale odor across the bedroom. They followed the words back to the tall shadow across the dark room. He stood in the corner by the window.

How could I miss him? Wilcox thought. *He wasn't there a minute ago.*

Wilcox moved his gun to the stranger. "Unless you can stop a bullet, I suggest you identify yourself," he ordered as he pulled the hammer back.

"Major T. L. Cankor."

"What in the hell are you doing here, Cankor?"

"Government business. Defense Intelligence Agency."

"Bullshit. Why would the DIA hide in a goddamn bedroom?"

"Hello Dr. Petty," he said. "I think you know why, Detective Wilcox. The Stargate Project is a top secret, government program. I should ask you why you're trespassing on private property."

"Seems I keep running into Stargate employees," Wilcox scoffed. "I find that interesting since the goddamn government killed the program twenty years ago. You're all lying bastards. Tell me Cankor, why is it when you psychos show up people die?"

"It's psychics, detective," he sneered.

"What did you do to Proust?" Wilcox snapped back.

"I saw a car outside. It should not be here. I suspected burglary and tried the doors and windows. I would have run-off or apprehend the intruder. This is a protected government site, Detective Wilcox." Cankor pointed. "I climbed a tree. This window was unlocked. Simple as that. I had nothing to do with Dr. Proust's death."

"I didn't say he was dead."

Cankor ran fingers down his lapels and stepped toward them undeterred by the gun. "You think you're a smart guy, Wilcox. The fact is you are over your head. I suggest you two forget what you saw here tonight. Leave Henryetta and return to Memphis. I will pretend you did not break into this government-secured crime scene. The DIA will take care of Dr. Proust."

"You know what I think?" Wilcox said. "I think you had something to do with Proust dying tonight. Here's the problem. I don't care if you did it with a gun, a knife, a baseball bat, or some weird, psycho, bullshit weapon. As far as I'm concerned, it's a homicide, I'm a cop with a gun, and you're a person of interest."

"You know nothing." Cankor stepped closer. Wilcox raised his gun. "There are bad people in this world. Stargate is a way to stop them. The day we fall behind is the day you will be speaking another language or dead. I suggest you stay out of our way."

"When innocent people die, someone's lost their way Cankor. Looks like the DIA is killing remote viewers and their families. I'll bet my pension you had something to do with Middleton's and Tantabaum's deaths, and the three innocent people in the wrong place that night. You gotta be one sick son-of-a-bitch to kill little, old ladies and college students."

"Wild speculation with no proof wastes time, Detective Wilcox. I suggest you . . ."

"You're boot print is in the garden, Cankor. I bet there's a mountain of photographs taken that day. Five homicides don't happen often around here. I'm sure we can confirm the eroded boot print out there happened the night of the killings. I'll bet we have pictures of muddy tracks on Elda Middleton's front porch and in the house. I'll bet we have your DNA and prints, Cankor. No, you're as dumb as any other scumbag feeding on society."

"I spoke with Alfred Baldwin," Petty said. "He's worried about the national killing spree and misuse of psychic-weapons. Is he looking for you, Major Cankor?

"DIA, not DOJ, is in charge here. We're the watchdog, Dr. Petty. Alfred Baldwin and his people will soon be managed by us. No need for you to be concerned."

"Admit it. You are killing remote viewers, Cankor," Wilcox pressed.

"You know the answer to that question. You met the killer on Main Street. You saw him at the Sterick building," Cankor spoke hypnotically as he eased around the bed.

"Don't move another step, Cankor. I only need one excuse," Wilcox threatened.

In the dark bedroom they could not see Cankor close his eyes for the first time. And they could not see the odd, flat smile of demented concentration. An invisible force pulled Petty from Wilcox's side and held her against the wall. Wilcox struggled, but could not even turn his head. Frozen in place, his gun dropped from his open hand and slid to Cankor's feet.

"I suppose cooperation is a foreign concept to you people." Cankor sighed as he raised his hand and watched Wilcox and Petty slide down the wall to the floor unable to move or speak.

"I'm tired of this house." Cankor looked around the bedroom and out the front window. He turned back to Wilcox and Petty, two flies entangled in an impossible web. "And I'm tired of people like you, always so judgmental. So pushy. Pathetic weaklings in my way like Elda."

Cankor huffed and closed his eyes a second time. He touched his forehead and his flat smile returned to his callous face. Within seconds Wilcox and Petty began to tremble. Blood started to leave their heads. Their muscles started to cramp. The overwhelming sense of terror crept in and their bodies responded.

THIRTY

"It is man who makes truth great, not truth making man great."
Confucius

"Leave them alone."

The words floated into the dark room. Petty and Wilcox were paralyzed on the floor.

Cankor opened his eyes. He knew the voice well. "I will not," he spewed.

"You know my capabilities."

Cankor turned to the paltry figure standing in the doorway. "They've not been tested for a while. Are you sure you want to risk it?"

"Don't make me hurt you."

Cankor's rage churned, but when he tried to move only his coat swayed.

"We cannot do this anymore."

Cankor tugged at his legs. He was bound to the floor. "You are evil like me."

Wilcox could only stare at his gun a few feet away. Petty struggled to turn her head. She had to see the one in the doorway. "Who—are—you?"

The shadow leaned into the room and turned from Cankor. "I am Hunter Keller, Dr. Petty."

On Keller's last word Cankor's boots broke free. He spun and dove out the open window.

Wilcox broke free. Without a word he scooped up his gun and dove after Cankor. Sliding on his belly down the wet porch roof, he grabbed at shingles and dug boot toes stopping at the edge. His head hung over the side of the twenty-foot drop as he watched his gun disappear into Elda's hedges and the old sedan fishtail down Dewar.

In the bedroom Hunter Keller helped Dr. Petty from the floor. It was the first time she saw the one accused of killing so many—she stared and wondered what just happened. Although Hunter Keller was a man, she saw a boy. He reached for her hand as if to give her a secret. A ribbon of moonlight touched his face and she saw his eyes. At that moment she knew he was different, and Hunter Keller's eyes would always say more than words.

He whispered, "No one can find me. People will die."

* * *

At two in the morning they pulled into Bald Knob Wildlife Reserve north of Little Rock. Wilcox picked another lock and swung open the gate as Petty shook her head—the risk of two counts of illegal entry. Staying in an Oklahoma or Arkansas hotel was not an option, and Highway 64 and Interstate 40 to Memphis were monitored. A night in the woods made sense.

"Who the hell closes a damn wildlife reserve—animals need a

break?" Wilcox muttered as he drove into the empty woods. "Since when are their hours of operation—never heard of it. You gotta have campers all over. How do they round em all up in a place that's gotta be twenty-five square miles of nothin'.'"

Petty ignored him and Hunter Keller was asleep. The storms moved out as the cold air filled the night and they snaked two miles into the dark woods. They found a small clearing with a weathered picnic table. Wilcox started a fire. They ate from a bag of random groceries picked up in Beebe—their only gas stop. Although the convoluted route from Henryetta to Bald Knob added miles and time, Wilcox had a plan. They would go to Jonesboro in the morning and then Memphis in the late afternoon. He would not lose Keller along the way.

"Why enter from the north? And why Memphis late tomorrow?" Petty asked.

"Because they're watchin' highways, hotels, the police station, morgue, and your place and my place," Wilcox huffed. He threw a rock in the woods like a major league pitcher taking out a batter. His frustration over the mounting, unsolved deaths with no end in sight was getting to him. "For a brilliant, forensic doctor, I wonder about common sense. Maybe you haven't noticed our passenger attracts attention and people die."

"We're all tired, Tony."

Leaning on the car puffing on his cigarette he studied the squirrelly little guy sitting at the picnic table. Keller did not look like a serial killer, but they never do. Wilcox met him on South Main two weeks earlier. Keller stirred-up his gut like every other guilty slime ball. Wilcox had razor-sharp instincts he didn't understand, his gut was always right. Now he stared at the killer who slept on his backseat all the way from Dewar. Driving in silence for hours, Wilcox stewed over the facts he understood and set aside those he could not explain—like what happened in the bedroom at Elda Middleton's house.

"You always sleep after a fight," Wilcox poked.

"What're you doing?" Petty whispered as she nudged him at the edge of the car.

He could not hide his ire any more. Too many were dead. He glared at the one his gut said to hunt the last two weeks, the one who always got away leaving bodies behind. Now, there he sat, his head down, a blanket draped over his boney shoulders, and his hair shooting in all directions.

What are you doing now? Wilcox wondered as he lit another smoke.

"Blocking," Keller answered. He moved his gaze to the empty diet coke can on the table.

Did you just read my mind? I don't believe that shit. You're playing games. Wilcox walked over to the table and sat on the edge. Like a hungry bear he hovered over the twig of a man. "What the hell is 'blocking'?"

"Preventing others from reading his thoughts, or locating him," Petty said.

"Something like that," Keller said.

"Are you blocking now?" Wilcox asked.

"Not now. No one's close enough to be a problem." He slipped his hoodie over his head and pulled the blanket over his chest.

"I'm supposed to believe this crap? Do you believe this crap, Petty?"

"I don't know, Tony. I'm still trying to figure out what happened on Dewar."

"Simple. Hypnosis. The power of suggestion. That Cankor guy hypnotized us, made us believe we couldn't move. Keller shows up and we snap out of it. They do it in Vegas acts— hypnotize a whole audience."

"I don't know about that," Petty muttered.

"What you should be thinking about is that another remote

viewer—Proust—got killed and this guy shows up. Seems to happen a lot." Wilcox turned back to Keller. "It's best you start talkin' to me. It's not looking good for you."

"I'm not what you think I am," he whispered still staring at his coke can.

"The evidence against you is indisputable and overwhelming," Wilcox slapped the can into the woods and leaned closer.

"Nice touch, Tony," Petty scoffed. "You think you're in your interrogation room at the police station? Do you really think you're going to scare him into a confession? Give me a break. You're better than that. You have nothing but a gut feeling. There's a lot more you cannot explain, nobody can explain." Petty approached the table. "You have no real evidence, and you know it. You don't even have enough to hold him an hour. He could leave right now."

"You're wrong. I can put this guy at every homicide. That's enough."

"No it's not, Tony. What you have is all circumstantial. So he's in pictures? No prosecutor's going to touch it if that's all you have. I know the evidence. You don't have any. I suggest you stop pushing him around and start listening to him. He didn't have to come to Dewar to save us—hypnosis or not. Let the man talk. Maybe you will get answers to questions. You can't explain a lot. It's time to listen."

"Why were you at my homicides, Keller? Why were you with the truck driver outside Blytheville, and why were you at the Sterick building, and at Broken Bow, and Middleton's house? Did you kill your parents?"

"Slow it down, Tony," Petty said.

"Are you gonna tell me you're innocent? Are you gonna tell me you were at all those crime scenes to help the poor bastards? If that's your story, you gotta be one miserable guy because you failed every damn time. They're all dead, Keller." Wilcox yelled.

Keller cringed and sunk into his blanket. Wilcox jumped off the table, found a tree, and slammed his fist into the trunk. Petty pulled his arms to his sides and said, "Don't do this to yourself, Tony. We can figure it out." She reached in his breast pocket and pulled out his silver flask and unscrewed the cap. "Take a few swallows and come back when you have control of your emotions. We have an opportunity to get a lot of answers from a remote viewer. There is more going on here than we have dared to imagine."

Wilcox nodded and tilted his flask. After he swallowed, his eyes met Petty's. His pupils dilated and brow relaxed. She put a cigarette in his mouth and lit it. "I don't approve, but . . ."

"I know what you know," Keller said. They turned back to him. Keller was now standing by the popping fire with his back to the dark depths of the woods.

"What does that mean?" Wilcox asked as the rage bubbled inside. Petty turned his head with a soft hand to his jaw. They looked at each other again. "Okay. I won't shoot him," he said and then winked.

They sat at the picnic table across from the fire and Keller. Wilcox stared at the skinny paradox in the hoodie. "You say you know what we know. Tell us what you mean by that statement. We can take it a lot of ways."

"It is more efficient to tell you what you do not know," Keller said.

"Okay. More efficient," Wilcox said, his ire moving to curiosity.

"Our time together is limited. This night is not over. More danger is ahead." Keller looked down on the fire and spoke like a prophet. "Tomorrow night it will happen."

"What will happen tomorrow night?" Wilcox asked.

Petty interrupted. "Hunter, help us understand by starting where you think you should."

He nodded. "The government's psychic-weapons program never ended."

"We know," Wilcox snapped. "Most people with brains know governments lie."

"You know, but you do not believe," Keller said.

"Why does that matter?" Wilcox asked.

"It puts you at a disadvantage. Like the others, you are outside my reality, what I have lived with all my life. Unless you believe, you will never find the truth you seek."

Keller turned to the dark woods and looked deep. Wilcox followed his line of sight, but saw nothing. Keller spoke without emotion. "You know my parents were remote viewers, but you do not know I am the reason they are dead."

"You killed your parents? Are you confessing?" Wilcox pressed.

"My mother carried me in 1978. She and my father would leave Gondola Wish that year. Our government lost its moral compass."

"What the hell does any of that mean?" Wilcox snapped.

"Gondola Wish was one of the several names given the government psychic-weaponry research program," Petty said. "You know it as the Stargate Project, the last iteration, the one the CIA supposedly terminated in 1995."

"Elda Middleton was my mother's close friend. Elda was the first remote viewer to see the bad people. She possessed the strongest precognitive skills—could see futures better than others. Elda knew first that one day the progeny of remote viewers would be hunted and—"

"—terminated," Wilcox said flicking his butt in the fire. "Are you the one Elda saw? Are you the one hunting remote viewers?"

Keller ignored him. He knew self-doubt fed his anger and

only Wilcox could fix it. "Most governments know remote viewing is the most advanced intelligence gathering tool in the modern age."

"Intelligence gathering is not killing people," Wilcox said under his breath.

"And they know psychic-weapons can be developed to kill," Keller added.

"You lost me at intelligence gathering," Wilcox said.

"I will explain. Imagine sitting in any meeting in the world whenever and wherever you wanted. You see and hear everyone and everything, and no one knows you are there. If you could do as I described, would you agree you would obtain accurate and detailed information?"

"Of course. That's why we have spies, Keller. They do exactly what you said."

"Remote viewing allows you to do what a spy does, but you are thousands of miles away from the meeting, you are invisible to your enemy, and you have no risk of compromise. RV intelligence gathering is more accurate than any existing espionage methodology. We can attend all meetings past, present, and future and no cost and with few people involved."

"If I believed in that psychic mumbo-jumbo, I agree those would be benefits."

"Governments understand the advantages of eliminating antiquated, complex, costly, and unsecured intelligence operations that expose them to the enemy," Keller said.

"If remote viewing is as you say, it makes perfect sense our government would want to control it and take it underground," Petty said. "The country possessing it would have a clear advantage in the world."

"It's fantasy," Wilcox mumbled lighting a cigarette.

"My body is here, Mr. Wilcox, but my mind is on the balcony at your Mud Island condo."

Wilcox blew a cloud into the conversation. "Parlor tricks, Keller. I'm not naive."

"I am looking at the cracked glass on the table. You refuse to let it go. It's the glass you threw across the room the night you returned from the Memphis Public Library. It was the night your partner—Alex Harris—was killed. You still blame yourself for his death."

"Easy narrative, Keller. I'm sure you visited my balcony while in Memphis. You probably saw the cracked glass. The rest of your scenario is logical. Of course I feel responsible for Alex's death. Every good cop who losses a partner feels they could have done something. All you're doing is putting together obvious pieces of information to create your mesmerizing story."

Keller ignored him. "Alex Harris was used, Detective Wilcox. You were returning from Cape Town, South Africa, a private jet owned by Albert Bell. You were returning from hunting for three very bad men. They were surviving board members, a secret society, Gilgamesh. You were under a church on Devil's Peak—a secret fortress. Max, the man with you, is now dead. The three men escaped—they too would die later at the end of a serial killer's knife. When you landed in Memphis, you got the call on the tarmac. The plane taxied to your car. You were instructed to go alone to the Memphis Public Library. Do I need to describe . . . ?"

"Stop," Wilcox demanded staring at the popping fire. *No one would know those details.*

"I count 183 cigarette butts in the ceramic flower pot next to the railing," Keller said. "You got the plant last year—October 15. It is a dried stick now. It never had a chance because you never watered it—you don't take care of living things. But you kept it on your balcony, the place where you drink your scotch and smoke your Marlboros. The place where you try to make sense of a world filled with bad people—there are just too many. You think you are not making a difference, Detective Wilcox, but you are. Since the beginning you took bad people off the streets of Memphis. Your actions allowed 347 lives to continue. You need to know that."

"Is he close, Tony?" Petty asked. But Wilcox's eyes were locked on Keller's.

"The potted plant is the last thing your sister gave you. She died the day after sending it to you—a car accident in Boston. You had a friend investigate. You thought you were responsible. You thought Gilgamesh. The plant came with a note, her last words. She said she was sorry for the distance after your parents died. She said it hurt too much. She could not lose you too. She said she loved you always. You burned the note, but the ashes are in the pot. You look at them every time you sit on your balcony. And every time, you look up and wink at Bethany."

Wilcox looked away. "You can stop now. I don't know why you are doing this."

"Because 'you' must believe in me, Anthony Wilcox. You must see the unexplainable is real. Like in your world there is good and there is evil." As the glow of the fire seemed to gather around the small man, Petty and Wilcox stared in wonder.

Keller lifted his eyes from the dancing flames and met Wilcox's cold eyes. They stared. Then Keller said, "The time will come when 'only you' can decide the outcome."

"Why me?" Wilcox asked.

"I can only tell you what is and was and will be, not why."

"This has always been about more than remote viewing. It's about the lesions." Petty said.

"I don't know if I can explain in a way you can comprehend," Keller said.

"You must try," Petty said.

Keller took a deep breath. Sparks left the fire and a breeze lifted his hair as if another presence entered their circle. "Imagine you are being carried away in the jaws of a lion—alive."

"Wonderful," Wilcox scoffed. "Going to be eaten." *My worst nightmare.*

"Yes. And more lions are coming. You are dinner for the pride. Soon they will tear your body apart. Your pain will be unimaginable. Your death is welcomed. If it was only up to your conscious brain, you would experience everything. But we have an unconscious process that takes over. We avoid the pain and experience on the way to death."

"What he says is medically true, Tony. The body responds to stimuli all the time on its own. In the case he described, the body would respond without conscious thought—an adrenalin release, heart rate and blood pressure rise, shock, atrial fibrillation (erratic heart beat)—and then without intervention, cardiac arrest. We have no control over any of it."

"Psychic manipulation of the amygdala creates unimaginable terror triggering the things Dr. Petty shared. The lesions on the amygdala are hidden. The visible signs you have seen—the eyes, and pale deformed faces, and rigid postures. These are all related to the terror experienced."

"You explained it well, and you just made my case against you," Wilcox said. "You've already demonstrated your psychic abilities. And you were at my crime scenes. I think you even tried to do it to me, but for some reason it did not work."

"I stopped them," Keller whispered.

"Tony, you said he pulled you from a burning car. Why would he try to kill you?"

"Did you pull me from my car, Keller?" Wilcox asked. "Or did you plant that thought in my brain?"

"You were heavy."

"Why would you do that?"

The campfire flames washed over Keller's boyish face. "They want to control it."

"You didn't answer my question." Wilcox pressed.

"Let him speak, Tony," Petty demanded.

"They want to control psychic-weapons. They must eliminate remote viewers and people most likely to be their enemy in the future—descendants of remote viewers. When they came for you—an outsider—their plan moved to another level. I could not run or hide anymore. Attacking law enforcement and unsuspecting obstacles confirmed my worst fears. They are close to reaching their goals. No one is safe. They must be stopped."

"Who are they," Petty asked.

"Bad people," Keller said as he cringed.

"Are you, or have you ever been, one of them?" Wilcox asked. The weight of the discussion was moving him. Is it possible Hunter Keller is simply telling the truth?

"I am alone. I am the problem." Keller said. "I am the alpha. They are attempting to develop something that comes natural to me—my psychokinetic abilities."

"Please educate us," Dr. Petty said.

"Psychokinesis is the psychic ability to influence a physical system without physical interaction," Keller said.

"Through psychic manipulation, the lesions are produced on the amygdala launching the emotion of unbridled terror," Petty reviewed. "That in turn triggers the cardiac arrest and leads to death. But Hunter, you said they are attempting to develop this psychokinetic ability. That means it is not mastered. This explains the stabbing and strangulation of our victims with lesions."

Wilcox sat in silence staring at the mystery in the hoodie by the fire.

"I see the future," Keller said. "I knew Dr. Proust would be attacked tonight. I did not stop it. I am responsible for many deaths. Detective Wilcox is right. I'm a part of this nightmare."

Wilcox pitched his butt in the fire. "Proust died with no one touching him. I think this Cankor guy has mastered this psychokinetics. If I'm right, they don't need you anymore, Keller. They don't need the alpha. Your days are numbered."

"Seeing the future does not make you responsible for the future, Hunter," Petty said.

"I feel responsible."

"You can't save the world," Wilcox said under his breath as he wrapped his head around the possibility Hunter Keller was as much of a victim as any of his cold cases.

"Your psychokinetic skills are genetic," Petty said. "Cankor's are learned. Inherited traits are stronger and more adaptive, genetic based. They evolve. Major Cankor would need to continually educate himself. That would require dedicated time and discipline to reproduce a genetic strength. But you still can't learn to be a Picasso. You must be born Picasso."

Keller nodded. "Major Cankor is much older than me. He does have natural physical and mental limitations that would present some limitations."

"That would explain why he ran from Dewar. When I asked Hunter who he was, the distraction was enough for him to break free," Petty said. "Your focus makes you stronger."

"Bone said they needed my DNA. I was the future of psychokinetic weaponry."

"This is about genetic engineering psychic-weapons, Tony. The U.S. Government is attempting to control the genetic aspects of psychokinetics. This explains Mr. Baldwin's involvement. Major Cankor must work for Baldwin."

The three stared at the glowing embers. Wilcox still struggled. The concepts went against everything he knew. It went against his instincts, too. He would have to choose.

Parapsychology research is progressing—albeit fringe science, Petty thought. *We use such a small portion of our brain—I guess it's possible. Why did Alfred Baldwin tell me they were working on levitation? How is that connected?*

A cold blast of air slithered through the pines. Wilcox watched a trail of sparks from the small fire snake into the night. "Keller, don't move," he said as he reached for his gun.

"What're you doing," Petty asked as she touched his moving arm. "You're not going to shoot him?"

Petty looked up. The glow of the fire fell on an enormous stag standing directly behind Keller. The bull elk was over five feet at its muscular shoulders. He had a three-foot rack. Seven-hundred pounds of wild animal stood a few feet behind Hunter Keller.

"He is one big buck," Wilcox muttered as he raised his gun. But he did not have a clear shot. The bull's head stayed behind Keller's torso. "If he's spooked, one sweep of those antlers will tear Keller to shreds."

They sat still. Wilcox cocked the gun and waited for an opening. Then the bull elk stepped even closer. He nosed the back of Keller's head. Wilcox had to shoot soon. He only needed a few inches right or left.

Without taking his eyes off the fire, Keller reached back and rubbed the thick neck of the bull elk. They watched the enormous animal bob its head and snort. It backed away and trotted into the woods where a herd of a dozen more took shape in the shadows. They melted into the trees and were gone.

"Ah—what just happened?" Wilcox asked.

"Animals like me," Keller said.

"Animals like you?" Wilcox left the picnic table to inspect the surrounding woods. "I know elk are in Arkansas, but I did not know they were so damn big." He approached Keller staring at the fire. "That bull wandered into our camp. They don't do those things, Keller. Bull elk avoid people. I guess their curious out here, this wildlife reserve. You're lucky he decided to leave."

Petty changed the subject. "When did you know you were different?"

"When I was ten-years old the headaches started. I saw things. At first I thought they were dreams. Then they turned into nightmares—I saw terrible things. I didn't talk about it until Bone. I trusted him. He listened and tried to help me understand. My parents tried to help too, but I guess like most kids I did not want to listen to them until it was too late."

"Help us understand. What do you see?" Petty asked.

"I see everything. It is like a movie theater without walls, hundreds of screens. Now I can move them around, shuffle them like cards. I can stop on any one I want, and watch that movie. It can be from the past, present, or future. When I was young it was confusing. There were too many. They never stopped. I had no control."

"How did Bone Jackson help you?" Petty asked.

"Sorting the movies in my head. How to focus. How to turn it off."

"Did you know your parents were going to be killed?" Wilcox asked.

"No." Keller took a deep breath. "I avoided those movies. Death is eminent."

"Were you the reason people were killed on Dewar?" Petty asked.

"They came for me. The killing was to send a message. It would not stop."

"They want more than your DNA," Petty muttered.

"Slow down," Wilcox said. "You keep saying they. Are you talkin' about Cankor and his people, or the government—Baldwin and Swenson—or a covert operation, or the Russians?"

Keller straightened up. "We need to leave immediately!"

On Keller's last word bobbing lights broke over a hill a half mile away. Wilcox poured coffee on the fire as the lights moved between the trees getting brighter, and the racing engine and grinding gears got louder.

"They're here for me," Keller said as they jumped into the car.

"Can we talk to them?" Wilcox asked.

"No. They will kill you and Dr. Petty. No negotiation."

Wilcox shoved the key into the ignition. The battery clicked and went silent. "What's happening? I didn't have a battery problem before."

The lights neared. "They're doing it," Keller said.

THIRTY-ONE

"I would rather trust a woman's instinct than a man's reason."
Stanley Baldwin

Nashville, Tennessee

The light under her door poured six inches into the dark hotel room until someone stopped and tried the lock. They found her.

Abby Patterson checked into the Drury Inn because she saw a silver Tahoe in the lot. After an hour of waiting back at the parking garage, her tail had found her empty car—their subject had gotten away.

Abby had turned the tables. For the next eight hours she tailed her tail. They pulled into the Drury. Abby went inside wearing her black wig and baseball cap, no longer the blonde. She blended into the crowd and observed. Then she got a room.

The shadow lingered at her door, and she considered her options. She could leap off the balcony into the pool three floors down, but the twelve-foot distance from the building made it a bad option. If the Russians stormed the room, they had her cold.

Watching the crack under her door, she pressed her cell to her head. *Marybeth, pick up.*

"Hi sweetheart," bubbled into her ear. "I've been thinking about you. Thought we were going drinking tonight. You never called."

"I'm in a little situation—kinda tied up at the moment. I need your help, honey."

"Are you on surveillance, another cheater?"

"In a way, dear. Right now I have some bad people looking for me."

"Oh God, Abby. Looking for you? Why would they be looking for you?"

She changed hands reaching for a cigarette. "I need you to focus, Marybeth. There are a couple of Russian guys looking for me. I'll explain later. These are the kind of people who beat you and take you away for a long time. I'm at the Drury in Nashville, room 307. I need you to get over here right now. Bring me an outfit and the red wig I left at your place."

"It's after midnight. Are we going out afterwards? Should I get dressed up?"

"Have you heard a thing I've said, girl?"

"Well yes, but I need to know if I should change into something more appropriate."

"Marybeth, just forget I called. This is too dangerous. I'm gonna do something else."

"I'm getting in my car now. I'm turning the key. I'm coming. I have your outfit and the red wig in a bag in my backseat. I was going to give it to you the next time anyway. This is no problem. I'm five minutes away. Don't worry, I'm not drunk. Well, I only had a few."

"Are you sure you can do this?" Abby asked watching her door.

"Of course I can. I'm not an airhead."

"When you get to the Drury, come straight to room 307. Do not look at or talk to anyone.

You are a hotel guest coming in late. Walk straight to the elevator. If someone gets on with you, get off and go to the girl's room at the end of the lobby. It is a very normal thing to do. You must take the elevator up alone. Press floors three, four, and five."

"I got it. I'm almost there, honey."

"Good. I'm gonna let you go. Don't forget the clothes and wig, darlin'." Abby disconnected and stepped onto the balcony with a cigarette. *There's no way I could make that jump . . .*

The clouds moved into Nashville stirring the wind. The rain neared. The forecast said thunderstorms around three in the morning. Abby saw the silver Tahoe parked next to her car. *How'd you figure that out?* Two men stood under a light. Abby backed into the shadows of the balcony, kicked her heels into the room. The next balcony was five feet away. She could make it.

Four minutes later Marybeth's BMW pulled into the parking lot with the top down. *God Marybeth, I said low profile.* Abby watched her roll the aisles for a space. The two backed up to the Tahoe. When she passed by she waved. *What are you doing?* The two watched her park. Abby swallowed as Marybeth approached the Tahoe. She stopped. *You're talking to them. My God, girl!* Then she pointed to the hotel. Abby sunk into the wall below the railing as they turned and looked at the third floor. *Why are you pointing to my floor?* One started running to the hotel. The other picked up Marybeth and carried her kicking to the silver Tahoe.

She had less than a minute head start. When she reached the

ground level she shot through the garden into the parking lot pulling her gun. She got to the Tahoe looking back at her balcony. The Russian stood with his fist in the air and ran back into her room—he was on his way. When Abby reached the Tahoe and swung open the door, she put her gun to the head of the Russian. Marybeth was half dressed in the backseat.

"Move it," she said. "You're in America. This looks like rape. I can shoot you." She pushed the muzzle into his cheek and he eased out of the SUV. She felt for keys in the ignition.

"You not shoot me. I go," he said.

"Run, you Soviet bastard."

The Tahoe fishtailed out of the parking lot onto the highway. "You okay?"

"I'm fine," Marybeth said as she finished dressing.

"What were you doing talking to these guys and pointing at my floor?"

"I was walking by minding my own business," Marybeth said. "They asked if I wanted to go dancing. Did I have any friends?"

"I told you Russians were chasing me. I said talk to nobody. I needed you here as a cover. What part did you not understand?" Abby found a quiet road and apartments. She watched her mirrors. *Never should have called you . . .*

"I'm sorry. I don't know what I was thinking."

She turned into the complex with the fewest lights and crawled through the lot. "We need to ditch the Tahoe. And you need to listen to me." She parked and they jumped out. Abby checked three cars before finding one unlocked.

"Get in. No questions."

"But you can't just take someone's car, Abby."

"I'm not real happy with you at the moment. Just get in and watch." Abby leaned under the steering column feeling for the wires. *I haven't done this in a long while.*

Abby Patterson did not see the black Suburban turn into the

apartment complex. And she did not see it roll up behind them with no lights. Marybeth was checking her nails and Abby was under the dash touching wires and cranking the engine.

Three got out with guns. The driver's door opened. The fist met the side of her head.

THIRTY-TWO

"There is love of course. And then there's life, its enemy."
Jean Anouilh

Memphis, Tennessee

"Do we just kill him now or take him out of here and kill him later . . . ?"

ICU released Baily to a private room the day Wilcox and Petty had left for Henryetta. Brain swelling went down and vitals returned to normal. They moved him because they needed the bed. They also pulled the 24/7 guard detail. Cottam was satisfied the Oklahoma shooters were not coming to Memphis— Baily convinced him Hunter Keller was the primary target. Although the director accepted Jackson and Baily were collateral damage, it would not alter the MPD pursuit. When a police officer is shot, they would not stop until the shooter was found.

Baily's visitors were homicide buddies, beat cops, and paramedics. The day his vitals stabilized the mayor came by with a small contingency of the city council and large contingency of news media—the mayor never passed up a "shot-cop" photo-op. The MPD director came every day. His visits were after hours and alone. When Baily was in critical condition, Cottam sat in the dark until they sent him home. Every cop was family. When they moved Baily to a private room in stable condition, the director came every other day. With his young detective now on the road to a full recovery, he could increase his focus on the hunt.

They required the head bandage until the stitches healed. But Baily kept pulling it off during his nightmares. The orders were to tie his hands to the railings at night.

The crescent-shaped incision line marked the position of the metal plate covering a third of his skull. The bullet shattered the right side of his skull and buried deep in the occipital lobe. When Baily arrived in the ER, they stabilized and concluded the damage was done and internal bleeding stopped. Surgical retrieval of the slug was too risky—more brain damage, paralysis, and possible death. The neurosurgeon closed him up. They left the bullet and hoped for the best.

Detective Baily appeared normal except for the shaved head, stitches, and selective loss of memory. Few knew his future was unpredictable. Baily could drop dead any minute or live a long, normal life. The prognosis for brain injuries was always the same —survival always a miracle.

Baily got the bad news the day after Wilcox and Petty left for Oklahoma. If Baily lived, he would be eating hospital food another two weeks. His stay was non-negotiable. After release he would sit on his hands a minimum of six months. Although it was not said, it was unlikely he would ever return to active duty. At the moment he was alive and improving. Six months is a long time away. A lot can happen. Maybe he would be the exception to the rule.

"Well hello Nurse Crowley," he said in his most alluring voice. He watched the attractive lady of color punch her keyboard on her mobile work center outside his door. She rolled it into the room never looking up. The night shift—with his favorite nurse—took forever to come. Baily was more than eager to get closer to the lady of his dreams, but he kept striking out.

"Good evening Mr. Baily," she said with eyes on the screen and fingers tapping the keys.

"You miss me, Nurse Crowley?" She smiled. "You know I'm very grateful you saved my life. I need to do something to repay you, like buy you dinner, or take you for a walk along the Mississippi River at sunset."

Crowley looked up for the first time. "I did not save your life, detective. The doctors saved your life. You need to take them for a walk on the river."

He leaned so he could see more of her. The tall, slender, curvy lady with athletic legs had to be a marathon runner. Her calves were firm with nice ankles. She fit well in her white uniform with the buttons up the front. Baily saw the top button undone as always, but he also noticed the bottom two were undone. That was new. As she propped her foot on the edge of the cart, her dress opened at least five inches above her perfect knee.

Did you do it for me? He wondered. *Are you warming up to me? Maybe you're playing hard to get—I know you like me. Or am I imagining everything—wishful thinking? If you're like other women, you have zero interest in hooking up with a homicide detective, especially one with a bullet in his head. It's the story of my life. Nobody wants to fall in love with a guy who could get killed every day. Hell, I'm lying in bed like a cripple. Ms. Crowley's gotta be looking out for her future—a stable man with a nine to five job. Someone without a bullet in their head. I need to start dealing with reality. I can't run around anymore. I need to make every minute count. I need to think about what I'm gonna do if I can't go back to the Memphis police department.*

"I'm sorry. Did you think I was asking you on a date? I'm sure Mr. Crowley would not approve. I was simply going to do something nice to show my gratitude."

"There's no Mr. Crowley," she said still punching data into the computer.

"A beautiful girl like you is single? I find it hard to believe." She flashed her soft, brown eyes at him, but this time with a smile. "Then you must have a fiancé or boyfriend or significant other. When I get out of here, I would be happy to pay for a dinner for two. You've taken care of me from the start, and I want to do something nice."

"There's no boyfriend or significant other, Detective Baily." She left her mobile work station, walked to the bedside, and reached for his hand. His heart beat in his throat. She turned his hand over and pinched his wrist looking at her watch. "Heart rate's a little high."

"Ah, I'm in shock," he teased.

Crowley put the BP cuff around his upper arm and stethoscope in her ears. Pressing the diaphragm inside his elbow, she held onto his elbow. She released the pressure. As the air hissed, she listened and watched for the first interruption in the dropping mercury. Baily perused her flawless complexion and full lips and high cheekbones—he was a visual person. He already liked her gentle personality and professionalism. He moved his finger on the back of her arm watching for a reaction—nothing. Nurse Crowley focused on her sphygmomanometer.

"Your pressure's a little high, detective. You need rest,

including your imagination." She set a cup with pills on the side table. "Take these, pain medication and antibiotics."

"I want to know you more than just as your patient." *Did I say it out loud? Where did it come from? Are you an idiot? Don't ever say what you're thinking.*

She draped the BP cuff over the railing. "It is one of my rules, Mr. Baily. I do not mix my personal life with my professional life."

"I have an idea," he said. "Give me your phone number, and have me assigned to another nurse. That way we can abide by your rules."

Nurse Crowley smiled as the door closed behind her.

Midnight rounds were over when the three men in hospital greens and hanging surgical masks eased out of the supply closet at the dark end of the third floor. Two led with guns tucked in their scrubs beneath their white lab coats. The third pushed the wheelchair with the squeaky wheel. On the seat, the stack of sheets hid the ropes.

As they approached Detective Baily's room, they could see the mobile nurse station in the doorway and hear a conversation. The three backed into a vacant room and waited in the dark. When the nurse left, the floor would be quiet for hours. They could remove Baily with little risk.

Oblivious to the impending danger, Nurse Crowley finished updating Baily's patient file and returned to his bedside. She put a note on his palm and rolled his fingers into a fist. "I'm turning you over to Anita Martino. Call me when you get out. I am Angelina."

Speechless, he watched the girl of his dreams push the bulky cart out of his room and the door close. Alone with the smell of perfume he unfolded his note. As the pain-meds took hold, he savored each word.

Lying on his side facing the window, the squeaky wheel entered his dream. Baily fantasized Angelina Crowley's return for one last visit, maybe even a kiss, before "her rules" forbade it. But when the fat, sweaty hands pinned his head to the pillow, and clamped down a damp rag over his mouth and nose, it did not fit his paradise. Caught between a dream and reality, Baily could not move. A foreign weight crushed his chest, pinned his legs, and pulled his arms over his head.

With one eye he saw the man straddling his massive chest like a mounted horse, and he saw another man draped over his legs, and he saw the third man pulling his arms. Baily fought through the drug-induced stupor, but the nausea grew.

The toxic smell poured from the rag held over his face, a familiar odor—metopryl. Each second Baily became more lucid. He learned about metopryl at the police academy. It was the latest and greatest knockout drug. He would be out under a minute. Although Baily could hold his breath more than a minute in a swimming pool on a dare, he could not last thirty seconds in the heat of battle. But maybe his attackers were unfamiliar with metopryl. Maybe playing opossum could work.

Baily gave-up the fight in increments. First he stopped moving his legs—the man left. Next he let his arms go limp. Then he relaxed his rock-hard body beneath the rag-holding straddler. Through slits he saw into the dark hall. The one off his legs dragged his Angelina into the empty room and closed the door. Baily saw red, but he had to sell them. He had to wait for the two to loosen their holds just a little—they had no idea.

Seconds later a docile victim put sick smiles on their faces—the metopryl did its magic. The big, black cop had been tamed. They would tie the wild beast and load him onto the wheelchair.

They would cover him with sheets and depart—another patient release.

What came next happened in just four seconds. Baily yanked free his arms and threw his head forward like a mountain goat. With all his pent-up rage and raw strength, and metal plate, he crushed the jaw of his straddler knocking him out cold. Before the unconscious, rag-holding, piece of garbage could flop to the floor, Baily grabbed the telephone from the bed stand and swung it into the arm-holding intruder. On the fourth, pounding thrust the phone exploded into pieces and another bloody face slid to the floor on top of his partner.

Baily stepped onto the cold linoleum barefoot and boiling. "Who are you sons-a-bitches?" he muttered under his breath as he yanked a gun from the unconscious man with a Russian tattoo.

Are you the guys who shot me in Broken Bow? He stepped on the necks, but neither moved. They would be out for a while. *I thought you were only after Keller . . .*

Baily approached the closed door across the hall, his hospital gown sailing behind. As he eased open the door he saw Angelina on the bed and the back of a man. Her buttons were scattered on the floor and her dress was torn open and her legs were gripped on each side of the dark figure with his pants at his ankles.

The head turned when the door squeaked closed. Baily's first blow jarred the man's head and buckled his knees. Baily pulled him from the bed and held him by the neck and squeezed. The bloody hand gripped his wrist as Baily pounded the face until his body hung like a wet blanket on a hook. Baily dropped him to the floor and stepped over the bloody heap. He gently covered Angelina with bedcover and carried her down the hall. When he rounded the corner he met three sets of wide eyes and open mouths at the nurse station—they had heard nothing.

"You know me—Detective Baily. Call the police. Do not ask questions. Just do as I say." He set Angelina in a chair—she was in and out wincing in pain, her eyes swollen closed. A nurse held her shoulders.

"Tell them we've got three guns on the floor. Tell them the perps came for me. They attempted to sedate and transport. They are armed. MPD will know what to do." His eyes jumped back to Angelina—she attempted a smile.

"You're gonna be okay," he whispered. "Do you hear me?" She nodded but could not open her eyes. "Get her out of here. All of you go, now. Leave the floor."

"We have seven patients on this floor," said the head nurse. "I will not leave them. I'm staying right here." She turned to the two nurses. "Take Angelina to the south elevators. Get her to emergency." They disappeared.

"Sounds like you're good at what you do—" Baily checked her name tag with a fleeting eye, "—nurse Sims."

"I am. These are my patients, detective."

"Are the seven sedated?" he asked.

"Yes. All are post-op, elective surgery."

"That means nobody's in critical condition, right?"

"Yes, detective. They are healthy surgical patients we hold overnight for wound drainage and basic recovery. We sedate so they get a good night sleep."

"Pain meds and sedatives intended to knock them out?" he asked.

"Yes. We don't want them moving in their sleep and popping stitches."

Baily looked back over his shoulder down the hall. "I got some caged, wild animals looking for a way out of here, Nurse Sims. Left alone, they'll avoid trouble and your patients. You saw what they can do when they are nervous. I don't want them nervous, Sims. I don't need them doing any more stupid things. Right now you're in the lion's cage with me."

"I stay with my patients," she said like a soldier watching a border.

"When you're in the lion's cage, you live when you do everything the lion tamer says. When you don't, you are eaten by the lions, Nurse Sims."

Her eyes darted from Baily down the dark hall. "What are you saying?"

"I'm saying your patients are safe. I'm saying your presence puts them and me at risk."

Baily turned back to Nurse Sims with brow dipped. "You're leaving the floor, now. You're telling security to shut down elevators and to keep people off this floor. You're telling the police that Memphis Homicide Detective Baily is armed. I have three pinned in the north corridor and want our people on all exits."

When the door closed behind Nurse Sims, Baily moved to the edge of the corridor and confirmed his borrowed Glock was fully loaded—he was going hunting.

Can't let you bastards get off this floor. And I sure as hell can't let you hurt these drugged patients. He slid in the clip. *Why did you come for me anyway? I can't be that important.*

With adrenalin pumping and heart pounding, Baily leaned an eye into the hall. *You guys botched this one up. What kind of idiot rapes a nurse while the other dumb-asses try to hold down a big cop? I saw the flag tattoo—damn Russians. This has gotta be what Bone said, some kind of weapons race is goin' on. The damn Cold War all over again. I gotta get this to Wilcox.*

He moved down the hall in inches. Someone could jump and shoot any time. *Probably should have tied you guys up. Probably not still unconscious, although I did beat the hell out of ya.* He backed into a vacant room. *If you're up and about, you would scatter, increase options. Or you could have left. Nurse Sims took too much time . . . and my damn head's killing me. Yeah. Good chance you idiots left by now. I can't be worth that much to ya.*

He backed into the next empty room, checked it, and eased on to the next. *Guess Wilcox and Petty get back from Oklahoma tonight.* He leaned out. A groan rolled from the other end. *Shit. Maybe I hit 'em harder than I thought.*

He slid out the room and moved to another set of rooms down the empty hall. Each time he checked for patients and his pursuers before moving on.

He counted seven sedated patients. *Everyone's out like a light. Damn good meds,* he thought as he chuckled and shook the metopryl fog from his head. Then he thought about Angelina. Baily backed into the next room and caught movement across the way.

The blunt force to the back of his head shot pain down his spine. His knees buckled, and he fell like a tree. Baily's borrowed gun broke from his grip on the cold linoleum and slid across the floor to a bloody hand and sinister smile.

THIRTY-THREE

"All that is necessary for the triumph of evil is for good men to do nothing."
Edmund Burke

Bald Knob, Arkansas

"They may screw with my car. Let's see if they can screw with my gun." Wilcox jumped out and shot at the bouncing lights. After three, both were out and red taillights spun to a stop.

Burnt gunpowder choked the air. Keller yelled from the backseat, "Focus off your ignition."

Petty slid over and turned the key—it started. "Tony, go around. I'm driving." The spinning tires fishtailed. A cloud filled the campsite. Wilcox felt for the trunk and ran his hand up the side. He found the door and leaped inside as they dropped down a slope into a dark abyss. Pushed against the seat, he reached for the door. It grazed a tree and slammed closed. The car leveled and shot into the air taking the tops off saplings as they descended like a piper cub with no engines. The landing was hard, but the battered cruiser whined forward cutting a swath in the tall grass between the fat trees.

"Thanks for waiting," juggled out of Wilcox as he searched for his belt after slamming into the ceiling twice.

"If we're lucky, I'll find a road out of here before we run off another cliff."

"Keller, tell me about these people," Wilcox said. "Who the hell are they? What do they want? Why the hell are they chasing us?"

"I can't see everything?"

"Shit. And I guess you don't know anything about the damn ignition either."

"Some psychics can interfere with electrical circuits. It's not difficult."

"You mean telekinetic bullshit, like bending spoons and levitation?"

"Not levitation. That is very difficult. Interfering with circuits and bending spoons is easy."

"You're killin' me, Keller." Wilcox attempted to light a cigarette as he bounced around the front seat. "That stuff was debunked a long time ago. Even Houdini exposed fakes."

"Psychics selling something are always fakes," Keller said. "You don't know real ones."

"So you admit most of this crap is pure trickery," Wilcox puffed.

Petty focused on the driving as she spoke. "By definition *psychic* means relating to or denoting faculties or phenomena inexplicable by natural laws, especially telepathy and clairvoyance. Hunter is not saying all psychics are fake, Tony."

"I hate photographic memories, too," he grumbled lighting his cigarette.

"Thousands claiming to be psychic were tested by the government," Petty added. "Twenty-three were contracted. That should tell you something."

"There are not many of us. We don't talk about what we see and can do. We hide to avoid persecution. It's not as bad as when we were called witches, warlocks, and Satan worshipers."

"Are you saying psychics are looked down on?" Wilcox asked.

"Yes, because people don't understand. Not too long ago we were burned at the stake, drowned, imprisoned, and put into insane asylums. My parents tried to talk to me when I started having my experiences. I thought they didn't understand. I saw bad things. I thought I was evil."

Petty snaked through the thick brush between small trees. With lights off she avoided the large shadows and hoped for no drop-offs. "Are you certain your parents were remote viewers, Hunter?" she asked.

"Government files. Signed contracts. They joined Scanate in 1972. They left in 1978. Then it moved to Fort Meade and was named Gondola Wish. The military took over the program."

"Why'd your parents get involved in the first place?" Wilcox asked.

"My mother believed something good would come of it. My father was recruited from the military. They met at Fort Meade. They were very powerful psychics."

"You have proof besides contracts that are easily forged?" Wilcox asked.

"They buried stuff in a metal box, a cornfield south of the farmhouse in Stringtown. I have government psychotronic program manuals, one for each decade. They are classified manuals, not the fake stuff the CIA released in 1996."

"I see them getting the 1970s manuals. How'd they get a hold of the 1980s and 1990s?"

"Remote viewers are close. They watched out for each other until they started to die."

"The end of the remote viewer underground railroad," Wilcox muttered.

"Because my parents were the most powerful in the program, they were tracked down and watched their entire lives," Keller said. "When they learned I was not adopted, that I am their biological son, everything changed. They knew my powers would be substantial."

Light cut through the trees a half-mile back. "Our company's back. Talk to me Keller. Tell us anything you have on these people. I need to consider options."

"I am limited. They have a psychic with them."

Petty navigated the winding course like Pac-Man surrounded. Lights popped over the ridge. "Fog lamps," Wilcox yelled. "Try harder Keller. Give me something."

"They work for Major Cankor. Two are local, hired to find us in Bald Knob Park. One is Russian, the leader, they call him Bender."

"What do they want?" The lights got bigger.

"As I told you before, they want to kill you and Dr. Petty. They know you are here. They know who you are. They know you are too close, know too much."

"Well I'll be goddamned," Wilcox muttered as he checked his gun one more time.

"They want to take me. They will say they won't hurt you. Do not believe them. They have no plans for you to leave this park. You present problems they do not want."

"What about this Cankor fellow, can you access his

thoughts?" Wilcox asked not believing he was buying into the psychic mumbo-jumbo. The impossible struggle he had coming into the park was almost over after he witnessed the scrawny man in action.

"I can access sometimes, but not often. Major Cankor is a psychopath."

"So what?" Wilcox asked.

"A psychopath's amygdala is often small and always dysfunctional," Keller said.

Petty cut sharp and flew by another fat trunk. The move forced the cruiser into a thick cluster of bushes. When they broke through the other side, they were airborne. Seconds later they crashed into a field. Petty cut the wheel sharp and spun a 360 to a dirt cloud stop. They sat in a grassy basin surrounded by trees. The lights behind were gone.

"There's an opening to the north," she said. "It could be a river or a road."

"It is a gravel road," Keller said.

"You are still killin' me, son. You've gotta speak up sooner. Go, Petty." She accelerated and the car ran toward the only gap in the tree line a hundred yards away.

"It is part of my problem," Keller whispered. "I don't talk much. I'm a quiet person."

"Around me, speak up Keller. I do not read minds. Hell, I have trouble reading anything." They bounced across the field, the trailing floods reappearing. "And why the amygdala, Petty?" Wilcox asked. "Why not some other part of the brain?"

"Some theories are the amygdala was once our primary communication organ," she said. "It is believed to be the home of ESP—sixty million years ago the method of interaction for animals and humans. Evolution happened. Humans developed other communication methods and most lost ESP. Many believe animals still use it. Instead of ESP, we call it instinct."

"Thanks, Doctor Science." The lights shot into the field behind them. Wilcox raised his gun. "I'm gonna shoot out those goddamn fog lamps. Keep this baby level."

"Shoot now," Keller yelled. "I'm sharing early."

Wilcox got one lamp with his first shot. Bouncing across the field and four shots later he got the second. Their car dove through the gap in the tree line. It flew over a wide creek bed and plowed to a stop on a gravel road.

"Good drivin', Petty. Now let's get out of here. I only have one bullet left."

The crooked board nailed to a tree said Huntsman Road, but they missed it. Petty kept the lights off and held the battered cruiser between the dark ditches. Ten minutes later they came upon the spinning blues.

"What do we have, Keller?" Wilcox asked.

"I'm getting . . . not good."

The squad cars were parked nose-to-nose blocking the road. "Says 'White County Sheriff's Office' on the doors." Petty slowed. "Not good? Do I accelerate, or do we stop and talk?"

"Push through," Keller said. "I mean, I suggest we do not stop."

"No," Wilcox said. "We're gonna stop. We don't need the county sheriff after us, too."

The two uniformed, white males stood by their doors with hands resting on their holstered guns. "Keller, get down on the floor under the blanket. Do not come out unless I call you," Wilcox said with his head straight ahead. He reached over and touched Petty's arm. "Let me do the talking please."

They stopped. The two sheriff deputies moved thirty feet off each fender. The older one did the talking. "Step out of the car, and show me your hands."

Petty and Wilcox got out. Wilcox held up his badge. "I'm Memphis homicide, Detective Tony Wilcox. With me is Dr.

Victoria Petty, the Shelby County Medical Examiner. We are on official business. What is the problem?"

"Anybody else in the car?" the sheriff asked.

"I just told you, I'm a cop." *Something's not right.*

The two pulled their guns and bent their knees.

THIRTY-FOUR

"The most dangerous thing is illusion."
Ralph Waldo Emerson

"I wouldn't move if I were you, mister." The sheriff cocked his gun.

"We're not moving. You can lower your weapons," Wilcox said.

"Been a killin' in Henryetta. Okmulgee County Medical Examiner's dead. There's a three state search for you two, and a man named Hunter Keller."

"If that's true, I'm sure it's concern for our safety. We were in Henryetta investigating a possible connection to unsolved homicides in Memphis. We met Dr. Proust at the Middleton residence, and were attacked, a man they call Major Cankor. He claimed to be with the DIA—I doubt it. Cankor killed Dr. Proust and fled. We were threatened and left. Dr. Petty and I have been avoiding Major Cankor and his people all night. We stopped at Bald Knob for our own safety. When I return to Memphis, I will file my report. The homicides are connected."

"You got Hunter Keller with you?" the sheriff asked again.

"Yeah," Wilcox shot back. "He's in my backseat hiding," he said. "Did you hear one thing I just said? I am a Memphis homicide detective. Dr. Petty and I are not the bad guys, sheriff. We are on police business. We witnessed a killing and are now hunted. There are dangerous people in your county, in your park now."

"Just tell me where Hunter Keller is, Mr. Wilcox." the sheriff ordered.

"I'm a goddamn cop like you. Where is the professional courtesy? Okay. Look. Here's how we'll do this. You can look anywhere you want for this Keller guy. You can climb all over my car if that will make you happy. However, if you have something on me or Dr. Petty, charge us right now. If not, get the *fuck* out of our way or there's gonna be trouble you do not want. I don't know how good you think you are, but I'm way better."

On Wilcox's last word the jeep flew past and skidded to a stop next to the squad cars. As the steaming cloud of dust settled, Wilcox saw the shattered headlights and pulverized fog lamps. Two meaty guys with shaggy hair jumped out with guns. They flanked the elder officers and smiled like imbeciles. The third—a tall, lanky albino with a bald head and snake beneath Russian flags tattoos on both arms—took the position between in the middle of the foursome.

"These people leave fire burning," he said in a thick, eastern bloc accent. His dark lips on his white face moved very little as he spoke with a caustic tone and destroyed the English language.

"Dangerous thing these person to do in woodland. Bad behavior burn trees to ground and kill animal. Shame on you bad people. And you drive car reckless through park. You shoot gun in my direction. You hit car lights. You make difficult to see where go in woods."

The white Russian pulled a gun from his waist and let it hang at his side. Wilcox felt his gun stuffed in his belt pressing against his spine. With one bullet and facing five guns, Wilcox had to find the words to talk their way out. Hunter Keller was right. He never should have stopped.

"You do something about this, yes Mr. Sheriff Johnson?" the albino said.

"Thank you, Mr. Bender. We can't have dangerous behavior in Bald Knob, Mr. Wilcox."

"It's Detective Wilcox."

"Give me your gun."

"It's in my car with the Keller guy. No more bullets either. I ran out shooting assholes chasing me in the park."

"So, you admit to Mr. Bender's claims." The sheriff took a step closer. "You may not know it is illegal to shoot in the park. You asked for a reason. I have one—the unlawful discharge of a firearm in a public setting. I will need to arrest you Mr. Wilcox." His smile said more.

Wilcox backed one step. "Let's cut the bullshit. You're not cops. You can't arrest a raccoon. I don't know how you got your outfits and squad cars, but I hope you didn't do something stupid.

"And for the record, I know your scumbag friends work for Major Cankor. You're probably a local boy looking for a big payoff. You best think it through. This is not your normal deal. Messing with a homicide detective and medical examiner will change your lives forever. I can promise you no one will stop until they get you old farts. You will die in the electric chair. Before you make a huge mistake, you best factor in we are not alone."

"You're not alone?" Bender said with his gun pointing at the dirt.

"Hey albino Gorbachev, I'm not talkin' to you. Don't know

how you do things in the Soviet Fucking Union but here we have GPS and Wi-Fi. My people know exactly where I am. I've been talking to them ever since you showed up in my mirror you little prick."

"You talk to people?" Bender said looking around. "I see no people."

"You will. The Memphis police, FBI, and the real local cops are coming. Their chopper will be touchin' down on this road soon. Damn amazing, all the modern technology makes it hard for idiots like you to get anything done."

"People know you here?" Bender asked.

"Did I forget to mention the roads in-and-out of this park are shutting down? A perimeter is being set. None of you will get out. I suggest you put down your fucking weapons before . . ."

Bender's gun exploded. Wilcox dropped.

"Do not move doctor lady. You next. Is very easy. You give Hunter Keller now."

Petty tried to see Tony on the other side of the car. "Please. Let me help him. I'll cooperate." The second explosion from Bender's gun sent a bullet off the fender inches from Petty. She jumped and froze.

"One warning for you doctor lady. You give Hunter Keller. We go. Then you fix big mouth detective man."

The lead sheriff deputy lowered his gun with doubt in his eyes. "Lady, just do what he says. None of this has to happen."

"But he's not here," she said.

"Why you lie to me." Bender walked to Wilcox.

"I'm not," Petty said. "You have the gun. You just shot a policeman."

"You lie to protect little man. You think I not serious. I need show serious?"

"He was with us. He got out. He left back in the park," Petty said.

"You remember car no start, yes?" Bender said. "I make happen. I do that. *I know* he close. I know what you know. I now make you tell."

"But I . . ."

"You tell Keller come now," Bender ordered. "You tell little man no more game."

"If you are a psychic, you know Hunter Keller can see the future," Petty said.

"I know this, yes," Bender said.

"You know he saw the blockade. Saw you. He left us."

Bender knelt over Wilcox and pushed the barrel of the gun into his head. In the steaming headlights Petty saw the ruddy complexion and twisted smile and chards of glass embedded in his wounded face. He looked at her with one eye, the other swollen closed. She saw a cold blooded killer.

"I shoot detective man first. I shoot you next. I find Keller alone." His eye danced.

"No! Wait."

"Tell him where Keller is," the sheriff deputy said. Even he could not hide his disgust.

"I'll give you Keller"

Bender cocked the gun.

"Don't shoot! Keller is here," she said. "He is here."

"Put it down Bender," the sheriff said. "Our orders are to get Hunter Keller."

Bender dropped his gun staring at the headlight.

Why did he do that? Petty watched in terror. There was no way out. But the gun on the gravel started to spin. *My God!* And like a fat rat running to a woodpile, it scooted across the road into the ditch. Bender's face changed. His lips began to stretch to his ears, and his eye pushed out of the socket. He grabbed his throat gasping for air, and then fell face down on the ground where he shook and kicked and then was still.

"Why'd he throw his gun in the ditch?" one said. "What's wrong with em?" the other said. In the still night came a light breeze. It cut through the dark woods and delivered the pungent smell of farm animals.

Confused but undeterred, the sheriff aimed his gun at Dr. Petty. "I don't know what just happened, but the guy said things could get weird. We got nothin' to lose lady. I'm gonna give you one chance to produce Keller. We're gettin' paid a lot of money to deliver that boy. Now I got two dead people to get rid of. Guess three's just as easy."

The bull elk jumped the drainage ditch and walked between the sheriff and Dr. Petty. It stopped in the headlights and turned its head to Wilcox's cruiser. The four guns backed a few feet, and for the first time saw the herd surrounding them.

"Think they're attracted to the light," one said.

"Don't get them riled. Don't need a stampede."

"They don't see a lot of bright lights in the middle of the woods."

The sheriff said, "I hunt elk around here. I never saw one that big."

"What killed Bender?"

"Gotta be that Keller psychic boy," The sheriff said. He cocked his gun at Petty."

"He's in the car," Petty said.

They squinted past the headlights. "Nope. He's standin' next to it. Come here Keller."

She turned. Keller had his hands in his pockets and hood over his head. His eyes were locked on the four with guns. When she turned back, it was different. The four were frozen like she and Wilcox back on Dewar, and their guns were spinning on the gravel at their feet. She watched as each slid across the road and into the ditch like Bender's.

"Hunter, are you . . . ?" But then she remembered Bender's face. She watched him die like Dr. Proust. She saw the crippling terror, the facial deformation, the atrial fibrillation, and the cardiac arrest. Hunter Keller is a killer.

"Do not kill these people, Hunter."

"They will kill you and Mr. Wilcox," he said. "They do bad things. More are hurt."

"I know you see the future. But it is not your responsibility to fix the world."

Wilcox moaned. Petty turned and ran to him.

"I see their victims. They must be stopped."

"I know you do, Hunter. But the only way you can live in peace is to live like the rest of us. We cope with tragedies and wrongs. We trust law enforcement and the courtrooms and juries of our peers. If you bypass the legal process, you become one of them."

"But I see those hurt before they are stopped," Keller said. "If I can save innocent lives before societal justice arrives, I must. These four men do not deserve to live."

Propped in her arms Wilcox opened his eyes and blinked his way back into the world. The muscular legs of the giant bull elk were a few feet away. Bender was face down on the gravel road. Through the legs of the elk Wilcox saw the four men in a frozen stance.

"Nobody's gonna believe this shit," he said. "Is Keller doin' this?"

Checking his wound she whispered, "He stopped Bender, Tony. He controls those men like Cankor on Dewar. They can't move. I told him not to kill them. He's not listening."

Wilcox struggled to get his head around things as he regained consciousness. *Are those guys floating a little off the ground or is this another illusion—hypnotism or some trick. This stuff is impossible: people frozen or floating, guns sliding, and wild animals standin' around.*

Wilcox tried to stand, but Petty held him down. "You're lucky," she said.

"Then why does my head and ass hurt?" he grumbled. "And I feel like puking."

"Bender shot you, Tony. The bullet clipped your rectus femoris and buried in the vastus lateralis, no orthopedic or vascular damage—minimal bleeding."

"You mean I took a bullet in my butt?"

"Yes. And when you fell, your head hit hard enough to knock you out. Assuming we survive the night, we can get the bullet out anytime. Best to just leave it alone for now. I don't want to encourage bleeding."

"Great doc. Now help me up. I can't let Keller kill these assholes."

Leaning against the front fender, Wilcox found Keller by the passenger door. The bull elk backed out of the light opening a clear path for Keller to do what he does.

"Keller, listen to me. I don't like these slime balls any more than you, but even I am not authorized to shoot the bastards. Do not kill these people, Keller. I was starting to think you were nothing like these people. You're not a killer. Show me I'm right about that."

"I killed the Russian," Keller said. "He held the gun to your head. He was pulling the trigger. I had to stop him. These four are very bad men, too. They will kill seven people before they die."

"You cannot kill people based on the future. Bender shot a police officer and had a gun to my head—that is justifiable homicide. But we cannot justify the execution of four people under our control. We have laws. These bastards are innocent until proven guilty in a courtroom. You cannot be their judge, jury, and executioner—not in America."

Wilcox pulled out his gun and aimed at Keller. "I have one bullet, son. I don't like everything about our legal process, but it works most of the time. Don't make me shoot you."

"Tony, don't," Petty said. "Just talk to him."

Another breeze crossed the road lifting debris. When it left, dead leaves settled and one of the four ran across the road, jumped the ditch, and crashed into a tree trunk. They watched him slide to the ground out cold. Wilcox lowered his gun. "Bet that hurt like hell."

Unsure of what she witnessed, Petty watched in silence.

One by one, they ran across the road, jumped the ditch, and slammed into the tree. Thirty seconds later there was a pile of four.

"Are they breathing?" Wilcox asked as he turned the gun back on Keller.

"They will wake in an hour," Keller said. "It will take two days to walk out of Bald Knob. They will be picked up on charges —they killed two White County Sheriff Deputies. The ballistics and DNA from the scene will convict them. The other two will be charged for petty crimes. They will kill again."

"Sometimes life is not fair."

"I see all of it," Keller said.

"You remember what you said to me? You said I can't stop all the bad people in the world. I live with that, Keller. But I do what I can. I believe in the end it matters."

Keller came around to the front of the cruiser. The bull elk stood like spectators. "I don't know what the hell happened out here, but we need to leave. We need to lock the guns in the trunk of the sheriff's car. We take the cell phones and break the radios. Keller, move the cars in the ditches. I want keys and distributor caps."

As Petty dressed Wilcox's wound, they watched him move the cars into the ditches. The herd of elk melted into the woods.

"I don't get the animals," Wilcox said.

"They communicate with him," Petty said. She patted the bandage. "Bleeding stopped." She flashed lights and Keller started to return to the car.

"Is it me, or did it look like those guys were a few inches off the ground when they moved across the road and hit the tree?"

"I didn't see that," Petty said.

"I think he caused the accident in Blytheville—the whitetail migration. They said they never saw anything like it before."

"You don't know," Petty said. "There could be a logical explanation."

"He was in the truck before it happened. I talked to the guy while he was driving. He said Keller was there. Got out after he said the trucker was gonna die that night."

Keller got in the car and they stopped talking. They went down the gravel road twenty miles in silence. Wilcox sat there with his aching leg and head, and rehashing the bizarre events of the last twelve hours. He worked hundreds of homicides, dealt with all kinds of killers. Looking back at Keller sleeping, he still didn't know if Keller was a victim or primary suspect.

Are you killing bad people, Keller? Is that what this is about? Wilcox rubbed his head, but nothing helped. *I get it—you know two of the four bastards back there are gonna kill again. You want to stop 'em before they do. You want to help the victims that get lost in the legal cracks. I just can't let you do it.*

They pulled up to the edge of the paved highway. "Now what," Petty asked.

"Take a right," Wilcox said.

"Where are we going now?"

"Lookin' for Highway 64. We'll take it to U.S. 49 and go north. Let's hope they won't be lookin' in Blytheville. We'll get some rest and leave in the morning for Shelby County. I got a place where we can hide and figure out what the hell to do next."

Petty pulled onto the highway and accelerated. "Maybe we'll survive this yet."

When they dropped over the first hill, lights popped on and left a second gravel road.

THIRTY-FIVE

"The mole has very small eyes and it always lives under ground."
Leonardo DaVinci

"Are they dead?" he whispered into the secured phone . . .
The private plane was 5,000 feet over Kentucky. It
would land in Memphis in the hour. High-tech equipment on the
government jet scrambled all communications. They could talk
freely, when the cabin was secured. Baldwin waited for the
attendant to latch the door.

His cover story was a visit to the National Civil Rights Museum
in Memphis. He would be receiving an award—the one held in
abeyance a year to fit the U.S. Attorney General's busy schedule.
Although Alfred Baldwin liked all forms of personal adulation, this
time he did not intend on spending more than an hour at 450
Mulberry. The award meant nothing to him. As a matter of fact, his
true Memphis agenda was far more in line with his veiled, liberal

philosophies. Few knew Baldwin opposed the fundamentals of liberty and justice for all. He preferred control of the masses. The hidden purposes of his visit to Memphis were known by even fewer.

"Not dead yet," Swenson said. "Dr. Petty, Detective Wilcox, and Hunter Keller are alive and well, somewhere between Bald Knob, Arkansas and Memphis, Tennessee. At the moment we do not know their exact location. We will before the night is out." He spoke without confidence.

Baldwin always pushed. He believed without his personal involvement nothing happened right. "Day after day I receive nothing but disturbing information from you, John. We missed Hunter Keller in Memphis four times. God knows we got absolutely nowhere in Sikeston, Broken Bow, or Dewar. What a damn big mess."

"He's getting stronger. We will find him. We must."

Baldwin poured bourbon on the rocks looking at his cell phone. *I've never liked you. You're a skinny, little man with pseudo-psychic skills that make you seem smarter than you are. You saw the answers to your tests all through medical school. You did not understand a damn thing. Still don't. Now I've got to deal with another wimpy associate who always falls short.*

"I don't need to remind you, we've been looking for him for five years now."

"I know, Alfred," Swenson replied with no emotion. "Where is this going?" With a half-smile he looked across the dark room. "What more would you like done, sir?"

Baldwin downed his drink and tumbled the cube in his mouth. *I'd like to arrange for your burial at sea,* he thought as he rolled the diminished sliver of ice to a cheek. "I don't want any more screw-ups, John. I want my trip to Memphis to be a productive one. I want Hunter Keller once and for all, no maybes or excuses."

"This is about Stringtown, isn't it? It's always about Stringtown."

"We could go there."

"You still blame me," Swenson said.

"Arnold and Alma Keller were the two most gifted remote viewers in the program. They suddenly decide to leave. They have a child we know nothing about for thirty years, John. How could you miss such vital information every step of the way?"

"They set it up as an adoption. There was no easy way to uncover it."

"You should have dug deeper. How many people find babies in boxes in snowstorms?"

"In the '70s adoptions were 175,000 a year," Swenson recited. "We've been over this ground many times. Even today more than a million people live with their adoptive parents. These kinds of numbers are impossible to work through rapidly. Even with an army of investigators, we would miss it. The Kellers were smart. They knew how to hide it."

"After learning he existed, Alma and Arnold are executed and Hunter disappears. We lose the most powerful psycho-kinetic man on the planet. I hold you accountable. He was your job."

"You know the problems chasing a man with his abilities. Psychokinetics are only part of his skill sets. His innate, precognitive skills allow him to avoid undesired futures."

"And now we lose him and Wilcox and Petty in Arkansas," Baldwin boiled. "Time's running out. Our enemies are closing in like piranha after fresh meat."

Swenson leaned back in his leather chair holding his cell phone in his palm. He made eye contact with the man on the sofa across from him, as Baldwin whined and complained on speaker. The man on the sofa sucked his fat cigar. It lit his hard face, and then the long orange ash waned and smoldered in the cloud that filled the room.

"I can say the Memphis program is back on track," Swenson crowed.

"What does that mean?" Baldwin asked.

"We've confirmed the five homicides in the region are remote viewers or their descendants. We confirmed cause and manner of death. We got to Memphis in time, and have an opportunity to get Hunter Keller. He was at each homicide. There will be more in the Midsouth."

"You fail to factor-in Mr. Keller's blocking skills," Baldwin said.

"We've developed another way to locate and penetrate. His blocks will not work much longer."

"How do you propose to do that?" Baldwin asked.

"It is best you not know, Alfred."

"I'm stronger than you, Swenson."

"I know. You tell me that often," Swenson said with a hint of disrespect. "I cannot share details because I know very little for the same reason. Different elements are held by different people. No one person has all. It is necessary to protect our advances." Swenson winked at the menacing shadow with the cigar across the room.

"We've had some successes in Memphis," Swenson said. "We've confirmed the forensics and learned more about remote-homicide. Green and Blanchard have been eliminated—the clearance and removal of Russian moles is a major step forward. And Dr. Tanner, of course, is no longer a leak. I'm sure that brought you some enjoyment."

"I do not draw pleasure from shooting a man. It was a military operation—simple as that."

"I'm sorry, sir. I stand corrected. Regardless, Memphis is pivotal."

"What are you trying to say?" Baldwin asked as his plane started its descent.

"When you arrive, we will be presented with the opportunity. Unfortunately, Wilcox and Petty have seen too much. They know too much. They know psychotronics is a weapon of mass destruction garnering the undivided attention of the U.S. Government. And they know we will not allow anything or anyone to get in our way.

"Very disturbing to say the least," Baldwin said.

"They will be in Memphis with Hunter Keller. We need to take care of everything tonight. Tanner was right."

"What makes you so certain they'll be in Memphis?"

Swenson got up and walked to the man with the cigar. He stood at the edge of the leather sofa looking down with a half-smile. "I just know."

"That's not very reassuring," Baldwin said lighting a cigarette.

"Check into the Peabody as planned. I will contact you with updates. In twenty-four hours your headache will be gone, Alfred."

The cabin door opened. "I gotta go." Baldwin pushed the phone into the arm of his seat and listened for the security beep to signal disconnection of the secured line. "What?"

"We will be landing in ten minutes, sir." The attendant backed his small head out the door. Baldwin heard it a hundred times before. His stent as attorney general was coming to an end, and his most important mission had to be successful. Baldwin moved his tongue over his teeth searching for residual bourbon and some peace. Memphis was the end of the road for him.

THIRTY-SIX

"How'd you get this number?" Wilcox said into the phone next to the bed in the cheap hotel. He held his hand over the mouthpiece and whispered to Petty, "We're leaving!"

"How we got the number is immaterial. The important thing is we're talking now."

"Who are you?" Wilcox asked.

"We've never met, officially."

"*Who are you, asshole?*" Wilcox barked a second time. "Your next words decide if we are done talking and I do a better job disappearing."

"Dr. Petty knows me. I worked with her recently. I had to depart unexpectedly. Something came up requiring my immediate attention."

"What do you want Swenson?"

"Very good, detective."

"Ten seconds to be relevant."

"We need you and Dr. Petty in Memphis tomorrow. And please bring Hunter Keller."

"And why would I do what you want?"

"Your friends mean something to you. If you fail to comply, we will terminate them." Swenson smiled as the cigar ash got bright in the dark room.

"I don't have friends. Goodbye."

Swenson laughed. "I was told of your wit. Abby Patterson will be the first. Cam Baily will go next. They were both quite the challenge to acquire—feisty."

Wilcox squeezed the phone, his eyes burned. "I don't believe you have them."

"Allow me to provide proof." Swenson put the phone on speaker and walked to the darkest corner of the room where they were tied and gagged. He pulled off Patterson's gag and kicked her in the stomach.

"When I get loose, I'm gonna kick your skinny ass," Abby said. Swenson smiled and pushed her gag back in her mouth.

He took off Baily's next. "Tee, we're in the Ster . . ." Swenson kicked his face.

"Cops are all alike," he chuckled. "They would rather die than do what's in their best interest. I hope you have more brains than this one, Detective Wilcox. You don't have a very good record keeping partners. Maybe you're ready for another and I'm out of luck."

"If you do anything to them, I will find you. You will beg me to let you die." Wilcox walked to the window of the cheap hotel. "And if you know anything about me, you know I will do what I say, you miserable punk."

"It's not nice for a police officer to threaten citizens. Your boss would be disappointed to hear such unlawful language from one of his homicide detectives."

Swenson stooped down and removed another gag. "Go ahead," Swenson said. "Tell your employee how you disapprove of his aggressive language and unlawful threats. Tell him how you would send an army of police officers to apprehend him if he killed anybody."

"Tony, this is Cottam."

Damn! Wilcox cupped the phone. "They have Patterson, Baily, and Cottam."

"Do not negotiate with . . . "

This time the one holding the cigar kicked a hostage. He smiled when Cottam fell on his side and created a new puddle of blood. Swenson stuffed the rag back in the director's mouth.

"We want you, Petty, and Keller."

Wilcox knew he was responsible. He pulled Abby into his nightmare—he broke all the rules doing it. If he had done his job the right way, Abby would be safe somewhere tracking another lame cheater. Her subjects were scumbags. He threw her to cold-blooded killers.

"Are you still there, Detective Wilcox?" Swenson taunted. "Are you going to save the people *you* put in danger. How could you expose a PI and rookie detective to so much danger? You are an irresponsible man. Even your director faces death because of your inept skills."

If Wilcox had stood his ground at Lamplighter's Baily would not have been shot in the head or taken by Swenson. Baily would be drinking a beer with his generation's cops talking about the senseless homicides. Swenson was right. Wilcox was irresponsible.

You must be desperate—kidnapping the director of the Memphis Police Department. I get Patterson and Baily, but not Cottam. Talk about putting the stick in the hornet's nest. And his kidnapping has been kept under wraps. MPD has gotta know he's missing, but they're not saying anything about it. What the hell are they doing? What kind of power do these people have?

"What do you want?"

"I'm a thoughtful guy, Detective Wilcox. If you do what I say, everyone lives."

"What do you want?" he said again.

We meet on Mud Island tonight. You and Dr. Petty bring Hunter Keller. We trade three for one and go our separate ways."

"Where on Mud Island? It's a big piece of real estate?"

"History says you're quite familiar with the place, detective. It was in all the newspapers. You and that world-renowned forensic pathologist tangled with a serial killer on that island. I suppose you're getting tired of the place." Swenson grinned as he returned to his chair and drink.

"Where, Swenson? Give me specifics."

"The north end is most convenient, yet remote. I'm sure we can conduct business and not be disturbed. We will meet where you found those disgusting heads on stakes, the sandy clearing near the bank. Surely you remember.

"We will meet at ten p.m. sharp. And please do not underestimate our capabilities. We are quite capable of monitoring and assessing situations from afar. If we feel the slightest compromised, your friends die and we simply move to our plan B. I advise against games, detective. I would not sacrifice my friends for a psychic-serial killer. Mr. Keller has killed many, although I am quite certain he has been on his best behavior while under your purview."

"You're an idiot, Swenson," Wilcox fumed.

"I've been accused of many things, but that one is new. We will take Hunter Keller off your hands tomorrow night, and everyone lives happily ever after."

"Who do you work for?" Wilcox asked.

"Is that information truly necessary?"

"Not really. Why do you want Keller?"

"I am certain you've witnessed his talents, a very gifted young man. I am equally certain you have seen but a fraction of his astounding capabilities. And I'm also certain you've spent most of your time doubting him. He needs to be with those who can appreciate him fully."

"What makes you think he'll share anything with you? You killed his parents and friends and remote viewers. Your minions have forced him into a life of hiding."

"You should know better than most that things are not always as they appear. We're not the bad guys here. Our mission is secret, and it goes beyond your narrow focus. It can withstand your judgement. I recommend you do the right thing tomorrow night."

Swenson dropped the cell phone onto the cold, cement floor and crushed it under his heel. "This is not going to go well," he said while staring at the shattered pieces.

"They will come. That is all we need." Light seemed to avoid the dark figure sucking the cigar on the long sofa. He pushed the stub into the arm and sparks rained down.

"No one leaves Mud Island alive tomorrow night. When we have Keller, we terminate the others and dispose of their bodies under the Harahan Bridge. We leave Memphis by water."

"Nasty currents down there. They'll be sucked under immediately," Swenson said. "They will tumble along the river bottom for miles. Their body parts won't make it to Vicksburg—fish bait."

"This time I'm ready for Hunter Keller," Cankor said.

THIRTY-SEVEN

"I will sleep when I'm dead."
Warren Zevon

T he bullet found his chest and they carried him away . . .
Another crisp November day on Mulberry Street in
south Memphis set the stage for the scheduled spectacle to be
covered by the national media. Satellite trucks sat in their
designated spaces and crowds began to grow outside the National
Civil Rights Museum. Since its opening in 1991, each U.S.
Attorney General and many high ranking government officials
found time to visit the hallowed grounds—the place of the Martin
Luther King assassination, and where the civil rights movement
gained its unprecedented momentum. The NCR Humanitarian
Award waited for Alfred E. Baldwin. Now, the event mattered.
He needed an excuse to be in Memphis, Tennessee.

The complex of historic buildings and museum grew from

the Lorraine Motel, the site where King died on the balcony on April 4, 1968. Now marked by a wreath outside room 306, the small motel is frozen in time and serves as an honored backdrop for NCRM awards ceremonies. Unlike other events in the city, the promotional campaign for Alfred Baldwin's visit to the city had a three day run. The last minute commitment from the attorney general left little time for the usual preparations. Some believed the brief promotion was for security purposes.

The honorees and local dignitaries mingled around the buffet table in the private quarters of the museum—the staging area for the event. Baldwin stood alone at the tinted windows looking at the growing crowds attending the special award ceremony.

The mayor took a position next to Baldwin at the window. "Dr. King never had a chance," he said staring across the plaza at the wreath on room 306 behind the stage waiting for them. "It was a terrible day. When it happened, I was twenty working at *The Tribune*, a cub reporter."

Baldwin stood silent. Although both looked out the same window, their thoughts were very different. Baldwin's eyes stayed with the churning crowd, not room 306. He was killing time. He had a reputation and had sent all the signals—he wanted to be alone. But the mayor persisted. Baldwin showed no interest in the mayor's lame anecdotes. His head was on important matters few could comprehend.

The mayor edged even closer to one of the most powerful men in the world. The Attorney General sets the legal agenda for the nation. He can change the course of history by ignoring gross travesties of justice, and by transforming the most innocent acts into politically correct barbarism. It was always about personal gain, and Alfred Baldwin was the master. He understood power.

"They're gathering," the mayor whispered. "Thank you again for coming to our city. We appreciate you fitting us into your schedule. These special recognition moments are important to the region and national community. Coverage of the positive helps offset the negative."

Baldwin stared straight ahead. "It was a single 30-06 round fired from a Winchester Model 760. The bullet entered the right cheek, broke the jaw, and went down the spine."

The mayor straightened his stance pushing his chest out. "Excuse me?"

"Shattered vertebrae and severed the jugular." Baldwin sipped his bitter punch.

"I missed something. What are you talking about?"

"It lodged in the shoulder—ripped off the man's tie." Baldwin turned with fire in his eyes. "This is your city. You should know how King died. You should know the details of this man's horrible tragedy. He didn't die so this shrine could be built. He was murdered by a savage element lurking in your city. Dr. King had more to do. But some racist fool thought differently. Your city gave that monster the opportunity because you were not ready."

"Sounds like you're scolding me," the mayor said attempting to recover from the awkward moment. "You have no idea what—"

"—Please! Enough. I heard you. You were twenty. How could you be expected to know? You weren't responsible. Nobody's responsible except the man with the rifle. But now you're the mayor and I'll bet you still don't know the details of the man's death—it's too messy. You'd rather lose yourself in the pomp and circumstance, and symbolism. While you do that, another piece of vermin is spawned in the bowels of your city."

The mayor stood a foot taller than Baldwin, and was in far better shape. Baldwin was an overweight bourbon-drinking cigarette smoking man. The cameras in the room caught the mayor's clenched fist and hard face bearing down on the chubby man at the tinted window. It would make the six o'clock news.

"I know more about my city than you will ever know," the

mayor seethed. "Your twisted arrogance is abominable, and an enormous disappointment. For a sitting U.S. Attorney General to reach such hair-brain conclusions with absolutely no information is concerning to say the least. I know how Martin Luther King died, sir. I know how he was rushed to St. Joseph Hospital. And I know how Memphians prayed for a miracle that day."

With a cold smile the mayor leaned down and into Baldwin's fat face—he would give the news media another photo-op. "You're not welcome in my city, little man. After you take your award, leave. By the way, it was not a Winchester. It was a Remington you pompous fool." The cameras followed the mayor's cold departure. Baldwin turned back to the tinted glass.

He enjoyed the reflection. He watched the mayor blend into the crowd behind him, and the whispers and turning heads. Once again he pulled all the strings. Baldwin created the perfect conditions. The news would run with the confrontation for the next twenty-four hours, a perfect distraction, and the room would leave him alone. He needed to focus on the more important matters. Although his perfect plan was unfolding, there were always surprises. He ran over the counter measures still making adjustments.

"Swenson, it's about time you made contact," he said into his cell looking out the tinted glass. "I waited last night." Baldwin looked for and found his lead bodyguard by the door touching an ear. They exchanged nods. "Talk to me, Swenson. Where are you?"

"Sorry for the delay. I can assure you it was in the best interest of the mission. It is also best we not discuss my current location." Swenson learned how to manage Baldwin long ago. He put at risk those things he knew Baldwin could not lose—control of outcomes. "When do you accept your humanitarian award, sir?"

"Soon I hope." Baldwin watched them check the podium

microphones. The stage was in the parking lot of the Lorraine Hotel under room 306. Bundles of cables snaked through the grass dropping off the curb onto Mulberry and feeding a half dozen satellite trucks. "I'd rather be at the Peabody on my third drink."

"Be specific on the window of 'saturated protection'."

"1:00 to 1:05. But, my protection is already in place. No need for you to do anything."

"I check behind the protection, sir. There are elements of risk you've not shared with secret service, elements posing a greater danger than the routine, political crackpots."

"You're talking about the Stargate Project. Let me remind you, the only reason I am in this backwater town is because you guaranteed me a success. This time it better pan out."

"I believe we have a good chance of accomplishing our mission right here in Memphis."

"I sense a softening of your position. Has there been a set back?"

"No, sir."

"Is *he* in the city?" Baldwin asked. Looking across the room his agent touched his tie with two fingers. "Talk faster. They're going to need me."

"*He* will be here," Swenson said.

"And the others?"

"Working on it." *You don't need more,* Swenson thought. *After one it won't matter . . .*

"I hope you get it right this time," Baldwin said.

Secret Service secured the area the best they could with an impossible setting. Barriers were in place on East Butler, St. Martin, Hulling and South Main to Nettleton. The zone of exposure had been dissected by the most prudent protection agency on earth. Incursion possibilities were weighed, and risks were eliminated, minimized, or closely monitored.

"Excuse me," said the program coordinator at the edge of the window. "I'm sorry to disturb you, sir." Baldwin turned with a scowl and holding his phone to his chest. "The ceremony is about to begin. There will be opening words from the NSM President followed by five smaller award presentations. You will be introduced at 1:00 p.m. and escorted to the podium as stipulated. There will be no variance."

"Thank you for the update." Baldwin turned back to the window and his phone. "They don't like this location for security purposes. They won't let me get past five minutes on the podium. I'll get out of here and back to the Peabody in twenty. You call in thirty with an update."

"Understood." Swenson disconnected and smiled at Major Cankor. They stood on the rooftop of the Sterick building looking south at the swarm. It was a clear day. They had a perfect view of the Civil Rights Museum parking lot and podium ten blocks away.

The small band started playing. Baldwin forced his cell into his pocket, his coat fit tighter than usual. The conferees filed across the lot flanked by cheering crowds. Memphis police lined their path ten feet apart. Local dignitaries, news media, and family members of the honored guests were seated in front of the small stage.

The positioning was odd. *People are a fair distance away,* Baldwin thought. *They're forced to stand in a tight, narrow formation to see the podium. It's like watching a football game from the wrong end zone.* Baldwin was told about the last minute change. They said it was a TV network. They had to have room #306 and Mississippi River in the background. Secret Service did not like the added *lanes of exposure.* They could cancel Baldwin's participation, but decided five minutes or less of exposure was an acceptable compromise.

He was alone in a non-smoking environment. The two

attendants cleaning the ravaged buffet, and two agents with fingers to their ears, would not say a word. Baldwin lit up. Blowing smoke at the glass he tapped speed dial. He held out the phone for the familiar squelch and waited for the crystal chime—the line was secure.

"Status?" Baldwin said.

The scrambler made the voice on the other end robotic. "Located, sir."

"Assemblage?" He asked and took another long drag.

"Ready, sir."

"Good."

Two cigarettes later, the side door opened. "We're ready for you, Mr. Baldwin." The agents stepped out first. The crisp November day hit him in the face. He crossed the lot with a tinny, off-key *America the Beautiful* playing. Baldwin put on his fake smile and waved to the public from the cluster of sunglasses, ear pieces, and bumps in black coats. Today would be the most important day of his life for reasons few would ever know.

Walking through the crowd, his elation did not come from the honor bestowed. It came from knowing he would soon complete the most important mission of his lifetime, and it was personal. Alfred E. Baldwin was a survivor. He was an elite Gondola Wish remote viewer, and the leader of the Stargate submersion program. Better than anyone, Baldwin understood the power of psychic-weaponry. He knew how it would change human intelligence gathering, and it would be how all future wars are fought. He knew in the wrong hands it would change the balance of power and course of humanity.

Six chairs were at the back of the stage with the five honorees and host. There was no chair for Baldwin—he could never sit out in the open again. Plain clothes Secret Service moved in the crowd and more black suits surrounded the platform. He took the stage flanked by crossed arms and scanning eyes. City officials rose and stood off to the side. The mayor glared at the AG. Baldwin adjusted two of the ten microphones as if it mattered. He flashed a smile at the crowd and looked down at his index card—show time.

It was 1:03 when he started to open his mouth. Baldwin always liked being the center of attention, but this time he felt strange. The image of an enormous ten-point stag was standing in crosshairs. Where did that come from? What did it mean? Was it nerves or something else?

A bead of sweat grew and left a sideburn. It rolled down and hung on his jaw. Baldwin's clothes felt heavy and tight. He rubbed his jaw and cleared his throat. Baldwin ignored the image and squinted into the flashing strobes. "I am honored to be . . ."

The distant crack of thunder rolled through the city to the Lorraine Hotel. Heads turned looking for lightning or storm clouds—there were none. Then splintered wood flew from the podium and Baldwin's index card took flight. His face was wet. His thigh burned. He froze.

Secret Service jumped into action, but it all happened in one second of surprise and confusion. Before they got to the attorney general, the second crack of thunder rolled and more splintered wood flew into the air. This time the impact knocked Baldwin back into the chairs. This time the bullet found his chest.

They surrounded him and carried him away as screaming crowds stampeded and knocked down barriers in a desperate attempt to find safety. The cluster of dark suits carried Baldwin into the museum as the chaos on Mulberry stirred terrible memories—another assassination.

Alfred E. Baldwin was taken away in a stream of black limos and flashing lights, and the Memphis police and federal agents swarmed the city. The flow from the National Civil Rights Museum was like red ants protecting the mound poked by a stick.

Ten blocks and four minutes away the Razar, long-range

scope and Remington 700 were disassembled with precision. The rooftop of the Sterick would be empty in less than a minute, the building in two.

THIRTY-EIGHT

"I would rather die a meaningful death than to live a meaningless life."
Corazon Aquino

Brent Mansion - Shelby County

"I'll be a son of a bitch. Baldwin got shot today," Wilcox said looking at his cell. "It's streaming news. It was around one, the Lorraine Hotel."

The old Brent mansion would be the safest place to hide. One mile into the woods of north Shelby County, the abandoned manor came to mind. Wilcox had spent time there; a serial killer lived in the basement. The overgrown property posted—no trespassing—was the perfect place to get some rest and to consider options.

"Mr. Baldwin's in Memphis? Wonder if it had something to do with Stargate," Petty said.

"They say he was here to receive a humanitarian award from the National Civil Rights folks. But those kinds of things get setup minimum of six months in advance, security purposes. Since it wasn't, I'll bet you're right."

The musty smell of rotting wood filled the old mansion in spite of the strong breeze passing through the seven-foot windows of shattered panes on all three levels. Even the remodeled sections were now weathered. Nothing could overcome the steady decay of a dying structure.

At the corner window on the second floor Wilcox had the best view of the long driveway. The weed covered road cut through ten acres of wildflower fields boxed-in by dense woods. The weaving route was the only way for wheels to reach the dilapidated structure. The network of creeks and marshes surrounding the estate—occupied by poisonous moccasins and black snakes—all but eliminated access on foot.

While standing guard at the window, Wilcox could not resist an occasional look at Petty's legs. Now bathed in the only square of sunlight in the room, her curvy calves, small ankles, and firm thighs took his mind off their mounting troubles. Although he admired beautiful ladies, this time was different. This time there was more than a physical attraction.

She always knew when Wilcox was checking her out. She felt his eyes and smiled at her cell as she read the news. Although they were beginning to know each other on a professional level, personal feelings were growing. Before she left Dallas, she knew the reputation of the top Memphis homicide detective. She knew the stories of his crudeness and arrogance and womanizing. But it did not take long for her to see through all of it. She was attracted to the gentle, honorable man inside. She saw character and unwavering commitment to justice. He reminded her of her father lost in the line of duty. He was a Dallas homicide detective.

She crossed her long legs for his wandering eyes and continued to scroll. "Thank you for my wood chair, detective. It is very thoughtful of you. I prefer to sit on something a nasty rat cannot make a home in."

Wilcox snapped out of his erotic trance. He turned back to the window and empty road. The sun dropped behind the tree line, and the shadows began to reach for them. Hunter Keller fell asleep on the old sofa in the center of the room. "He can sleep anywhere. Rat infestation doesn't seem to bother our psychic friend," Wilcox said.

"Bald Knob took a lot out of him," Petty said.

"He is different."

"I think the nasty rats like him, too. You know the elk herd?"

"Yeah. They just stood there hypnotized by the damn headlights."

"They weren't looking at the headlights, Tony. Every one of them was looking at Hunter. It was like they were waiting for instructions."

"I seriously doubt that. I can't explain much, but that's a reach, doctor."

Keller lay on the sofa, filled with rat holes and stuffing poking out. It looked like the sofa was used as a shield in a machinegun fight. Keller's hood covered his ears, only his nose visible. The shredded arm cradled his head. His black Converse high-tops hung off the end.

"Hey, Keller, wake up," Wilcox barked.

"Let him rest. We have time," Petty said turning off her cell phone.

"We don't have time. Somethin's supposed to happen tonight. The sun's going down. Mr. Keller, I need you to conjure up some of those skills. Tell me about the Baldwin shooting. Are you awake, Keller?"

One eye opened. "I'm awake," he said. "The shooting is not political."

"I need more, please. Don't be like a teenager with an attitude," he poked.

"Tony. Don't harass him." Petty dragged her chair to the sofa. "Hunter, we have a meeting in four hours with people we know little about. We need your help. Did the people we are meeting have something to do with this shooting? Can you tell us anything? Is Albert Baldwin a problem for them?"

"I don't see everything," he said. "I see pieces. It takes time to sort through faces and events because I don't know everyone. After, I see relationships and intentions."

"Give us the *Cliff Notes*, Keller. Petty and I will fit the pieces together."

"Mr. Baldwin was shot by someone I do not know. He is new to me."

"Maybe it is a political hit," Wilcox muttered.

"The man is professional," Keller said. "He is a sniper."

"Do you know who he works for? Was anybody with him when he shot Baldwin?"

"They are on a rooftop—the Sterick building," Keller said.

Petty leaned closer. "You said *they*."

"He did not know Mr. Baldwin. They paid him $200,000. It was another assignment."

"Who are they? Look around the roof," Wilcox pressed.

He slipped his hood off and stared at the ceiling. "Dr. Proust gave him money. Dr. Swenson went to Henryetta to terminate Dr. Proust. It was time for him to go."

"Time for Proust to go?"

Dr. Swenson was in the car on Dewar that night. Because

you and Dr. Petty were in the house, Major Cankor did it—he killed Dr. Proust.

"Dr. Swenson is a remote viewer," Petty said.

"Yes. He is not strong. He was going to try to kill Dr. Proust. Major Cankor took over when he knew you were there."

"Swenson's with Cankor," Wilcox said.

"He is on roof with the shooter," Keller said.

"Swenson is Baldwin's mole," Petty said. "He had to be the one who killed Green and Blanchard. He was protecting his position."

"If Swenson and Cankor eliminated Russian moles and assassinated Baldwin, they could be at their end game."

"Hunter, tell us what you know about Cankor, Proust, and Baldwin," Petty said.

"They've been close a long time. They met in 1978, the Gondola Wish Project."

"I bet the assholes wanted to control psychic-weapons from day one."

"They killed my family and friends. And Bone is dead because of me."

"We can't go there now," Wilcox said. "The world's full of bad people. You gotta give Bone the respect he deserves. He chose to get involved in your life. He knew the risks. You were important to him. Don't take that away from him by blaming yourself for his death."

"But I am the reason so many people die. It's killing me inside."

Petty and Wilcox were not going to overcome a lifetime of confusion and pain with a few words of wisdom. They could not begin to comprehend Keller's complex world, the burdens he carried. They had to take a different tact if they were going to get his help with Mud Island.

"The three of us will put our lives on the line tonight,"

Wilcox said. "We have no choice because nobody's going to believe any of this shit until it's too late. Swenson and Cankor and their minions are the bad guys. I don't know how Baldwin fits in all this crap. God knows who else these people have killed. They will not stop until they get what they want."

"If they get control of psychic-weapons, the world as we know it could change a great deal," Petty said. "We've got to stop them."

"Now is the time to put aside your paranoia and blame. If you want to make a big difference, tonight is your night. I don't get any of this psychic shit, but I've seen you do things. If you got 'em, use your gifts to help us stop these sick people before it's too late."

"They have the advantage," Petty said. "They are choosing the venue, time, and there are two of them. There is only one of you, Hunter."

"The training wheels come off. Tonight is about your parents, your friends, and the remote viewers and their families slain by monsters. You gotta find a way to do what Bone and your parents taught you."

They sat in silence as the second floor in the old mansion grew darker and the occasional gust lifted the torn curtains and swept the room. Keller looked up at Petty and said, "I don't think that is the case."

"What are you talking about?" Wilcox asked. "She didn't ask you anything."

"I did, Tony. I did ask him. I just didn't say it out loud."

"What did you ask him?"

"Why is Major Cankor afraid of you?" Petty said. "Why did he run away from you on Dewar Avenue?"

Keller clarified. "I don't think he is afraid of me. I think he is choosing his time."

"You stopped him on Dewar," Wilcox said. "Or was that something else?"

"I distracted you, Hunter. It broke your focus," Petty said.

"He sure wanted out of there," Wilcox said. "He's afraid of you, Keller. Whatever you did to him, and those jerks at Bald Knob, you need to do again on Mud Island."

"There will be two remote viewers on Mud Island," Keller said. "They did not setup a meeting they could not control, Mr. Wilcox. They want me. It is best I go with them so the others can live. Maybe I can convince them. Maybe I can escape another time."

Tony lit a cigarette and blew. "I must be psychic, too. You know as well as me, when those freaks get you under control they kill us—they toss our bodies in the river. You know they chose Mud Island for that reason, Keller. The movie is in your head, but you're afraid to look. It is time to grow up and to do something about it. It is time to use these gifts to stop this evil."

"We will do our best to protect you," Petty said. "But Tony's right. They've killed many innocent people. Now they are killing each other."

"Who does Cankor and Swenson work for?" Wilcox dropped his butt and turned a shoe as he looked out the window. "Save it. We have lights in the woods."

They watched them emerge on the road through the field to the mansion. Petty said under her breath, "How did they find us?"

"These people are relentless," Wilcox said checking his gun. "Talk to me Keller—who?"

"I'm blocked. There is a remote viewer with them."

"Gotta be Cankor or Swenson or both. A surprise visit. Impatient bastards."

They watched the last car in the line stop at the edge of the woods. The headlights popped off. Three cars continued to the mansion in a slow, tight line with only parking lights.

"Grab your things," Wilcox said. "Our car's in back. Let's move!"

"I thought you said there was only one way on wheels," Petty said.

"Let's hope I'm wrong."

THIRTY-NINE

"The sun also shines on the wicked."
Seneca

I t was a beautiful night to die . . .
Wilcox parked by the overgrown boat launch ramp at the north end of Mud Island. Standing in the shade of an oak, the three took in what could be their final moments. The pale half-moon washed over the river brush, and the hot engine popped in the cool November night. Wilcox could not stop memories—they flowed like the Mississippi a few hundred feet away. Six months ago the terror and carnage he experienced on the island was unbearable. He found seven dead men and met a serial killer. Somehow Wilcox survived. This night he returned to the sandy clearing on the east bank and would face impossible odds against another monster with unimaginable weapons. Death would return to Mud Island before the fingers of the morning sun touched the muddy river again.

"Everyone knows what to do—right?" They stood at the top of the narrow path on the edge of the ravine. Keller and Petty nodded with wide eyes. *I wish I could do this alone,* Wilcox thought. "If you have any questions about the plan, let's go over it now." They stood in silence.

"We stay together until it's time. Is your gun loaded?" He asked Petty, although he knew the answer. Wilcox checked all three guns at the Brent mansion and again in the car. He had two, Petty one. Keller refused to carry.

"Yes, for the third time," she said.

"Good. You got it where nobody can find it?"

"Depends if they're perverts, I'm wearing my thigh holster."

"They don't have to be perverts to look up your dress," Wilcox said as he led the way down the incline reaching back for her hand. A gust ballooned her dress like a spinnaker sail. "Never mind, I see it. And I see you're still wearing damn heels —unbelievable."

"You're not a pervert, more like a pain. And my shoes, it's not like I could run home and change into Nikes. You left my suitcase in Henryetta. Don't worry, I can still outrun you."

Hiding his smile, Keller followed down the weed-covered slope. Wilcox and Petty reminded him of his parents—always poking fun but always watching out for each other. Although Keller tried to stay away from personal thoughts, he knew where their relationship was going. With his hood up and hands in pockets, he jumped to the bottom.

Wilcox lead the way across the river scrub covered in a blanket of gray mist. They reached the last stand of trees. Less than a hundred feet away, the tall grass stopped at the edge of the infamous clearing. Beyond the barren patch there was a sparse line of trees lining the river bank. They could see the wavering white ribbon marking the moon's path from the other side.

"Keep low from here forward, and whisper. I prefer no talking. Pay attention."

They moved through the tall grass on the narrow trail. When they reached the edge of the clearing, they left the trail for the tall grass and watched and listened. But the churning water of the Mississippi River sliding by swallowed sound, and the gusting winds moved shadows. Although they were early, they would not know if they were alone.

Inches from Keller's face Wilcox whispered, "Do not deviate from the plan. We can't change anything without screwing up everything. Petty and I go to the clearing. You wait here. You stay low in these weeds. Do not move around—the top of the grass will shake and give you away. And for God's sake do not poke out your head. I will call you when the time is right. Do you understand, Mr. Keller?"

He nodded with a distant stare. Petty leaned into the huddle. "Are you blocking someone?"

"Yes."

"Do Swenson and Cankor know where you are when you block?" Wilcox asked.

"They cannot locate me, but they know I am nearby. I know they are nearby, too. There are seven others with them, trained combatants, mercenaries paid a lot of money. They have guns."

Wilcox rubbed his face like he took a hit in the jaw—*we don't have a chance.*

"There's no going back, Tony. You've done all you can. This is an impossible situation. Let's hope the plan works."

Wilcox pulled Keller to him like a father pulling a child from the path of a car. "Listen to me," he said with urgency in his tone. "You can do some strange damn things, but you cannot stop bullets. If you don't think you can beat them your way, you must leave the island. Do not try to save us, Keller. We understand the significance of this moment. You must live to fight another day.

You may be the only one alive who can stop these people. All the conditions must favor you, or you leave. Do you understand me?"

"I understand," Keller said.

"We must get Patterson, Baily, Cottam, and Petty off this goddamn island before you come into the equation. It is the only way." Wilcox turned to Petty. "And it is your job to take them up that trail, get them into the car and out of here. You don't look back." He folded his keys into her hand. "Take them to The Med. I will meet you there when this is over."

We both know we are not making it to The Med. Petty grabbed his neck and kissed him hard. She would do everything but drive away without him. She would not leave him behind. "Don't show off, Wilcox. You can't stop bullets."

He nodded. "If the rest of our plan materializes, we have a chance. If it does not, we are all pretty much screwed. Keller, you said the lesions on my brain may protect me for a while from that psychokinetic shit."

"That is a real possibility."

"It does make medical sense," Petty said. "Lesions are scar tissue. It will alter brain function and disrupt neural connectivity like a short circuit tripping a breaker. You may not get hurt, but it could knock you down or out. Don't forget we are dealing with powerful psychics."

"It is our only advantage. I'm the bait with an attitude," he said, and then pulled a gun from his waist. "Keller, I need you to break one of your rules. Take this. I know you don't like guns, but this is different. Tonight we all need to do things we don't like."

"I cannot," Keller said.

"Only if you need to protect yourself." *Take the gun.*

"If I kill, I will lose control. I almost did when I stopped Bender. You pulled me back. If I need a gun, you will not be there to bring me back from the evil part."

Wilcox tossed the gun at Keller's feet. "There it is if you change your mind."

Petty and Wilcox left the tall grass and stepped onto the mound of sand that cascaded down the bank to the sliding black water. "Guess we're early," he said without turning his head. "Be careful where you look. We don't want to give Keller's location away."

She jabbed him in his ribs as she pulled a sinking heel from the sand. "You do know I spend some of my life outside the morgue. I have some street smarts, Tony. You can be so arrogant."

They waited in the cool night air. "You know this is not an island. It's a peninsula, the Mississippi River to the west and Wolf River Harbor east. They meet at the south end of this strip of land. The city rerouted the Wolf River back in the '6os creating a land bridge at the north end. I suppose that made the harbor possible."

"Thanks for the geography lesson, Detective Wilcox."

"These bastards can take the land route like the wild animals."

"I don't do wild. I dislike furry things looking for something to eat."

"I'm talking raccoon, opossum, armadillo, deer, skunk, and your basic river rats."

"This just keeps getting better." Sinking in the sand, Petty kicked off her heels.

"They could come from the south end, but it's a hike through thick scrub and sticker bushes. If I were them, I'd come by boat. Can land anywhere on the east bank. Easy exit, too."

"What's really on your mind, Tony?"

He leaned closer. "You like him. You are convinced he's a victim in all this."

"I've considered the evidence thus far. It is not an emotional process for me," Petty said.

"We still do not know him," Wilcox said out the side of his mouth. "We don't know who killed his parents or who's responsible for all these killings. I don't have enough facts to be sure of anything right now."

"You've watched him for two days," Petty said. "Those men were after him at Bald Knob. He stopped them. He protected us."

"Yeah but . . ." Wilcox muttered.

"You heard Cam. He's convinced Keller's not a serial killer. Keller saved your life twice, Tony. He's more a boy than a man, and he's scared and alone. He's not driving this nightmare. He is running from it."

"You saw what he did to Bender," Wilcox said. "And you saw what he did to Cankor. He can kill with his mind. He just admitted he can't control it."

Petty whispered. "I think he's now hunting his nemesis."

"Or is he the problem? Is that why the government is trying to stop him?"

"I don't know, Tony."

"That's my point. We need to watch our backs."

The meeting had been set for ten. At midnight the small boat with no lights neared the island. Wilcox and Petty watched the black mass nose into the bank, the stern sliding in the stiff current. A small shadow jumped onto land and climbed the bank.

"Hello Dr. Petty. Detective Wilcox. Where is Hunter Keller?" Swenson asked.

"You're late. We almost left."

"Precautions. And you would not leave. Where is he?"

"You're the one with the psycho skill sets. You should already know he'll be here after my people are safe, you sawed-off prick."

Swenson looked back at the boat. The standing shadow nodded. "I hope you don't do anything stupid. It could go very badly for you."

The next shadow to depart was much larger. It glided up the bank. The flat-brimmed hat and long, billowing coat broke from the obscure darkness as he left the shadows of the trees. "He's on the island somewhere—blocking."

"I feel him too," Swenson said eyeing the tall grass.

Wilcox confirmed Major Cankor was the man Keller described on Main the night Randle Johnson died in the small bank. Now Wilcox was sure Cankor was the man in the dark bedroom on Dewar. When Cankor reached the sandy mound, his presence dominated. The moonlight washed over his massive hulk stopping at his face hidden beneath his wide brim.

"We meet again," Cankor said. An acrid mist shot from his mouth into the night air.

"You gonna run like you did at Dewar?" Wilcox said.

Cankor ignored the inflammatory words from the man he would watch die. "Hunter Keller was busy at Bald Knob. Impressive. But still unable to finish the job."

"Why'd you kill your friend today, Cankor?" Wilcox taunted. "I thought you and Baldwin were best buds." But the words only added to the suffocating impossibilities—there were too many innocents exposed and at a weapons disadvantage.

"Odd choice of words, detective—*kill* and *friend*," he scoffed. "I only kill my enemies."

Four shadows emerged from thick grass south of the clearing. From the corner of his eye he saw each had a gun pointed at his head. *Now there are six. Where are you?* "You didn't answer my question, did you Cankor sore?"

"It's more complicated than we have time for tonight. It is in your best interest we make our little trade and go on our separate ways expeditiously. The banter is wasting my time."

Three more guns got off the boat and stood on the shoreline. Wilcox watched them unload one hostage at a time. They pushed each up the bank. They were bound at the knees, hands tied behind their backs, blindfolded, and gagged. Then one stumbled and moaned—it was Abby.

"It's really not so complicated, Cankor. You want what doesn't belong to you, and you're willing to kill for it. You're no different from any other pathetic cold-blooded psychopath."

Cankor ran his long fingers across the brim of his hat and slid a cigar in his mouth. It didn't move when he spoke. "Maybe you're wrong. Maybe I'm doing something good and you don't know, Detective Wilcox."

"If it were true, we would not be here," Petty said.

He put the match to his cigar. The flame danced on his empty face. His cold black eyes locked onto Petty. She flinched—she too was an obstacle to be removed.

"We know the truth about Stargate," Petty said. "We know Swenson, Proust, Baldwin, and you met in 1978."

"It was when you geeks decided to take over the world," Wilcox scoffed. "Did you realize back then you had to kill your competition—all the other remote viewers and their families?"

"You know nothing," Cankor rebuked.

Wilcox smiled shaking his head. "You couldn't have people like you running around the world. You would not be so special."

"Shut up," Swenson said as he slid into Cankor's shadow.

"I'm curious," Wilcox pushed. "Just help me with one little thing and I'll shut up. I see a lot of this in my line of work. You know, when the bad guys start killing off their partners. Tell me Cankor, when did you decide your lifelong partners had to go? Was it always your plan, or did you just get there one day? When did you decide Proust and Baldwin were excess baggage? When did they stop being partners and start being a pain in your skinny ass? I suppose you had to build your confidence, believe you could control the psychic-weapons alone."

"Are you finished?" Cankor asked.

"I bet I won't be able to shut you up when you're sitting in your cell writing your book, *The Errors of Ugly-ass Monsters*. Hey Swenson, if I were you, I'd watch my back, or head."

Wilcox watched the last hostage thrown to the ground. It was Cottam. They dragged him up the bank. "Any dummy can tell. You're next on Cankor's list."

Cankor blew smoke into Wilcox's face. "All things important require personal sacrifice and elimination of enemies. It is how countries are born, detective. It is how change happens and power moves in the world. American doctrine is no different from Nazi Germany, Castro's Cuba, radical Islam, or other controlling regimes with a vision and ability to dominate."

"You're a sick man." *Now I got you talking . . .*

"They scoffed at the idea of psychic-weapons. The research was misguided, underfunded, and misinterpreted. The program was moved around. They did not know what they had. When they began to understand, it was too late."

"So you thought you'd take over. You would be the one to decide which global ideology would prevail and how the world should evolve," Petty said.

"No, he's in it for the power and money," Wilcox said.

"It is my mission," Cankor growled.

Wilcox leaned in. "There are greater purposes in the world than the missions of men. There are things like compassion for humanity, integrity, and freedom, of which you were once a part.

"At least be honest with yourself. Your mission has turned you into a monster. You've killed many and often. It brings you a creepy pleasure. You two are no different from a wild animal looking for the next meal."

"It is not important that you understand. Give me Hunter Keller, now."

"Not until my people are safe. That was our deal."

"Wilcox is blocking me," Swenson said. "Keller taught him."

Cankor smiled. "I'm impressed. What else can you do detective?"

The lesions stopped them from getting inside me, Wilcox thought, but would not share. Let them think they had a new risk. "Release Patterson, Baily, and Cottam or I will show you."

"You think I will give them to you without Keller?"

"There are nine of you and three of us. Why are you worried?"

Cankor removed his hat. Like the sun, the moonlight found his bald head and hideous smile. He panned the pale fields in silence. Then he stopped on Dr. Petty. His brow dipped. She began to tremble. Her back and legs stiffened. With a whimper she leaned on Wilcox. He held her.

Like the others her eyes bulged in their sockets as the terror consumed her. She grabbed her head and screamed. Wilcox dropped to a knee holding her as she slumped into unconsciousness.

Foam dripped from her lips. "Stop hurting her." Wilcox felt for his ankle holster. *Where is the help I was promised?* He wrapped a finger around the trigger. *You don't control time, asshole. It's the great equalizer. My bullet goes 1,700 miles per hour. In a fraction of a second it'll be coming out the back of your head with half your skull following. I'm taking control. I'm taking you out of Petty's amygdala. And the next bullet is for Swenson.*

Wilcox started to pull his gun from the holster. It would be one fluid motion and both monsters would be dead. But the seven would kill him and the others. It was a no win.

"*Stop!*" Hunter Keller stood in the river brush.

FORTY

"You don't need strength to let go of something. What you really need is understanding."
Guy Finley

Seven guns moved to the skinny man in the tall grass. Cankor turned and Petty sunk on Wilcox's knee—the demon released his grip. Hunter Keller gave himself up.

"There you are," Cankor said. Swenson salivated.

Wilcox let go of his gun and rested Petty on the sand.

God, are you already dead? Did he—? Or, maybe you're unconscious. Wilcox put his ear to her lips—shallow breathing. *But if you're alive, will you ever know? Did Cankor destroy your brain?* Wilcox's eyes found Cankor and Swenson staring at Keller. *I'm gonna kill you bastards!*

He reached a second time for his gun. It was at his feet—this time he would not hesitate. But his hand did not move. *You're controlling me like on Dewar.*

"It is time. You're the last." Cankor put on his hat and backed into the shadows like a rat backing into its hole. "Come to me. Make this easy for everyone."

Keller pushed through the grass onto the sand. "This needs to be over. Let me help Dr. Petty. She is innocent. Let the others go. I will go with you and make this easy."

Swenson smiled like a child waiting for a prize. "We decide when it's over, not you."

Keller's eyes stayed on Cankor. "Let me help her, please."

"You are still blocking," Cankor said. "Why?"

"You are making a mistake," Keller said.

"Someone's blocking. I feel it, too," Swenson looked over his shoulder. "There are only three of us. It must be Keller."

"Shut up Swenson," Cankor boomed. "What are you hiding from us? Do not test me."

Keller looked down at his feet. His hood fell around his face. Cankor moved closer but stopped at the edge of the moonlight like a vampire afraid to burn. With slow eyes, he studied the southern fields as if he could see anything with a heartbeat.

There's someone out there, Cankor thought. *Don't they know it is too late? Don't they know Keller is already dead and nobody can stop me? That's right. There's no way they could know.* He smiled.

"Hey freak," Wilcox yelled. Cankor spun around to the irritating homicide detective. "Keller is here now. You and Bambi win. I need to get Petty to a hospital. Let us go as we agreed."

"We're in control here," Swenson said.

"Стреляйте его," Cankor said with a wave of his gnarled finger.

What the hell—Russian? Wilcox thought as he tried to move his hand to his gun.

The explosion rolled across the river and was swallowed by

the night. Like Bald Knob, Wilcox was hit—but this time in the chest. He dropped next to Petty's lifeless body.

"You know that was necessary," Cankor said. The smoking gun lowered behind him.

Keller started toward the blood-covered detective. The seven guns rose. "You don't need to do this. I'm going with you. No more death."

Cankor puffed his cigar. "Detective Wilcox moves on slivers of opportunity. The man does not fear consequences. He is dangerous. I will not allow heroics this night."

Keller's eyes moved up the leather coat to the face of the man who hunted him for a decade. *You really don't know what is going to happen tonight,* he thought. *You hide your weaknesses from others, but I know them all. You do not see the complete future, only parts.* "You killed my parents."

"I was forced to. I did not want to. They were among the few to talk to me in the beginning—Scanate, 1975. The others stayed away, ignored me." Cankor pointed to his face like he was auditioning for a part. "*This* scared people—no hair and the scars. Did you know my parents tried to kill me? They didn't know about congenital hypotrichosis or clairvoyance. They thought scars and hair loss and visions were signs. I was evil. I was a child from hell. But Scanate saved my life. They shipped me off to the government program instead of poisoning their monster. Your parents were just as bad."

"Major." Swenson touched his shoulder, but Cankor shrugged him off like an irritating child tugging on his coat.

"Your parents were given an opportunity to live," Cankor said. "They refused to help me. Deep down, they rejected me, too. They kept you from me. I could not allow it. Your parents gave me no choice."

"You did not need to kill them. You did not need to kill the remote viewers. We all have always wanted one thing—a normal life. We wanted to be left alone."

"They were a risk. And you are dangerous," Cankor said leaning his brim into the soft moonlight. "The gifted Hunter Keller, son of most powerful psychics. They gave you everything and more. I did not know your capabilities. I did not know I could control you."

"I'm not special. I'm not what you think."

Cankor's cold grin melted. "You're right. You're not special, not anymore. You're an abject failure, no discipline, and no purpose, and no balls."

"I did not ask for this."

"Contemptible. You were given gifts you never worked a day in your life to develop. You squandered a miracle, an unparalleled genetic advantage over every living thing on the planet."

"I rejected it," Keller said.

"I developed mine. I sacrificed to understand, to be strong." Cankor smiled at the empty night sky and reveled in the moment. His plan was coming together. "I see more than any man alive. I stop life with my mind. I terminate anyone, anytime, anywhere, and leave no trace."

"It is evil. The world will reject it."

"You're wrong. I'm unstoppable. Now, even you can't stop me."

Keller turned to the north field and scanned the dark tree line along the leading edge of the land bridge. "Did you ever consider something else can stop you?"

Cankor followed his gaze into the empty field. "This is not some *Marvel* action adventure. This is real. I change outcomes. Every government wants the ability to vanquish their enemies, to control their destinies regardless of the cards they are dealt. I can give it to them."

"If you see the future, you know it will be abused. There are those seeking power without concern for human life. The outcome will be catastrophic."

"I'm in control of it," Cankor boasted.

"You don't control it. It controls you. That is why you must be stopped."

"What's Keller saying?" Swenson asked. "Kill him now. Kill all of them. We need to go."

"You are weak now. I know. You did not save your friends because you cannot." The three hostages squirmed in the sand and seven guns stayed on Keller.

"The Cold War rages on—underground. The balance of power is about to change. I will lead the change. It has become too expensive and time consuming for nations to engage in outdated, military conflicts to achieve political objectives. Everyone wants their fair share of the world's limited resources. Now it is possible. I level the playing field. Psychic-weaponry is the great equalizer, the most significant weapon of mass destruction since the atomic bomb. Armies will be stopped without putting one soldier on the field of battle. Thousands will drop where they stand without a single shot fired. Those who live will run from an invisible enemy. War will become obsolete. Countries will try to live together."

"No. Others will learn and more innocent people will die."

"I bring a civilized solution to uncivilized, international conflicts."

"No. You will destroy the human race. Psychokinesis is too dangerous to exist. Those who control it will abuse it."

"You could have been a part of the vision, but you ran from me. You hid from the world. Why did you climb out of your hole now? Is it the carnage? Is it a feeling? You could not control the urge to kill me. You know the rage unleashes the monster within. You must control your kill instinct. If you kill me, you will kill others. It's the way it works. You can't turn it off once you turn it on. You are here tonight because you can't stop—*you are evil like me!*"

He said nothing because Cankor spoke the truth. Keller hid from the world because the evil inside would consume him. He could not let it happen.

"There was once a time we needed you," Swenson said. "Now, we need you *gone*."

Cankor's and Swenson's eyes fell on Keller and their pupils contracted. Their combined psychokinetic strength penetrated his blocking shield. Keller began to tremble. His face paled. A single drop of blood rolled from his nose. He collapsed onto the sandy mound as they sunk the psychic-dagger into his spine. His heart pounded and body went rigid. The soft moon exploded into a blinding sun, and the gray mist floating above the fields burst into white fire. A thousand needles pierced Keller's brain as air left his lungs and his throat collapsed.

FORTY-ONE

Like lethal toxins of the Box Jellyfish, Cankor's psychic venom penetrated Keller's amygdala and triggered primal fears. His adrenaline burst into his veins. His memory clouded as crippling spasms spread through his body. Anxiety mounted. Blood pressure climbed. Keller ran for his life in his mind causing the hyperventilation that starved his brain of precious oxygen. In seconds he drifted into shock.

Cankor knew well the stages of the psychic-kill. Keller's body would shut down like helpless prey in the jaws of a beast. The fear and pain would be catastrophic. The body's defense mechanisms would take over. Keller would revel in a euphoric peace. In seconds his spastic heart beats would stop. Like the others his amygdala would trick his body into suicide.

Keller tumbled in the tunnel—the one traveled at birth and in death. Inside the swirling portal of existence between worlds, all things that once mattered evaporate. He forgot about the remote viewers killed. He forgot about his self-imposed mission and his dead parents and dead friends. He forgot about clandestine, government research out of control and the threat to the world.

Keller forgot the years of horrific crimes against the innocent. He was no longer on Mud Island with Cankor and Swenson. In the tunnel, real monsters mean nothing.

Swenson broke away blinking back into the present—Keller was helpless now. "I'll give you the honors."

Cankor would savor the final moments with his nemesis—it was part of the gift, the part that Keller feared most and ran from all his life.

Swenson walked to the hostages and kicked each one—they were his now. None reacted to his boot. They were worn from abuse, all hope gone. A few feet away Petty and Wilcox lay silent and Keller squirmed like an earthworm caught on a sidewalk in the hot sun.

"You seem depressed," Swenson said as he poked Abby Patterson. "Not having a good day?" He ran his hand up her leg, something he could never do with an unbound lady. She recoiled, pulling knees to her chest and turning her covered head away.

"Maybe if you were nice to me you'd have options." He stroked her leg again. But this time her feet shot out crushing his face. The mangled wire glasses, bloody nose, and three-piece suit tumbled backwards into the tall grass like a garbage bag caught in a stiff wind.

He returned and kicked Patterson one last time. He ordered, "Kill these people, now." Three guns pressed against three heads as Swenson turned to the glow of the city less than a mile away. "Best use silencers."

Velcro pouches ripped open in unison.

I've earned this, Swenson mused. He took in the crisp night air and sweet smell of victory. *Since Stargate I out-maneuvered them all—Proust and Baldwin. I knew Cankor had the will and the ability. He would be the one to confuse the architects of the government's secret project. Now, twenty-one remote viewers are dead and their lineage nullified. Keller is the last obstacle. After tonight only Cankor and I will possess the telekinetic knowledge and power to kill. We will decide who gets our services. We will define the next millennium. I will get the respect I deserve. And for now, I'm okay with the number two position.*

While in captivity the hostages listened to Swenson's and Cankor's ongoing conversations about Hunter Keller and his astounding psychic gifts. The two openly discussed their twisted plans to corner Keller so his gifts could not be used to turn the tables on Mud Island. Now—the hostages lying in the sand bound and hooded—it was clear Hunter Keller was not the most gifted one. If he had been, he would have foreseen the events on Mud Island. Keller would have protected Detective Wilcox and Dr. Petty. He would have foiled Major Cankor's sinister plans.

The three gunmen screwed silencers onto their muzzles. Swenson stared at the glow of downtown Memphis waiting for the muffled pops and the rush. But another feeling came. It was like a soft gust of cold air in his face. Swenson's hair lifted. His smile faded. His gaze moved from the glittering skyline to the soft, pale scrub. When he opened his mouth, it was too late. The high pitched whistle crossed the island in a fraction of a second. Cankor broke from Keller and watched Swenson's eye explode and body drop face down, the back of his head gone.

"Shoot the hostages," Cankor ordered as got up and dragged Keller behind a tree. "Shoot all of them. We will prevail."

More hollow-points whistled across the southern field, and more chunks of brain and shattered skull flew into the cool night air. In seconds three more empty bodies holding guns with silencers sat down in the scrub. One by one they flopped over and disappeared in the grass.

Cankor's four remaining soldiers moved up the bank into tall grass returning fire. But they had no targets. After the flurry of shots they stopped to reload. The island was quiet, the cloud of burned gunpowder thick. Then four more whistles cut through the grass and four more heads exploded. Their lifeless bodies fell over like rotted trees in a soft wind.

Cankor dragged Keller toward the boat. *How did this happen?* His distraction left him vulnerable. Now he would complete his mission and escape. When Cankor reached for the rope, white light flooded the bank. Like a UFO hovering above the river fifty yards out, the intense beams widened, and spinning blues and reds emerged, and the grumbling hum of diesels swallowed the river sounds.

Someone's blocking this, Cankor thought. *Keller's unable to block. Who am I missing?* He watched shadows approach the clearing—he knew they had orders not to engage. Grabbing Keller's ankle, Cankor dragged the ragdoll body up the bank into the north field.

"*Major Cankor.*" The words echoed from a bullhorn on the water. "*This is the Memphis police. Do not attempt to leave Mud Island. You are surrounded.*" The words rolled down the river as boats nosed onto the shoreline and lights climbed the bank. But Cankor pushed into the grass dragging Keller behind.

Only two on Mud Island knew the national security risk. The intimate details of the top secret U.S. psychic-weaponry program could not be shared, not even with the commanders of the MPD elite force or director. However, U.S. counter insurgency forces were briefed—the mission was to recover two rogue members of a classified government program. Orders were explicit. Take Major Cankor and Hunter Keller alive. Under no circumstances allow Keller to leave Mud Island.

Clutching Keller's boney ankle, Cankor marched toward the land bridge off Mud Island. It was not covered—an inexcusable, tactical error. He and Keller would disappear in the north woods of Shelby County. They would escape because Cankor was focused. He knew their every move well in advance.

FORTY-TWO

*"All we know is still infinitely less than all that remains
unknown."*
William Harvey

Disoriented, she stayed low squinting into the white light.
Twenty feet away she saw lumps on the sand. Pushing up,
her hand touched something—Wilcox, his chest covered with
blood. Petty crawled to his side and felt for a pulse. It was strong.
Under moving shadows, she slapped his face hard. "Wake up."

"Damn Petty."

Inches from his face she whispered, "Hold it down."

"What'd you hit me for?" Wilcox whispered back.

She ripped his shirt open and wiped his wound. "You're not
bleeding now." She applied pressure and looked around. "You've
been shot again. Do you remember anything?"

"Am I gonna die?"

"Yes."

"Shit! Then there's somethin' I gotta say." He struggled to sit up.

Petty held him down and climbed back in his face. "Save it. You've got another forty years if we get out of this."

"I just got shot in the chest. Show a little compassion. I know I can be a hard ass, but . . ."

"Actually it's the shoulder, and whisper. We don't know who's in control of this island. You've been shot twice in two days by people you piss-off. You're running out of luck. This bullet found a muscle too—no major arteries, nerves, or bones. The impact must have knocked you out, or you're a sissy."

"You're so nice to me when I'm weak. It hurt like hell." He lifted his head and squinted. "Where are Cankor, Swenson, all their people? And where are the hostages?"

"I think Patterson, Baily, and Cottam are over there—those lumps on the sand. They're moving. I do not see Cankor. Swenson's over there, by the hostages."

"I need to find my gun and shoot that Swenson twit."

"That's not necessary. Swenson's dead, missing the back of his head."

"Sniper fire?" Wilcox pushed Petty's hand off his chest and sat up. "Is our backup here? Hence, light everywhere. The moving shadows on the bank gotta be the good guys."

"You think?" Petty teased.

"You better hope, or we are both dead." Wilcox started to stand.

"Be careful moving around, you're still injured. You don't want to start bleeding again."

"I don't see Cankor's henchmen anywhere, or Keller. He was supposed to stay over there." They both saw the trampled path in the tall grass. It crossed over Keller's hiding place.

"Does Cankor have him?" Petty asked. "And why would they let Cankor get away?"

"They're not gonna shoot Cankor or Keller—they're government assets."

Wilcox looked around and found three shadows standing in the scrub at the south edge of the sandy clearing, each in camo holding a high-powered rifle with scope. "I'm Wilcox. This is Petty. Are you boys with us?"

Three thumbs went up. Wilcox turned back with a smile, but Petty was gone. Then he heard Baily in the distance. "We've been kept in the dark forever."

Wilcox approached the hostages as Baily rambled on to Petty. "Thought it was all over when we heard the shot and Wilcox stopped talking. Cop killers have no limits."

"He's okay," Petty said as she untied Baily looking back for Wilcox. "Where'd you go?"

Wilcox lifted Abby kicking. "Whoa now. It's me, Tee." She stopped. He cut her ropes and pulled off her hood and gag. She pulled him close and kissed him hard.

Petty and Baily watched. "Guess she's appreciative," Baily muttered. Petty rolled her eyes and slid over to Cottam who was not moving.

"You took your sweet-ass time, Tee," Abby said.

Wilcox untied her ankles. "Sorry to get you into this mess—didn't see this coming. And it's not over yet, so keep low. The guys with rifles are on our side."

Baily wobbled to his feet, Petty helped Cottam stand, and Abby and Wilcox got up. The five stood in a line on the sandy mound. They watched the lights combing the north field. Less than fifty yards out they saw someone moving toward the land bridge.

"Cankor's getting away," Wilcox said.

Behind them, the sniper rifles were down. To their left the MPD elite force jumped off boats and swarmed the bank like army ants. They too stopped and lowered their weapons at the edge of the clearing. A tall man in dark fatigues climbed the bank with a hand on his holstered gun. "Detective Wilcox, I am lead commander of this operation. Call me Derby. We have covered all fronts except the land bridge."

"Well the land bridge is a problem, Derby. This guy's a psychic. He knows it's open. It is how he will escape. That's him out there. We gotta get people to that tree line ASAP."

"Limitations are never acceptable. When we arrived, we had no intelligence on the location of targets. At this time the northeast flank is populated from the southern flank. Unfortunately, targets have a window."

"Well that's just great."

"It's a lot of ground to cover in a short time," Petty said.

"Then let's shoot the bastard now," Wilcox boomed. "Someone give me a rifle."

"We have orders. They are to be taken alive."

"Well, that's not gonna happen, Derby. Did they tell you what we're dealing with?"

Baily blurted out, "Whoa! Look at that."

"What in the hell . . . ?" A line of shadows emerged from the woods northeast of the land bridge a hundred yards out. "Are those your men, Derby?" Wilcox asked. "Looks like a battalion."

"Someone put a scope on that," Derby ordered. Sniper rifles went up in unison.

"Sir. Deer. A lot of them. No sir. Correction. Elk, sir. Big ones."

"Bald Knob again?" Wilcox said under his breath as they all watched the enormous herd move from the woods onto the land bridge.

"What's Bald Knob?" Derby asked.

"It's hard to explain. Let's just say I've seen a lot of bull elk before."

"Major Cankor had something in his left hand," Petty said. "I saw him drop it. Now he's waving both arms at those animals."

They all watched. "He had Mr. Keller," Derby said. "He dragged him from this location."

"Keller's alive?" Wilcox asked.

"I doubt it, sir. He was not moving."

"He could be alive. He could be unconscious," Petty said.

"Who's running this operation Detective Wilcox, you or Derby?" Cottam asked.

"You won't be able to stop this." The words came from behind the snipers. Heads turned. "I suggest we keep guns down and watch. We're out of this now."

Flanked by Secret Service agents, the man in the three-piece suit and blood stained shoulder bandage walked up like he owned Mud Island.

"You're late," Wilcox said. "And still couldn't find a clean change of clothes."

"Sorry, detective. You gave me a lot to do, and little time to do it."

"You screwed up leaving the land bridge open."

"Who are you?" Cottam interrupted.

Wilcox made the introductions. "This is U.S. Attorney General Alfred Baldwin. He was supposed to be here at ten— that was our deal." Wilcox leaned into Baldwin's face. "Your delay got Petty's brain fried, me shot—I could have died—and Cankor's got Keller in God-knows-what condition. Not good, Baldwin. This is typical government incompetence. We talked about this at the Brent Mansion. You are goddamn late."

They watched the herd close around Cankor.

"I am sorry, detective. But not everything goes according to plan. Securing and deploying needed resources on short notice proved enormously challenging, even for me." Baldwin winced and rubbed his chest eyeing Cankor in the field. "We're here now."

"Damn bullets hurt even when you're wearing a vest," Wilcox grumbled.

"So true. And the one that missed clipped my shoulder and made a bloody mess. Knocked me down, too."

"And sold your assassination on camera," Wilcox said. "I still gotta give you credit. I don't know if I could have stood on that podium knowing I had to take a bullet or two."

"What we do for our country," Baldwin said under his breath.

"I've missed a lot," Cottam said as they watched the herd grow and close on Cankor.

"You were tied, gagged, and hooded the last twenty-four hours," Baldwin said. "I am sorry sir. I was assassinated at your Loraine Hotel today. I was there picking up a humanitarian award. My people knew there would be an assassination attempt. I had to allow it."

"That makes perfect sense. Sorry I missed it," Cottam chided.

"There's gotta be a hundred out there now, sir," said one sniper.

Baldwin was unimpressed with the animals. He saw it before. "Director Cottam, your abductors—Dr. Swenson and Major Cankor—had to believe I was dead."

"And why is that?" Cottam asked.

"Because I too am a remote viewer."

"A remote what?"

"It's a long story. Let's just say a psychic with unique capabilities."

"I see. And I assume Mr. Keller is one too," Cottam said.

They stared at the lights flooding the north field of Mud Island. "Mr. Keller is something very different," Baldwin said. "Let me be very clear. The United States Government cannot allow either to leave Mud Island. The national security risks are too great. We must contain."

"I do not see Keller. Are we sure Cankor had him?" Wilcox asked.

"He is lying somewhere in the field. The herd forced Cankor to release him."

"Those animals are a problem for Cankor," Wilcox said.

"That massive herd can't be good for Hunter either," Petty said.

"Both are going to be trampled," Cottam said. "I've never seen anything like this."

"Actually I've seen it two times before—Bald Knob and Sikeston," Wilcox said.

"They won't hurt Hunter Keller. He is safe," Baldwin said. "The elk protect him—dead or alive. I suppose they don't know the difference."

"I'm a hunter," Cottam said. "Wild animals run from people. They don't make friends."

"As Mr. Wilcox said, we've seen this before," Baldwin said. "Our scientists say it is extrasensory communication tied into the animal's instinct mechanism. Animals respond to stimuli. In this case the stimulus is sent by Keller, his subconscious reaction to danger. He knew he would face danger here tonight. The animals picked up on it. They came, driven by protective instinct. They see Keller as one of them. They see Swenson and Cankor as predators."

"That sounds bizarre," Cottam mumbled.

"Mr. Keller connects with animals like his mother did years ago—the Scanate Project. The particular skill is rare. I know of no other with the capability. Mr. Keller possesses even more gifts beyond our understanding," Baldwin said.

They stared at the undulating herd beneath the rising dirt cloud.

"You see the largest bull elk with the enormous rack? The animal is holding his head high. He's maybe twenty feet away from Major Cankor."

"He's gotta be seven-hundred pounds," Cottam said.

"See how he stays to the edge of Cankor's line of vision?" Baldwin said. "When Cankor turns, the bull moves to hold his position in the periphery."

"What about it?" Wilcox asked.

"He is the alpha male in the herd. He's measuring Major Cankor. He is going to charge. It is now about timing. The alpha bull elk sees Cankor as a threat to Keller and his herd."

"They had to travel a long way," Cottam said. "Seems like that makes them the predator, not the defender."

"That doesn't matter in the animal world, Director Cottam. The concept of first and second means nothing. Instinct drives everything. Major Cankor's aggression triggered the threat and created the confrontation," Baldwin said.

"How can you be so sure Hunter Keller is dead?" Petty asked.

Baldwin leaned out and found the doctor. "If Mr. Keller were alive, he would be fighting back. I believe the psychic confrontation is over. It appears Major Cankor was the victor."

"If Keller's dead, why would Cankor drag him off?" Wilcox asked.

"To destroy his remains, to burn him, to obliterate the Keller family DNA. Major Cankor's objective is to secure his total dominance over the global, psychotronic initiative."

"So you admit psychic-weaponry does exist," Petty said.

Baldwin smiled. "Yes. I speak in general terms."

"A psychic-weapon of mass destruction is something our planet really needs," Wilcox said.

"I'm afraid it has had the attention of the superpowers for

four decades. What began as an intelligence gathering tool soon became much more."

"Killing people with 'thoughts' sounds like science fiction to me," Cottam said.

"I still have trouble that one man can cause so much trouble in the world." Wilcox said.

Baldwin said, "If Cankor was not occupied by this elk herd, one look this way and people would die. Don't deny what you do not know or understand."

"I hear you, but still find that hard to swallow," Cottam said.

"Director Cottam, you have multiple psychic-homicide victims in your county morgue. I am quite certain Dr. Petty has now seen enough to share her professional opinion on the matter."

Eyes turned to Dr. Petty as she scanned the herd still looking for Hunter Keller. "Psychic manipulation of the amygdala produces an overwhelming sense of terror triggering life system shutdown and cardiac arrest."

She turned to them and said, "In layman terms, you are mentally manipulated into being scared to death—a kind of lethal hypnosis. The hypnotist is far away."

"William Harvey, an English physician in the 1600s, was ahead of his time. When medical intervention was viewed a last option, he said something profound. I believe it fits this moment. He said, '*All we know is infinitively less than all that remains unknown.*'"

"Never heard of the man," Wilcox puffed.

Petty chuckled. "He was the first to describe the systemic circulation and properties of blood pumped to the body and brain by the heart. In his day he was thought to be crazy, too. Four-hundred years later, he's a genius."

"Today a third-grader knows more than the world population back then," Baldwin said.

"Maybe this Harvey guy got it right," Wilcox said. "The stuff I've seen over the last few days is from the unknown."

On his last word the alpha bull elk charged Cankor and pushed him to the ground. Cankor jumped to his feet and waved his hat and arms backing up the herd. The bull elk hesitated and backed away. Then it lowered its head and charged a second time. A cloud of debris lifted.

"They're going to kill him," Petty said. "We can't just stand here. It's not right."

"Shooting the animals would create a much bigger problem," Baldwin said. "We would confuse the herd. They'd come our way—we would be the predators. Major Cankor could escape and a lot of us get trampled. I don't care how many guns we have, we'd lose the battle. Trust me, we cannot intervene. We must let this play out."

Wilcox stepped into the tall grass. "Baldwin, you don't know if Keller's dead."

"I do not know for sure."

"He could be alive. He could be lying out there needing help."

"Keller stopped blocking," Baldwin shot back. "Cankor and Swenson got in his head. Hit him with everything they had. Even Keller could not survive the onslaught."

"Explain Dewar, then. Cankor ran when Keller showed up," Wilcox said.

"Cankor was caught off guard. Maybe he was injured on Dewar and had to leave to do battle another day. Regardless, it appears he has recovered. He and Swenson took Keller down."

"I will not stand here and watch. I'm gonna do something," Wilcox said.

"I can't stop you. You're making a mistake. Those animals are crazed. If they don't kill you, Cankor will." Baldwin turned to his team. "Everyone, stand down. That's an order."

"Commander Derby, it goes for your people too," Cottam ordered. "Detective Wilcox is on his own. He's always been," he said under his breath.

But Petty heard him. "And he's often right." She ran into the deep grass. "Maybe I can help." She caught up to Wilcox. Together they approached the edge of the snorting herd of moving shadows.

"I have no idea what I'm gonna do with Cankor," Wilcox whispered.

"Knock him on his ass," Petty said.

"You never cuss," Wilcox said. "Don't try to get on my good side."

They inched forward. Even though Cankor was a despicable serial killer, allowing wild animals to gore and trample him to death was not the justice they sought. And in Keller's final hour, they would not abandon him. The frail, young man from Stringtown with the bizarre gifts was now more alone than ever. He did not need to confront his nemesis on Mud Island. He did it because Wilcox and Petty gave him the courage to face reality. Now, they would not leave his body in the field beneath the sharp hoofs of a hundred bull elk. He deserved better.

"I know why he came here tonight," Petty said as they pushed through the grass. "We helped him reach a turning point. Hunter believed he was evil like Cankor. He was afraid of what his gifts could do to him. I think tonight he was . . ."

"Was what?" Wilcox turned to her.

"I think tonight he was . . . too afraid to run."

They approached the edge of the herd and stopped. The massive heads turned. A path opened. "What's this about?" Wilcox whispered with his eyes on the path.

"I suspect we are more of a curiosity than threat, at the moment," Petty said.

They walked the narrow path. With each step forward the

animals opened before them and closed behind. Forty yards from the sandy mound and onlookers, they saw Keller lying on his back on the trampled grass. The bull elk maintained an open circle around his lifeless body.

"Baldwin was right," Wilcox said. "They're protecting him. I'll be damned."

Elk eyes locked on Wilcox and Petty as they knelt by Keller. The muscular animals could close in on them at any moment. Petty felt Hunter's carotid. "No pulse." She put her ear to his chest.

Wilcox stared at the snorting heads and black eyes and three-foot racks of sharp boney spikes waving in the moonlight. They were in control.

"Is he deh . . . ?"

Before he could finish the word, Petty started CPR.

Wilcox could do nothing for Petty or Keller. He had to find Cankor. He had to do the impossible—convince a psychopath to stop killing. Maybe Cankor would return to Stargate if he knew Baldwin was alive, on the island, and willing to make a deal.

He got to his feet and pushed forward through the herd. He peered over a hundred bobbing heads and through the choking dust cloud. Then the elk opened another path as if they knew he was going to stop Cankor.

I'm doing it again—way over my head. Keller's dead and Cankor's my serial killer. I can't let that monster get off this island. Wilcox moved deeper into the herd. As he progressed, the bull elk were bigger and more agitated. *You guys must be the warriors.* He took each step unsure if it would be his last. *Whoa there. I'm one of the good guys. I don't need to be gored tonight. Did I mention I've never hunted a day in my life? Animals, anyway . . .*

Wilcox was nudged down the path with curious noses, challenging snorts, and huge eyes. He looked away from the few rearing up on hind legs. They dropped back to all fours and let him pass. *I'm on my way to die with some psychic asshole,* he mused. *I'll never get this power-crazed freak to give it up. Why do I attempt the impossible? What is my problem?*

There was movement ahead, in the murky haze and undulating shadows. He found Major Cankor—his back ten yards ahead. The bull elk maintained another circle around Cankor, but the purpose was different. They were going to kill the man.

But before Wilcox could open his mouth, the psychic-killer waved off the last charging bull elk and spun around; his long, black coat lifted in the air like a hideous cape.

"Too bad," Cankor spewed. "The bullet would have been a more comfortable way to die, Detective Wilcox."

His chest wound burned under Cankor's stare. Wilcox winced and tried to blink away the spiraling pain. "Stop. Wait. You win. Everybody's dead. You're the last one standing with the weird skill sets. You are a valuable commodity, Major Cankor. Nobody's gonna mess with you now. Swenson's missing half his brain, Keller's a carp in the grass. All the RVs are dead. You win. Let's get out of this pissed-off herd of elk before we both get gored."

"Alfred is here," Cankor said. "He survived the sniper's bullets."

"He did. But you control psychic-weaponry. Your first customer is the U.S. Government. Baldwin is standing over there ready to make a deal. Don't screw this up."

"You underestimate me because you're a common man with a narrow definition of right and wrong. You live in a one-dimensional world, Mr. Wilcox. Your small brain cannot comprehend extreme, existential concepts. I don't need to make any deal. I have all the power now."

"What are you talking about?" Wilcox inched closer. *How much time do I need to reach my ankle holster, pull my gun, and put a bullet between the eyes of another delusional monster?*

"You're a fool." Cankor smiled. His brow dipped. "It is time for heroes to die. I will kill you first, and then Dr. Petty. I will kill the others and save Alfred for last. You have underestimated me. You have woefully miscalculated the dimensions of the moment."

"Listen to me, Cankor. Alfred Baldwin's your old, school buddy. He's here to cut you the best deal and take you back to Stargate. You're on the top of the heap with a deal." Wilcox looked back at the white lights and knelt inches closer to his ankle holster.

"You think I don't know what you're doing?"

"I have not underestimated you, Cankor. The government's not gonna let you off this island if you don't work with them. You can't stop bullets. You can't stop all the snipers tonight. You can't stop a world hunting you. We will not let you take psychic-weapons to our enemies.

"Take the deal on the table. Work with the most powerful country on the planet. You'll get everything your little, black heart desires. Any other way means the end for you."

Cankor smiled at the moon. "I will be the only one leaving Mud Island tonight."

He raised a hand and plunged a psychic-dagger into the top of Wilcox's head. Like a sizzling bolt of lightning, the pain shot through the core of his brain and down his spine. His knees buckled, and he dropped to the turf gasping for air. Like all the others under telekinetic attack, his arms and legs stiffened and back arched to the snapping point. Cankor's unspoken words dripped with controlled rage, and burned the inside of Wilcox's skull.

"Soon you won't care," Cankor said as he turned his back to the next dying man.

Baldwin was right. Petty and Wilcox should have stayed on

the sandy mound and let the animals have their way—Cankor's skills could not stop a herd. He was an evil predator on a sinister mission.

Cankor was right when he told Wilcox what would happen next. Wilcox lay paralyzed on trampled grass. He struggled to manage his final thoughts. With all he could muster, he willed his cramped fingers down his calf to his ankle holster, but he was attempting the impossible. His frozen body would not find a way to remove the gun from its holster, to aim, and to pull the trigger one last time. Cankor was right—Wilcox did not care anymore.

When he touched the pearl handle of his 357 magnum, his hand flopped to the ground. The terror, manufactured by his manipulated amygdala, took over. Wilcox lost reason and the will to live. The side of his head sunk deeper into the flat grass. Surrounded by the muscular legs of bull elk, his heart raced and eyes ached under the mounting pressure. He touched the pearl handle a second time and inched his finger to the trigger. Through wet, paper-thin slits his eyes found Major Cankor one last time. But Cankor was no longer standing in the middle of the herd. He was floating above the herd in the swirling dust cloud raining debris.

Am I dead? Am I dreaming? This is an illusion.

FORTY-THREE

"Gifts make their way through stone walls."
Proverb

From the sandy mound they watched in silence. The flood lights lit up the north field of Mud Island like an NFL stadium night game. Lights poured to the tree line northeast of the land bridge. All could see Major Cankor floating above the herd.

Cottam spoke first. "Is that man levitating?"

"There is a logical explanation," Baldwin said. "It is not what you think."

"He's gotta be thirty feet up and climbing," Baily said.

"More like fifty," Patterson said.

"What in the hell is our government doing?" Cottam said as he rubbed his eyes and witnessed the silhouette climbing and his coat lifting in the river breeze like a demon's cape.

"I did not see this coming," Baldwin said. *You should not be seeing this.*

Director Cottam said. "Tell us the government did not know that man could levitate." He shook his head in disbelief as the others blinked in silence. "I suppose if I were running things in the government, I'd want to keep this a secret too."

"Major Cankor is not levitating," Baldwin said.

"Right. We believe you. He's not be levitating," Cottam said tongue in cheek.

"Hunter Keller is doing it." Baldwin pointed to the wisp of a shadow standing in the center of the herd. "There he is. He is alive. And he is in control of everything, including us."

"Keller is levitating Cankor?" Baily asked.

"No. Keller is controlling our minds," Baldwin said. "This is nothing more than a mass-illusion. He is manipulating us. We see what he wants us to see."

"Are you saying we are hypnotized?" Cottam asked.

"Not the way you think. This is not hypnotism by the power of suggestion. It is more like pheromones—excreted chemical factors that trigger a response. In nature it is most often of a sexual nature. Pheromones are well documented in the insect world. They come into play with some vertebrates and even plants. They are well understood."

"How does that apply here," Patterson pushed.

"Hunter Keller releases telepathic-pheromones, in a sense. He is impacting perceptions and behavior of receiving individuals. But unlike chemical pheromones with limited reach due to diffusion issues, Hunter Keller's T-P is effective in large areas."

"How large?" Cottam asked.

"At least a city. Maybe more. We have not been able to test him."

"Is it possible Keller is actually levitating Cankor?" Baily asked.

"No. He is creating the illusion of levitation in our minds. We are seeing and feeling what he wants."

"Does Major Cankor believe he is floating fifty feet above the ground?" Cottam asked.

"Yes," Baldwin said. "All of this is for Cankor. We are in range to receive the telepathic pheromones. Mr. Keller is attempting to negotiate with Cankor, get him to surrender."

On Baldwin's last word they watched Hunter Keller turn to them and drop his head. Seconds later Cankor plummeted to the ground.

"It appears the Major was unwilling."

The herd melted into the woods and the dust cloud settled on Mud Island.

The Memphis Tribune: Gunshots on Mud Island Kept Under Wraps

Memphis, TN, November 6 – Early today gunshots were fired on Mud Island. The MPD Elite Force was called into action. At least one died at the scene. Details surrounding the shooting are unknown at the time of this report.

MPD Director Cottam was interviewed leaving the scene. "The nature of events occurring on Mud Island is classified," he said. "I am pleased we could assist the FBI and Homeland Security on a matter of national importance. The citizens of Memphis were never in harm's way. The operation was professionally managed and carefully monitored to insure the safety of our community."

The MPD Harbor Patrol was called into action around midnight last night to assist the U.S. Coast Guard and the elite force. After completion of the operation, a body was removed and transported to the Shelby County Medical Examiner's office. Dr. Victoria Petty was unavailable for comment. All other participants departed Mud Island by water to an undisclosed location. The north end of Mud Island is a restricted (crime scene) area until further notice.

Sources close to the operation said U.S. Attorney General Alfred Baldwin was on Mud Island. Rumors he died following the shooting at the National Civil Rights Museum have been corrected. "Mr. Baldwin was never in danger. The failed attempt on his life resulted in minor injuries. Perpetrators are being pursued." Asked if the failed assassination attempt was connected to Mud Island events, there were no comments. Memphis Homicide Detective Tony Wilcox, the lead investigator on a series of unsolved homicides, was not available for comment.

Wolf River Harbor residents reported an unusual number of large, bull elk in their neighborhoods the morning of the incident. The Tennessee Wildlife Resources Agency was contacted and could not explain the migration phenomena. Elk are rare in the region.

EPILOGUE

"Life is a mystery to be lived, not a problem to be solved."
Soren Kierkegaard

Three Weeks Later

D r. Petty stood at the door watching Tony push green Jell-O cubes with a fork. She pulled the file close to her chest and walked into the hospital room. "Knock, knock."

"Where the hell have you been?" he groused.

"You gonna poke those green Jell-O squares to death, or are you gonna to eat 'em?"

"Nobody's talking. I think I'm being handled, kept in the dark. I ask questions and I get irritating smiles and more stinkin' food. I'm about ready to jump out the damn window, but they got me tied to the bed except one arm. Where the hell am I?"

"The restraints are for your own good, Tony. You've been thrashing about." The door muffled closed behind her. "You are at Walter Reed in Washington DC."

"A damn military hospital? Am I a prisoner?"

"Not yet," she said. "Seriously, we almost lost you."

"What're you talkin' about?"

"You've been in a coma for twenty-one days." Staring at the ceiling he stopped poking his green Jell-O. Petty patted his arm. "I received the call two hours ago. You just woke up, Tony."

"I did? They called you first?"

"Yes. I was cleared to be here first, following some standard tests and you eating something. You pulled out your feeding tube before you woke up. You broke one restraint."

"Why's nobody talkin' to me?" Wilcox asked.

Petty closed the blinds and slid a chair to the bed. "We don't have much time." She pulled a piece of paper from her file and held it like she was reading. On the back it said—room bugged. Wilcox blinked. She slid the paper back into the file.

"What the hell's going on?"

"Do you remember anything?" Petty asked.

"I remember everything."

"You were unconscious when I found you in the field. What is the last thing you remember on Mud Island—we'll start there?"

"Watchin' Cankor float above the herd of bull elk." Wilcox rubbed his forehead as if the thought gave him pain. "I think I was crazy by then. Cankor fried my brain. I tried to reach for my gun to shoot the bastard, but had no strength. I lost the will."

"What else do you remember?" Petty asked.

"I remember Keller. I remember he was dead, white as snow. The skinny guy laid there like all the others, our homicides. You tried to help—I don't know why. I guess Cankor escaped."

"Something happened after you left me with Hunter," Petty said.

"Sorry. I've seen a lot of dead people. He was dead and I needed to stop Cankor."

"He responded to CPR."

Wilcox stopped rubbing his head. His eyes locked on Petty's. "Keller is alive?"

"Yes. Tell me, how soon after leaving us did you find Major Cankor?"

"Half a minute. He was less than twenty yards away, deeper in the herd. The asshole saw me right away. Said he knew I was coming—the psychic prick."

"So you did speak with him?"

Wilcox looked at the ceiling. "He spun around. I saw his beady, black eyes on me. Ya know, I don't know if our exchange was verbal or mental. I guess it was probably mental. His lips didn't move."

"That explains it. That is why Hunter was able to come back. Cankor was distracted. You distracted him. Cankor's psychic grip loosened," Petty said.

"Guess the poor bastard can't multitask." Wilcox resumed poking his green Jell-O cubes. "So, Keller survived that night on Mud Island, too?"

"Hunter survived. Cankor did not."

He stopped poking as a smile grew on his face. "There is a God. Tell me. Did the hostages make it off Mud Island in one piece?"

"Director Cottam had four broken ribs, a dislocated jaw, and sprained ankle. Detective Baily had a broken wrist and fractured skull. Your friend, Miss Patterson, had cuts and bruises, mostly the knuckles on her right hand." Petty smiled. "I like strong women. Abby gave those two more than they bargained for. The good news is none of them had damage to their amygdalas."

"What about the snipers and MPD elite force?"

"They got off the island without even a grass stain," Petty teased.

"And Baldwin and his people?"

"They're fine, too. Alfred Baldwin's on his way. There are some things you need to know before he gets here. Cankor's body was taken to the Shelby County morgue. The bodies of Dr. Swenson and their seven mercenaries were removed by boat, their deaths undisclosed."

"How in the world does Baldwin get away with that bullshit?" Wilcox complained.

"It was classified as a government covert military operation. Insurgents killed by federal agents are viewed as enemies of the state, military deaths on a battlefield subject to military law. There are no requirements to report numbers or names or details."

"This was no military operation. We used the MPD elite force. We were hunting serial killers responsible for domestic deaths. I am goddamn tired of governments breaking laws."

"Major Cankor's death was classified differently," Petty said.

"Why? Didn't they shoot the bastard?" Wilcox chided.

"His death fell under the jurisdiction of the presiding county medical examiner. By law it was my responsibility to conduct the inquest and rule on cause and manner."

"If they didn't shoot him, how did he die?"

"This is where it gets complicated, Tony. You saw Cankor levitate."

"Yeah, but I was in lah-lah-land. I'm sure that was him messin' with my brain."

"We all saw the same thing, Tony."

"I don't understand. What are you trying to tell me?" Wilcox sat up in bed.

"Alfred Baldwin told us it was a mass-illusion created by Hunter Keller. He says Hunter used psychic skills to manipulate

Cankor into believing he was in great danger hovering a hundred feet above the ground. Baldwin said we were in range to experience the illusion."

"After what I've seen the last few days, that makes a hell of a lot more sense than levitation," Wilcox said. "So, Keller created this illusion to force Cankor to cooperate. I assume he did his thing—tried to escape. How did the bastard die?"

"Baldwin believes the herd of bull elk trampled and gored Major Cankor to death." Petty looked down at the file on her lap and closed her eyes.

Wilcox knew something was wrong. "You did the autopsy. What do you say happened?"

"Baldwin claims Cankor never left the ground, Tony. He claims levitation is impossible."

"You're the forensic pathologist. What do you say happened, Dr. Petty? And I don't care who is listening to our goddamn private conversation," Wilcox yelled into his empty room.

"I don't know, Tony."

"Trust me. They can't do anything to you for telling the truth."

She opened her file and read, "Severe compression of spine, all vertebrae fractured. Base of skull fractured. Two broken legs—tibia and femur—compound, spiral fractures, and two broken ankles. All ribs fractured. All major organs, ruptured."

"Even I know a compressed spine is not your typical trampling injury," Wilcox said. "He died from a fall, didn't he?"

"Yes. Cankor had to fall a long way to get those injuries on that surface. He had to fall at least a hundred feet to produce the damage I saw. It was textbook, Tony."

"So I did see him levitate. It was not an illusion," Wilcox said still poking at his Jell-O. "I guess our skinny, little friend has even more gifts than we thought."

"You remember Bald Knob?" Petty asked.

"You talkin' about the part when Keller made those guys run into the tree?"

"Yes. They weren't running, Tony. They were floating. They were a few inches above the road. I didn't want to believe it. I thought I was seeing things. It would be impossible."

"I saw it too. But I couldn't get my brain around anything I saw with Keller."

"Hunter did not kill those men at Bald Knob, Tony."

"Okay. And why is that significant now?"

"Up until Mud Island, we only have evidence of Hunter using 'lethal force' one time."

"You mean the Russian guy, Bender."

"Yes. He shot you and held the gun to your head, Tony. Hunter saw the future. He knew Bender would pull the trigger. That night Hunter had to use lethal force. I think for the first time in his life. He was different after that, even more introverted. He was battling something inside."

"Cankor was his second," Wilcox muttered.

"And again, Hunter was the only one capable of stopping Cankor. He knew it, Tony."

"Where's this goin'?" Wilcox pushed.

Petty leaned close and whispered. "Hunter is deathly afraid of his psychic powers. He's been running from them all his life, especially after his parents and closest friends were killed. But he knew he had to do something, Tony. Hunter knew exactly what Cankor was doing. Hunter was at your homicides for a reason. They were all remote viewers or direct descendants. He knew they were going to die."

"And he was there to warn them, to help them. But he was afraid to use his powers to protect them because why?"

"The ability to kill with his thoughts petrified him, Tony."

"That would explain him showing up at homicides and doing nothing, except he did call 911 on South Main."

"He didn't know how to help. He feared his powers. It explains why he felt the blame for the deaths." Petty said. "His psychic powers come with a price. He knew if he used them to kill, they could take control of him like Cankor. They could possibly change him into a monster."

"Turn him into a heartless monster like Cankor," Wilcox muttered.

"After Cankor had you shot on the sandy clearing, he came back to me. I thought he was going to finish his work, kill me like he killed Dr. Proust on Dewar. But he was using me to get Hunter Keller. Cankor knew Hunter would not let him kill me. And Cankor stopped."

"Why?" Wilcox asked.

"Hunter gave himself up. When Cankor saw Keller, he let go of me."

"I missed all that."

"You were unconscious, remember? I was paralyzed, but I could hear. Major Cankor said something odd. I didn't understand the significance until later."

"What did he say?"

"He said to Hunter—now you are evil like me."

"Keller believed the use of lethal power would lead to being taken over by the *evil* inside of him."

"That is why he could not help the others. He had to risk it at the end," Petty said. She leaned closer and whispered. "Now we must help him, Tony."

"Why? I would assume Baldwin's gonna help him," Wilcox said. "They need the guy."

"Our U.S. Attorney General suppressed the autopsy findings. All my inquest documents have been altered. I was forced to sign off."

"How much change are we talkin'?"

"Cankor's death was changed from a homicide to an

accident. They eliminated pathology associated with a fall, and over-stated pathology supporting a trampling. They're covering-up levitation, Tony. Baldwin's taking control. He is employing legal maneuvers citing national security."

"Pushy little twit," Wilcox muttered poking at his green Jell-O again.

"You and I are prohibited from discussing events leading up to and including Mud Island. Violation is punishable by heavy fines and imprisonment."

"You are a stickler for truth, justice, and the American way, Petty. You need to get over it in this case. The government's protecting their psychic-weaponry secrets."

"It's not right, Tony."

"Frankly, I don't give a rat's ass what the documents say about Cankor as long as the bastard is takin' a dirt nap. Revel in the moment. He's off the streets. Our unsolved homicides come off the books. We go back to chasing common criminals."

"The world may be a little bit safer, but I don't like my government manipulating the truth. The ends never justify the means."

"I hear you, but let's focus on getting out of here. We need to get back to Memphis."

"I am worried about Hunter," Petty said.

"If he's with Baldwin and the Stargate people, I would relax," Wilcox said. "They'll treat him like a rock star. The kid's got unbelievable gifts. Our government wants to understand and protect them. I'm sure they'll take good care of him."

"Then why are they holding him in a secret, secured structure under the DOJ building?"

"They have something like that under the DOJ? What are you talking about?"

"I have reliable sources, Tony. The government cannot risk losing Hunter Keller again. They are charging him with Cankor's death and the deaths of remote viewers. If he does not cooperate, they will prosecute. He will face life in prison or execution. Hunter will never see daylight again. He is their lab rat, or a dead duck."

Wilcox pushed his food tray. "That is unadulterated bullshit."

"He is too powerful to ever be free. He will not survive. You know him. Hunter's not physically strong enough. He will wither away. He is an introverted man alone in the world, a man scared to death of his gifts. He will die. He will use his powers to kill himself."

"Have you spoken with him?"

"Not since Mud Island." Petty wiped her eyes.

Wilcox turned back to the tray table over his lap. Poking the green Jell-O cubes with his fork helped him think. Anger filled his eyes as the door swung open and Alfred Baldwin entered the room. Two secret service agents took positions in the hall as the door closed behind.

"How's my favorite homicide detective?" Baldwin asked as he nodded at Petty.

Standing at the end of the bed in his three-piece suit, he checked his watch. "I got here as soon as I heard you were back among the living. How do you feel?"

"I'm good." He swallowed his ire. "I heard I had a Rip Van Winkle moment."

"You had us worried for a while. This stuff is unpredictable. You remember anything?"

"Some." He touched his shoulder bandage. "I remember I got shot, and a herd of bull elk."

"You don't remember your last moments with Hunter Keller and Major Cankor?" he asked as Petty looked down at her file. "We're big boys and girls now. It's okay. We can talk openly. We're on the same team."

"Are we?" Wilcox said. "Or are you on a team and we're on a team?"

"I know what you think you saw, detective. And I know Dr. Petty brought you up-to-date on the important things. Why do you think we let her in here first? You got the *Cliff Notes* on *War and Peace*."

"You're such a crafty Attorney General," Wilcox chided. "What you gonna do next, ex-communicate a homicide detective and medical examiner to protect your goddamn secrets?"

"We're more civilized than that." He rounded the bed as his smile melted and eyes sharpened. "I don't have much time to play, so I'll be direct. Under no circumstances will you or Dr. Petty share your experiences, philosophies, or closely held views on people or events leading up to and or including Mud Island. Comprende' amigo?"

"Oh. You speak Spanish—such a talent. I guess you mean I can't tell the world about the psychic-weapons our government's perfected and may use on us one day?"

"Don't do this Wilcox," Baldwin said.

"I'm sorry. Did I already cross a line? I just want to be clear. You don't want me to talk about you developing unstoppable, killing machines soon to visit cities across America—the telekinetic homicidal maniacs brought to you by your untrustworthy U.S. Government."

"Very funny," Baldwin said as he pinched the knot of his fake tie.

"And levitation, God knows we should stay away from that one."

"Mass-illusion," Baldwin said. "You don't understand. You will never understand."

"What about Cankor—your elite force of remote viewers was terminated by a psychic serial killer you guys developed and could not control. Is that mass-illusion too?" Wilcox poked.

"Major Cankor is dead," Baldwin said.

"Right. The monster was trampled to death in Memphis by a random and massive herd of bull elk never before seen in the Midsouth." Wilcox tugged at his arm restraint with his free hand. "Be glad I'm tied up Baldwin. You don't scare me."

"I hope you do feel better soon . . . come to your senses." Baldwin's smile returned. "You won't talk."

"You're a devious, power-hungry prick on your way to oblivion. History will get it right."

"I know you don't want to see anything bad happen to your friends. It would be a shame if Miss Patterson lost her PI license and went to jail for interfering with a government investigation. And Detective Baily, he has such a promising career in law enforcement. I'd hate for his medical clearance to be denied. Of course, Dr. Petty has her own problems. The government is looking into pressing charges on her unlawful tampering with evidence in five homicides. To protect our national interests, we sent three experts from Bethesda Research to work with Dr. Petty, to straighten things out. They are all dead now. I wonder why? Who could be implicated? What is the less than obvious motive? Did Dr. Petty come to Memphis to work closer with Dr. Tanner, a Russian mole?"

"You're a monster. This is not Nazi Germany," Wilcox seethed.

"When it comes to national security, it might as well be," Baldwin said.

Wilcox looked at Petty. They had zero options. Baldwin held all the cards. They watched him walk to the window and open the blinds. The sun fell into the room. "Hunter Keller is a national treasure. His psychic gifts are beyond imagination. He is a rarity, the son of two very powerful psychics. He is the perfect storm, the ultimate weapon of mass destruction."

"And now you kids can dissect him like a frog in biology class," Wilcox said.

"We're not monsters. I don't have to tell you we live in a very dangerous world. There are bad people out there, people who wish to do us great harm. I and others have a responsibility to protect our nation. If our enemies obtain the powers of a Hunter Keller, they could destroy the world as we know it. Power is a very complex thing. Once one has it they use it."

"And you are the exception?" Petty said.

Baldwin turned from the window. "Yes. I would like to think so."

"It is not your right to imprison and experiment on an innocent man," Petty said. "No matter how you try to justify it, Hunter Keller has human rights."

"He has been avoiding people like you all his life. The man has lost everything, his parents and friends. He just wants to disappear, be left alone," Wilcox said.

Baldwin returned to the end of the bed in silence and a troubled gaze.

Wilcox studied the man he now despised. "You're not telling us something." Baldwin looked at his feet. "I remember that face. You had it when you stepped onto the porch at the Brent mansion. That night you were lost. You needed our help. You were desperate."

He looked into Wilcox's eyes and cleared his throat. "You both are free to go when the doctors give you medical clearance," Baldwin cleared his throat again. "You have my word I will not interfere. Contrary to your negative opinion of me, I do appreciate your assistance in Memphis. Maybe one day you will understand. Your government thanks you." He attempted a smile, turned, and walked to the door. "Keep in mind our little talk." He gripped the handle and paused.

Wilcox looked down at his food tray. One green Jell-O cube

lifted off the pile and quivered several inches above the bowl. Petty's eyes widened. Wilcox froze.

"Hunter Keller has escaped," Baldwin said with his back to them. "He thinks you're his family now. When he makes contact, I am sure you will do the right thing."

Baldwin pulled open the door and left the room. Wilcox's eyes smiled as he stabbed the floating green cube. Petty wiped a tear off her file—*we are family.*

BOOKS BY STEVE BRADSHAW

The Bell Trilogy
Bluff City Butcher
The Skies Roared
Blood Lions

Evil Like Me

Serial Intent

ABOUT THE AUTHOR

STEVE BRADSHAW is a forensic field agent and biotech entrepreneur writing his unique brand of mystery/thrillers. Steve's training and experience investigating thousands of unexplained deaths for the medical examiner's office, and as the founder-President/CEO of an innovative biomedical device company enables him to put his readers on the front row in the fascinating worlds of fringe science, modern forensics, and the chilling pursuit of real monsters.

Steve enjoys sharing his experiences and perspectives as a forensic investigator, President/CEO, and mystery/thriller author. Visit his website and join MEMBER GUEST so you can interact with the author, get insider information and updates, arrange for an author visit, and to be the first in line for new releases.

For more information:
www.stevebradshawauthor.com
steve@stevebradshawauthor.com

www.ingramcontent.com/pod-product-compliance
Lightning Source LLC
Chambersburg PA
CBHW020238200626
46816CB00001BA/20